BLUE CAP

THE BUSHRANGER;

OR,

THE AUSTRALIAN DICK TURPIN.

—

ILLUSTRATED.

—

LONDON:

HOGARTH HOUSE, 32, BOUVERIE STREET, E.C.

INDEX.

BLUE CAP, THE BUSHRANGER:

OR,

THE AUSTRALIAN DICK TURPIN.

CHAPTER I.

THE FLIGHT OF A CANARY AND THE OATH OF A BLUEBOTTLE.

IT is Illawarra Bay, on the eastern sea-board of New South Wales, and it is a summer's night in the January of 1859.

The great white moon, gleaming like a vast silver shield from out a sky of indigo, shines down upon the still and glassy waters, the densely wooded shores, and on the dim mountain peaks in the distance.

Along that shore gleams not the light of a single human habitation, but over the still and glassy waters comes the dismal howl of the warrigal, the shrill squeak of possum, the plaintive wail of the mopoke and coocoo bird, mingled with now and then the jocund "He-haw-ha-ha-ha-ha" of the laughing jackass.

From the shore, too, is borne the delicious perfume of the mimosa and the gold and silver wattles, whose long green trailing branches and white and yellow blossoms droop into the very waters around the vast semi-circle of the bay, while the tall tree ferns flutter and wave above them, and in their rear the white-trunked blue gums, and the lofty iron bark and peppermint trees, rear themselves proudly upwards towards the star-spangled heavens, from whence the great Southern Cross gleams down in a galaxy of light, only second to that of the moon herself.

In the middle of that bay rides at her anchor a solitary vessel.

She is a schooner, rigged after the fashion of the American clippers, but with a somewhat broader and bluffer bow, and masts which do not rake so boldly—a so-called Sydney schooner, like those which sail along the Australian coast, at times visit the adjacent isles, or even venture across to New Zealand, in defiance of the mountainous billows of the great southern ocean.

And what can this strange schooner be laden with? and what does she there in that quiet, forest-bordered bay?

We will answer the latter question first.

She has put in here for the night to avoid the sudden gales, called "Southerly Busters," that, without a minute's warning, come sweeping up the Pacific sea-board of Australia during the hours of darkness, scattering destruction in their course; and she is laden with "canary birds," which she is exporting to a very healthy part of the neighbouring island of Van Dieman's Land, called Port Arthur.

And are they very pretty little canary birds? and do they sing sweetly?

Oh, no, not at all.

They are surely the most ugly birds that were ever fledged, and the songs of the majority of them—were they allowed to give utterance to any sounds at all—would, without doubt, consist of the most frightful string of blasphemies and obscenities that it is possible to conceive.

Canary birds is, in fact, their nick-name, but the appellation of wasps or hornets would be much more fitting; for the cargo of the schooner Yan Yangs consists of heavily-ironed convicts, who are attired in tightly-fitting dresses of broad yellow and black stripes.

A horrible looking lot of wretches they are—shaven headed and shaven faced, ankle fettered and wrist fettered, and lying scattered about the deck in sleep in every variety of attitude, for, even at this hour of the night, the thermometer stands at 86° in the captain's deck cabin; and down in the close stifling hold these striped rascals would all be dead before morning.

And so, like the torpid wasps or hornets that we have before likened them to, they lie sprawling all over the main deck, in company with a number of troopers of the New South Wales mounted constabulary, who have brought their mattrasses, blankets, and pillows on deck, and who are all as sound asleep as the convicts that it is their duty to guard.

For that matter, the officer of the watch is asleep, and the man at the wheel is asleep too, for the New South Welsh are naturally an indolent race, and do no more work than there is strict occasion for; and where is the use of a man being at the wheel when a schooner is riding at her anchors in the middle of a calm land-locked bay? and where is the occasion of a watch being kept where there is nothing to watch for, where a ship may not be again seen for years, and where no hostile natives inhabit the shore?

But the convicts—ay, the convicts—might not they seize upon the advantage of such a lax guard being kept to escape?

Well, at first thought, such a thing would seem probable, but then, be it remembered, the Yan Yangs is at anchor a good mile away from the shore; that the bay swarms with sharks, and that the weight of the yellow birds' wrist and ankle fetters are very great.

Their attention had been attracted to the sharks when the troopers brought their beds up, and they had been laughingly told, whilst their fetters were being carefully examined, one by one, that whoever thirsted after liberty might jump overboard, and swim ashore, if his irons and the sharks would let him. But most of the rascals shook their heads, and some declared, with an oath, that they would wait for a better chance.

The troopers, therefore, with the greatest confidence that all was right, went asleep, and slept soundly, as men generally do who have light work, little care, plenty of food, and good constitutions.

And most of the convicts were fain to follow their example; all save one, a herculean fellow, who sat huddled up in the only corner of the deck where the moonlight didn't penetrate, with his head bent forward on his knees, and snoring most naturally.

He wasn't slumbering, though, for his black, beady eyes often took a covert glance around; and, what was more, his hands were hard at work upon his leg irons, for, during the day, he had found and secreted a long rusty iron nail, and with it he was now endeavouring to break his fetters.

He had been at work for three hours, and his

looks were far brighter than they had been at the commencement. Another hour, and there was a faint rattle, a fainter cry, and a dead stillness.

The leg-irons had parted in twain—that was the rattle.

The convict had been unable to repress a smothered exclamation of joy—that was the faint cry.

But then he thought of the many dangers that still surrounded him, that the dual noise might have disturbed the slumbers of one or more of the troopers, who all slept with their loaded revolvers under their pillows, and so he curled himself up again, and lay as still as still could be—and that was the dead silence.

No one moved, however. No one stirred hand or foot, and so, after ripping a broad band off his striped jacket, and with it tying up his riven fetters to each leg, so that they should not ring or clatter as he moved, the convict rose to his feet.

It was then apparent that he was a very tall man, as well as a very big one, and that he was the possessor of one of the most hideously revolting faces that it is possible to conceive.

For a moment he leant on the bulwark, regarding with his grey eyes the far-distant shore; then he tore off another piece of his yellow jacket, and dropped it over into the water.

He regarded it anxiously for a moment, and then his eyes brightened up wondrously as he muttered to himself—

"I thought we were anchored close to the great inshore current. Now, that is fine! I could not well have swam ashore with all this dead weight of iron hanging to me; but I think I can keep myself afloat, and the current will bear me on to within a score yards of the bank, and then one short spurt, and I am ashore."

His thin lips expanded in a grin, but it died out as he saw the black dorsal fin of a shark cleaving the waters like a knife.

But though the smile vanished, the sullen look of dogged determination did not.

The shark had shot athwart the bows.

Well, he would crawl aft and drop himself over the stern, that was all. Ah! and the current ran swifter there—that was better, too.

He could tell this because every yard that the little piece of torn cloth drifted astern, and yet shoreward, the faster it sped, and, taking the long steel chain that united his wrist-cuffs in his hands, so that it should not jingle, he crept aft.

He had just reached the poop of the little vessel, and, pausing for a moment, was reflecting whether it would be safe to pass the seemingly sleeping helmsman in order to drop over the taffrail, when a trooper suddenly sprang up from behind the after hatchway, and stood before him.

"Go back, man!" he said, sharply. "Do you want to feed the sharks?"

"What's that to you, you cursed, prying, sneaking, bluebottle? Let me pass, I say! Don't move your hand towards your pistol, or I'll brain you! What, you will? Take that for your pains, then!" retorted the convict; and, shaking out the long heavy wrist-cuff chain, he clasped his hands together, raised them high above his head, and the chain descended with crushing force on the trooper's head.

With such force, indeed, that his skull was eaten in, and his brains were scattered about the deck in all directions.

The sound of his fall awoke the man at the wheel.

"Murder! a convict escaping!" he roared with all his might.

But they were the last words that he ever uttered, for the next instant the ruffian had served him as he served the trooper; and then, although the alarm had spread, and both constables and convicts were waking up in every direction, he raised his victims one by one in his stalwart arms, and launched them over the side, exclaiming, with a guttural laugh, as they plumped into the water—

"There's a feast for you, friend sharks—eat and enjoy yourselves; you needn't take the trouble to swim after me now, and ye'll have too much sense to do it, that I know very well," and before the last word had escaped his lips he had run across the deck to the other side, and leapt overboard.

Leapt overboard amidst a rain of bullets, too, for a score of troopers were rushing towards him, firing as they ran along the decks.

The greatest confusion reigned on board.

The convict dived, and everybody thought that the weight of his irons had dragged him down at once and for ever beneath the waves.

But no, a minute later his head bobbed up like a cork, a good two hundred yards astern of the Yan Yangs, and he was perceived to be drifting at a great rate towards the shore.

"Over with the boat!" cried the captain, as he came on deck. "Over with the boat! We'll soon overhaul that fellow."

"The boat won't float, sir—the seams are all open; the heat of the sun has made 'em gape like a shark's mouth," quoth the carpenter.

"And how the devil does that happen, Chips?" asked the captain.

"Well, sir, you would have it turned upside down on the decks, instead of towing it astern, and the blazing sun has blistered off the paint, and drawn the timbers," said the carpenter.

"But water should have been dashed over it continually."

"What was everybody's business was nobody's business, sir."

"So it seems, and that rascal will escape."

"No, he won't; not if the troopers' revolvers can bring him down—and they fire more coolly and steadily now."

At last he was hit, for by the light of the clear moon and the Southern Cross they could see a bloody track upon the water in the convict's wake, and a loud shout was raised as the black dorsal fin of a shark was seen in close proximity to him.

They could plainly perceive the grim monster of the deep drawing gradually closer and closer to what they now thought to be the doomed swimmer.

They knew that the hyena of the ocean had as keen a smell for human blood as the ban dog or the sleuth hound.

If the monster once scented him, he would be irrevocably lost; but it was evident that it had not scented him as yet.

The current was carrying him swiftly towards the shore; he was already midway between it and the ship, and out of pistol range.

Every instant the fierce watchers expected to see him go down, for his mouth seemed to be scarcely above water—every instant, too, they expected to see the shark's tail wriggle with joy, and to behold the leviathan tear through the water in pursuit of his prey.

And the convict presently saw his danger, too.

Tired of being borne along upon his chest, he turned over upon his back for a rest, and thus caught sight of the great black fin moving to and fro like the tail of a dog above the turnip-tops or mangold wurtzel when retrieving game.

His scream could be heard from the deck of the schooner, but he only uttered one, which was wrung from him by the horror of his position, before he had time to think.

When he had thought, however, he cursed himself for having uttered a sound that might have brought his grim foe down upon him, and henceforth he was dumb.

And so he floated shoreward, staring with eyes dilated and full of horror at the horrible fin, which seemed to him to draw nearer and ever nearer in rapidly shortening circles.

The monster evidently suspected something, and was trying to hit off the scent.

He would not take very long at that.

How slowly he seemed to float, and his strength was failing.

He could but just keep his under lip above water, and he dared not turn his head to glance over his shoulder towards the shore, for fear he should make a ripple and the shark should notice it.

Oh, it was a horrible position, hovering between two deaths, and not knowing which would claim him for a victim!

But suddenly the leviathan stopped in its course, and its fin poised rigidly upright; then it swam rapidly backwards and forwards twice or thrice, stopped again for nearly half a minute, and suddenly raised its huge head half out of the water, and the convict saw its white gleaming saw-like teeth and its green glassy eyes fixed upon him.

Then, all at once, the shark hastened forward with such terrible velocity that more than half of the glistening, scaly monster was visible from the schooner's decks, as it shot, with the speed of an arrow, in the direction where the convict's head was bobbing up and down.

And the convict saw him, too, and all hope died out in his heart, to return an instant later, however, when he most unexpectedly found ground beneath his feet.

He was upon it in a twinkling, and rushing through the shallow water shorewards as hard as he could.

It was up to his hips, and so his progress was necessarily slow—his terrible foe could still swim, and was close behind him.

The drops of perspiration ran down his face; but suddenly the water shallowed to just above his knees.

Then he heard an angry snort, and a great splashing, and, glancing round, he saw the white silvery belly of his grim foe turned upwards, its mouth gaping open, and the flukes of its tail beating up the mud and sand.

In its over eagerness it had grounded, and was now as harmless for mischief as a flounder.

The convict chuckled grimly, and, walking back half a dozen yards, hit the monster heavily over its under gaping jaw with his wrist-fetters, causing it close with a crash.

After which feat he sauntered leisurely out of the water, across the narrow strip of golden sand beyond, and from thence up into the silent bush, where he was lost to sight amidst the trees.

*　　*　　*　　*

"He's got clear away, the scoundrel!" exclaimed the captain of the Yan Yangs.

"For the time," answered one of the troopers—"only for the time."

"How do you make out, only for a time?" asked another.

"Because the trooper he killed and threw overboard was my twin brother, as you are well aware, Matthews, and here I swear before you all, by everything I hold sacred—ay, by my hope of salvation hereafter—I swear it, that that man shall be brought to the gibbet by me, and by me alone! How soon can I land, Captain Waddle?" and he turned to the master of the schooner.

"You can land at once if you like to jump overboard."

"No, thank you: a shark might destroy a life that has suddenly become too valuable to risk needlessly," was the reply.

"Then Chips shall coddle up the boat, and I will put you ashore before we trip anchor in the morning. Will that do?"

"Thank you, sir; it must do," was the reply. "The fellow will get a seven hours' start of me; but it won't avail him in the end."

CHAPTER II.

SPEAK OF THE DEVIL AND HE'LL SHOW HIS HORNS.

ON the same night as the events occurred which have been described in the last chapter as having taken place on the margin of the beautiful bay of Illawarra, three men were sitting round the fire-place of a small and partially ruined hut, at the edge of a small patch of cleared land in one of the deep and wood-sheltered gullies lying between Mullet Creek on the north, and of Millagong Range on the south.

The night was far advanced, and the light gusts of wind which occasionally passed down the gully towards the bay, waved the branches of two or three lofty trees which had been left standing near the hut with a dismal and melancholy sough, and caused the dilapidated roof and the loose slabs of the old shanty to shake and rattle fitfully and weirdly.

The window places were nailed up with pieces of old timber, and the door—which had long before fallen from its hinges—was propped up with a couple of the slabs of which the hut had been originally constructed, but which had broken away from the framing of the roof, and fallen, leaving narrow slits in the wall, which slits, however, had been patched up with sheets of bark.

The fire-place was piled up with smouldering logs, and on a rudely-made table was a bush lamp, consisting of an old rusty tin pannikin filled with grease, and having a piece of cotton rag stuck in some clay at the bottom, to serve for a wick.

This primitive contrivance afforded a dim and smoky light, which, with the occasional flaring up of the fire, was sufficient to render visible the interior of the hut.

On the table stood a "billy" of tea, still emitting a faint curling steam, and the remains of a rough meal of damper and mutton, the latter of which had evidently been hastily cooked by being thrown on the embers and burnt in that manner until sufficiently done.

A half-emptied bottle of rum also stood on the table, and near it a pannikin which smelt strongly of the same spirit.

In a corner of the hut, and thrown carelessly down, lay an empty bottle which had also contained rum, but which had apparently been finished by the companions.

The three men were smoking, and in deep converse.

One, by name Dick Evans, was barely twenty-five years of age, and, setting aside a peculiar downward cast in his twinkling blue eyes, which never could look anyone boldly and openly in the face, was rather a presentable young fellow, though he certainly looked much older than he really was, for drink, riot, hardship, and anxiety had done their work, and whilst his face was sunburnt and storm-beaten, it looked sallow and unhealthy, and the lines therein were hardened into an appearance of ferocious recklessness and insolent boldness.

Of his two companions little need be said, except that, being older than himself, they were rather more deeply steeped in infamy and hardened in vice, although they lacked somewhat of the dash and effrontery of their leader, and suffered themselves to be governed by sheer impudence and assumption.

This precious trio, then, were seated over the fire in the dilapidated hut, amidst gloom and smoke, planning a scheme of villany by which they might repair the decline in their treasury, impoverished by excess and licentiousness.

"Look here," growled a voice from the smokiest corner of the fire-place, and belonging to the most disreputable-looking of the party; "I want to know what you've brought us here for at all—here, where we've been stuck like possums hiding in a hole for the last six or seven days? We're near out o' grub, and as for lush, why, that's all a chance. If we're goin' to do anythin', let's do it, and if not, let's hook it, for I'm tired o' this game; and, I tell you what it is, I ain't goin' to stand it no longer."

"Ax no questions, Jack—ax no questions and you'll be told no lies," coolly responded Dick Evans; "you'll stop here as long as I like, and, until I like, you won't move a foot. Do you think I'm such a fool as to waste my time hanging about here in hiding without a good reason for it?"

"But what's the reason? I'm not goin' to put my neck into a rope without knowing the why and the wherefore," replied the one addressed as Jack.

"I'll tell you what my reason is," replied Dick. "Ten miles down the river, and at the foot of the big ranges, is the Marrang head station, where many a good heifer and foal have I lifted afore I come to grief, and there, to that station, must we go to-night."

The two listeners looked at one another, but said nothing.

"It isn't cattle nor horses we'll go there for this time, and that you know right well; but it's money and valuables, and whatever we can lay our hands on. There's only one old woman and a young girl there, and the servants, and they won't resist, for——"

He did not proceed to say why, but, with a villanous twinkle of his dull and watery eyes, and with a ferocious and hideous smile overspreading his sallow features, he slowly drew from the breast of his jumper a revolver pistol, clicked the lock, nodded, replaced it in his breast, and said, drawlingly, "Because they won't."

"Why, you don't mean to say——?" commenced Larry.

"But I do mean to say," interrupted Dick. "Come, none of your humbug! You know very well what I mean to say, Larry Doyle, and you know, or you may know if you don't, that what I say I'll stick to, and I know that if you are the man I take you for, what you'll say. What do you say, Jack? Will you go in for neck or nothing? Will you jump out of this frying pan into the fire?"

"I'll have no hand in anything where there's a chance of bloodshed," said Larry Doyle, vehemently.

"No, nor divil a bit will I," said Jack Cooper.

"You brace of cowardly curs," roared Dick. "I wish the devil, whom you apostrophise, would turn up at this moment, and I would ask him to join me on this expedition."

"Done, young master, I am here, and I will join you hand and glove," said a voice behind him; and Dick, turning suddenly round, saw a hideous face glaring in at them through the great crack in the door.

CHAPTER III.

DISSOLVING A LONG-ESTABLISHED PARTNERSHIP.

"COME in, matey," roared Dick, though not without turning a shade paler. "Come in, no matter who the devil you are."

"In his name you summoned me, and in his name I'm here. Ready—ay, ready—to go on any business," replied the voice; and then ensued the rattle of chains, the tumble-down door was lifted and thrown back, and a big man, all black and yellow stripes, entered the hut.

"Who are you?" asked Dick, taking a step backwards.

"I thought you knew my name; you used it very pat."

"Yes; but I'm not going to believe that you are the devil."

"Not the great original, perhaps; but I'm the greatest one in Australia, at any rate," and the giant laughed a laugh of the damned.

"But what do you here? You wear the livery of a convict."

"The livery of a man, you mean! None but men wear these stripes, and yet they always cast them off as soon as they can. Ha! ha! ha! ha!" and the canary bird laughed until the hut shook.

"Well, I believe you are a man and a devil both," said Dick, "and being such you can give the assistance I want."

"And ain't I willing to give it," growled the convict. "A half share in the plunder, though, and a good tuck out before we start."

"All right; but come nearer the fire. Why, you're dripping wet."

"Well, I've had a goodish swim of it," laughed the convict.

"With those heavy fetters on? Can it be possible?" exclaimed Dick.

"Rather, youngster. I'm a strongish man, you see; but these fetters you may knock off as soon as you like."

"And how am I to knock them off?" asked Dick.

"With your poker. Take it up, and I'll soon show you the way."

Dick did so, and then with one hand he lightly took hold of the long steel chain that united the convict's wrists.

But no sooner had he done so than he let it go again, exclaiming, with an air of disgust as he looked at his fingers—

"What is on them?"

"Bah! 'tis only two dead men's brains," laughed the convict. "I should have thought the sea would have washed all that away."

Dick shuddered. He half repented the partnership he had entered into; seeing which, Jack Cooper, who had been watching him intently though never speaking a word, suddenly said—

"I think, my lad, you are about to jump out of the frying pan into the fire. That ugly scoundrel will manage to put your head in a noose if you don't look out—take my word for it."

"Let the spalpeen go his way, and bad scran to him, and let we three stick to the ligitimate, as we've always done," added Larry.

"Ha! ha! ha!" laughed the convict—"and what could a brave, dashing young fellow like my new friend here ever hope to accomplish with a brace of whining, slinking, cowardly curs like you? I'll help him to build up a fortune within a year, and steer him clear of trap, judge, and Jack Ketch, too."

"Ye don't seem to have been able to keep yerself clear of the two former, at any rate; and as for our being whining, cowardly, slinking curs, why just prove it, my fine yellow bird," said Jack Cooper, whipping up a knife, and advancing upon the convict.

But the latter, with a snort such as might have been uttered by a furious horse, took three steps forward to meet him, and then, with glaring eyes and set teeth, raised his wrists on high, and sent the chain clattering down behind his back.

Jack Cooper saw the murderous intent, and, though he might have lunged forward and found his antagonist's heart before the heavy chain could come swinging down upon his skull, he dropped his knife, slunk back to the fireside, and vowed in whining accents that he meant no offence.

"There, there, you've proved yourself to be the mangy cur that I said you were," sneered the convict. "If your companion has enough pluck to attack a bound and fettered man, let him try it on, and, perhaps, I'll own that he has the spirit of a mouse."

"Larry Doyle ain't of a quarrelsome turn o' mind," remarked that individual, as he puffed away assiduously at his pipe, "and he never cares for a fight unless there's something to be gained by it."

"In that case, as the gentlemen are of such a

peaceable turn of mind, let us proceed to business," said the canary bird with a chuckle, and, depressing his wrists, he dropped his chain with a ringing jingle in front of him, and Dick, taking up the poker, set to work as the convict directed him.

Three sharp strokes, and the chain broke with a clang.

"That will do," said the convict; "I can manage the rest myself."

He went over to the fire-place, and, taking up a stone, hacked away in turn at the fetters that girt his ankles and wrists.

In less than five minutes he had knocked them all off.

"Hullo, you have been lately wounded, then?" said Dick, as he noticed a broad crimson patch on the convict's left shoulder.

"A furrow from a revolver bullet," laughed the giant; "the salt water has stopped the bleeding, though, so it counts for nothing."

"I should think you were pretty anxious to get rid of those togs; though where you will be able to get others I can't guess," said Dick.

"I can, though," quoth the giant, shortly. "What I most want, at present, is something to eat and drink—I could eat a man, I could!"

Dick therefore placed before the stranger what was left of the damper cake and the remnant of the half raw, half burnt, mutton, in quantity about a pound and a quarter, together with the rum bottle, that might now have held about a quartern of spirit.

The convict tossed this off first, and then cleared the mutton and damper to the last fragment and crumb, even grinding up the smaller bones between his great teeth as a dog might have done.

"That's a very handsome revolver of yours," he then remarked, pointing to the stock of the one that emerged from Dick Evans' jumper pocket; "hand it here, and let's have a squint at it?"

Dick immediately did so, flattered by the compliment.

"Are you a good shot?" asked the convict, as he inspected it.

"Well, I can hit the ace of spades at twenty-four paces, ordinarily."

"Humph! Could you hit a man's left eye at the same distance?"

"I might, if he didn't blink; but, in fact, I never tried."

"Oh, you never tried? Is this revolver loaded in every chamber?"

"Yes, in every chamber. Why do you ask?" exclaimed Harry.

"Because I want to dissolve the old partnership before the new one is entered upon," answered the convict with a laugh.

Then there was a double report, a double groan, and Jack Cooper and Larry Doyle fell over each other, half in and half out of the fire.

"Heavens, you have killed them!" exclaimed Dick Evans.

"As dead as door nails, my boy," replied the other; "Larry Doyle's clothes will about suit me, and he and the other cove would have betrayed you, out of revenge for deserting them, at the first opportunity."

"Well, I daresay they would," rejoined Dick; "but this is horrible, and I have known them so long too!"

"Humbug, man! he who has the devil for a partner mustn't cry over spilt milk," and the convict chuckled, and crossed the hut floor to turn poor Larry Doyle "out of his skin," as he called it.

He was soon dressed in the dead Irishman's clothes, even to his slouched billycock hat.

Then he searched Jack Cooper's pockets, and uttered a grunt of disgust when he found nothing therein.

"What are we to do with the bodies?" exclaimed Dick Evans.

"Drop 'em down the old well at the back," was the reply.

"How the deuce do you know there's a well there? I don't."

"Perhaps I knowed summat about this hut before you was born. But come, make haste, we have no time to lose," was the reply.

Thus adjured, Dick helped his partner to carry the dead men out of the hut one by one, and in the middle of a thick copse close at the back they came across the well that his partner had spoken of.

Oh, mercy, what a depth it was! How the dead men rebounded from side to side with dull, heavy thuds in their descent, and with how hollow a splash they at last fell into the gurgling waters far, far below!

When this terrible work was done, work which seemed to change the once blustering and vaunting Dick Evans into a shivering, shaking, decrepit old man, though the convict seemed rather to enjoy it, the moulted yellow bird said—

"Of course you have horses at hand?"

"Yes," replied Dick; "three splendid nags, too."

"Then let us be off at once," quoth the other, "for the night wanes."

"Yes," replied Dick with a faint laugh; "we have heavy work before us."

"Work from which I shall take a new name," was the answer; "a name with which Australia shall ring within a month!"

Five minutes later the two men were sweeping at a swift gallop eastwards towards the doomed station.

CHAPTER IV.

THE ATTACK ON MARRANG—THE HUT.

"CURSE it all, we are too late to do anything! There's daylight showing in the east, and the people at the station are up and stirring. Look at the blue smoke beginning to curl upwards from the chimneys," said Dick Evans, rising up sharply directly they came in sight of Marrang, and pointing out these facts to his companion.

"Ugh," he grunted, "I thought it would be so. Well, what matters it? What are a few hours to us? There's another night not sixteen hours away. It will serve our purpose just as well, and there is plenty of good hiding ground within a mile or two of the station."

"Yes," assented Dick Evans. "There are some tidy little bits of scrub that it would puzzle an army of traps to flush their game out of, and I think I know of a cover wherein we can lie as snug as snug can be."

"Let us get on to it, then, without loss of time," said the convict, "for in another half hour the stockmen will be out and about, and our appearance will arouse suspicion, if nothing worse."

Dick Evans made no reply, but spurred up his horse, and the two men rode on for a good quarter of an hour at a gallop, when the open park-like bush changed into long reaches of dense, dark Mallee scrub, just a little higher than their heads, and into this they rode for a considerable way in Indian file, Dick Evans following up one of the many thousands of narrow paths with apparent confidence, for he never once drew rein at fault.

Whoever has trodden the bewildering maze at Woodstock can form a dim conception of what the Mallee scrub is like.

Travellers lost therein have wandered in what they thought to be a straight line for hours, and then have found themselves back at the point from which they started in the morning.

It is all sombre-leaved undergrowth, from six to seven feet in height, salt to the taste, funereal to the eye, void of all form of insect or bird life, and in some places scores and scores of miles in length and breadth.

It was some three miles within a desolate, lifeless, waterless region like this that the two foul birds of night took refuge, and there they rested all day, smoking and sleeping by turns, but seldom talking, for men who live much in the desert or the wilderness become almost as speechless as the other denizens thereof.

And when night again veiled the scene, they shook themselves together and got up and yawned, and took the hopples off their horses, and saddled and bridled them, and, mounting them, rode away in Indian file as they had come, Dick Evans leading the way.

When they got out into the open bush, the mopoke, or Australian cookoo, had just begun his lay, and a huge flying fox nearly knocked Dick out of his saddle.

They had already made their plan of operations, and they were very simple.

There was a hut where a stockman and a shepherd slept, at the bottom of the home-paddock, and within two hundred yards of the house.

This it would be necessary first to attack, and to secure the inmates, so that they should not be able to render any assistance in case of alarm, and also to prevent their pursuing should it become necessary to fly.

The superintendent, who usually slept in the house, was at one of the out-stations, superintending the sheep-shearing (of this Dick Evans had made himself assured), so that there was only a lad who did the handy-work of the station, two women servants, Mr. and Mrs. Beaumont (the proprietor and his wife, an elderly couple), and their grandson and grand-daughter, on the premises, and these the convict swore he would keep quiet with his revolver while Dick ransacked the house.

Noiselessly now they rode through the yeilding tea tree and gum bushes, their horses muzzled so that they could neither neigh nor whinny, and approached the station.

Then at last they dismounted, hid their steeds in a small patch of Leptopspermuns, and proceeded on foot.

After reconnoitring for a short time, the sound of their footsteps being concealed by the rustle of the night wind amongst the surrounding trees, they got up to the men's huts, and, peering through a chink in the window shutter, they discovered its two inmates sitting, smoking over the fire, after having eaten their suppers preparatory to turning in for the night.

There was a small terrier dog standing near the fire, and smelling uneasily about, occasionally emitting a short, low growl, as if he suspected the presence of danger, but did not exactly know from what quarter.

"Lie down, Jerry," said one of the men. "What makes the dog so uneasy, I wonder, Bill?"

Bill expressed himself, "Blowed if he knowed," and declared his intention of immediately "going to roost after looking out to see what sort of a night it was."

Although the watchers outside could not hear what was said by the men in the hut, they could see by the movements of the one who had been called Bill, that he was about to open the door, and therefore quietly stepping on one side of it, they waited until he came outside, when springing upon him, Dick Evans kicked his legs from under him, whilst the convict, covering the other with his revolver (who had sprung to his feet on hearing the noise), ordered him to "bail up," which, seeing the utter inutility of doing anything else, he quietly did, subsiding down upon the log on which he had been sitting, with an air of the most profound and stupid astonishment.

The other one was tied up, the operation being performed by his ankles being bound together and his hands tied behind him before he had recovered from his sudden terror at being thus unexpectedly assailed, and was dragged into the hut and thrown into a corner, where he lay helplessly on the floor.

The little terrier, however, was not so easily silenced, but rushed about barking and yelping at the heels of the bushrangers, until a well-directed kick from the boot of the convict, who had tried in vain to stab him with his knife, drove him into the same corner with his master.

"We don't want to hurt you, mates, nor the dog either," he growled to the man on the log; "but if you don't keep both yourselves and him quiet, we shall be under the painful necessity of cutting all your wizens. You understand, don't you?"

The one who lay in the corner wanted to know, with many expressions more strong than polite, "What they wanted there?"

"Keep a civil tongue in your head, or we'll want your life amongst other things," hissed the convict between his teeth; "and keep that dog o' yours quiet, too, or I'll precious soon cut his throat for him."

The man was subdued by the convict's blood-thirsty glance even more than by his words, and instead of making him an answer, he called to his dog, which lay whining and licking the place where it had been kicked, but at his master's voice went and crouched near him trembling and thoroughly cowed.

Meantime the other man, who all this time had set perfectly dumb-foundered, and apparently unable to comprehend the novel situation in which he and his mate were placed, was also bound and secured, and Dick and the convict, first making sure that the barking of the terrier had not alarmed any one up at the house, proceeded to sit down and discuss what was left of their prisoners' supper, for neither of them had tasted any food, save a few berries, since the preceding night at that other hut, the memory of which was seered in Dick Evans' brain for ever and ever.

It did not impair his appetite, however, and he and his truly devilish mate made such a meal as only famished men can make.

When they had done, a mouse would have found it very hard work to subsist even for a day on all the food that was left in the hut; but the mutton, the damper, and the bottle of colonial wine that they had found in a dark corner had instilled them with new strength, vigour, and ferocity.

"Let us shoot these fellows. Dead men tell no tales," said the convict, in a whisper.

"No," replied Dick Evans. "If we are to remain pals, there must be no more bloodshed than is absolutely necessary. I'm firm on this point, mind, however I may give in on others. The men are bound so as to be quite helpless, and I will gag them so as to make all doubly sure, and then as a last precaution we will lock them in. So what more can you want, matey, I'd like to know?"

"Oh! I dare say that'll do," said the convict. "You won't be so squeamish when we've been acquainted a bit longer, I'll be bound. However, do you gag the men, whilst I search the hut. There may be a note or two lying about."

He rose from table, and set to work without another word, and Dick followed his example.

Five minutes or so after the convict had gone to forage in the inner room of the bark hut, he returned, cutting a rather remarkable figure.

He wore on his head a cap of bright blue cloth, fitting close like a skull-cap, and with two long lappels that fastened under his chin. From the summit of this cap stood erect a dozen or so of bright crimson and blue feathers, to a height of nearly a yard. It was easy to be seen that they consisted of the entire tail of a blue mountain macaw.

This singular head-dress covered the whole of

his shaven skull, and gave him a half Indian, half Morisco, and wholly savage and demon-like appearance.

"I have been tailoring as well as plundering," he said, with a laugh. "This old cap, made to keep a traveller's ears warm in a colder climate than this, will give me a name, and in return I will give it fame. Henceforth I am known, and known only, as

'BLUE CAP, THE BUSHRANGER!'

Within a month or two Australian mothers shall hush their brats to sleep with the terror of that name."

CHAPTER V.

THE ATTACK ON MARRANG—THE STATION.

A HAPPY family party were gathered within Marrang home station that night.

A bright wood fire burned in the open hearth, for old Mrs. Beaumont would have it that the autumn evenings were chilly, though in reality the thermometer stood at seventy-two degrees in the outside verandah; and around it sat the old squatter, and his dame, and their two grand-children, Frank and Katie.

The old couple need no particular description, and anon we shall take a better opportunity of picturing the young ones; suffice it, therefore, now to say concerning them, that Katie Beaumont was a very pretty blonde of eighteen, and her brother a particularly handsome boy of some two years younger.

Supper had just been discussed, and now the old squatter had his glass of grog by his side, and his pipe in his mouth, whilst the old lady was busily engaged at her knitting, her grand-daughter with the last monthly part of "Bow Bells"—just out by the mail—and young Frank in carving a stock-whip handle out of a piece of Myall.

It was a beautiful bit of knife work already, though not nearly completed. The straight-grained piece of wood, delicately tapered in a hollow from the full butt to the thin point, was carved at the top with vine leaves and fern foliage, underneath which kangaroos and emus found shelter; but around the butt were cut two horsemen—a bush-ranger and a mounted trooper—the former falling beneath a bullet from the levelled revolver of the latter.

"There, grand-pa," said the lad, presently, shutting up his knife, and passing the stock-whip handle to the old gentleman; "it's getting on finely towards completion, isn't it?"

"Yes, my boy, yes," said the squatter; "you've great talent at wood carving. I wish, however, that in that, and in your drawings as well, you would restrict yourself to the beauties of vegetable and animal nature. Why is it, that in everything you attempt you must introduce a scene of blood?"

"My father died a bloody death, grandpa. He was slain by a villanous bushranger. Is it strange that I like to depict bushrangers meeting a fate that they so much deserve? Oh, why will you not let me enter the mounted police? I would then spend my whole time hunting up the demons," said Frank Beaumont.

And, as he spoke, the boy's face flushed, his eyes flashed, and he gave a little gasping sob as though he were choking.

"Frank," said the old squatter, severely, "these feelings do you anything but credit. We should leave vengeance to the Most High, and earthly punishment to the lawfully-constituted tribunals. Your father's murderer, Frank, is a prisoner for life—a striped and heavily-iron felon—worse off than the very beasts. He has to toil day after day at the most laborious labour, without pay, without thanks, without hope—at all events in this world."

"But they should have hung him, grand-pa. He killed my father; my mother died of a broken heart, and they did not hang the villain. Our laws are weak and unjust;" and again the youth flushed angrily up to the very roots of his bright golden curls.

"Don't revile the laws, Frank, until you are old enough and wise enough to make better," said his grandfather, severely. "The links of evidence were not quite sufficiently strong to convict the assassin of the capital offence and the law gave the criminal the benefit of the doubt. It always does in such cases."

"But my dear, dear father pointed the man clearly out as his murderer, and, though he couldn't speak, intimated by signs that the attack was wholly malicious and unprovoked," said Frank Beaumont, vehemently.

"I know all that, boy—I know all that; but not every one could understand and interpret the meaning of his gestures as you did. There was just a doubt in the minds of the jury, and so they brought in a verdict of manslaughter, instead of wilful murder, and I can't say but what I am glad. I disapprove of capital punishment altogether."

"So do not I," said young Frank. "When I grow older, I will shoot down a bushranger whenever and wherever I see one, regarding them as the wild beasts that they truly are. I wish I was a mounted trooper, so that I might make it my special business to hunt them down, and take them, either dead or alive, just as I pleased. As for the villain who killed my father, if I ever come across him working in any road gang, I shall be unable to refrain from shooting him if I chance to have a pistol about me—I know that very well."

"I forbid you to speak in such a manner, forward, impulsive, hot-headed boy. See, your sister and grandmamma are in tears. You are ever affecting them thus, by reverting out of season to the painful subject of your poor father's death. As for encountering his assassin, that you will never do, for, with a batch of other convicts, he sailed at the beginning of the week for Port Arthur, in Van Diemen's Land, a veritable hell upon earth, if all reports of it be true. So take back your stock-whip handle and go upstairs to bed. It's close upon ten o'clock."

At this moment, and before Frank could grasp his grandfather's outstretched hand, Katie Beaumont sprang to her feet with a shriek.

"What on earth is it?" asked everyone.

"Oh that face, that awful face?" was the reply.

"What awful face, my dear?" asked the old squatter, in soothing tones; "you have either fallen asleep and dreamed, or Frank's bombast has strangely affected your nerves."

"No, no," said Katie. "No, no; I was wide awake, and my eyes were fixed on that window, when the most ghastly and revolting face peered in and grinned and mouthed at me. The face, almost of a devil, with a closely-fitting skull-cap and a fantastic top-knot of feathers rising straight therefrom," and she stood trembling, holding on to the edge of the table for support, or she would have fallen.

"Now, I know that you must have been dreaming, my dear, for who wears skull-caps or feathered head-dresses in Australia?" laughed the squatter. "You have been reading some sanguinary Indian tale, I'll be bound, and dozed off to finish it in your own way."

"No, grandpapa, no. Thrice no," retorted the fair girl; "it was a real face that I saw, and hark! there is a heavy step on the verandah."

"There is, indeed. I heard it," exclaimed Frank; "let me run upstairs for your revolver, grandpapa; robbers may be about the place."

"Nonsense, foolish boy; if it's anyone it's one of the stockmen come to ask about the branding tomorrow. Hi! come back; where the deuce is the boy off to? Come back, sir, I say!"

But Frank didn't come back. He dashed on to

his father's bedroom as hard as ever he could to possess himself of the revolver.

He had not got half way there when a terrified servant rushed into the room, exclaiming—

"Oh, master! oh, missus! there's two strange men a breaking in through Miss Katie's bedroom window. Oh! we shall be all murdered."

The squatter seized upon the poker at once on hearing this, the old lady sank down on the floor in a swoon, Katie began to run distractedly to and fro, and the servant girl hastened to conceal herself under the table.

Then screams rose at another part of the house, and a hoarse voice was heard to shout—"Stow that row, or I'll blow your brains out precious quick!" and then all was still again.

All still, at least save the sound of heavy feet coming directly towards the parlour door.

Another moment, and that door was thrown open, and in the aperture stood Blue Cap, a revolver in either hand pointed at the assembled company, a look of satanic exultation on his dead white face, and a snaky glitter in his blood-lustful eyes!

"Bail up, I want food and lodging I tell you, and perhaps something more besides. How d'ye do, Mr. Beaumont; I hav'n't set eyes on you since that cursed trial five years ago. You weren't exactly friendly disposed towards me then—I hope time has healed all animosities!" he exclaimed, with a laugh.

"Norton, the murderer of my son William! Villain, what do you here?" faintly gasped the squatter.

"He has come here to meet his fate; he has come here that I may avenge my father's murder! It is heaven's will!" screamed an exultant boy's voice —and there stood Frank, in the opposite doorway, with his revolver pointed at the bushranger!

"Crack!" went Blue Cap's weapon.

"Crack!" went young Frank's, in turn. And then he gave an exultant and fierce cry of joy, as he saw Blue Cap fall with a crash to the floor!

CHAPTER VI.

TREATS OF BLUE CAP'S DOINGS AT MARRANG.

"IT was to be, Frank—it was to be," said the old squatter, when he saw the murderer of his son lying prostrate on the floor. "You have been a blind instrument in the hands of the Almighty; but it was to be."

The boy made no reply, but thrusting the revolver into the breast pocket of his jacket, he crossed the room, and bent over the body of the prostrate bushranger.

He lay still and motionless, in a strange huddled up position, and his wide open eyes seemed to have a film gathering over them, but there was no blood.

Frank essayed to turn the body over with his foot, to discover where the wound was; but finding his strength to be unequal to the task, he bent down and endeavoured to effect his object with his hands.

But suddenly he felt himself clutched in a grasp of iron, a voice hissed in his ears, "Ha! ha! my young cornstalk, I was only playing spider," and then a heavy blow between the eyes made him see stars, and a second dashed him insensible to the floor.

"Dick, bind that young tiger cat. He'd have deprived you of a mate if I'd let him have his own way," growled the convict, with a grin of malice.

Poor Frank's face was streaming with blood; he was stunned and senseless.

Blue Cap drew forth the revolver from the pocket of his jacket, and transferred it to his own belt.

Then, whilst Dick Evans was strapping him up with the fifteen foot long thong of a stock-whip, that he had found in an adjoining room, Blue Cap walked over to where Katie was tending Mrs.

Beaumont, with hands that trembled, and lips that quivered with terror even whilst she uttered words of comfort, and, lifting her in his arms, he pressed his thick tobacco and spirit tainted mouth to hers in a succession of hot, lustful, passionate kisses.

Blue Cap had not saluted the face of woman, or held a young girl's soft yielding form in his arms for years, and he strained Katie in his muscular embrace until she screamed with the pain, kissing her meanwhile wherever he could, and as greedily as a starving schoolboy devours jam tarts.

Yet a blow from her little fist in his dexter eye so quickly changed his amorous feelings to murderous ones, that with an oath he first made his teeth nearly meet in her shoulders, and then hurled her from him with such force that her head coming in contact with the wainscotting, she fell huddled up and senseless on the floor.

Blue Cap spat at her as she lay there with her beautiful face turned upwards, and pale as monumental marble. Then he gave the moaning and groaning old lady a kick that broke one of her ribs, bidding her "Stach that row, or he would boot her brains out;" and when she only groaned the louder, as was very natural, with the pain, he carried his threat into execution, and kicked her about the head until she, too, lost consciousness.

"What's that old fool threatening?" he then exclaimed, glancing fiercely at Mr. Beaumont, whom Dick Evans was holding down in his chair, with the whispered counsel that "he'd better keep quiet if he valued his life;" advice which, however, the old squatter was deaf to, for he kept exclaiming—"Let me get at the villain! Let me get at the villain!"

"Let him be. Let him be," said Dick. "We came here to rob the station, matey—not to fight with boys, women, and old men. Let us bind the old gent down in his chair and go to work."

Blue Cap glanced keenly into his companion's face, and there read strong disapproval of, if not disgust at, the unnecessary brutality he had been guilty of.

He replied with an oath—

"You invoked the devil to aid you on this expedition, and he answered your call. If you expected him to be a namby-pamby kind of a personage— half saint and half sinner—why, you mistook his character very much indeed."

"I'll dissolve partnership with him if he don't behave more like a man and less like a fiend. I'm game for thieving—ay, and for shooting too in self-defence, but I won't see women, nor boys, nor men old enough to be my grandfather ill-used when there's no need of it; and if my plain speaking offends you, come out into the paddock and we'll blaze away at each other till one falls," and Dick clapped his hand on his revolver-stock.

Blue Cap's face grew black-red with passion, the foam worked itself up around his jagged yellow fangs, and for a moment he seemed ready to accept Dick's challenge, and fight with him a duel to the death.

But then, in an instant, the expression of his face changed; an oily smile spread itself over his features, and, with a mocking bow, he said—

"The devil never quarrels with his patrons as long as they stick to him. Patience, friend Dick; will soon teach you to be as fond of blood, violence, and cruelty, as I am. Like smoking, 'tis an acquired taste and only comes of habit. You're but a youth yet—a youth in crime, I mean—well, we'll soon change all that; meanwhile, I give in to you. No more violence or bloodshed than there is need for— that's our motto, eh? Ha! ha! ha! Well, so be it!"

And Blue Cap burst into a paroxysm of laughter that he did not recover from until he saw Dick Evans' face flush with passion again.

Then he recovered himself, and said, briefly—

"Is he bound securely?"

"Yes, he is," replied Dick, curtly.

"Then, old gentleman," quoth Blue Cap, "you'll just hand me over your keys, and explain to me, to save time, what they open. We chiefly want coin of the realm, and portable articles of gold and silver; but we don't object to colonial notes, or anything of value that we can carry in our saddlebags. Come, be quick!"

"Villain; murderer of my son!" groaned the old man.

Blue Cap's face grew dark as night again.

"Come, governor," said Dick. "If I preserve you from my companion's peppery temper, at the cost of incurring his anger myself, you must, at all events, keep a civil tongue in your head. He may have killed your son; but that's not the case in point at present, you know. So just give up your keys, and tell me, whilst you're doing it, have you not two three-year-old racing colts in training here?"

"And what if I have?" said the squatter.

"We are in need of them, and shall take them."

"But the Baron and Rosella are worth three thousand pounds!" stammered the squatter.

"They may be worth as much more if their speed saves our necks from the troopers," quoth Dick.

"A dashed deal more," quoth Blue Cap as he received the keys from the squatter's hand. "You are a sharp lad, Dick, after all, and a credit to your mother, whoever the good lady may be; so where are these racing tits kept, old cock?"

"They are in the stable to the right of the home paddock," said the squatter, turning away from the convict with a shudder, and addressing Dick.

But the former tugged his face round by his grey whiskers, and forced him to explain what rooms, what desks, what drawers, &c., the respective keys opened, and what was in such depositories worth the taking; often, during the investigation, hinting with an oath, that false information would sign his death warrant, spite of comrades or anything else.

"Now, whose agoing to do the rummaging and the searching?" he asked, when he had elicited all the information that he wanted. "Someone will have to stop with these people, although two or three of them is pretty quiet still. But nobody knows when they may come round, and then, like as not, they'll be screeching and bellowing again."

"I'll stop with them," said Dick. "You go and gather in the harvest. If 'tis too heavy for you to carry, just give a shout, and I'll come and help you."

"Right you are, Dick, and you can investigate pockets while I am away. I'll take this candlestick and leave you the other. I want the one as gives the best light. I won't be long, never fear," and the ruffian stalked out of the room with a revolver in one hand, a candlestick in the other, and the bunch of keys dangling from a little finger.

Directly he was gone, Dick deprived the squatter of his watch and chain, his rings, his studs, and all the money that he had in his pockets.

Then he went round and served the old lady and the young one in the same manner.

But he raised the old lady's head on a tilt, and bade Katie—who had recovered consciousness—not to be frightened, for he would see she came to no further hurt.

"Oh, look to my brother," quoth Katie, grasping his hand; "though a bushranger, you have a kind heart. If he is not killed already, promise me that you will protect him, too," and she essayed to rise.

But she was so giddy and faint that she fell again.

"You'd far best lie where you are, and as if you was dead, until we are gone," said Dick. "Your brother is a very long way from death's door, and he shan't get a step nigher to it through any act of me or my comrade."

Then without waiting for her reply, he crossed the room to where Frank was just wiping the mist of blood from before his eyes and wondering where he was, and, first feeling that his lashings were secure, said—

"Cheer up, youngster; but remember that a still tongue makes a wise head. If you get better before we go do not attempt to fight your father's murderer with your tongue, or he may reply with a bullet. You are bound and helpless, but your time may come some day if you are discreet, and don't throw your life away."

"But my sister, my grandfather, and my grandmother—the villain will kill them, too," gasped the boy.

"No he won't," said Dick; "but, hush! he comes. I daren't say a word more," and he hastened away to the opposite end of the room.

Blue Cap re-entered with a flushed face and eyes that flashed with a savage delight.

"A good booty, Dick," he exclaimed—"a downright good booty, lad. I forgive the old fellow his want of politeness. I forgive the old girl her snorts and groans, and as for the young one—I forgive her that blow in the face, although it was so heartily bestowed. Never mind, we'll kiss and make it up," and Blue Cap began to cross the room towards the spot where Katie lay, now in only a pretended swoon.

"Stop, mate," said Dick. "Be content with what you've got, for kiss that gal you won't and me a standing by. If we've done all that we've got to do here, let us find the two racing colts, saddle 'em, and show Marrang our heels. Delays are dangerous."

"Blow danger," quoth Blue Cap. "Larder and cellar come before stables. I'm as dry as dry can be, and hungry too. We shall be fools to leave before we have had a good blow out, matey."

"Listen to me," said Dick Evans. "There's a police camp within three miles of this, and I'm not altogether pleased with the way we lashed those fellows in the shepherd's hut. Cowhides is stiff, I know, and oncommon hard to burst, but if that darned little terrier dog is half as 'cute as I takes him to be, and his master puts him at it in the right way, he'd do the mouse and lion business in about a quarter of an hour with his little sharp white teeth. A hoss would then take one o' them coves to the police camp in a quarter of an hour, or shank's mare in half a one; and if so be they've done it, we've only got bare time to get clear off in. We each of us knows what walley our bodies is to the traps; if you've nothing to fear, why stay, but it's a very different case with me."

Blue Cap grinned until the corners of his mouth almost reached his ears.

"I reckon—valuable as you thinks yourself—the police, for every crown they'd get from Government for your ugly head, would get for mine a pound. Therefore, I thank you for the hint, Dick, and off we will go," he said, with a laugh.

"Shall we unbind the squatter?" asked Dick.

"No!" roared Blue Cap. "They as is in faints will come round, sooner or later, and release them as is bound. Let him be, and come way."

Dick was too glad, now that the spoil was all safe, to get his bloodthirsty partner away on any pretence whatever, and so he briefly replied, "Come along, then," and they quitted the room together.

CHAPTER VII.

A TIMELY RESCUE.

WHEN the footsteps of the two bushrangers suddenly ceased, betokening that they had quitted the house, Katie Beaumont staggered to her feet.

"Grandma, grandma, do you live?" she first of all exclaimed, bending over the old lady.

"Yes, my dear," came a faint, low response; 'I'm alive, but I'm in great pain. Where's your grandfather?"

"Here I am, my dears, as helpless as a trussed fowl," came the quick retort. "But Frank—see to Frank; he's a plucky boy, and I'm afraid that the villain who murdered his father has killed him, too."

"No, he hasn't grandpa," came a feeble voice from the opposite side of the room, "and if Katie will only come over here and cut my lashings, I'll have him yet before he's off the run. There's poor father's revolver upstairs, and powder, caps, and bullets in the case. Quick, Katie; hurry, hurry, or it will be too late. Don't thwart me. If I can't kill that bad, wicked fiend in human form, I shall break my heart."

"Don't release him, Katie—don't release him; he will rush on his death," whispered the old man in the young girl's ear. "Say anything; but don't release him."

Katie nodded, and glided across the room.

She knelt down and kissed her brother's blood-stained face.

"Not that, Katie—not that; I want you to release me, or I shall be too late," he said, querelously.

"But, Frank, I do not see a knife."

"Well, run into the kitchen and fetch one."

"Oh, Frank, I'm so afraid. The robbers may not be off the premises yet," she exclaimed.

"Oh yes, they are. I heard them pass out of the front door and close it behind them. Do hurry, Katie; don't you see that you are losing valuable time—time that can't be regained. If I can't creep upon them before they have saddled, led out, and mounted the Baron and Rosella, they may snap their fingers at me; so come, sissy, make haste."

Thus urged, Katie proceeded to the kitchen, and presently returned, bringing with her the bluntest knife that she could find; and therewith, seating herself by Frank's side, she pretended to make as much haste as she could in cutting asunder his bonds; he moaning and complaining the while at her slowness and stupidity as he called it.

But presently she uttered a shriek.

"Good heavens! Have you cut yourself, dear?" asked Frank, anxiously—for he was very fond of his sister.

"No," was the reply; "but he has returned—there!"

Miss Beaumont pointed towards the open door, just within which stood the bushranger, with the towering blue and scarlet feathers of his strange head-dress sweeping against the top of the doorway, whilst a devilish smile lighted up his perfectly hairless face.

"My mate dragged me off, without even suffering me to bid you good night, but I've slipped away from him, whilst he is saddling the horses, to do so, and to apologise for his real, and my apparent rudeness," he said, with a chuckling laugh. "Good-bye old gentleman; pray remember me in the next world," he continued; and, levelling his revolver, he shot Mr. Beaumont dead in his chair.

"Now for you, old lady," he ejaculated, and crack went another barrel, and Mrs. Beaumont also gave up the ghost, with an ounce of lead in her brain.

"As for you, my little lass, you shall be a bush-ranger's bride, whether my mate and your friends sanction it or no," then laughed Blue Cap; and he returned his revolver to his pocket, and, springing forward, for a second time seized Katie in his arms.

She shrieked and struggled, but he was as strong as a bear, and pressing her soft bosoms against his broad chest, that caused her to moan between her clenched teeth with pain, he covered her face hot, burning kisses.

that supreme moment of agonised dug the blunt knife that she

retained in her hand with all her strength into Blue Cap's left cheek.

The stroke hardly drew blood, though no doubt it inflicted great pain. Anyhow, it was sufficient to turn all the convict's passion into hatred.

For a second time he dashed her to the floor, and this time he followed up the act of wanton barbarity by leaping on her, and then deliberately braining her with his pistol butt, laughing at Frank as he struggled vainly to burst his bonds, calling down the wrath of heaven the while upon the slayer of all his kindred.

When he had killed the girl he advanced upon Frank, with—

"Now, then, my lad, it is your turn."

He plucked forth his deadly weapon and pointed it full at Frank's chest, but the youth never blanched.

"Aren't you afraid of death?" asked the bushranger.

"You sha'n't see that I am, anyhow," was the reply.

"I will kill you with a dozen shots, then, instead of one, and see if you mind pain," laughed the bushranger.

"Do as you like, vile wretch, but you won't draw a cry, or tear, or groan, or supplication, I forewarn you."

"We will see, I repeat," chuckled Blue Cap, and he now pointed his revolver at Frank's left shoulder.

But ere he could pull the trigger there was a cry of "Hold, villain, on your life! Murderer of my brother, your time has come."

Then ensued the crash of broken glass, and a man in the uniform of the mounted constabulary leapt into the room, revolver in hand.

CHAPTER VIII.
THE OATH OF VENGEANCE.

BLUE CAP wheeled round like an angry bull on the intruder.

"Crack!" went his revolver, and the trooper's blue shako was dashed from his head.

"Crack!" again, and away went a silver button off his chest and his left shoulder strap along with it.

The third shot flew wide, and then there was a dull "snap, snap, snap!" as the hammer came down on the three already exploded caps.

Blue Cap was defenceless.

It was now the trooper's turn, but he was too excited to take cool and deliberate aim.

He fired four barrels of his revolver rapidly.

Then he peered through the smoke in search of the prostrate body of his foe, but uttered a cry of astonishment and rage when he saw that he was gone.

At the same instant a loud "C-oo-ee!" came from the direction of the home paddock.

It was Dick Evans halloaing out to his companion.

Receiving no immediate answer, another "C-oo-ee!" awakened the silent echoes of the night, and then there was the trampling of horses' hoofs, and a loud voice bellowed angrily out—

"Where the devil are you, mate? Not a-murdering the prisoners, I hope."

"No, no, I'm coming; ride towards me; here, this way. The troopers are in the house," responded another voice, and the young constable dashed out of the window into the verandah again, in time to see Blue Cap vault over the post and rail fence into the home paddock, and Dick Evans sweep towards him at a gallop with a led horse.

He was out of pistol range, even though the voices in that wondrously clear climate could be heard so distinctly; and when the trooper saw by

BLUE CAP RAISED HIS HANDS HIGH ABOVE HIS HEAD, THEN THE CHAIN DESCENDED WITH CRUSHING FORCE.

the white moonlight the quality of the horses on which the flight would be effected, he turned back into the room with an oath, for he knew that to dream of pursuit on his own tired and jaded steed would be madness.

"The villain!" he muttered between his teeth. "He must have as many lives as a cat, and his friend, the devil, seems to be ever at his elbow to give him a helping hand when he most needs one. Well, the race is not always to the swift. The tortoise beat the hare in the long chase, and I'll run you to earth yet, you wolf, or my name isn't Ted Hogan."

"I'll help you, Ted Hogan, if you'll permit me," said a faint voice from the opposite corner.

"What, is there anyone alive, here?" exclaimed the trooper, "I thought I was alone with the dead."

"Eh? Are all the others really dead? Quite dead?"

"They look like it; but come and examine their bodies with me. We shall soon find out, then."

"But how can I? I'm bound hand and foot."

"Oh, I see!" exclaimed the trooper, with a low whistle. "Well, it won't take me very long to set you free."

He drew a clasp knife from his pocket, opened it, and, finding out Frank, proceeded to cut his bonds.

"Ah, it was you the villain was standing over when I entered the room. I had forgotten it. I recognised only the murderer of my brother. I had eyes and thoughts for nothing else. How I missed killing him I can't think; I am considered a good shot in the service. He must bear a charmed life—he must indeed," said the trooper, whilst engaged in this operation.

"He killed my father, years ago," replied Frank, "and now he has killed my sister, and both my grandparents. Oh, he is a ruthless fiend!"

"And what is his name?" asked Ted Hogan.

Frank Beaumont looked at his questioner in surprise.

"Don't you know the name of the man who killed your brother? Well, that is strange!"

"Hardly, for I've only been in the colony, and in the service a month. He killed my brother last night, in escaping from the vessel that was carrying him and scores more yellow birds to the penal settlement at Port Arthur, in Van Dieman's Land. I only know him as No. 144, for that was painted on his jacket," explained the trooper.

"Oh! I see. Well, his real name is Norton, but he calls himself Blue Cap, and he is a bushranger. His companion is called Dick, and isn't a bad sort of fellow. When we tackle the two, and kill Blue Cap, we must spare Dick, because he tried all he could to prevent his mate from killing us."

At this juncture the last bond was cut, and Frank, scrambling to his feet, staggered across the room—for he was so stiff that he could hardly use his limbs—to where his sister lay.

He felt her pulse and heart, but they were for ever still.

Unconvinced, however, he ran upstairs for a little hand mirror, and held it before her lips.

Then, when he withdrew it and saw that its polished surface was undimmed, he knew that she was dead.

We will not attempt to describe his grief—our efforts would be all too feeble to depict it. So great was it, that when the trooper told him that his grandfather and grandmother were dead also, he had no tears or extra emotion to bestow on them.

But suddenly he checked all outward manifestation of his inner agony, and said brusquely—

"It will be time enough to mourn when they are avenged. Ted Hogan, are we to hunt down this demon in human shape together or separately? I will not thrust my company upon you if you do not wish it; but still, if you will let me go with you, I shall be very glad. There are two of them,

you know; and together we should be far more likely to succeed."

"But you are such a boy," said the trooper.

"Well, I'm only sixteen; but I'm five foot nine high, and strong in proportion. I'm a good horseman, and a very fair pistol shot too; added to which, I know every inch of the country for many a score of miles round."

"In that case," said Ted Hogan, "I shall be right glad of your company; that is, if you may come."

"May come!" repeated Frank, sadly. "There is no one alive now to say me nay. I'm the owner of Marrang, I suppose, but I've no kith nor kin in the world except a few distant cousins in England, whom I have never seen. You see I am my own master."

"I've no relatives in Australia, and I'm my own master, too, for eight or nine days, at the termination of which time I shall have to report myself in Sydney, I suppose; so that I shall be very glad of your company for a portion of, or all that time," said the trooper.

"Then let us swear that the wretch Blue Cap shall die by our hands!" said Frank excitedly.

"But why should we swear such a thing? We will certainly do our very best to find and kill him."

"Never mind. Let us take an oath of vengeance. I feel that we shall be more likely to succeed then," persisted Frank Beaumont.

"If such is your belief, I will take the oath readily."

"Stay a minute, then, until I rejoin you," said Frank; and he hurriedly quitted the room.

Presently he returned with a revolver.

"It was my father's—my father, whom that villain slew. I will swear on it, and do you swear on yours, that with these weapons we will kill him," he said.

"I am ready to do anything that you wish. Dictate the words, and I will repeat them after you," was the reply.

Frank thought for a moment, and then said slowly—

"I swear that I will fire six bullets from this revolver through the bloodthirsty and cowardly heart of the miscreant who calls himself Blue Cap the Bushranger."

He looked up after kissing the pistol, and then Ted Hogan went through the same form of words and the same action at their close.

"It is well," said Frank, grasping the trooper's hand. "Let us go up now and release the servants whom Blue Cap's mate has locked in one of the rooms at the back," and away they went together.

The servants were soon set free, and they assisted Frank and the trooper to carry the dead bodies out of the dining room and lay them on their respective beds.

Frank then ordered a substantial meal and the best wines that the cellar contained to be laid on the table.

"We must eat and drink in order to keep up our strength. If we grow weak, these men may be able to cheat us out of our revenge," he said.

Then he sat down to write a letter to the station superintendent, who was out at the other end of the run, telling him all that had occurred, the errand he was bent on, and what he wished done in his absence.

"Send a messenger with it at once," he said, to one of the servants; "and tell Jack to give a feed of oats to Gin and Lubra. They are our strongest and fleetest nags, now that the scoundrels have stolen the two racing colts. We will start in half an hour from now."

Then he and the trooper ate as much as they could, and partook moderately of the generous wine; and by the time that the horses were led round, they were quite ready to mount them.

They filled their saddle-bags with meat and bread, placing a bottle of wine in each.

Then they clapped their revolvers in their right-hand holsters, filled the left-hand hand ones with cartridges; and mounting, rode away on the track of the bushrangers.

———

CHAPTER IX.

STICKING UP THE WOLLONGONG MAIL.

BY this time, however, the two bushrangers were a good nine miles away over the Illawarra Ranges, across the Cataract River, and heading for Narcho, with their steeds just as fresh as at starting.

They were not journeying on the most friendly terms.

Blue Cap had admitted that his motive in returning to the station was to murder its inmates; and Dick had told him plain and pat, that "If he'd a known he'd killed that pretty young gal, he'd ha' helped the trap to riddle him with bullets, instead of galloping like wildfire across the paddock to pick him up."

"But I'd all the spoil about me," quoth Blue Cap.

"You might have taken it down below with you, and offered it as drink money to the devil and his imps," retorted Dick. "I like a man as will shoot another when there's any occasion for it; but to kill for the pleasure of killing, and old men and women too. Bah! it's tigerish, that's what I call it—terrible and unearthly."

"Well, I'll try and control my instincts in future, Dick, on my word I will. But I do love smashing people up, there's no gainsaying it. A fellow once as felt my bumps, said I'd the organs of combative-ness and destructiveness, and that they was a growing very large; and do you know, I 'spect he was about right. But I'll control 'em, Dick—I'll control 'em, for your sake, my boy," and the elder bushranger laughed until the woods rang.

"You'd best do that if we are to continue mates," quoth Dick; "and you'll find it a deal safer to work with a strong determined fellow like me, than alone, I can tell you. I own I take to you because you do not funk at things like Larry Doyle and Jack Cooper did; but I won't have needless slaughter—so there."

"Well then, man alive, I agree to that, don't I? But how the dickens is it that you have never asked me what I picked up at the station, eh?"

"Because the horrors you perpetrated there drove it clean out of my mind; but what was it?"

"Well, twenty-five pounds in gold, forty-five in colonial one-pound notes, about three pounds in silver, and a jewel case, small and compact, but pretty nigh full of costly trinkets. This, however, is, I guess, the gem of the lot," and Blue Cap fished out of the breast pocket of his jumper, and held up to sparkle in the moonlight, a ring whose great rose diamonds glittered and scintillated like stars.

"That's a three hundred pounder, and the gems 'll bring two hundred at any Jew fence's in Birckfields Hill or Parramatta Street," said Dick with flashing eyes.

"Yes, about," assented Blue Cap; "but it strikes me, Dick, that it's a pity to knock off work at such an early hour of the night; much more might be done."

"How?" demanded Dick, reining up his horse.

"Well, half a league further on we strike the Wollongong Road at the Ten Mile Creek, and Cobb's coach is due there half an hour after midnight."

"I know it is, and 'tis now about a quarter of an hour to midnight. You propose to stick it up?"

"I do. Why the deuce shouldn't we, eh?" quoth Blue Cap.

"I don't know, except that in all probability the troopers are in full pursuit, and it would be rather awkward if the delay enabled them to come up with us."

"Oh, the delay won't extend over half an hour, or at the most three quarters, and the traps are a good hour to the bad, take my word for it. Besides, on nags like these, as long as we don't let them come within pistol range, we can shake them off at will."

"Blue Cap, your arguments are convincing; I'm on."

The two men spoke no more, but rode on at a steady pace through the silent bush, in the direction of the Ten Mile Creek and the Wollongong Road.

They had not yet met or passed a solitary human being, for the neighbourhood was a thinly settled one, people considering themselves near neighbours if their homes were not more than a score of miles apart.

Here and there kangaroos grazed in flocks, a long legged emu now and then strutted past, happy that his lot was not cast near broken bottles and old nails—which, however, he would have unhesitatingly swallowed had it been—for an emu will devour anything and everything that comes in his way.

Up in the tree tops the wakeful possum sometimes squealed, and the Australian cookoo shouted "More pork!" as loud as he could bawl, answered ever and anon by the "he-law, he-haw! ha! ha! ha! ha!" of that comical big-headed bird the laughing-jackass.

These were the only sounds save the rattle of dead bark against snow-white tree trunks, the drowsy hum of the locusts amid the leaves, the shrill trumpeting of the bush mosquitos, and the occasional howl of some prowling warrigal in the distant gullies, that disturbed the silence of the warm, breezeless Australian night.

On, and on, and on, over the grassy plains and slopes, and at last the two horsemen rein up.

"This should be the Wollongong Road," says Dick.

"It is the Wollongong Road," adds Blue Cap.

It was curious how either of them knew it.

There was no road apparent.

It was still open, park-like bush, with grass underneath, and box, peppermint, shea-oak and ironbark trees growing singly and in groups all around as far as the eye could reach; and yet it was the road, nevertheless, for a very close inspection showed the faint marks of wheels and of horses' hoofs on the green turf.

"We will hide behind that clump of trees," said Blue Cap, "and when the coach gets to this point, where the driver will have rather a ticklish bit of work to round that prostrate tree trunk and then escape grazing that shea-oak just beyond, we will ride out at a gallop and bid them bail up."

"Very well," replied Dick; "there couldn't be a better place, and success is pretty nigh certain. But no useless bloodshed, mind, Blue Cap; that I insists on."

"All right—all right. What's the good of bothering about that? Of course, if any of the passengers has fire-arms and presents them at us, we aren't a going to be outdone in politeness nohow," growled the elder.

"No, no. Shoot as many fighting cocks as you like, but not the harmless barn-door varieties, nor no pretty chicks nor sitting hens," quoth Dick.

"Oh, I've promised that. It's all right, that is."

And away they rode behind the clump of trees.

About a quarter of an hour later, away in the distance, appeared three great red lights in the form of a triangle.

They belonged to the approaching coach.

Then ensued the "pad—pad—pad" of galloping hoofs upon the soft turf; and, presently, full out into the moonlight, appeared a scarlet and gold circus-band-carriage looking vehicle, drawn by six fine horses, and driven by a tall slab-sided Yankee, whose white felt hat was at least a yard high in the crown, and of prodigious breath in the brim.

"The coach is crammed chock full of passengers, and they're all men," muttered Dick to Blue Cap.

"If 'twas chock full of devils, 'twould be all the same to me," was the excited reply. "Now, do you attend to the driver and his cattle, and I'll tackle the coach full of men. If he dares to drive on after you tell him to rein up, shoot the off leader—if you feel merciful towards the man. 'Twill be all the same."

"All right," responded Dick; "you'll find that I'll do all that's proper and needful anyway, old boss."

"Now, this is the right moment. Away!"

He dug his spurless heels into the sides of his mettled racer as he spoke, and, with reins drawn taut, and his reloaded revolver grasped tightly in his right hand, bore down on the coach like a comet.

"Bail up! Whoever dares to resist, in goes lead and out goes brains," he roared, with a horrible laugh; and, at the same instant almost, "Bail up!" yelled Dick Evans. "Curb in your horses, or you die."

Then there was a pistol shot, a horse shrieked and fell, the rest snorted and reared, the coach rocked, ran partly up a bank, toppled over, and came crashing down; and, whilst Dick Evans, addressing the prostrate driver, exclaimed wrathfully, "You brought it on yourself, you fool," Blue Cap ejaculated in a fierce and a shriller key, "Guard, out with the letter bags; don't lie snivelling there like a stuck pig. Leg broke? Well, what the deuce is that to us? Out with the mail bags, or I'll smash in your head. Now you dod rotted shunks, your purses, watches, chains, and rings. Do you want to be quickened with a pistol bullet, eh?"

"Die, robber!" exclaimed a voice.

There was the report of a pistol, and away went Blue Cap's macaw plume.

"Die, fool!" retorted the bushranger, and he gave the rash firer a bullet through the skull.

Then, his blood being up, he would have gone on firing at others, had not a cry at this instant been raised, "Rescue, rescue! here comes the troopers!"

And Blue Cap and Dick Evans looked round, to perceive what they took to be two troopers—one in uniform and one in plain clothes—approaching at a gallop.

CHAPTER X.
THE MIDNIGHT CHASE.

BLUE CAP gave vent to a horrible imprecation. Dick Evans was every whit as annoyed. But at the same time he was not so surprised.

Blue Cap would have stopped and fought the new arrivals.

But Dick Evans saw the madness of such a course.

He knew that the proximity of the two troopers, as he took them to be, would give the cowed passengers of the coach hearts of spurious valour, and that whilst they were exchanging shots with the police, they would be quite courageous enough to fire at their backs.

"Come away, man," shouted Dick therefore.

"Not till I've stopped those fellows' running cackle," growled Blue Cap, wheeling round.

"Nonsense. 'He who fights and runs away will live to fight another day.' I aren't going to help you tackle a score. No, no, Dick Evans is not a coward, but he's still further removed from a fool. If you aren't an out-and-out idiot you'll follow him sharp, and live to thank him for setting the example," and with these words the younger bushranger rode off at a gallop.

"The sneaking cur!" growled Blue Cap, fiercely;

and he had half a mind to stand his ground and fight his battle out single handed.

But a moment's reflection showed him the insanity of such a course, and so, shooting a couple more of the coach passengers as a balm to his wounded feelings, and hurling a volley of fearful maledictions at the survivors, he wheeled round his mettled racer and dashed off in pursuit of Dick, throwing himself well on his flying steed's neck to avoid the bullets that now began to whistle around his head from the pistols of Ted Hogan and Frank Beaumont.

But it is impossible to take good aim whilst dashing forward at a gallop, and so every bullet flew wide of its billet, and Blue Cap chuckled as he rode on unhurt.

Perhaps he thought that his pursuers would draw up to render assistance to the occupants of the shipwrecked coach, but they did no such thing.

"There are enough of you left unhurt to help the rest, and we have sworn to take that ruffian alive or dead," sang out Ted Hogan, as he sped past.

"Ay, though we chase him thrice round the world," added Frank Beaumont.

And in another minute the flight and chase had swept out of sight.

"That's yer sort," ejaculated the Yankee coachman. "The real grit and no mistake. Pity 'tis that the rogues has got the best horses. They'll give 'em leg bail as safe as pumpkins."

"You'd better see about your own horses, and getting the coach to-rights," said one of the passengers, brusquely.

"All right," retorts the slab-sided one. "A delay of ten minutes for refreshments, gentlemen, and off we go again. This'll be the third time that Cobb's Royal Mail has discharged the duties of hearse and stage coach in one. However, we will lay the dead gentlemen along the bottom, and then, as there'll be more room, you can clap your feet up on the opposite seats; and then don't think of what is, but think of what's pleasant. That's road philosophy, that is."

And chuckling, and laughing, for violent deaths were no new sight to them, the coachman and the guard set to work getting the gaudy vehicle and the five remaining horses into proper trim for performing the rest of the journey.

Meanwhile, Ted Hogan and Frank Beaumont rode on, with no thought but of overtaking Blue Cap and his mate.

They spoke not, for the guidance of their horses required all their care; and, besides, they had often to maintain the chase by sound, as every now and then patches of tea tree and box scrub hid the chase from view.

But though the night wind hummed its melancholy song through the sombre eucalyptic foliage, and the clouds which had been coming up from the south all the evening and early night had now blotted both moonlight and starlight out of the dull firmament, there was a kind of phosphorescent glow in the atmosphere that revealed the immediately surrounding objects distinctly, whilst the air was so heavy and still, that when hidden from the eye, the "pad—pad—pad" of the galloping hoofs in front could be distinctly heard on the soft turf.

And though in mere point of speed the stock horses, Lubra and Gin, were no match for the racing colts, Baron and Rosella, the nature of the ground over which the chase lay was such that the ready knack of the stock horses in clearing and rounding fallen timber, their sure footedness and their ready obedience to snaffle and heel made up for their shortness of stride.

Besides, over such a country the bushrangers dared not put the racing colts to racing speed, or they would have dashed themselves to pieces against some obstacle or other in the semi-darkness before they perceived it.

And thus it was that the bushrangers found it impossible to shake off their pertinacious pursuers, and though Blue Cap often wished to wheel round and fight, he recollected that, like a fool, he had emptied his revolver upon the harmless inmates of the coach, and at that headlong pace there was no time to reload.

On, and on, and on.

An hour had passed away, and twelve miles of bush had been traversed.

The horses were not so fresh now, and their laboured breathing told of an early breakdown.

The tempest, too, which had been brewing the whole night long, now suddenly broke forth in all the terrific grandeur of a semi-tropical Australian thunderstorm.

The southerly-buster howled in wild gusto amidst the lofty tree branches, beneath which the four horsemen were madly flying like phantoms in the murky gloom; the artillery of heaven roared, rattled, and crashed almost incessantly, and the bright lightbolts which shot, flashed and quivered in awful splendour across the leaden sky, lighted up at every instant the murky gloom, dazzling the eyes of both man and horse, and when they disappeared, leaving, until their sudden reappearance, a void of black and almost palpable darkness behind.

But still guided by the glimpses that they caught of the chase during these flashes, and still dimly discerning them through the gloom when the interval was longer than usual between them, and their eyes had become accustomed to the darkness again, Ted Hogan and Frank Beaumont kept on the track of the bushrangers, who now seemed to be riding recklessly forward, urging their horses to the very top of their speed.

But the pursuers, one with his twin brother and the other with his whole kith and kin to avenge, would not be shaken off, and as relentlessly as the black ban-dogs of hell pursued the wicked baron who followed the chase on a Sunday, so Ted and Frank kept on their headlong course, urging their now flagging steeds—whose flanks heaved and fell, and from whose quivering nostrils the white breath just streaked with blood streamed convulsively—with voice, hand, and spur.

Neither pursuers nor pursued had as yet gained any advantage; their relative positions were as much the same as when they had swept out of sight of the coach.

It was evident, however, from the exhausted state of their horses, that the long race was nearly run.

Ted and Frank had not exchanged a word since its commencement, and now every baleful lightning flash showed their faces darker and sterner as the staggering and roaring of their steeds convinced them every minute more fully that the bushrangers would get away.

At length the trooper's horse stumbled and fell; but with almost superhuman exertion, his equally exhausted rider kept him on his feet.

It was only a short respite, for a minute later it caught its fore foot against the root of a tree, and, staggering forward a few steps, fell with a heavy crash to the ground, hurling its rider over its head.

At the same instant, the poor animal coughed up a volume of blood from its mouth and nostrils, and rolling over with a spasmodic gasp, died.

Its heart had burst!

But in his excitement and his thirst after vengeance, young Frank noted not the fall of either horse or man, but sped past the one and over the other with a yell that would have done credit to the lungs of a Comanche Indian.

As for Hogan, he scrambled to his feet half dazed, and scarcely knowing where he was, or what brought him there.

He reeled on mechanically, as it were, on foot; but he had not gone many paces, when a vivid sheet of pale blue lightning streamed across the heavens, almost blinding him with its intensity; and a second later, a clap of thunder seemed to rend the very firmament in twain.

Another flash, and another roar succeeded; but the latter was almost drowned by the downward crash of one of the monarchs of the forest that had been stricken by the forked quivering tongue of flame.

The trooper felt the earth shake beneath the concussion; he saw huge boughs and wrenched-off splinters flying in all directions through the air; and then he heard a piercing scream, and, by the next lightning flash, saw the white, agonized countenance of a man who lay crushed beneath the great red-gum, and a grey horse, whose bridle had become entangled around its prostrate rider's foot, plunging and struggling violently to free itself.

One glance sufficed to show Ted Hogan that the poor wretch under the tree was not Blue Cap, and then he knew that he was the other bushranger, and that the horse rearing and plunging there was one of the Marrang racing colts.

His eyes lighted up with renewed hope then.

He freed it somehow, calmed it with a few words, flung himself into the saddle, listened for the sound of galloping hoofs—heard them—and dashed off swift as the lightning's flash in fresh and hot pursuit.

He could hardly help giving a yell of delight, when he found that the beautiful animal he now bestrode was comparatively fresh—good for another half dozen miles at the least; and Frank uttered a cry, half of joy and half of exasperation, when, five minutes later, the trooper dashed past him like the wind, and took up the running.

Then his own horse went down, giving our hero an ugly fall.

He did not feel it, however, in his then state of excitement, but, springing to his feet, sought to induce his gallant stock horse also to rise.

But it was of no use; the animal was thoroughly broken down—was as weak and helpless as a two months' old babe, in fact.

Poor thing, it would never rise more.

Frank saw that the race, as far as he was concerned, was over, and so he strained his eyes, in the hopes of with them being able to follow it to the end.

But bushranger and trooper had alike swept far beyond his range of vision—the hoof-strokes even of their galloping horses had died out; the lightning flashes revealed nought but the grim and silent bush.

CHAPTER XI.

JOHN AB HOWDEEDOO?

FRANK hesitated what to do for a few moments. He did not like to leave his poor horse, and yet he wanted to be in at the death, for he had made up his mind now that, barring accidents, Ted Hogan would run Blue Cap down, and shoot him like a wild beast.

He ran on, therefore, heedless of the few large warning drops of rain, precursors of the coming storm, that now began to fall heavily on the leaves over head, oblivious of the thick pattering that quickly followed, and unmindful of the perfect deluge it rapidly developed into, and which drenched him to the skin in a less time than it takes to record the fact.

He heard and heeded, however, the double report of a pistol that rang shrilly forth on the night air in the lull of the thunder; and when, an instant later, a bright sheet of flame spread, for a brief moment, over the entire heavens, he thought he saw two mounted figures showing blackly against the blinding light on the summit of a gentle eminence, a good mile away.

He thought he saw one of these figures throw up its arms and fall, and the other wheel round and gallop towards him, but the deep darkness suddenly veiled the scene, and the wild, weird note of a laughing jackass rang in his ears with a burst of mocking laughter.

He walked on and on, scarce able to see his way now, for the thunder storm was over, and no lightning flashes came to illumine the path with their momentary, fitful glow, though the rain continued to descend in torrents.

On, and on, and on, footsore and weary, with his forehead bleeding from a great cut he had received from a stone, when his horse went to earth with him.

Often he stopped to listen for the returning hoof-strokes of the trooper's steed, but he heard them not.

He could not make it out.

He felt assured that he was in the right path, and that he had seen Blue Cap fall.

What, then, could hinder Ted Hogan from returning?

He "Coo-ee-yed" every now and then, to direct him towards him (and this peculiar native call, when uttered properly, can be heard at an immense distance), but he received no reply, and he at last awoke to the fact that he was alone, and lost in the midnight bush.

He came upon patches of scrub.

Presently, he thought they grew denser and thicker.

He picked and tasted some of the leaves.

In spite of the rain, they were salt.

It was the Mallee scrub there.

He guessed where he was, and, shudderingly, he resought the open bush.

He breathed a fervent prayer when he found it, and he hurried away from that hated scrub—the grave of so many a lost wanderer—as fast as he could.

And then, still "Coo-ee-ying" at intervals, and still receiving no answer, he, at last, found himself on a little hill bare of trees, where he stumbled over something, and, picking it up, found that it was a revolver.

Whilst he was looking at it, the clouds rolled away from the face of the moon and the stars shone out.

By their light, he saw that the revolver he had picked up was a government one.

"It must have belonged to Ted Hogan," he thought to himself, and then came the query—

"Where was Ted Hogan?"

Ha, that was a difficult question to answer.

The ground was cut up by horses' hoofs, and in one place the emerald turf bore the dark stain of blood. A desperate struggle had evidently taken place there; but then, where were the dead and the living?

Frank "Coo-ee-yed" once more, and this time was answered by a horrid croaking.

He looked up to see two enormous carrion vultures rise from a strange erection on his right, and fly lazily away.

This erection looked like a rough wicker-work hammock stuffed with straw, and supported on four wooden uprights, at a height of about nine feet from the ground.

Over one side of this seeming hammock, a long skeleton hand and arm hung supinely down, and a white bleached human skull seemed also to grin mockingly from behind the mouldering straw.

Anyone fresh from England would have stared aghast at such a horrid sight; but Frank knew that it was only the tomb of one of the black fellows, who, objecting to burying, and not having heard of cremation, expose their dead to the intense heat of an Australian sun, which, when the vultures do not find them out, turns them into very respectable mummies in a month or so.

Frank only bestowed one glance on this spoilt mummy, for the vultures had scented it out and preferred changing it into a skeleton, and then he commenced to search the ground for other tokens of the deadly fray that he felt convinced had taken place there.

Presently he found a piece of torn blue cloth with a silver button attached.

Heavens, that must have been a portion of the trooper's coat!

Frank became very concerned now, for he saw that the fight must have come to grappling, and yet what had become of the combatants?

Over and over the ground he stalked again and again, and presently perceiving something gleaming white and round amongst the undergrowth, he went and gave it a kick in order to turn it and see what it was.

It gave a strange sound and felt stranger still to the sole of his boot, and whilst he stared in astonishment at the odd thing, he saw what looked like a great black ugly snake firmly affixed thereto.

He stepped back in terror at first, but perceiving that the reptile did not uncoil itself, but seemed to be in a kind of torpid state, he took firm hold of it close up to what he conceived to be its throat, and compressed, and twisted, and tugged at it with all his might.

But like other snakes it wasn't cold, and unlike other snakes it was hairy, and whilst astounded at these two novel facts, yet tugging still the harder for their discovery, a piteous voice exclaimed in the shrillest of accents—

"Oh mine big tail! Oh mine big tail! Chin, chin! chow, chow! let um go, let um go; me ain't strong."

Frank stood amazed.

He had read of gorillas and apes, ourang-outangs and baboons, but he knew that neither of these were indigenous to Australia, nor had he even read of their being able to speak.

Perhaps another kick would solve the riddle.

Frank bestowed it most heartily, eliciting a groan, as deep as it was fervent, in reply.

And then the thing upreared itself, and revealed, not legs, but a face underneath—the face of a frightened Chinee, with a smile that was child-like and bland.

"Who the dickens are you?" exclaimed Frank.

"I'm John—I'm John Ab Howdeedoo? So glad you come. Poor John welly much frightened."

"What are you frightened at?" asked Frank.

"John frightened at pig ugly debbil in cradle up dare, and two oder ugly debbils dat come here to fight and fire pistol bullets all round him. Oh, belly bad men to fight like dat, and John so near too."

"Who fought—who got the best of it?" asked Frank.

"Both fought, an' both got de best of it, John thinks. Man in grey gallop up fust, and man in blue obertakes him jus dare. Man in grey he turn round an' swear; man in blue say, 'Ah, I have you at last, have I?' den dey both blazes away, and John belly his head in de ground and nebber bob up till you kick him on top and pull him tail, and say, 'All right, John; I'm your friend. Nobody hurt you.'"

"I never said anything of the kind; and do you mean to tell me that, close by as you were, you don't know how the fight went, or who killed the other?" said Frank Beaumont in accents of disgust.

"John thinks um killed all round and den de grinning debbil up dare eat um all up; but John nebber look to see. Him stop up ears, shut up eyes, berry um head in de ground like ostrich, and wait till goot gennlemum knock at um head an' say, 'Honest John, you um too good to be killed. No danger now—me take care you. No harm happen you, John.' Then um wake up and see kind gennlemum," and the heathen Chinee smiled again till his expressionless face seemed to be dividing into two portions.

"You are a fool," said Frank, "and I've a great mind to punch your head. But just think, and surely you'll be able to recollect if there were more than two men fighting, and, if there were only two, which got the best of it. Do try to remember."

Frank spoke very earnestly, and the Chince seemed to try, oh so hard, to think.

Once or twice a ray of intelligence lighted up his sallow, beardless face, but in an instant it would die out again, and leave his countenance an expressionless blank most comical to behold.

"It um no good, it um not one lilly bit of good," he said, with an air of the utmost dejection and despair; "John see nothin' an' hear nothin'. He shut um eye and stop um ear, an' berry um head, an' hide umself altumgader, an' wish umself towsand miles away."

Frank fumed internally, but he saw that not an atom of reliable information was to be obtained from the flowery celestial on the point next his heart.

However, he determined to try him on another.

"John," he said, "do you know of a bush inn or a shanty anywhere near, where I could get food and shelter?"

"Bush inn or shanty?" replied the Chinaman, scratching his bald pate. "Dars de Currency Lass; dat all I know."

"And how far is the Currency Lass off, John?"

"Twenty, forty, two hundred steps off, mabbe, sar."

"Oh, close by, is it?" exclaimed Frank, brightening up. "Guide me to it, and I'll give you a shilling."

"Shilling?—shilling for John Ab Howdeedoo! dat belly good. John sleep in comfortable stable now in de straw, not out in wet bush. No, no, no, ear, not at all."

And the heathen Chinee performed a grotesque dance in the shadow, that Frank would have found very diverting had less serious matters occupied his mind.

He was glad, however, that he had got a guide to a place where he could obtain shelter until the storm was over, and dry his clothes, and gain some slight repose ere another morn brought with it fresh labours.

He fancied, too, that there he might come across Ted Hogan, who might have been wounded, and sought the place as the nearest where aid could be secured.

He hurried the Chinaman to set forth therefore, and when he had finished his dance—but not before—he obeyed, with many gesticulations that Frank didn't understand.

In a strange shuffling run he led the way, our hero following him at a walk that was just as fast.

Presently, however, he stumbled, and fell over something.

When he got up he looked to see what it was.

The spot was wrapped in profound shadow, but by putting his face closer to it, he could just make out that it was the body of a man, nearly divested of his clothing.

A still closer scrutiny convinced him that it was the body of a murdered Chinaman, for it was clotted with, and lay in a pool of blood.

"John," shouted out our hero, "here is a slain countryman of yours. Come, and have a look."

The celestial uttered a little cry of alarm at this hail, but he came back at once, and after inspecting the dead body for a minute or so, exclaimed—

"Poor lilly Ab Sin. It's my matey, Ab Sin. De fighting men kill him, cos he no hide like him's friend, John Ab Howdeedoo. He no shut um's eye, and close um's ear, and berry um's head, an' so um lose um's big tail, and um's life. Yah!"

"They've stolen his clothes, too. That's odd," said Frank.

"But lilly Ab Sin had belly good clothes, sar."

"But who but a Chinaman would wear them?"

"Don't know, sar, but Ab Sin's belly good clothes all same. Kill him for his big tail, s'pose! Ladies wear um for chignon—worth gould sobberin each, heard say."

"Well, John Ab Howdeedoo, you may thank your stars they didn't see yours, for it is a whopper."

"Lilly Ab Sin's just as good um tail as mine. But Gor a massy, sar, let us get along, or dey kill us, too. Currency Lass nearly in sight now."

And he started off at a quicker shuffle than before.

Frank followed him, for the dead Chinaman was nothing to him, and about five minutes later he saw a light a little way ahead, and as they drew nearer he discovered that it shone through the window of a long rambling wooden house, evidently a bush shanty.

Indeed the creaking sign-board, with "The Currency Lass" painted thereon in tarnished gold letters, was the next thing that attracted his notice.

The deep growl of dogs greeted their near approach to this inhospitable looking caravansera, but there was nothing peculiar in this, and the Chinaman exclaimed—

"Dey welly good bow wows. Dey know John. Now he creep round to snug straw in stable loft, an you knock at front door like gennlemums. Shilling, please, sar."

Frank gave his guide the promised coin, and would have questioned him further about the shanty, for candidly he didn't like its look; but by the time he had formed his first query to suit Mr. John Chinaman's limited comprehension, he looked round, and John was gone.

CHAPTER XII
IN A DEN OF THIEVES.

THERE was nothing for it now but either to avoid the bush shanty altogether or to pluck up heart of grace, knock at the front door, and demand admission.

The pelting rain and the general discomfort of the early morning, together with a kind of aguish shivering that had seized upon him, determined our hero upon the latter course.

He knocked heavily with the stock of his revolver at the closed front door, and a voice presently responded—

"Pass on, whoever ye are. Ye get no rest here to-night. They pay high who put up at the Currency Lass at such an hour in the morning, I can tell you."

Frank felt annoyed at this uncourteous reception, and, giving the door a kick, he responded sharply—

"Come, my good man, you can't have the heart to refuse the shelter of your roof and a meal this bitter night, to a traveller lost in the bush. I've a well-filled purse, and I will pay liberally for the accommodation."

He had hardly spoken, when steps were heard within, the door was thrown open, and a rough voice said—

"Oh, if you've a long purse, nothing more need be said, for you are heartily welcome. I thought you might be a penniless loafer, or perhaps a bushranger."

He was a great, big burly man of fifty, so big and burly that he filled up the entire doorway.

He cast a very sharp glance at Frank as he spoke.

"I've been hunting bushrangers," quoth our hero, "and they only escaped me owing to being better mounted. By-the-by, has my companion, a mounted trooper, reached here before me. He's called Ted Hogan."

"No trooper has been here nor no bushranger either," quoth the landlord; "but walk in, sir, and dry yourself."

Frank did not need a second invitation, and a minute later be had followed mine host into a roomy kitchen, wherein the first object that caught his eye was a gaudy American clock, with its hands pointing to half past twelve o'clock in the morning.

Seated before a blazing red-gum fire were two young fellows, about twenty-eight and twenty-six years of age respectively, whom the landlord introduced as his sons.

They were both strongly built, but would evidently neither of them ever attain the almost herculean proportions of their father, who looked a perfect Samson in the ruddy firelight, which now enabled Frank to view his countenance and note the general appearance of the place.

The man had his first attention.

He was attired in the ordinary costume of a bush shanty proprietor, who was also a farmer in a small way, as they generally are.

He was nearly seven feet in height, and broad chested and strongly built in proportion; in fact, his well-set muscular figure showed great strength.

His short black hair was turning slightly grey, and his face was pleasing and open, save when in perfect repose.

Then only a kind of half sneer, half scowl, rested on it, seemingly caused by some malformation of nature, rather than by habit.

The room was plainly furnished, as is usual in the bush. A roughly hewn table, a chair, half a dozen three-legged stools, and the American clock before referred to, formed the main portion of it.

The fire consisted of a few logs of wood kindled on the hearth, whilst two iron bars laid across it, and resting on a brick at either end, supported the tea-kettle and a saucepan or two, from whence issued a savoury smell, strongly suggestive to an empty stomach.

The walls were decked with an atrocious print of "The Babes in the Wood," a rifle, a fowling-piece, a double-barrelled gun, and a brace of old flint pistols.

The weapons attracted Frank's attention, because they were all capped and on half-cock.

Still he was fain to confess that in such a lonely situation, so far away from another habitation, and the country around swarming with bushrangers, escaped convicts, and rascals of every description, there were but very slight grounds for injurious suspicion in all this.

"Come, lads, let's have some supper and some hot grog. The gentleman is almost famished, I expect," said the landlord, approaching the fire.

"It's lucky for me that you sup late," replied Frank, with a searching glance at his host.

"Well, sir, we've been very busy, making an underground cellar to keep the liquors cooler. We can't spare much time in the day, what with the customers and the farm; and so we sit up a few extra hours of a night whilst the job is on. We are generally between the blankets two hours the other side of midnight, I can tell you," was the explanation.

By this time the supper was turned out, which, if wanting in quality, was certainly ample as to quantity.

A boiled leg of mutton was fished out of one saucepan, and a huge mess of potatoes out of another. Then damper cake was lifted from the hearth, and an immense can of ale, in company with a bottle of whisky, brought from the adjoining bar.

Despite the awful events that had occurred during the past half dozen hours, bodily exercise, excitement, and rude health, had combined to make Frank very hungry.

He did ample justice to the substantial fare set before him therefore, and drank more than he should have done of the strong heady ale, listening patiently, meanwhile, to the landlord's account of the recent death of his wife from typhus fever, of the marriage of his only daughter to a rural policeman, of the murrain in the cattle and the rot in his sheep, of the last great bush fire, and other like matters, until at last he felt so drowsy that he asked to be shown to his bedroom—but to be called at the first gleam of daylight, so that he might search for his friend, the trooper, who was so mysteriously missing.

It was high time to retire, too, for the fire had gone out, the clock pointed to half after one, and, as Frank rose yawning from his chair, the remains of the solitary candle sank in its iron socket and left them in darkness.

"Here is a pretty go," said the landlord, after a fruitless rummage in every nook and corner of the room. "We have not another scrap of candle in the house, were it to light us to purgatory—or farther. You must go to bed in the dark."

"Never mind that, 'tis no great hardship; and besides, the moon once more shines out. So lead the way, and I'll follow close at your heels," said Frank.

"Will you not leave your revolver down here to dry by the warm hearth. If the rains get in the nipples of the barrels, it'll take you half a day to clean it else," said the host.

"Oh, I don't mind that; but we are so attached to each other, you see, that it would break our hearts to part company, which we never do on that account," replied Frank; and again his old suspicions of the evil character of the bush shanty returned with redoubled force.

But he wished the younger men "good night," heartily and genially, and then followed their father to his room.

This was no easy or pleasant matter.

He had to grope his way after him along a dark passage, at the end of which he was ushered into an apartment illuminated by no other light except that of the moon, which shone dimly through a small window glazed with little panes of coarse glass.

Here Boniface wished him good night, and with many apologies for the poorness of the accommodation, left him.

The room was small.

In one corner stood a bedstead of that shape commonly called in the colonies a "stretcher," which, with a dirty painted basin-stand, a broken chair, and a ship looking-glass, made up the furniture.

Frank's first impulse was to bolt and otherwise secure the door, but it was destitute of both bolt and lock, and only fastened with a small thumb latch.

Dismounting the wash-ware, Frank piled the stand, together with the chair, against the door, in such a manner that no one could enter without making, at all events, a sufficient noise to wake him.

He then carefully examined his revolver and put on fresh caps, ere he slipped it beneath his pillow.

Then, without undressing, he threw himself on the bed, and, weary and well-nigh worn out by his night's adventures, endeavoured to woo slumber.

For a time a species of nervousness possessed him.

The moaning of the passing wind, the flapping of a loose board on the roof above, the fitful shadows of a gigantic iron-bark thrown by the moonlight on the damp and discoloured walls, and above all the deep bay of dogs in the yard beneath his window, baffled every attempt at slumber.

And when at last he did drop off into a half-doze, the whispering of human voices in the next room put him once more on the qui vive.

He was as wide awake as ever now, and could not help fancying that he was the subject of conversation, and that amongst the other voices he could distinguish those of Blue Cap and of the Chinaman Ab Howdeedoo.

He rubbed his eyes, and the wider awake he grew the more convinced he was that his suspicions were correct.

Creeping from his bed he put his ear to the wall, and, thanks to the loose jointing of the boards of which it was composed, could peer into the adjoining room as well as hear every word that was spoken therein.

To his surprise, by the bright moonlight that shone into that apartment far more clearly than into his own, he saw the landlord and his two sons in close converse with—Blue Cap and the Chinaman in one.

Yes, Frank knew Blue Cap well enough now, for he had washed certain lines and marks off his face, and the Chinese expression was gone, in company with the celestial tail.

He still wore the blue cotton dress, however, and the clumsy shoes, and he was telling, with much action and in a very audible whisper, the way in which he had gammoned the Johnny Raw, as he persisted in calling Frank.

"After we'd disposed of the trap, I stumbled upon that Chinee proper. My right hand was so hurt with that half-spent ball, that I knew I couldn't hit a house at a dozen yards. However, I knifed Johnny with my left hand through the heart whilst I blarneyed him with my tongue, and then I slipped on his loose, ugly togs over my own and cut off his pig tail, for the Government had already made me a Chinaman about the head and face, and no sooner had I put my wig and false beard in my pocket than up comes young Johnny Raw.

"Well, I knowed that he'd his shooter ready, and that I couldn't use mine. I knew that you was too far off by that time to be of any sarvice to me, and so I falls down in the shadiest corner I could see, hoping to escape notice.

"But he spies my bald head, and comes over and kicks it; then he spies my tail and pulls it as though 'twere a bell rope; but I held firm, for I'd untwisted two plaits and held 'em down under my clothes, so that I could take a firm hold on 'em with my hands in my breeches pockets.

"'Twas a stiffish tug o' war though, and more than once I thought that he'd have had my scalp lock. But I gets up at last, and then I blarneys him proper—deceived him even after he'd discovered the real Chinee's dead body and all, and then he pays me to bring him here, where you must settle him, my friends, for this hand o' mine is getting worse every hour. By the Lord Jingo, if you hadn't come up at the right moment, Jem Norton would have been made food for warrigals by one rascally trap."

"We couldn't make out why you didn't keep up with us whilst we were dragging him along down the hill," said the eldest of the landlord's sons.

"Well, the fact is, I was too dead beat at the time to keep up with you. Knifing the Chinaman seemed to revive me a bit, but I'd hardly ha' done it if I hadn't thought I'd a pursuer close behind me on horseback, who it would be difficult to give leg bail to. But, by-the-by, here I'm blarneying away, and you've never told me what you've done with the trap. You seemed to be up to some precious queer game with him, I thought," and the bushranger grinned.

"Let the full tide in an hour's time tell. We've staked him in the middle of the river. The water was only up to his waist when we left him, but it rises twelve inches an hour, and now it must cover his shoulders. Once more round the clock and he dies of water on the brain, we'll say," was the reply.

Frank's blood ran coldly within him.

He listened with the intensest eagerness to gather, if he could, a knowledge of where abouts his unhappy friend and companion had been left, and in which direction lay the river.

But the conversation of the men now turned upon himself—upon what they were going to do with him.

"In another hour he will be at his soundest, and then we can knife him and bury him," said the landlord.

"What, in your new cellar?" asked Blue Cap, with a grin.

He had been told that joke, Frank could see.

"No. In the swamp," replied the landlord.

"Well I've no objection to the programme in the main, except that I'm left out as an actor therein. I shall knife him—I can use my left hand still, you know, and it will afford me a sort of pleasure," said Blue Cap.

"Very well," said the landlord. "You do it if you like."

"And I don't see why we should wait another hour. He's sure to be asleep now, and if he ain't it don't much matter; we're four of us, and he'll be certainly too drowsy to use his revolver until 'tis too late," continued Blue Cap.

"All right; if you think proper, we'll go now certainly," said the evidently obliging host of the Currency Lass.

"Come along, then; I hate to be kept waiting for blood, wine, or food," responded Blue Cap, with a hideous grin.

Then they all rose to their feet, and handled their weapons.

And Frank recoiled from his peep-hole in horror.

The villains would be on him in an instant or two.

The feeble barricade would not stay there a second

Frank glanced around the room, and espied a rope in one corner.

A long rope.

It suggested an idea.

He secured one end of it to a leg of his bed, which was close against the window, opened the casement and dropped the other end out through the opening.

Then he got out in turn, and curled his left leg and arm around it.

But he had no intention to descend yet.

He slipped down a yard, and then his right foot found a resting place on the end of one of the projecting logs of which the house was built.

Here he steadied himself, with only his eyes and the six barrels of his pepper-box revolver showing just above the stone window-sill.

He had resolved to bid his hospitable entertainer farewell.

He had resolved to shoot Blue Cap the instant he entered the room.

CHAPTER XIII.
A PARTING SHOT—A HOT PURSUIT.

HE had not to wait long.

The moonlight presently showed him the handle of the door opposite turn, the door itself opened half an inch, and a nose appeared, then a couple of feet and a head was thrust in.

It was that of Blue Cap.

Frank waited no longer.

He took as steady an aim as he could, and "Bang, bang, bang!" went three barrels of his revolver.

A shriek of pain, followed by a hoarse curse, told him that he had not burnt powder for nothing; but the next instant, the landlord and his two sons rushed into the room, and Frank saw that it would be madness to delay longer.

"Good-bye, landlord. I'll pay my reckoning in leaden coin the next time we meet," halloaed out Frank, and he began to slide down his rope.

He had begun to congratulate himself on a possible escape, when a deep angry growl below caused him to look down.

And there, directly below him, he saw the red fiery eyes of an immense dog glaring up at him.

Ais deep muzzle, broad chest, and greyish white coat of wiry hair, showed him to be a bloodhound; and with a thrill of horror, Frank saw that he must drop right at his feet.

It was a case of Scylla and Charybdis however; and so Frank levelled his pistol at him, and tried to steady himself on the rope, so as to be able to take sure and deadly aim.

His first shot missed him, the second gave him only a slight wound that rendered him far more dangerous, and ere he could discharge a third he felt the rope give way.

It had been severed with a knife above, and Frank fell some eight or nine feet—almost into the dog's jaws.

He beheld the fierce brute about to spring on him, and at the same moment a clattering volley rang out from the window, and half a dozen bullets whistled by his head, and buried themselves with dull thuds in the earth around.

Though intended for quite a contrary purpose, that volley saved his life.

Every ball missed him; but one passed through the head of the hound, who fell dead across his body.

It was a providential escape, Frank thought; but he was not yet out of the wood, and if he would escape, there was evidently no time to lose about it.

He could hear the muttered curses of disappointment, and the ramming of fresh charges home, as those above saw him move.

With a prodigious effort, he threw off the dead brute whose weight nearly stifled him, and firing the last barrel of his revolver at the window, he with intense satisfaction saw the giant landlord clap his hand to his face, which in a instant became covered with blood; and then, springing to his feet, he ran for his life, he knew not whither.

Almost immediately he was checked by a high fence.

At any other time he would have found it an obstacle difficult to surmount; but now a love of life gave him strength and expertness, and in a moment he was at the summit.

The sharp crack of a rifle rang out on the still night air.

Frank saw his wide-awake hat fly from his head, and felt a scrape, like that of a blunt razor, traverse his scalp; but he did not stay even to rub his sore head.

Springing down on the off side of the stiff cockatoo fence, he again took to his heels, ramming a ball cartridge home in each barrel of his revolver, as he ran blindly on.

Five minutes later he halted to regain his breath, and from behind a gum-tree glanced back at the den of thieves and murderers from which he had just escaped.

It lay about three-quarters of a mile away, and was clearly visible by the bright light of the moon, which now shone down from an almost unclouded heaven.

The early morning was so still, that even the spring of the grasshoppers could be heard; and Frank Beaumont listened with breathless anxiety for the sounds of pursuit.

Presently the deep fierce bay of dogs smote on his ear, mingled with shoutings and fierce execrations.

An instant later, he saw two men and two dogs emerge from the shadow of the cockatoo fence.

They were powerful hounds, and the men with voice and gesture were urging them on the fugitive's trail.

Frank turned round, and again continued his flight.

He had not, however, run many yards, when he caught his foot in a hole, and was brought to with a sprained ankle.

He ground his teeth, and groaned in despair.

He then glanced round, and saw that the dogs were only a hundred yards or so in his rear.

They were running neck-and-neck, their great tongues lolling out of their mouths, thus displaying their formidable fangs, their eyes flashing fire, too eager for his blood even to give tongue.

Frank looked wistfully around.

A ray of hope dawned upon his soul.

A yard from him stood a tall gum-tree, and thicker with foliage than its fellows.

With great difficulty Frank clambered up its trunk, hid amongst its densest fronds, and with his revolver on his knees, prepared to sell his life as dearly as possible.

He knew that they must come well within range before they could see him.

They could not use their rifles otherwise, except at hap-hazard.

From the dogs he was now quite safe.

Those brutes were howling with baffled rage at the foot of the tree.

Frank did not notice them.

He waited for larger game.

His bullets were for their masters.

Presently these latter drew near, not advancing boldly—for they knew that he was armed, and had shown them practically that he was not a bad shot—but dodging from tree trunk to tree trunk.

They were the landlord's two sons—the landlord and Blue Cap were, no doubt, hors de combat; dead Frank devoutly hoped, but bad men are not so easily killed.

At last the villains opened fire, but, thanks to the sheltering foliage of his tree, the balls flew by him harmlessly.

He returned the compliment whenever a head showed itself from behind a trunk, but for some time with equal ill success, the rascals were so quick in their movements.

At length a bullet from one of the young men grazed Frank's left cheek, and, half mad with rage and pain, he swore that he would soon repay the shot with interest.

He had not to wait long for a chance.

The elder bushranger incautiously exposed his side whilst reloading, and Frank covered him steadily and fired.

He saw him clap a hand to his side, and blood spout out from between his fingers.

He then quitted his tree, and with many oaths staggered over to the trunk of the one in whose branches Frank was concealed.

The next instant he perceived him.

Their eyes met.

Frank fired two shots at him and missed each time.

Then his foe's barrel covered him.

"Curse you!" he muttered; "that was a dead shot of yours, but I aren't going to die alone. You'll have to take the dark journey with me, my young cockchafer."

His finger was on the trigger of his weapon.

His eye glanced along the barrel.

Frank felt that his time was come.

But, ere he could fire, his brain reeled.

Death's hand was laid heavily on him, and he fell at the root of the tree a corpse.

Frank had only one foe now.

One foe and the two dogs; but he soon shot them down, and then he reloaded all his barrels, and waited for his last enemy to put in an appearance.

He forebore to do so, however, and, after waiting

for about a quarter of an hour to convince himself that he was gone, he descended the tree to the ground.

Then he recollected the critical position in which the bushrangers had declared the gallant trooper, Ted Hogan, to be in, and Frank determined to use every effort that in him lay to discover and release him.

About half an hour out of the hour that the landlord's sons had declared would settle him had already sped away.

Would there still be time to effect a rescue?

Frank asked himself the question anxiously, but he could not answer it at all satisfactorily.

For first he must find the river—and where was it?

Knowing that, at all events, to get to it he must descend, and there being a gentle slope in the ground he was traversing, he took to his heels again and ran, or rather limped, for his failing strength and injured foot would allow him to do no more.

He had not gone very far when a cold breeze, as of one blowing over an expanse of water, blew upon his heated face, and halting, he could plainly hear the ripple of a rising tide just at the foot of the slope.

A minute later he had hobbled somehow to the edge of the stream, and the moon, which had been clouded for a brief while, becoming revealed again, he saw a rather broad expanse of water lying before him.

Hope now returned to him, and he strained his eyes to the utmost to catch sight of some object rising above its surface.

For a long while he could see nothing, and he began to fear that the tide already flowed over the head of the unhappy trooper, when he heard a faint "Coo-eey" in the distance.

He replied with the whole strength of his lungs.

Then came a response.

He threw himself down on the river bank, and swept the whole surface of the stream with his eyes more on a level with it in the direction of the sound.

And then he saw a round, dark object resting like a ball on the surface of the water, and knew that it must be a human head.

He limped to as near a point of the shore as he could, and then halloaed out—

"Is that you, Ted Hogan?"

"Yes," came the faint reply back again. "If that's you, mate, save me if you can do it in time. The water's nigh up to my chin; it'll be all over with me in ten minutes."

"All right," shouted back Frank, "I'll try my best."

But, hardly had he uttered the words, when he remembered that he couldn't swim, and that, with no doubt a strong current running up mid channel, the unfortunate trooper was far beyond wading distance.

What was to be done then, for not a boat was to be seen—perhaps, indeed, a boat had never floated on that dim and silent stream?

CHAPTER XIV.

INTRODUCES JOB SHORT—A GENIUS.

WHILST debating anxiously within his mind what he could do to aid his friend, and dismissing every idea as impracticable, Frank noticed the mouldering embers of a camp fire within the little patch of Leptospermum bushes on his left.

Where there was a fire there were sleepers, and where there were sleepers there was help, Frank thought.

He rushed towards the spot, therefore, but just as he reached the fire, someone jumped up on the

other side of it and presented at his chest a rusty sword, shouting—

"Thy name and purpose, Saxon? Stand!"

Frank recoiled a step or two in abject surprise.

"These are Clan Albyn's warriors true, and, Saxon, I am Roderick Dhu. How de dhw? See the pun? No! Why then intrude you upon my midnight visions? Why shake your gory looks at me? Avaunt, I say? Avaunt!" and the strange being flourished his sword around his head, and then, digging the point into the ground, leant upon the hilt, and regarded our hero with a melancholy stare.

Frank then saw that he was a youth of about nineteen years of age, very tall, and dressed in garments of a most strange cut and fashion.

They were identical, in fact, with those of a stage Hamlet, but very old and worn, and adorned in places with patches.

Frank jumped to the ready conclusion that he had stumbled across a madman, but his friend's position was critical, and any aid would be welcome.

Besides, madmen have oft-times clever ideas.

"I have a friend drowning. Can you swim?" he asked.

"Prate not to me of friends," roared the strange youth. "Friendship's but a name—a dream—a phantom."

"Well, then, an acquaintance," said Frank. "He is in the middle of the river, bound to a stake. Do you hear?"

"Plainly, foolish youth; and so has many a good man been before him. So was the heroic Joan of Arc, and so were Gardiner, Latimer, and Ridley. It matters not so that he hath not recanted. Tell me, has he recanted?"

"He will drown if he be not rescued in five minutes. The water is up to his chin, and I cannot swim a yard."

"What's this you say?" quoth the sorry Hamlet, passing a hand rapidly to and fro across his eyes, as though to gather together his scattered faculties and wandering fancies. "A man drowning, did you say, and close at hand?"

"Yes," answered Frank. "You can see his head from here. The rascally bushrangers have bound him to a stake in the middle of the river, and the water is fast rising above his head. An ordinary swimmer could save him with ease; but, alas! I can't swim a stroke."

"Job Short can, though. Job Short can swim like a fish and dive like an otter—neglected genius, and poet, and actor, though he is. Show me the man, and I will speedily bring him to the bank," quoth the strange youth.

Frank was delighted at this assurance.

He seized hold of Hamlet's, alias Job Short's arm, and literally dragged him down to the edge of the river.

"There," he ejaculated hastily; "there! His head still rests on the surface of the stream like a ball. I don't think that the water has yet reached his lips. Oh, try and save him, if you can. It is such a dreadful death."

Job Short made no reply.

If he was really cracked, he was certainly enjoying a most lucid interval at present.

He sat down on the bank, and took his clothes off like steam, then clapping his rusty sword between his teeth, he darted right into the water.

"I wonder what he's got that thing with him for," Frank murmured to himself, alluding to the rusty sword. "I hope he won't go cranky again, and cut poor Hogan's head off, instead of rescuing him from drowning."

He had half a mind to hurry after Job Short and urge him to give him his sword, and then he thought—

"Why, of course, he wants it to cut Hogan's bonds. A capital idea. If he took a knife he'd have to dive, but with a long sword he can manage

"I WANT FOOD AND LODGING, I TELL YOU; AND PERHAPS MORE BESIDES," CRIED BLUE CAP, AS HE POINTED THE PISTOL AT THE TERRIFIED GROUP.

to reach them without putting his head under water. Hang it, the fellow isn't half as mad as one would think."

It certainly did not seem like it, for Job Short, as he designated himself, swam well and swam with a method.

He might have walked out three-fourths of the way, but he preferred swimming, as a faster and easier mode of progression, and he took care to do 't in such a way as to derive full advantage from the set of the in-shore and the out-shore currents.

He reached Ted Hogan just as the water was rippling against his moustache.

Another minute and his nose would have been submerged, and then it would have been all over with him, for he could not have breathed.

"Thank God," he gasped faintly, as his rescuer, keeping himself afloat by resting his left hand on the top of the stake, passed his sword below water, and felt with it for its lashings. "Thank God, you are just in time."

Job Short made no reply; he could not think of a play quotation at such a time, and he seldom spoke in ordinary language.

He found a rope that encircled the trooper's body under the arms, however, and he cut it.

'Twas a hard task, for his sword was none of the sharpest, and the rope was tough as rope could be.

But he succeeded, and was rather surprised that the body of the trooper did not come to the surface.

"I'm bound below, around the legs," he gasped, blowing the water away from his lips in order to utter the words.

Job Short, puffing and blowing a little, now proceeded to make search for this second impediment.

For some seconds he couldn't feel it.

"Another—minute—I'm—dead," gasped the trooper.

He had to hold up his chin, and to blow away the water to be able to articulate each word.

Job Short instantly dived below.

"He has gone down," frantically exclaimed Frank Beaumont from the bank. "He has gone down, and poor Ted is lost."

'Twas quite true that he had gone down, but he soon came up again, and the trooper's feet now found the surface just as quickly as the body of his rescuer.

"Turn over on your back. I'll push you before me towards the shore," said Job.

Ted Hogan did so, and directly Frank saw what he was about he rushed into the water and reached out as far as he dared, to render all the assistance in his power.

Job Short had quite enough work on his hands.

The cutting of Ted Hogan's bonds had almost exhausted him, and he had very little strength left for pushing him towards the shore, whilst the trooper was so weak that, with his clothes on, he could hardly keep his nostrils and lips above water whilst he floated.

"I'm done," groaned Job, when they had got about a score of yards from the stake. "I'm clean done. I can't push you a yard further—I can't save myself, even."

"Try, try—don't mind me," responded Ted Hogan.

"Oh! that's all right, but we'll sink or float together. A few yards further, and we should touch ground."

Hearing this, Ted Hogan turned over on his chest and tried to swim.

But his limbs were so benumbed with the cold that they refused to obey his will, and down he went.

Seeing this, Job Short instantly dived after him, and as he did so felt himself grasped by the hair.

He hardly knew what had got hold of him, for though he had gone below with his eyes open, through the darkened water he could see nothing.

Whatever it was it towed him on, however, and he knew that his feet were dragging along the bottom of the river the while.

Presently, with a twist and a turn, out came his head, and he found himself sitting on a soft bed of mud with the water just above his waist.

A yard or two away sat the man he had three-quarters saved in a same position.

Frank Beaumont had completed the task that the chivalrous Hamlet had begun, and without getting out of his depth had succeeded, though not without some danger and great difficulty—owing to the slippery mud that coated the bottom of the river—in half towing, and half dragging, the near moribund youths into shallow water, where they soon began to recover.

"'Tis not in mortals—to command success—but I've done my best—to deserve it," gasped Job Short directly he could articulate, spitting out lots of river water at each quarter-dozen words.

"You've saved my life, anyhow—you and Frank here. I'm deucedly obliged, I'm sure," said Ted Hogan, in much the same voice, and with very similar interruptions.

"Directly you feel strong enough, you had both better try to get up and wade ashore," said Frank presently. "I can give you a shoulder, and help you on somewhat."

They had to rest a good time longer ere they could move, and then they crawled out of the water and up the bank beyond into the bush on their hands and knees.

By this time Frank had got some branches and dry bark, and lighted an immense fire, and very glad of its genial warmth were the two water-sodden ones, when, eel like, they had gotten within the influence of its rays.

Job Short was in great distress at the loss of his sword, which he had been fain, through exhaustion, to let drop out of his mouth whilst pushing the trooper before him towards the shore.

"Never mind; you shall have mine if we can only find it. The wretches who doomed me that lingering and horrible death threw it into a bit of scrub not far from here. I daresay we shall come across it with the day light, and Government must supply me with another," said Hogan, surveying Job Short with some astonishment.

This astonishment grew apace when a few minutes later he saw him slowly don his Hamlet costume.

CHAPTER XV.

MARKING OUT THE CAMPAIGN.

JOB SHORT, once in the costume of the royal Dane, was, to use his own phraseology, "Richard himself again."

He produced a wallet from amongst the bushes, and the wallet contained a cold boiled fowl, an ox tongue, a damper cake, and a bottle of Hollands, rather sumptuous fare for a travelling swagman, to be sure.

"I picked them up by the way," he condescended to explain. "From a long and a sad experience of the world, I find that genius is its own reward, and if it would be paid at all it must pay itself. always pay myself when the chance occurs. I d my best to atone for the ingratitude of an un appreciative world."

"You have certainly won my eternal gratitud to-night," said Ted Hogan. "But for you I should be now dead."

"And mine, too, as but for you I should have been deprived of a brave comrade," said Frank Beaumont.

"Express your thanks by pitching into the prog. Let tongue speak to tongue, and fowl fall he who first cries hold, enough," and Job Short felt for the hilt of his sword, and uttered a deep groan as he found it not.

"You are a tragedian, I see," exclaimed Ted Hogan.

"By heaven intended for such, my friend, but by envious man foiled. I have trodden the boards of the Theatre Royal, Melbourne, as a banner bearer, a warder on the outer wall, a Tartar, a Cossack, a modern dummy flunkey, ay, even as a silent demon in a pantomime at a wage of fifteen bob a week, and thereon have seen a Kean, a Jefferson, a Montgomery, a Barry Sullivan, whom I could have eclipsed had I been allowed to open my mouth, receiving more than as many guineas a night. Ah! my friend, I'm a blighted being, and though I was kicked off the stage for taking the leading tragedian's part out of his mouth one night, when he forgot a line, and was listening for the prompter's cue, my declamation would have brought the house down had it not been that I was in the costume of a sorry jester. But a time will come. Oh, yes, a time will come!"

"No doubt of it," exclaimed Ted Hogan with a mouth full of tongue. "And I'll take the tickets for your first benefit."

"And so will I," echoed Frank Beaumout.

Ted Hogan alone of the three made a hearty supper.

But then Frank had supped at the Currency Lass an hour and a half before, and Job Short had also supped just before Frank had intruded on his privacy.

When the trooper had done Frank pressed him to relate how he had got into the unpleasant predicament from which Job Short had freed him, which he did as follows:—

"I overtook Blue Cap about ten minutes after I gave you the go-by on the racing colt, and fired at him.

"Then we stood face to face, and there ensued a moment of agonising suspense.

"I fired again, and that shot, I think, would have taken his life had not his horse suddenly reared at the sight of a black fellow's skeleton up in a mi-mi, and thrown him, thereafter tearing like mad through the bush.

"I was about to shoot at the scoundrel as he lay writhing on the ground praying for mercy, when I was caught a tremendous whack across the head from behind, which half stunned me, and another over the right wrist that caused me to drop my shooter, and then two fellows set upon me and pulled me off my horse, hitting me over the head and shoulders the while, so as to keep me half stunned and wholly unable to resist.

"I've a dim idea that I saw a third ruffian, a gigantic fellow, walking off with my horse, but I was too dizzy and confused to be sure.

"My captors evidently were old friends of Blue Cap, for one of them said, 'I thought when you was lagged we should never see you more;' and he answered, 'No bolts nor bars could keep me, Jem,' and then he begged of them to do for me, and they responded, 'All right; but we'll have some fun with him first,' and then they dragged me along down through the bush and the scrub, and out into the river, where they bound me to that infernal post.

"The water wasn't much above my knees then, but they were kind enough to tell me what would be my fate, and then they waded ashore, laughing."

"The inhuman wretches," responded Frank, and then he proceeded to tell Ted his adventures at the inn, and how he had heard through the thin partition to what doom they had sentenced him.

"The cowardly curs," hissed the trooper between his teeth. "But you say you have shot the chief miscreant, Blue Cap."

"Yes," replied Frank; "but I don't know that I've shot him dead. I believe 'twas a hard hit; there was so much blood, and he was not able to put in an appearance after. But I believe that that rascal has as many lives as a cat."

"Never mind, if he has twice as many we will have them all at last. But you shot the landlord, too, you say?"

"Yes—and I believe the bullet went right through his head, and as for the son, who fell under the tree, from whose boughs I shot him, he is dead, I know."

"Then you have killed a man worth exactly a thousand pounds," said Hogan. "Whilst they were binding me to the stake I recognised them as two brothers, both notorious bushrangers, by name John and James Clarke."

"A thousand pounds, a thousand pounds!" exclaimed Job Short, gaspingly. "Then in this unappreciative world a dead bushranger is worth a dozen living actors. Oh! genius, how art thou rewarded."

"It's a queer present, but as it seems to be a valuable one, I will beg you and Hogan's acceptance of the dead man. You can send him to the proper market and divide the thousand pounds between you," said Frank.

"But he is your prize, not ours," quoth Ted Hogan.

"Yes, he is the captive of your bow and spear," echoed Job.

"Say rather that he is a pheasant that I have shot, and which I send as a present to my friends," laughed Frank. "As the events of this night have made me the possessor of more wealth than I shall know what to do with, I have no need of blood money. Perhaps his father may be worth something too, and, if Blue Cap is dead, there ought to be a couple of additional thousand as safe as the Bank of Australia. I want none of it. I only want revenge."

"I am ready for both," said Hogan. "The labourer is worthy of his hire, and whoever rids the colony of these human tigers, does as good a service to the state as a bishop, judge, or member of parliament. A couple or three hours' rest will make a new man of me, and then I vote that we visit this inn without loss of time."

"My foot does not hurt me at all, now," said Frank. "It couldn't have been a real sprain after all, and the cold water seems to have done it a lot of good."

"Well, let us snatch a couple of hours' rest, for we want it badly, and we must not knock ourselves up, at, perhaps, the beginning of the chase," said Ted Hogan.

"Discretion is the better part of valour," observed Job.

Frank agreed with both these observations and truisms.

He helped to replenish the fire, and then lying down around it with their feet towards the cheery blaze, the thoroughly tired-out youths soon sank into a sound deep and dreamless sleep.

In a couple of hours Frank Beaumont awoke.

To his surprise it was broad daylight.

He forgot that dawn was almost on the point of breaking in the east ere he sank into slumber.

He aroused his companions, who, at first, were as surprised as he. It was, however, but seven in the morning, and they had not been asleep two hours.

Breakfast was hurriedly partaken of, and then the fowl, the tongue, and the damper cake were polished entirely off, and washed down with river water, flavoured and warmed with Hollands.

Then, after a good wash in the ebbing tide, Frank gave Ted his revolver that he had picked up in the bush, and carefully proceeded to recharge his own.

"I am weaponless," said Job Short, dejectedly.

"Not for long, I hope. My sword can't be far off; we will look for it as we go along," said Ted Hogan.

Within ten minutes the sword was found.

Job was then in his element, and, buckling it on, he evidently thought himself the leader of the expedition.

"Now I must be your guide," said Frank, "for I alone know the way. By George, I hope I haven't forgotten it."

They walked on in silence for some little way, and then Frank said—

"Yonder is the tree in which I took refuge, and from which I shot Clarke and his dogs."

They went up to it, and there were the dogs lying stiff in death, and one almost hidden from view by millions of red soldier ants, who would, in the course of a very few hours, reduce it to a skeleton.

But the dead bushranger was gone, leaving nought but a pool of blood behind him.

"His friends must have removed the body," said Frank. "I daresay we shall find it at the Currency Lass."

"Let us push on as fast as we can then, or we may find the birds flown," said Ted Hogan, rather anxiously.

Job Short was silent, but he carried his sword drawn, and was bent upon doing mighty deeds.

At last the shingle roof of the bush shanty became visible between the trees, and very soon the trio were clambering over the high cockatoo fence that Frank had topped and cleared so lightly and swiftly when the bushrangers were firing at him from the inn window.

It was a very different obstacle now, and Frank wondered how he had done it; but it was scaled at last, and the inn yard gained where the big blood-hound lay dead just outside his house, and the severed rope by whose aid Frank had escaped from out his bedroom window lay in loose coils over him."

"Let us first secure the stables," said Ted. "Then we take away their means of escape if the bush-angers are still in the house.'"

CHAPTER XVI.

THE DISCOVERIES AT THE CURRENCY LASS.

THE stables were by no means difficult to find. They formed one side of the dirty, unpaved back yard.

A huge dung-heap was quite sufficient guide, and, besides, there was an inverted horse-shoe nailed on each door.

The trooper tried one door.

It was unfastened.

He went in, and found the stable empty.

He was not very much surprised, however, nor was Frank, for in Australia horses are seldom stabled in the summer season, when the open bush is near.

"I feel sure that we shall find Blue Cap and the landlord lying either dead or mortally wounded within," he said. "I've no doubt the unwounded son has escaped, and very probably on his way he dragged the body of his brother into some patch of scrub, hoping that it would not be found. Let us enter the house at once."

"Yes," said Ted Hogan, "I don't see why we shouldn't; but we must exercise caution, for we don't know how many rascals may be there waiting to receive us."

"Come one, come all, these rocks shall fly, their native heath as soon as I," shouted Job Short, flourishing his sword in the air in close proximity enough to jeopardise Frank Beaumont's nose.

"Not so much noise, old fellow. I'm more afraid of the past tense of the verb to fly applied to the bushrangers, than the future tense applied to you. So don't frighten them, but come along silently and discreetly," he said.

This speech put a stop to poor Job's heroics, and finding the back door unlocked, into the house they went, Ted and Frank revolver in hand.

The bar, the bar-parlour, and the kitchen were empty, but the ashes upon the kitchen hearth were still warm.

"The fire has been relighted since my escape," said Frank.

"Are you sure of that?" asked Ted Hogan anxiously.

"Quite, for it was half-past one when I went upstairs to bed six hours ago, and the ashes would not have kept warm on that great open, draughty hearth all that time. Besides, here is a tin billy with tea in it, still lukewarm. Somebody has breakfasted, and not very long ago."

"I think we had better search every room as fast as we can, and then take a good survey of the country round from the windows, or even from the roof," said the trooper.

"So do I. Whoever has been here, depend upon it they are here no longer, and our business is to discover by the surest means possible which way they are gone," said Frank.

"Charge Chester, charge—On Stanley, on!" shouted Job.

"Hush!" said Frank, almost fiercely, for he and Hogan spoke only in whispers. "You will ruin all."

He pulled off his boots, and Hogan hastened to imitate his example.

This, however, gave Frank a half minute's start of him, and that enabled our hero to gain the head of the stairs first.

Then he glided into one after the other of the three rooms, and standing on the threshold of the last, exclaimed, with a burst of passion—

"Fools that we are to sleep and take our ease. The wretches have stolen away!"

"Stolen away?" exclaimed Ted Hogan, with an oath. "How, in the fiend's name, can that be?"

"I don't know. I could have sworn that I had given each his death-wound. It is most strange," said Frank.

"Perhaps they have managed to crawl forth and hide themselves in the bush," exclaimed Ted Hogan. "If that is the case we will soon find them, and dispatch them."

"I don't know what to think," quoth Frank. "However, let us scan the country well from the windows."

They did so, but not a sign of life was to be seen in any direction.

Scores and scores of miles of sunlit bush could be seen all around the shanty, but they might have belonged to an uninhabited world, for all evidence to the contrary.

The searchers looked at each other dismayed.

There was a great pool of blood close up to the window out of which Frank had escaped, and another larger still on the threshold of the door.

From this latter there was a trickling stream all down the stairs and up to a cupboard door in the kitchen, where it suddenly ceased.

"That cupboard is big enough to hold a man," said Frank.

"If it had no shelves in it," answered Hogan, dubiously.

"I smell a rat! Stick him behind the arras!" shouted Joe Short in his most tragic accents, and like Hamlet he lunged forward and ran his sword not through the arras, but through the cupboard door.

No shriek followed the thrust, nor did the panelling give way.

Ted Hogan had to open the door in the usual manner, and then the cupboard was discovered to be empty.

But it was a very deep inside, and Frank, glancing into it, exclaimed suddenly—

"Why, there is a flight of steps leading down into a kind of vault."

"So there is," said Ted Hogan, equally surprised.

"Away with him to the deepest dungeon!" shouted Job Short, flourishing his sword again.

But whether he meant Frank, or the trooper, or

an imaginary bushranger, it was very hard to tell, as he glared at space the while.

"The landlord was saying that he and his sons had been digging a new cellar. That must be it. Let us explore it—they may be hiding down there," said Frank.

"If they are, we have them," replied Hogan. "And, by George, it may be so. Let me go down first."

"No, me," exclaimed our hero, and scarcely had the words escaped his lips when he was running down the steps into the pitchy darkness below.

Hogan hastily followed, revolver in hand, and Job Short, flourishing his sword, brought up the rear.

Ere the trooper got to the bottom he heard a dull call, and a hollow rattle.

Then the voice of Frank was audible shouting in accents of terror—

"Don't come down without a light—for heaven's sake fetch a light! Something has hold of me and will not let go. It rattles as I drag it along. Oh hasten, hasten, its horrible."

The strange noise still continued, and Ted rushed back to the kitchen for a candle, Job Short preceding him like an usher of the white rod.

Candles and matches too, he found on the mantelpiece, and to strike a light did not take long.

Then, with as much rapidity as he could use without extinguishing his light, he returned to the cellar, Job Short again falling judiciously into the rear.

When Ted Hogan had descended half a dozen of the steps that led down to the subterranean, he held his light up to get a better view of it, and beheld a sight that almost caused him to let fall the candlestick in horror.

Frank Beaumont was standing in the midst of a damp dismal vault, with his right leg entrapped within the ribs of a skeleton, which he dragged along with him at every step he took across the slimy floor.

And that slimy floor was strewed with other skeletons, all white and shining as though they had been polished after death, and lying in every conceivable position, whilst over and around them crept monstrous centipides and scorpions, fat white bulldog ants, and monstrous hairy legged triantelope spiders.

Ted Hogan had dashed down into this ghastly charnel-house, and set free his friend in less time than it takes to record the fact, and in less time than it took Job Short to thunder forth Hamlet's soliloquy on a skull, which he evidently thought the proper thing for the occasion, skulls being all around.

When Frank was led up out of the cellar he was much paler than he would have been had he found half a dozen living bushrangers there.

Ted Hogan brought him some brandy out of the Jar and after drinking a glassful he felt much better.

"Heavens!" he then exclaimed, "those must be the skeletons of the unhappy wretches who have slept and been murdered here. Isn't it perfectly horrible?"

"Yes, they let the ants make skeletons of them in the bush so as to remove all possibility of recognition or identification, and then they dug this cellar for them. I'll warrant me, that hadn't this little affair cropped up, they'd have been buried, and the entrance to the cellar stopped up," said Ted Hogan.

"And in the lowest deep a lower deep, still threatening to devour me, opens wide, to which the hell I suffer seems a heaven. Milton," quoth Job sententiously.

"Let us get away from this vile den," said Frank; "our prey is not here, that is very evident, and every minute's delay will give him the start of us."

"Yes," replied the trooper. "Let us go into the bush; doubtless there are some horses to be had for the catching.

"Right, right! A horse! a horse! my kingdom for a horse! exclaimed Job Short, waving his sword.

They went out of the house together and made a kind of a wide cast in search of horses.

Presently they saw three grazing some little way off.

They were not long in rounding them in to the stock-yard, but whilst they were doing so they were surprised by the sudden appearance of an armed native.

He held his long slender yelemen in his right hand, and his narrow shield on his left arm. At his waist hung his nullah-nullah and his boomerang. His face was painted red and blue, and a gaudy head-dress of parrot and cockatoo feathers surmounted his raven locks and dusky face. He was a tall and slender savage, perfectly destitute of clothing.

"Hurrah!" exclaimed Frank, "this black fellow, if we speak him fairly and pay him a trifle, will guide us on the trail of the fugitives as untiringly yet surely as a sleuth hound. I will have a yabber, yabber with him.

And whilst Ted Hogan and Job Short were saddling the horses he persuaded the native to be their guide.

CHAPTER XVII.
OPPOSED BY KING FIRE.

ONCE treated to a glass of rum and given a large fig of tobacco, and the black fellow was ready to follow his new acquaintances to the death.

He was offered plenty more such treats if he succeeded in following up the trail to its termination, and plenty of money as well, and black fellows know something of the value of money, preferring white, however, to yellow.

"We have no horse for him," exclaimed Job Short.

"Lor' bless you, he don't want a horse," answered Ted Hogan. "That nigger would keep up with mounted men for days, and pass them whenever he liked."

"Is it possible?" retorted Job, looking at the tall, lithe, sinewy native, whose naked limbs shone like polished ebony. "But you don't think he'll lead us amongst his own tribe, do you, and get us killed and eaten?"

"No fear of that," laughed Frank. "The Australian black fellows aren't cannibals, and they never injure those who put faith in them. Hogan, let us fill our saddle bags well, for we don't know where the chase may lead us, and there's lots of cold meat, cheese, and bread indoors, which it would be a sin to leave behind."

"All right," answered the trooper. "The same thought had occurred to me. We will provision ourselves for a week."

Five minutes later Frank, Ted, and Job were in the saddle and watching the movements of the native, who was running about with his head near the ground, his wide nostrils quivering, his eyes gleaming, his whole form trembling with the excitement he was labouring under.

No fox, stag, or wolf-hound ever littered feels the same delight in the chase as does the Australian native. No sleuth or ban dog ever more surely tracked an offender to his doom than can the naked black fellow, given the same opportunities and advantages.

After a little while his circular runs grew shorter, and presently he threw up his head with a snort and a gleam of triumph in his red, blood-shot eyes.

He showed his white teeth as he stood erect, and

pointing to the ground with his yeleman, he said—

"Two fellow top o' yarramans; put him long a bush like it in myall down ayonder. Bail, I think, I find them. Bungy find them by-an'-by, no doubt."

"All right; go ahead then, Bungy. Plenty of rum, baccy, and white money when we've run them down, never fear," said Frank Beaumont with a smile.

The black fellow's eyes glittered, and his wide lips expanded in a grin.

Then he put a big plug of tobacco into the hollow of his left cheek, and started off at an easy swinging pace across the grassy plain, his head bent forward and his eyes cast downward, so as not to miss a trace of the footsteps of the horses, which had in many places become obliterated by the high winds that had blown the fine sand, with which Australian plains are covered in the summer time, into ridges and furrows in all directions.

Frank, Ted, and Job cantered along after him, but poor Job was not so good a horseman as he was a swimmer, and when his half-bred horse took to buck-jumping, Job had to embrace his neck with both arms to maintain his position on his back.

And even in this he was successful but for a brief while, for when a horse buck-jumps properly he claps his nose between his knees, blows out his belly, humps his back as does a cat at sight of a dog, and then commences to dance the "Perfect Cure" as high as he can, with both fore-legs on the ground at once.

And thus did Job's horse, contrary to Job's most earnest wishes and entreaties, the result being that Job was ere long deposited on the grass.

The buck-jumper was soon caught, however, and Job was helped to remount, not without considerable fear and nervous trepidation on his part.

That fall had the effect of banishing the drama from Job Short's mind for many a long day, for he was too nervous to remember a single quotation as long as he remained in the saddle.

For the first twelve or fifteen miles the pursuers rode through fine, open, thinly timbered country; then came a vast mass of forest, and next for a score of miles there were undulating hills, occasionally opening woods, and now and then a grassy flat or green creek would appear, to relieve the eye with its emerald brightness.

All this way the black tracker never once came to a fault.

The scent evidently was hot and strong.

At noon the party came to a halt beside a sparkling river, and partook of a substantial repast, after which they again pressed on.

They had travelled some six miles further through the eternal forest, when the scene suddenly changed to the wild and the terrible.

A hill went sloping downwards, as steep as the roof of a house, for at least nine miles.

At its base appeared dark masses of forest-covered ranges, rolling like enormous ocean billows through a broad but dark and sombre valley, at the other end of which rose another nine or ten mile hill of equal steepness with the one that now lay at the travellers' feet.

They were looking down, in fact, into a vast chasm—a gully similar in nature to the Devil's Dyke, near Brighton, only a dozen times as deep, and a millions times more grand and imposing.

In the lowest depths of this ravine flowed a red, rushing river, and its hoarse murmur could be distinctly heard above the sullen moaning of the wind-tossed leaves of that mighty forest.

Altogether the scene was one of a wild and melancholy grandeur, such as no country but Australia could show, bringing weariness to the soul and oppression to the eye, with a sense of infinite desolation.

Bungy paused on the brink of the abyss, and signed to Frank, Ted, and Job to hide themselves, or rather to keep under the cover of the trees.

Then with his keen eyes he swept the horizon and pierced the depths of the wooded gulf.

"Ay, ay! Bale, me see 'em. I believe bale sit down," he then said, pointing to a thin wreath of smoke that curled skyward from half way up the distant, though clearly visible, opposite range.

"He thinks it is Blue Cap's camp fire," said Frank to Ted Hogan. "If he's right we have him for certain."

"Yes; it's not more than nine miles away," replied the trooper; "or, at least, it don't look so."

"Ay, ay! Budgery you. Nine miles eagle fly cross. Bale me one, two, three times dat go down dis side, cross bottom gully and yarra, yarra, den cross up dat range, one, two, three times nine miles," said Bungy, excitedly.

"Twenty-seven miles. Well, I suppose it must be so after all. I was looking straight across from hill side to hill side. Dash it, what a start the fellow has got of us to be sure. He must still have that infernal racing colt under him, and your shot could not have been half so serious a one as you fancied it, mate," said the trooper.

"Indeed it could not; and yet I argue from his early camping—if that, indeed, be his fire—that he feels himself too weak to proceed further. It is too late for a midday halt, and in his present peril he would not camp so soon for the night unless fatigue or exhaustion compelled him to do so. I, therefore, fancy that he has run to the end of his tether, and that we have only to move on and take him," said Frank Beaumont.

"To be or not to be, that is the question," quoted Job.

Ted Hogan began to entertain Frank's view of the matter. The black's opinion of the case they did not take the trouble to solicit, though, perhaps, it might have been the most valuable and trustworthy of all.

The four pushed on now with renewed spirit when they saw a possible end of the chase.

They had to dismount and lead their horses, however.

And then the difficulty was to keep going down themselves and keep their horses from advancing too quickly on their footsteps.

The consequences of a slip, a stumble, or a fall would have been to bring a horse staggering and crashing down on the unlucky slipper.

As they descended the silence became oppressive, save when it was broken in a startling manner by the shrill cry of the native companion or the clear liquid notes of the bell bird, that unfailing informant of the proximity of water, and consequently the saviour and preserver of many a poor wretch lost in the bush, who would never have discovered it unaided.

At last the bottom of the range was reached, and a quarter of an hour later the river.

It was bank high almost, but a tea-tree bush which reared its head above water in the middle of the stream indicated where it was fordable.

The black fellow and the trooper were both of opinion that the current was not so strong as to render crossing dangerous, and Frank said—

"We will make for yon tea-tree bush, and, as long as our horses feel the bottom, keep their heads well up stream. Should they get out of their depth, that instant we will give them every inch of rein, and their instinct will take them across, never fear. A horse will swim like a dog if he has his head."

Scarcely had the words escaped his lips when Bungy, with a cry, leapt into the stream, and, snorting like a hippopotamus, struck out for the opposite shore.

Then Frank and the trooper spurred their horses into the water, and they took to it kindly, swimming like otters, and very soon reaching the opposite shore.

But when they looked round they saw Job Short still on the opposite bank, vainly striving to urge his steed into the rapidly rolling and swollen stream.

The animal had his fore feet resolutely planted in a straight line before him, within a couple of feet of the river's bank, while his quivering nostrils and thrown-back ears indicated mischief.

"Be careful," yelled out Frank. "Speak soothingly to him, pat his neck, coax him in. If you whip him, he'll toss you over his head as safe as eggs."

"But he is a beast," responded Job. "He won't listen to reason! So-ho, good fellow! so-ho, good horse! Go it hot and strong," and Job patted his steed's neck, and begged and entreated it to take to the water.

But his prayers and solicitations were as vainly applied as his previous blows had been, and his steed's ears were only thrown still further backwards, whilst he showed the whites of his eyes, as vicious horses ever do when on mischief firmly bent.

"Good horse! good horse!" began Job again; but the sorrel steed, doubtless resenting the words as a foul libel, threw up his heels with a snort and a neigh, and away went Job into the water clean as a whistle, whilst with a toss of the head the sorrel trotted away into the darkness of the bush.

Job sank underneath, but quickly rose to the surface, and struck boldly out for the opposite shore.

During the half minute of semi-consciousness, however, the strong downward current had swept him a good score of yards below the spot where he had been submerged, and its opposite patch of tea-tree scrub, and here the waters ran with a much greater force.

He was a fine swimmer, but he had never struggled in a raging torrent like this.

The roar both deafened and frightened him.

He put forth all his strength for a spurt, and exhausted himself too soon, so that by the time he was two-thirds of the way across he was powerless to struggle further.

He gave utterance to a cry and turned on his back to float, but the current was running at the rate of nine miles an hour, and he would soon have been hurried heaven alone knows whither, had not the aboriginal, who, wearing no clothes, was the first one ready, jumped in to his rescue.

An Australian native swims like a fish, and so Bungy presently brought Job to the bank, where he was very soon himself again.

"How can I get on without a horse?" he then said disconsolately. "You will have to leave me behind."

"It is time enough to think of that when we ourselves can get on beyond a walking pace," said Ted Hogan.

"And ere that we shall be able to catch a wild horse very likely. There must be hundreds of them in a neighbourhood like this," added Frank.

"You won't find me ride him when he is caught," said Job. "That brute who has left me in the lurch was quite bad enough, I can tell you."

"Well, I'll mount him, and you shall have mine," quoth Frank; "but let us be moving, or you will catch cold and ague, and we shall lose time."

They crossed the narrow patch of valley that lay between the river and the opposite mountain side, suffering their horses to crop away at the wild oats that generally grow in such localities, as they forced their way through them, and then came another tug of war.

Job Short was certainly as well off on foot as on horseback, for the ascent was every whit as steep as the descent had been.

They performed it in silence, for they had little inclination and breath for talking.

Sometimes they halted for a brief rest upon the landing place, which lay between the steeper parts of the hills, and at other times to watch some vast fragment of granite, which, loosened by their horses' feet, plunged headlong to the bottom, occasionally bounding so high in its career that a horseman might have passed under it unharmed.

At last they got close up to the spot where they had seen the fire burning, but there was no sign of it now, not a trace, not a single wreath of pale blue smoke.

They proceeded very cautiously, however, for at any instant it might become revealed.

They had muzzled their horses, so that they could not neigh, and they led them, so as if possible to prevent them striking their feet against the rocks or boulders.

Such a sound would have assuredly alarmed Blue Cap, were he in the neighbourhood.

And the black tracker averred that, fire or no fire, he was not very far off, as the scent was warm.

It seemed like it, too, for presently a shot rang through the primeval forest, and the trooper's hat was dashed from his head with a pistol bullet through it.

"A good shot, whoever fired it," he said, picking it up and re-adjusting it in its proper place, though perhaps giving it a fiercer cock than before. "Egad, if he will only show himself, I'll return it with interest."

But the baffled marksman did not show himself—he knew a trick worth two of it, and though search was eagerly made, not a sign of him was discoverable.

At the close of it, however, the hunters came across the nearly extinguished embers of a camp fire, and Bungy, with a broad grin, exclaimed—

"White fellow fire! white fellow, sit down like it long o' that to-day, one hour gone. Yawr, ah!"

"No doubt about that, Bungy," said Ted Hogan.

"One white fellow down! Two white fellow sit down large fire, I go bail. My word two fellow come like it long a land plenty baked. Two Yarraman baked too. Then go way, but think no far with Yarramen so baked," quoth Bungy.

"He says that two white men have camped by that fire, and have only just ridden off. That their horses are very tired, and can't go much further, so that we must soon come up with them," said Hogan.

"Let us push on at once, then," quoth Frank.

And push on they did, at the rate of at least three miles an hour, a tall pace, considering that the ascent was still as steep as a house roof.

They had no doubt that Blue Cap had fired the pistol shot, not so much to kill, though he had no objection to that, as to cause a search to be made and time to be lost in beating about the bush, whilst he went straight away like a rocket. At last the pursuers fairly reached the top of the mountain, and glanced down in triumph upon the enormous masses of eucalyptus now far beneath their feet, which, when they stood on the river bank, had towered above their heads in sombre majesty for miles and miles skyward.

But looking in the opposite direction there was, as is often the case with Australian mountains, no appreciable descent, but instead a table land, stretching miles and miles away under the moonlight and covered with immense forests interspersed here and there with grassy plains.

"Now you must leave me behind," quoth Job.

"Not a bit of it," rejoined Frank; "my horse is still as fresh as when we started. Jump up behind."

"All right," said Job; "if you think he will bear double, that will be fine."

Frank rode up beside a fallen tree, and by its aid, Job managed to get astride behind him.

Then they once more pressed onwards.

But Bungy, who had started in advance at his usual run, with eyes directed downward at the track which he had never once lost since starting, presently came to a full halt, threw up his head and snorted ominously.

He came back with a countenance many shades whiter than it was by nature, and pointed with a long skinny arm in the direction they had been pursuing, and where about three miles further on was now visible a cloud of white, but flame-tinted smoke rising above the tree tops.

"Budgery white fellow, he fire um bush. He go on safe. Wind not blow his way. We turn, or it obertake us and burn us all up."

And it was evident that he was very frightened, for his eyes rolled from side to side, as only a black fellow's eyes can when under the influence of terror.

"He has played us a deep and clever trick," exclaimed Frank, "but I would sooner wade through a sea of fire than give up the pursuit," and he took off his hat and wiped his forehead, on which great beads of sweat had gathered, not from fear of the approaching bush fire, but from a dread that it would enable Blue Cap to get away.

"We might be able to do that three miles before the fire gains sufficient ground to form an impassable barrier across our path," said Ted Hogan. "I will take up Bungy behind, and we will dash on without minding the trail; we can pick up that afresh when King Fire is broken through and overcome."

CHAPTER XVIII.

THROUGH MANY PERILS.

WHEN Ted Hogan, Frank Beaumont, and Job Short looked round to see what Bungy thought of his proposal—but Bungy was gone.

Gone as though he had never been.

He had evidently taken fright at Ted Hogan's proposition, and had made himself scarce.

"It is no good our troubling ourselves about him," said Ted Hogan. "We could never catch him if he determined that we shouldn't, and we should be losing precious time in the attempt. It is only one less to carry, and black fellows should be as thick as peas about here. Let us get along."

This advice Frank Beaumont deemed sound. He hurriedly told Job Short to sit firm and hold on like grim death.

Then they urged their steeds to a gallop.

If they could only pass through the fire ere it assumed proportions to form an impassable barrier, all would be well, and they would be pretty certain to take Blue Cap before the night was over; but if they didn't—— Well, as they did not anticipate failure, neither will we.

They could hear the roar of the flames, and a sharp crackling like file-firing, as they seized upon and devoured the dry eucalypti leaves, dying out in a galaxy of twinkling stars.

"It will spread like lightning before this wind," said Ted Hogan. "Yet never mind, we will flash through it like an express train through a railway tunnel, the devil taking the hindmost."

He was in a state of strong excitement, as was but natural under the circumstances, and Frank Beaumont shared his enthusiasm.

As for Job Short, he had so much labour in keeping his seat that he could give attention to naught else.

Certainly the clattering of his sword scabbard against the horse's flank accelerated his speed as much as did Frank's spurs.

But presently both horses came to a halt, and neither words nor blows could induce them to proceed.

They trembled, snorted, and betrayed every symptom of abject and overwhelming terror.

They had caught the red glow of the flames flashing through the tree trunks and the onward rush of the smoke, white as a sea fog.

Ted Hogan saw the cause of their fear in an instant.

"Wheel them round," he said. "I will blindfold them ere we proceed further, or they will run away with us."

Frank pulled off his Chinese silk scarf, and gave it with his pocket-handkerchief to the trooper.

He soon blindfolded the horses, and then they once more resumed their mad gallop through the now fire-lit bush, but they were no longer scared by smoke or flame, and dashed steadily on without giving any heed to the roar of the fire, which now could have been heard for miles.

Every moment the hope that they would be able to gallop through the cordon of smoke and flame grew less and less, for the fire was spreading with enormous rapidity, and when they came fairly in view of it Ted Hogan exclaimed—

"A salamander would not dare to run that fiery gauntlet. The scoundrel has defeated us."

Frank Beaumont's face grew redder than the redness of the flame.

He gnashed his teeth with rage.

But presently a thought struck him, and he brightened up.

"We must outflank the flames," he said.

"We will try it on," responded Ted Hogan, dubiously; "but the fire is sweeping onward at a pace of six miles an hour, and spreading laterally at a rate of two at the very least."

"It's blistering my face, at any rate," said Job. "I've a strong notion we shall be burnt alive."

The sight that now presented itself was sufficiently awful in sober truth to strike alarm into the breast of anyone.

The roar of the on-rushing flames was louder than the loudest cannonade, and to appal the eye there was a perfect wall of fire rushing onwards right in their faces, with lambent-tongued skirmishers in advance, that overcame the dark tea-tree bushes with a rush and a roar, springing from spray to spray and twig to twig, likes quivering, writhing snakes, and in an instant consuming all that they alighted on.

The heat was so intense that it was impossible to stand it any longer, and Ted and Frank wheeled round their horses and fled.

But when they found that they could easily gain on the fire they grew more calm, and Frank said—

"Now, let us incline to the right, and round the conflagration. We must ride against the wind, for the other way we should have no chance owing to the rapid advance of the flames, urged on by the gale—for it is blowing a gale, I vow."

"But not a favouring gale," groaned Frank.

Ted Hogan made no reply, but wheeled his horse round to the right, and then away they sped again as hard as they could go.

The roar of a horrible Babel surrounded them on all sides.

Parrots and cockatoos in thousands wheeled and circled overhead, possums screamed from the tree branches, scaly serpents glided hissing amongst the grass, and even under their horses' feet, and the dismal howl of the warrigal was mingled with the roar of wild cattle, the neighing of wild horses, the squeal of the wombat, and the bumping of invisible kangaroos.

"We shall have to overcome many dangers and difficulties ere we round the fire," said Ted Hogan.

"None but what we can snap our fingers at."

replied Frank, who could not bear to think of obstacles.

"I don't know that, but we shall soon see," replied the trooper, urging his horse on afresh.

They had not proceeded far when the sonorous, deep-toned roar of a bull seemed to be answered by a thousand echoes, and then ensued a trampling of feet, that caused the solid ground to tremble and shake, as does the treacherous margin of a morass or bog beneath the footsteps of the incautious traveller.

"What on earth is it?" asked Job Short.

But there was no need for a reply, for a rolling sea of heads, surmounted by a tempest of tossing horns, were at this moment seen rushing right down upon them through the forest vistas.

"Wild cattle! Let us spur on for our lives, or they will overwhelm us and trample us into the ground," said Frank in alarm.

He and Ted Hogan dashed on, but Job Short fell off, and then roared—

"Stop, stop! I shall be killed! Oh! oh! oh!"

But though sorry for him, Ted nor Frank dared stop.

It would have been sacrificing their lives, the herd was now so close.

"Climb a tree!" yelled out Frank at the top of his voice, and that was all that he could say.

Ted and Frank twice glanced backwards, but no Job Short was to be seen, and then they had to think wholly of evading the on-rolling cattle.

Like the waters of a vast rushing river that has burst its banks they came rolling on, the leaders with their heads and horns lowered, the rear ranks with their heads reared on high, and their terrified eyes striving to pierce the gloom ahead in search of safety from the flames.

The red glow of the fire in the rear illumined the scene, giving it a light and shade that made it grotesque and horrible.

There were at least a thousand cattle in that galloping mob, most of them as wild and fierce as lions, for two-thirds at least had never been enclosed by stock-yard fence or submitted to the brand of slavery.

The rest were composed of runaways, who, however, liked their wild life too much to return to the well grassed runs of their former possessors.

But hand and voice were now no longer needed to urge on the tried steeds.

They at last saw the danger, and were as anxious to escape from it as their riders.

All that was wanted was a tight rein, to prevent their fleeing before the cattle, instead of endeavouring to shoot past them laterally.

They escaped, to use a common but inelegant simile, by the skin of their teeth, or by the closest shave possible.

The flank of Frank's horse received such a blow from the buffeting shoulders of the outer side of the galloping herd, that the animal span half round and nearly fell, and the next instant a vicious young bull rushed out from his companions, and, with a rear and a snort, dashed right at Ted Hogan.

Never was Spanish matador, with his lance broken, a lamed horse, and not a picador near, in greater peril than Ted Hogan at that moment.

A wild Australian bull will chase a well-mounted horseman for a dozen miles without being shaken off, taking as high fences and as desperate leaps en route as ever the pursued will venture on, for they are close, well knit, active, and not overfed, seldom exceeding a mule in size.

This particular bull was evidently as fierce as a lion, and as thoroughly bent upon mischief.

He charged the trooper with head down, his long, close set, and shining horns looking as uncanny as though they had been bayonets

Hogan wheeled his horse round just in time for it to escape with a ripping up of the flesh to the depth of about the eighth part of an inch, as the bull's left horn grazed its right shoulder.

But the good steed, now thoroughly terrified and smarting with pain, began to snort and rear, and become utterly unmanageable, whilst the bull wheeled round and prepared to make a fresh charge upon his foe.

Disastrous would that charge have been, for Ted's horse was beyond all control now, had not Frank drawn his revolver and dashed upon the foe.

He knew that his thick skull might turn a ball, in which case it would be all over with his friend; so, as the bull charged Ted, he charged the bull, and, encountering it half way, leaned over in his saddle, and fired right into his ear in passing.

Then, with a roar, a moan, and a stagger, the fierce brute fell dead, and Frank exclaimed—

"That's the way to dispose of 'em, Ted."

"I owe you my life," was the response, "and I'll never forget it. I wonder what's become of Short."

"Trampled and gored to death, I'm afraid," quoth our hero. "However, we will ride back and see."

"If we've time before the fire is upon us," said Hogan. "It's coming on with prodigious strides."

They rode back without exchanging another word.

The herd of wild cattle had all swept past, and were nearly out of sight; but warrigals (red, wiry-haired, wolf-faced furies) were tearing along in mad panic, and kangaroos were bumping through the long grass.

At last they discovered Job, not dead, but lying snugly under the protection of the prostrate trunk of a big tree.

The cattle, in clearing the trunk, had, perforce, cleared him, without noticing him, too.

"Well, you are pretty chaps, to leave a fellow in the lurch," were his first words; but Ted and Frank soon convinced him that it had been a matter of dire necessity, and then he was easily persuaded again to get up behind Frank and proceed.

But the bush fire, on account of the highly inflammable nature of the foliage whereon it fed (the eucalypti leaves being full of turpentine and gum) had by this time reached close upon them, so close that the heat was actually painful to bear, singing their hair, eyebrows, and moustaches, and causing the skin to peel off their faces.

"It will be impossible to round the fire now," said Ted Hogan. "We shall have quite enough to do to escape from it. 'Tis outflanking us both to right and to left."

A glance showed Frank Beaumont that this was, indeed, the case, and he answered, decisively—

"You are right. We must ride for our lives."

They pursued their way as fast as they could, but their horses were now regularly exhausted, and for a long while it was doubtful whether the fire would not overtake them, its progress was so rapid.

They had no time to bestow upon Blue Cap now; their own lives hung on the veriest thread. Did their horses give out, or merely turn lame, all would be over with them, for their grim pursuer was travelling at the rate of half a dozen miles an hour.

On, and on, and on, Job groaning, and now and then declaring that the horse's tail was being singed to a stump; but neither Frank nor Ted took any heed of him, for they had enough to think of.

Kangaroos still bumped, and dingoes galloped past, but only singly now.

The young and the active were far ahead.

These were the old, the crippled, and the infirm. Yet, urged by terror, they gave the riders the go-by somehow or other.

And long, many-jointed centipedes, curly-tailed scorpions, and great bulbous-bodied, hairy-legged, triantiwallagong spiders dropped on and around them as they rode on, terrified by the heat and the smoke, and not knowing how to escape.

And the smoke overtook them, and rolled on in front, and they could no longer see their way.

It was all blind steering now.

They could hardly see their horses' heads before them.

But they knew that the fire was behind, and that alone guided their flight.

Soon the fire coloured the smoke, and then it was like riding through a sulphurous cloud, a cloud that blinded and scorched, and seemed to wither up their brains, as it did the forest leaves.

It was an awful ride, that.

Many a time Ted and Frank thought that the end had come, that another minute and they would be unable to maintain their seats in the saddle; and as for Job Short, he seemed to have collapsed altogether.

And yet it was Job who suddenly exclaimed—

"Here's water just in front. I'll swear to it."

"I'm afraid you're wrong; I see nothing of it, and, besides, it's impossible for any fellow to pass through this smoke," growled Frank in response.

But even as he uttered the last word his horse gave a kind of a lurch, and thousands of drops of cool, limpid water seemed to splash over his face.

He was afloat; his horse was swimming. There could be no doubt about it.

But whither? Ah! that was impossible to tell, for the smoke-cloud still enveloped him closely in its folds.

He heard, however, another splash, and knew that it was caused by Ted Hogan's horse leaping into the stream.

Presently he heard the trooper shout—

"We are saved, mate, by a miracle."

A minute later the horses were swimming abreast.

Presently, too, the smoke-cloud grew less dense.

They then saw that their horses were breasting the waters of a wide and placid river, and that they were close to a little scrub-covered island.

To guide their steeds towards it was an easy matter, and in a couple of minutes the horses were scrambling up the bank, much refreshed by their immersion.

"Well, here we will rest until the bush-fire has burnt itself out," said Ted Hogan, throwing himself from the saddle. "There is abundant feed for our horses, and perfect safety for ourselves."

"Yes," said Frank, "and in a dozen hours we shall be as fresh as ever, and will follow up the trail of the villain, Blue Cap, more hotly than ever."

"Ah! that's if we can strike it again," quoth Ted Hogan. "I don't know what we shall do without Bungy. I don't suppose he'll turn up again."

"There must be lots of other black fellows in this region. So, if we don't come across him, I daresay we shall find another," said Frank. "However, let us now light a fire, dry ourselves, eat, and sleep; then we shall be ready for the morrow."

This was too good advice not to be followed. The horses were unharnessed and turned loose, sticks collected, a fire lighted, a very good meal partaken of; and then, after a smoke and a talk, all three composed themselves to slumber, with their heads on their pillows and their feet towards the cheery blaze.

Overcome by fatigue, they soon fell fast asleep, undisturbed by the roar of the brisk fire or the lurid glow that rendered every tree and bush on the little island as clearly visible as at noonday.

Poor Job Short, however, had troubled dreams. He fancied that Blue Cap had hold of him by the hair, and was proceeding to scalp him.

"Oh, take my money, but spare my life!" yelled Job; and then he woke up in a fright, to find that he was being tugged by the hair, and that some sharp instrument was at the same time hacking away at his head.

"Help! Murder! Help! help! help!" yelled Job, sitting upright; and then he raised his hand to his head; but withdrew it with a yell of anguish.

His cries awoke Ted and Frank, who, at sight of his lachrymose face and its cause, could hardly help laughing, for there, perched atop of his head, was a little native bear, not much larger than a kitten, its sharp claws maintaining a firm hold, whilst he waged battle with a cockatoo, who, perched on Job's shoulder, was pecking fiercely at him with his bill, but just as often striking poor Job's skull as its foe.

It was not without considerable difficulty that the doughty duellists were driven from the field; but it took a much longer time to soothe the terrified Job's nerves, and to convince him of the very harmless nature of the creatures who had interrupted his slumbers.

CHAPTER XIX.
THE CORPSE DOWN BY THE CREEK.

THE little incident narrated at the close of the last chapter created a great deal of amusement and laughter, and then Frank, Ted, and Job relapsed into slumber once more.

They did not wake up again until it was broad daylight, and then the bush fire had swept on and past them, its lurid glow and smoke canopy being visible nearly a dozen miles away.

Before them the road was clear, a scorched, blackened desert, with millions of sooty leaves blown hither and thither by the wind, like grimy butterflies, and a billion sparks flitting to and fro in their company, like fire flies.

Here and there a denuded tree-trunk still rose red hot, a veritable pillar of fire from the blackened earth, and every now and then one of these would fall with a crash, creating in the act a pyrotechnic display that would have done no discredit to North Woolwich or Cremorne.

"This island turned up most opportunely for us," said Ted Hogan, as he cut off some tea-tree branches to make a fire. "Had not our horses stumbled into the river they and we should have been dead enough by this time."

"Not a doubt of it," answered Frank; "and no doubt the fiend who lighted the fire thinks that such has been our fate. Well, we will undeceive him when we overtake him, that's one comfort."

"If we do overtake him," groaned Job Short.

"Oh, there are no ifs about it," responded Frank. "Overtake him we must and will, and I fancy he will make it easy for us by travelling slowly and carelessly now. He will never imagine that we have been able to escape the ruthless pursuer that he let slip upon us."

"I wish we could come across that fellow Bungy," quoth Ted; "and yet his tracking powers would be of little service now. The trail will have been effectually rubbed out, or rather buried, by cinders, ashes, and charred leaves."

"We will have him for all that," said Frank.

"Oh, yes, we'll have him in the end, no doubt!" assented the trooper, but rather dubiously.

"Well, then, I don't believe we ever will," quoth Job Short. "I think he's one too many for us."

"Not a bit of it, friend—not a bit of it. We are three too many for him, as he will find to his cost when once we overtake him," persisted Frank.

"And, in order to overtake him all the quicker, let us now to breakfast and recruit our strength and energies by a hearty meal," said Ted.

This was too good advice to be spurned, and the three set to work with a will.

Half an hour later the river was recrossed, and the trio were riding north-westerly, which was unanimously voted to be the likeliest direction in which to overtake Blue Cap, the bushranger.

Mile after mile they pursued their melancholy course over the blackened plain.

Sometimes their horses would stumble, through catching their feet in holes caused by the ravenous fire in pursuing the roots of the resinous gum-trees down into the ground, and it was only by rare good fortune that on these occasions they escaped sprains or broken legs.

They had set forth at early dawn, but noon had arrived before the domain of King Fire had been passed through.

Then a beautiful open country, consisting of well-grassed plains, opened to their gaze, and on these plains herds of kangaroos were grazing, whilst here and there long-legged emus, singly or in pairs, were seen crossing it at a run that would have put to shame many a horse's gallop.

The three youths could not help giving vent to a cry of delight.

It was like emerging from the gloomy plains of Tartarus into the Elysian fields.

"We shall soon have him now," said Frank.

"I hope so," answered Ted, more dubiously than ever.

"We shall never have him at all now," quoth Job.

"Why do you say that?" asked Frank sharply.

"Because how can you find out in what direction he has travelled over these vast plains?" answered Job with a wise shake of the head.

Frank's jaw fell. He saw the force of the observation.

"What lies beyond these plains?" asked Ted Hogan.

"Well, the Argyle Road to Sydney, and eighty miles away on the left the Manangle diggings," said Frank. "Then there is the rich pastoral district of Yan, too."

The trooper made no reply for a minute or two, and then he said—

"You may make sure that Master Blue Cap is making tracks for the Manangle diggings. Amongst ten thousand other rascals he will hope to escape observation, and, give him a few weeks for his hair and beard to grow, he will stand a good chance of doing so."

"But we won't give him the time," quoth Frank with fiery ardour. "If you think he is bound for Manangle, we can reach there by to-morrow night, and the next day he will be ours, I warrant."

"Well, let us hope so," replied Ted; "and now the quicker we can find water the better, for our horses are nearly choked, nor are we much better off."

The horses were, indeed, not only in dire distress from thirst, but were lame as well. The heat of the ground and the constant treading on burning cinders had scorched the horn of their hoofs.

To ease them the trio dismounted, and walked on foot for many miles, until at last they came to a gully, down the centre of which flowed a clean, rapid, and narrow stream.

In it they watered their horses, which refreshed them mightily, and then they prepared to camp for the usual and very necessary siesta.

The strongest and most enduring of horses would soon break down without this mid-day halt, which is never departed from.

But though the horses had plenty of the richest of grasses whereon to feed, their riders found on overlooking their haversacks that they were very nearly empty, whilst their stomachs happened to be in a very similar condition.

This was a most unpleasant state of affairs, but Frank proposed that they should set forth and try to stalk a kangaroo, the flesh of whose tail and hinder quarters is, when roasted, every whit as delicious as venison, whilst the rest of its body is so coarse, tough, and stringy as only to be fit for dogs.

Ted Hogan fell in with Frank's views at once, but Job Short declared that he was tired out, and would sooner stay behind to keep an eye on the horses and light a fire against their return.

When they had gone he set to work to collect the necessary wood for this latter purpose, but soon found that, as far as the labour of the thing was concerned, he might as well have gone kangarooing.

Sticks were almost as rare as diamonds, and he trudged to and fro and up and down a good four miles before he had collected from the widely scattered leptospermum bushes sufficient for his purpose.

Then he went down to the creek to fill the billy with water to boil for tea, tea being the prevailing drink in the bush at all hours of the day, being partaken of at breakfast, dinner, and supper indiscriminately.

But close to the bank of the creek he started at sight of the ashes of another camp fire.

And he started again, and this time uttered a wild cry, for a second glance showed him a corpse lying amidst the tall, rank grass and the neroda flowers.

A corpse? Yes, a corpse unmistakeably, for it lay on the broad of its back, with its stony eyes glaring unwinkingly up at the mid-day sun, and with a knife buried to the haft in its chest.

Job noticed that it was the body of a man of some forty-five years of age, and then he perceived with some surprise that a piece of paper, with writing thereon, was affixed by the knife to the murdered man's chest.

Job knelt down.

It was a stiff, cramped hand, and in pencil, but easily perusable.

Thus it ran—

"Caution to my Pursuers:

"The scent lies cold, so I give you a clue. Make the best of it. I'm afraid of no one in heaven or earth. My course is not yet run. They who think or hope so are fools. Catch me who can. I defy you all. I'll give you many a token of my power to do mischief, and will laugh at all your puny efforts to take me. Hurrah for rapine and robbery! Hurrah for

"BLUE CAP, THE BUSHRANGER!"

Job Short read this choice effusion with a shudder.

Then he looked round with his hand on his sword hilt, fully expecting to see the horrible face of the bloodthirsty villain they were pursuing glaring at him from some point or other.

And whilst he glanced nervously first up and then down the river, he was hugged from behind in a tight and suffocating embrace, a strange, and, to him, terrible voice muttered an unintelligible something in his ear, the owner thereof giving him at the same moment a hearty kick in the region that is generally used for sitting purposes.

"Coward," exclaimed Job—"coward, to pin a fellow from behind so that he can't help himself. Let me go, and with swords, face to face, I'll— Oh, he's sticking a knife into my pos—pos—posterior! Ah! he! ha! Don't do it again! It hurts! Oh, good Mr. Blue Cap, dear Mr. Blue Cap, take my money, but spare my life! Oh, take my money, but spare my life!"

But good, dear Mr. Blue Cap didn't seem to feel inclined to let his victim off so easily.

His grasp on his throat tightened.

He uttered strange chuckling sounds of pleasure and glee whilst he shook the seedy Hamlet, until he hardly knew whether he was on his head or his heels, and all the while he continued to lance his unmentionables *and their contents* until Job's

TED HOGAN AND BLUE CAP WERE FACE TO FACE AT LAST, AND THEN ENSUED A MOMENT OF AGONIZING SUSPENSE.

No. 4.

agonised appeals for mercy might have been heard miles away.

And all this time, turn or twist his head as he would, he could not catch a single glance at the ruffian who was so cruelly using him.

Then presently he fainted, nor recovered until he felt someone sprinkling refreshing water over him.

"Have you secured him? Have you shot or taken the murdering villain prisoner?" was his first questions.

"No, he was too fleet of foot for us," replied Frank.

"I'm sorry for that. I did my best. Directly I saw him I attacked him sword in hand, but he was a wonderful fencer, and, though a first rate one myself, he at last disarmed me. Then I grappled with him, but he was stronger than me too, though not possessed of nearly the science. Three times I threw him, but on every occasion he got uppermost. 'Let me go!' he often screamed. 'Villanous Blue Cap, never!' was my inevitable reply, and I stuck to him like a leech, but at last, unable to overcome me face to face, as man fights man, he dodged round and seized me behind. He very soon did for me then, though I kept tight hold of his jacket until reason forsook me, hoping that you would come up," and Job looked as if he were telling the truth, the whole truth, and nothing but the truth.

"You are a brave fellow, Job, but I wonder for how long Blue Cap has turned himself into a boomer kangaroo?" laughed Frank.

"What do you mean?" asked Job Short, indignantly.

"Why, that your doughty antagonist was not a human being, but an old man kangaroo," was the reply.

"But I assure you, 'pon my honour," began Job.

"We saw the whole of the fight," exclaimed Ted Hogan, interrupting him, "and we hurried up to the rescue as fast as we could. The boomer hopped up to you from behind, upreared himself, threw his two short fore-paws around your neck, and then struck at you again and again, as is their wont, with the cock-like spurs that adorn their hind-legs, and which are nearly as big and as sharp as pocket knives. We heard you shriek out, 'Good Mr. Blue Cap! Dear Mr. Blue Cap!' and then at last we frightened the kangaroo away—you falling like a log as he let go his hold."

"Oh, was that how it was?" said Job Short. "If you saw it all of course you ought to know. I didn't, and so thought things had happened as I described them. As you are acquainted with so much, of course you know all about the dead body too," and poor Job spoke very snappishly, for he was very annoyed that his tale of "dering do" had met with the lie-courteous.

"Dead body! What dead body?" asked Ted Hogan.

"We have seen no dead body," echoed Frank.

"Then it seems after all that you don't know and haven't seen everything," retorted Job Short, triumphantly. "Follow me, and I will show you where it lies concealed."

He scrambled to his feet, though not without difficulty, and limped before them to the spot.

For a minute or two the trio gazed in awe-struck silence at the weird, awful sight.

Then Frank, stooping down, read Blue Cap's vaunting challenge, and, rising to his feet, exclaimed—

"I now feel more sure than ever that we shall have him. He is playing the bold and reckless game. We defies us. Well, be it so, he will live to regret it."

"A man like that isn't bound for the diggings either. He don't mean to play at bo-peep. Depend upon it, mateys, he is up to some bold and dare-devil game, such as seizing and holding the Argyle and Sydney coach road, and levying black mail at the revolver's muzzle upon all who pass along it," said Ted Hogan, oracularly.

"I believe that's what he'll do," said Frank, "but if that's his little game his reign on the road shall be a very short one, and, that it may be so, friends, let us set about getting dinner at once. We have shot a fine little Joey, Job, whose meat will be as tender as lamb after half an hour's cooking."

Frank's prophecy in respect to the succulency of the young kangaroo turned out a true one, and a most hearty meal was made thereof.

Then what was left of the edible portions of the animal was carefully packed away in the saddlebags for future use, and, the horses being resaddled and recaprisoned, the three young men mounted and once more continued their journey.

CHAPTER XX.
JOB SHORT HAS ANOTHER TROUBLED NIGHT.

THE horses had been much refreshed by the two hours' halt and the plentiful feed of grass.

The water had cooled their burnt hoofs and cleansed their smoke and dust-filled nostrils, besides slaking their intolerable thirst, and the effect of all this was that they now journeyed blithely along at the rate of a dozen miles an hour or so.

"We can't reach the Argyle road to-night, can we?" asked Ted Hogan at length.

"Well, hardly," responded Frank. "'Tis more than fifty miles away yet, and I don't think our nags are equal to it."

"Nor do I," responded the trooper, "but we'll get as close to it as we can anyhow, won't we?"

"Yes," answered Frank, "for nobody knows what may turn up. Blue Cap keeps to the front well."

They rode on for some hours over the same beautiful down-like country, and as the shades of evening fell they saw the dark form of a solitary horseman thrown out in bold relief against the saffron-tinted horizon.

Every curve and outline of this man and horse showed out distinctly.

They could see his round, bullet head and the long, straight feathers that rose from its apex.

"It's Blue Cap!" exclaimed everyone.

"No doubt about it," added Ted Hogan.

"But he's a good five miles away," said Frank Beaumont, "and it'll be dark in ten minutes."

This was true enough, for there is little or no twilight in Australia, where a quarter of an hour after the sun has disappeared it is pitch dark.

It is during that brief twilight that distant objects are seen so distinctly, the rarity of the atmosphere being so great that an English rifleman would sight for a thousand yards an object that was a couple of miles away, whilst wooded ranges a score of miles distant look to be an easy hour's walk.

"Thou art so near and yet so far," Ted Hogan began to sing bitterly.

"That's just about it," observed Frank. "Our horses are dead beat when within view of the game. It is not a bit of good pursuing him. A stern chase is proverbially a long chase, and we should not come up with him for many a long mile if once he sighted us, which he could not help doing on this open treeless waste before long."

"No," assented Ted. "It would be a fool's game beginning the chase after sundown across such country as this. In my opinion we'd better camp, be up a little before the dawn, and try to nab him before he is awake and astir."

"That's my opinion, too," said Frank; "so let us tumble off our horses and into the grass at once, lest he should glance round and perceive us. If he does not take it into his head that we are close up with him he will camp soon, and then on these plains we must see the light of his camp fire."

"It's too late—he has turned round and spotted us," exclaimed Ted Hogan, with an oath. "See, he is waving something at us derisively."

"Yes," replied Frank. "But see, now he sets spurs to his horse and is off like the wind. His nag is as fresh as a daisy."

"Which is far from the case with ours," growled Ted. "I see some water down at the bottom of the next gully. Let us walk, our horses will follow us. Tisn't worth while to remount them."

"No, it isn't," assented Frank, "for the creek don't seem more than a mile away."

They strode along through the knee-high grass, carrying their bridles on their arms, and their horses following close after, cropping as they went.

But when they got to the creek they found it in possession of a fat, paunchy Chinaman, who was cooking something over a remarkably bright fire.

The aroma of this something was delicious, and as it turned round on a kind of impromptu spit, slowly roasting, it looked as a fine, fat possum might have looked if skinned and turned in a similar manner.

It suddenly struck Frank, Ted and Job that it would be fine fun to appropriate the Chinee's savoury repast, giving him in exchange some pieces of their cold kangaroo.

In all parts of Australia poor "Johnnie," as he invariably calls himself, is the butt of all practical jokers, who no more consider his feelings than if he were a wooden puppet.

"That's a nice savoury little roast, John, and it was very good of you to make us such a good fire against our arrival," said Ted Hogan to the Chinaman.

"Belly good of master to hab him little joke," was the grinning reply. "But master mustn't be too hard on poor John, who hasn't eatee eatee for all de day."

"No, no, John, you shall have some nice kangaroo steak," said the trooper; "and we will eat your roast possum for you. Come, that's quite fair."

John Chinaman didn't look as though he thought that it was, but he grinned and bore it, as it was the custom of his countrymen to do, and Ted, Frank and Job, sat down round the fire, and, opening their bags, each gave him a rasher of kangaroo—rather a dry and tasteless meat when cold.

But the celestial devoured it eagerly, as did the trio, the hot and savoury roast, when once it was sufficiently cooked, everyone declaring it to be delicious.

"I never tasted a possum with such a delicate flavour," said Frank Beaumont, when he had made a hearty meal.

"It was prime, and the stuffing delicious!" exclaimed Ted Hogan. "The Chinese aren't such bad cooks. Until now I've always fancied that possums tasted so very strong of turpentine."

"And so did I. It's because they feed on the gum leaves, which are full of turpentine," said Frank. "How our friend John has contrived to extract the objectionable flavour, and introduce one so entirely delicious, I can't understand."

"Belly easy dat, sar," said the Chinee, with a well-pleased grin that expanded his mouth from ear to ear. "Belly easy to get taste out that never was in. Dat no possum. My golly, no!"

"Not possum?" ejaculated Ted Hogan. "What the deuce have we been eating, then?"

"A fido, sar, only a fido," retorted the Chinee, with his mouth very full of kangaroo.

"And what the devil's a fido? I never heard of such an animal," exclaimed the trooper.

"What! Not know fido?" said the Chinaman, in

tones that seemed to betoken that the non-knowledge of fido betokened himself unknown.

"Fido de sweetest lilly bow-wow poopy dawg dat ever was seen. But him fur come off, dem him no good; but eatee eatee—belly tender so."

"What?" roared Ted Hogan, springing to his feet, with a face as red as beet-root; "do you mean to tell me I've been eating a mangy cur?"

"No, sar! Cur—no. Only lilly fido stuffed with snails—belly best snails, too, so fattee fattee. Pick up an' fill pockets wid dem, all de way from Yackandandarah. Belly pretty bow-wow poopy dawg," and the fat Chinaman looked disparagingly at the trooper's flushed and angry countenance, but with his mouth full of kangaroo the while.

"A dog stuffed with snails, three days in a Chinaman's pocket. Oh!" groaned Frank. And he beat a precipitate retreat.

"Oh, 'tis too much—by far too much!" moaned Job Short, hurriedly following his example, and sounds of dubious portent were almost immediately heard behind a little tea-tree bush that grew close by—sounds which betokened that that delicate poopy dawg was rising in judgment against them.

Ted Hogan laid the ghost of the defunct, as far as he was personally concerned, with a small modicum of brandy, but he glared at that Heathen Chinee the while, as if he would have liked to have choked him; and he then and there registered a mental resolve that he would never again, under any circumstances, rob a celestial of his supper.

It is astonishing how perseveringly Ted, Frank, and Job smoked for a whole hour after they had reseated themselves by the camp fire.

They were very pale and squeamish-looking, and never once alluded to their late repast.

They spoke little, and looked at John Chinaman with no friendly eyes; but they were far too polite and considerate to turn him away from his own camp fire; and so they resigned themselves to his presence as a necessary evil.

And by-and-by, feeling sleepy, they rolled their blankets around them, allowed their heads to fall back on their saddles, and with their feet to the blaze, one after the other sank into slumber.

Lastly, John Chinaman crossed over from the other side of the fire, and having no rug of his own, listened for a minute or two to detect which was the soundest sleeper, and discovering him in Job Short, hastened to make his blanket accommodate two; and wrapped up therein, with his back to the very widely strolling player, he was soon buried in a slumber as profound as his own.

But Job Short's sleep changed its character ere long, and he began to toss and turn, and throw his arms about in a most eccentric manner.

In so doing, he somehow or other got the sleeping Chinaman's long pigtail around his throat, and thereafter every movement that he made tightened it until he was half strangled.

At length an acute sense of choking awakened him, and he clapped his hands up to his throat, to find it encircled, as he at once concluded, by a venomous serpent.

"A snake!" yelled Job, in shrill accents of horror.

"De hang-hang rope!" shrieked the Chinee, awaking at the noise.

"Oh, de hang-hang rope!" he croaked again, and, rising to a sitting posture, he struggled to free himself.

But poor Job was struggling also, and, as the two men were back to back, they naturally, half awake and half asleep as they were, tugged in different directions.

"Help! help! help!" yelled Job, finding that he could not, unaided, divest himself from the coils of what he little suspected of being a pigtail. "Oh, it's a boa—it's a python—it's strangling me. A knife, some one; cut it in two, and release me. Oh! oh! oh!"

"Cut me down! Oh, de hang rope, de hang rope, de hang rope. My head's coming off. Belly hard en John, dis belly hard indeed!" blubbered the Chinee, giving his head yet another and another duck forward.

Of course by this process he mightily increased poor Job's tortures as well as his own, but Job pulled back again, and for a minute or two there ensued a most lively game of see-saw, the players screeching, yelling, and praying for assistance the while.

By this time Ted and Frank had awoke, but they enjoyed the comical scene so much, that for some time they were totally unable to render assistance.

Then, however, Ted Hogan rose to his feet, and to increase the fun, he drew his knife and cut off the Chinaman's pigtail close to his head.

Then he uncoiled it from Job's throat, and threw it on the grass in front of him.

"Oh, what a big snake!" exclaimed Job. "Thank you for killing him, Ted. He was nearly the death of me."

"Tank, you sar, for setting me free; Johnny belly grateful. Belly bad, hang-hang rope, dat for sure!" exclaimed the Chinaman in turn.

But then, clapping a hand to his head, and feeling only the little hairy shaving-brush shaped tuft that now alone remained of his once magnificent pigtail, he exclaimed in accents of horror—

"Oh, mine bigtail! oh, mine big tail! De hang-hang rope tear him all away! Oh, mine bigtail! Better mine life dan mine bigtail," and the Chinaman dug his knuckles into his eyes and began to blubber.

And by this time Job Short had also discovered the nature of the thing that had caused him so much uneasiness and fright, and his terror being thereby subdued, his anger began to rise in its place.

Turning upon the sobbing Chinaman, he therefore exclaimed, "Bother your pigtail, sir—blow your pigtail."

Finding that this did not sufficiently relieve his pent-up feelings, he sprang to his feet, grasped the offending article, and, striding over to John Chinaman, began to belabour him soundly therewith.

Now, to be thrashed without any conceivable reason with one's own pigtail, particularly after it has been surreptitiously cut off, must be to a Chinaman a very great indignity, and, as such, very hard to endure.

The celestial bore two or three strokes most submissively, but when he had rubbed his eyes clear, and perceived exactly what the gentleman in velvet was about, he yelled in no very amiable accents—

"Give me mine bigtail—give me mine bigtail!"

"I'm giving it to you as hard as ever I can," retorted Job, delivering a slash over his upturned face.

That was the last hair, or rather the last collection of plaited hairs that broke the camel's back.

The celestial sprang to his feet, lowered his head and charged Job Short like a bull.

Being utterly unprepared for such an attack, down Job went, and then the Chinee essayed to dance atop of him.

He had already executed two or three heathenish steps, when Job caught hold of his thin spindle legs, and tossed him over on to his nose.

Then, never letting go his hold, he sprang to his feet, and tightening his grasp on the Chinaman's own ankles, said gruffly and sternly—

"Now you do wheelbarrow until I let you get up."

The celestial did not at first know what doing wheelbarrow meant, but as the revengeful Job pushed him on by his legs, he progressed on his hands instinctively, and in this manner Job wheeled his novel barrow round and round the camp fire,

until, unlike most barrows, it grew quite faint and giddy.

The barrow had at first indulged in all sorts of groans, upbraidings, and complaints, such as—

"First you eat John's lilly bow-wow poopy dawg; den you hang John; den you turn him into one dam-dam wheelabout. You belly hard on John, but John's turn come one day. Yah! yah!"

But he at last got tired of complaint and invective alike, and indeed he wanted all his breath for other and widely different purposes.

Job didn't stop wheeling him until his hands gave way with sheer fatigue, and he sank on to his arms.

Then, and not till then, the offended Hamlet dropped his legs, and intimated to him, in language more forcible than polite, that he might go to the devil.

But John didn't take the hint—he merely sank down on the grass, and began to blubber again about the loss of his beloved pigtail.

"I tell you what, lads, it is about time for us to be off now," said Ted Hogan. "We ain't likely to get more sleep even if we lie down again, and we shall have a rare chance of catching Blue Cap napping. It's just three o'clock in the morning, and the sun won't be up for another hour and a half."

"I'm ready," said Frank; "I quite approve of the plan."

"I'm ready, too," quoth Job; "I suppose the beggar hasn't let his fire go out. If he has t'will be hard to find him."

Little did either of the speakers imagine that Blue Cap had been a hidden witness of everything that had passed during the preceding half hour, or that his revolver had covered the sleepers when Job Short and the Chinaman had awoke, and by the mere act frustrated his deadly intentions by instilling into his heart one of those sudden panics that at rare intervals he was subject to.

Yes, he had meant to slay them all in their sleep, but when he saw Frank and the trooper awake, with their hands on their revolvers, some inner voice told him that he would be rushing on his doom if he attacked them there and then, and so he withdrew his ugly head from behind the bushes, and after a little while slunk away into the gloom, and hied back to the spot where he had hoppled his horse.

And if his three pursuers calculated on nabbing him now, they calculated sadly without their host, for before they had even caught their horses the bushranger was galloping onwards towards the Argyle road.

He had grand schemes in his head, and he recked as little of the three self-constituted avengers, who thought that they were hunting him to his doom, than if they had been five-year-old babes, mounted on hobby-horses, and armed with wooden swords and pistols.

CHAPTER XXI.
A MISS AS GOOD AS A MILE.

IT did not take Frank, Ted, and Job very long to catch and accoutre the horses, and then they mounted and bade the unhappy Chinaman a laughing farewell.

It was still dark—dark at least but for the brilliant Australian starlight, which is very different to that of the northern hemisphere, where there seems to be more sky than stars, whereas at the antipodes there appears to be more stars than sky—stars that blaze forth from the dark-blue vault of heaven like little moons, and effectually dispel the darkness.

The cicadas were humming in the leaves, and the melancholy howl of the warrigal could be heard in different directions far off over the plains, as the trio moved noiselessly on with the amiable intention of shooting Blue Cap whilst he was napping.

In vain they looked for his fire, however.

It had gone out, or they must have seen it.

This was the conclusion that they naturally came to.

And it had gone out. There they were right.

But they little thought that the game had flown.

"We must find him when the sun rises," said Frank.

"Yes, there aren't many hiding places on these vast plains," assented Ted Hogan, with a laugh.

But day dawned, and for a circuit of miles and miles there was no sign of man nor of horse.

"He has given us th. slip again," ejaculated Frank.

"That's about it, I'm afraid," observed Job Short.

"Well, never mind," quoth Frank. "Another twenty miles, and we shall enter upon a more populated region, and, five miles further still, gain the Argyle and Sydney road. Then he won't baffle us so easily."

"We shall be more likely to pick up information concerning him, certainly," said the trooper; and then the conversation turned into other channels.

They rode on and on for hours, as fast as ever they could push their horses, but still no sign of Blue Cap.

At last they heard the cracking of pistols some way ahead, mingled with the sound of voices.

"Blue Cap's in that little game, whatever it is, I'll wager," said Frank, his eyes flashing with excitement.

"It's the devil's game, then, you may be sure of that," replied Ted Hogan. "It's the game of murder."

"It seems to be the only game he can play," retorted Frank. "But hark! what comes here?"

The exclamation was caused by the sound of horses proceeding at a mad gallop through the bush.

They had for the past half hour exchanged the open plains for thickly treed bush, so they could see only a little way ahead of and around them.

But almost ere the ejaculation had escaped Frank's lips, two harnessed steeds, covered with sweat and their eyes glaring with terror, shot by them so fast and so furiously, that no sooner were they seen than gone.

"There go two more in that direction," cried the trooper. "They are coach horses. The mail has been stuck up close by, the traces been cut, and the horses set at freedom."

"And there are more pistol shots," ejaculated Frank. "Come along; we have spoiled Master Blue Cap at that little amusement once before. Pray heavens that we stop him for ever now."

They dashed on with fresh hope and ardour now. They made sure that they should catch Blue Cap in the very midst of his cruel work, and checkmate him a moment later, at once and for ever.

But they were doomed to a sad disappointment.

There were the evidences of Blue Cap's work, but Blue Cap himself was gone.

It was the Sydney road that they had reached, and there, lying over on its side, was the Sydney mail.

The two pole-horses were as dead as horses could be, and the driver lay half under the coach, swearing and shrieking by turns with mingled rage and agony.

A woman and child lay dead in the coach.

In the middle of the road were two ripped-up letter bags, whilst scraps of envelopes and letters were being blown about by the wind, like a snow shower.

"The infernal rascal. I have never heard of a bushranger slaughtering women and little children before," said Ted Hogan, with intense disgust.

"Nor I," echoed Frank. "However, he can't be far off, and we will soon avenge them. Come on; we are losing time."

"For God's sake do what you can for me first," said the wounded driver, piteously. "The devil wouldn't kill me, because he said I should die with greater agonies if he let me be. Curse him, perhaps I may live yet."

"I hope you will," replied Frank, and then he, Ted Hogan, and Bob Short, exerted all their strength, and at last managed to drag him out from under the coach.

"Are you in much pain?" asked Frank then.

"Awful," was the groaned response. "Both of my legs are broken, and my thighs shattered. I'll never handle the ribands again. No, that's certain."

"Never say die—you can't tell that yet," quoth Frank, encouragingly. "Here, take a taste of this brandy; it will make a different man of you," and, as he spoke, he raised the flask to the poor fellow's lips.

He drank a deep drain, and then said—

"It has made a different man of me. Leave me now, and ride after that infernal fiend with the blue skull-cap and the macaw feathers on his head. If I see him a bound and fettered prisoner, I may get well again, or, if not, I'll die happy."

"I will stay to keep the poor fellow company," quoth Job. "You'll go on faster without me."

"We shall, and I was about to suggest your staying," replied Frank. "You can keep the ants, and the flies, and the hornets off him, at all events; if nothing more."

They then mounted their horses again.

"Good luck go with you," said the mail driver. "You'll bring him back this way, won't you, that I may look at him."

"Yes, decidedly," answered Frank; "we must. Don't you see that we have a comrade to pick up."

They then rode quickly away in the direction that the driver had told them Blue Cap had taken.

Not very far had they got, when they saw him a mile or two on ahead, and they at once gave chase.

He perceived them coming, when they had shortened that distance by one-half, and waved his hand to them.

Then he started off at the top of his speed.

"His horse is lame," said Frank presently, with a fierce exultation in his voice; "we will have him this time, never fear."

And it really seemed as though they would, for the bushranger's horse was unmistakeably lame. They gained on Blue Cap very rapidly.

Presently his nag stumbled and fell heavily. Blue Cap was on his feet in an instant, but not so his horse—its race was run.

Seeing this, the rascal ran in amongst some patches of scrub that grew near, and now, with frantic yells of delight, the two pursuers, revolver in hand, spurred on their horses to what they felt sure would be a certain capture of the miscreant.

But the devil stood his friend yet once more.

The patches of scrub were small, not one of them larger than an English plantation, but though they beat them in every direction, they could not flush their game.

And then, when they at last emerged into the open, whom should they see but Blue Cap, mounted on a fresh horse (a magnificent creature, as black as the raven's wing), a good three miles away, and sweeping along the sparsely wooded glades in a northerly direction, with the speed of the wind.

CHAPTER XXII.

THE DEVIL TO PAY, AND NO PITCH HOT.

IT was clearly no good following up the bushranger on his new mount, and Ted and Frank knew that well enough, for their horses were all but knocked up, and the powerful black animal that Blue Cap bestrode was good for a twenty-mile spin over any kind of country whatever.

"Let us ride back to Job," said Ted shortly.

"Let us first catch Blue Cap's abandoned steed," said Frank; "it's our three-year racing colt, Lubra. She has borne him well, and I don't suppose she is much more knocked up than the nags we are riding. If not, she will be a good mount for Job."

"Well thought of," exclaimed the trooper, and they forthwith hunted through and through the patches of scrub, until they at last came across the horse.

She was in a sorry plight, her legs being much swollen by hard riding, but she did not seem to have suffered other damage.

She knew Frank in an instant, and suffered him to approach and capture her.

They then rode back to the overturned coach.

"What! Haven't you got him?" were the first words of the mail driver as they drew near.

"No," replied the trooper; "he came across a wild horse in the scrub, though how the devil he managed to catch him, control him, and transfer his saddle and bridle in so short a time to his back is more than any fellow can well make out."

"It matters not; he's gone, and my life goes with him. If I could have beheld that fellow a hand-cuffed prisoner, and on his way to the gallows, I think I should have recovered. At all events, I fancy I should have lived to have seen him hanged, but as it is—as it is—as it is——why it's all over with me," and the unfortunate coachman fell back dead, with the last words on his lips.

"Come, it's of no use to stop here," said Frank, directly he and Ted had convinced themselves that the unfortunate man had really ceased to breathe; "we can do no good, and we must follow up the trail as long as we can. You mount this animal, Job—you will find her tame enough. When we can change for fresh steeds, we will."

"But how am I to ride this creature without either saddle or bridle?" asked Job, in sore dismay,

"Oh, a pull of the mane will guide her whichever way you like," laughed Frank.

"I never could keep on her, though, without a saddle and stirrups," urged Job.

"Very well, then, I'll ride her, and you shall take my nag. There, will that please you?" quoth Frank.

It seemed to please Job very much, but the next instant he espied a saddle and bridle amongst the luggage of the coach, and he pointed them out.

"The very things we want," said Frank, and he proceeded to appropriate the handy articles forthwith.

Not only that, but he also gave Job one of the dead passenger's revolvers, and made a general collection of bullets, caps and powder, after which they all rode away, knowing that, at the longest, ere many hours had elapsed some upward or downward coach or waggon would come across the wrecked mail, and do all that could be done for the dead.

* * * *

We have not space to follow them mile by mile and hour by hour in their onward march.

The doing so would swell out our tale to inordinate proportions; and, as it is, we have incidents that must be told, sufficient to fill a three-volume novel.

For three days and nights after Blue Cap had given them the slip, on the black horse that he had so strangely come across in the scrub, Frank, Ted, and Job perseveringly followed up his trail.

At a little townslip, called Wararoo, they had exchanged their tired steeds for fresh ones, and thereon they had ridden two hundred miles in thirty-six hours, Blue Cap giving them plenty of clues whereby to follow him up, whenever there was station or hut to be fired, or a coach, buggy, dray, or horseman, to be attacked and pillaged.

One night, as Frank, Ted, and Job were riding through a dense piece of bush, they saw the well-known form of Blue Cap ahead of them, still mounted on the great black horse, and still wearing the peculiar head dress from which he had taken his name.

They immediately started in pursuit, but Frank, being mounted on the slowest nag, after a sharp brush was left behind.

This annoyed him sadly, but spur and thrash his horse as hard as he would it still was utterly out of the running, and so at last he resigned himself to the inevitable, though with a particularly bad grace, for the mere idea that by no possible chance could he be in at the death was maddening.

He rode on for more than an hour at as swift a pace as he could get out of his sorry nag, listening anxiously the while for pistol shots, but not once hearing them.

At length, however, he did hear the rattle of galloping hoofs, and not knowing whether it might be one of his returning comrades, or Blue Cap doubling on his pursuers, he drew his revolver and stood ready for any emergency.

But a moment later adown the forest vista he saw a young, golden haired girl, riding at a headlong gallop, which she never relaxed until she reined in her handsome chesnut stock horse—whose foam-flecked sides and quivering nostrils told plainly of the pace at which it had been ridden—at his side, exclaiming—

"Oh, sir, for the love of heaven aid me! Our house is stuck up by bushrangers. They have turned it into Bedlam. They have beaten the servants, and are threatening my father and mother with death ere they leave, and I know that they will fulfil their awful threats unless aid and assistance arrives. Can you offer it?"

"Well, I will certainly give you all the aid that I can," replied Frank; "but how many of the rascals are there?"

"Half a dozen at the least, and our station hands have all run away. My father and mother are tied down in their chairs, the women servants are the same, and I let myself down from my bedroom window, made my way to the stables, and led out and mounted my chesnut at the risk of my life," was the excited and hurried reply.

Frank had now time to notice the young lady's personal appearance, and he perceived that she was tall, and the possessor of a superbly modelled and rounded figure, whilst her dazzling complexion, snowy brow, bright blue eyes fringed with the longest of golden lashes, her arched brows, and above all her dimpled little chin, and the richness of her glossy hair, that flowed like a cloud of golden glory around her, composed a host of charms that would have made Frank Beaumont their servant and slave in any desperate service whatever.

But when the young lady proceeded to tell him that, amongst the half dozen bushrangers was a hideous looking man, wearing a blue skull-cap with a plume of macaw feathers rising therefrom, his eagerness to serve her received another spur.

"Come," he said impatiently; "if I am to be of any use we must not linger on the road. I will do what I can, and I shouldn't wonder if we were reinforced by a couple of better men en route."

He explained to her as they rode along how matters stood, and frequently he "Coo-ee-yed," and discharged his revolver to attract Ted and Job's attention if they happened to be within hearing.

For the first five miles of their journey neither spoke a word, and no sound was heard save the low plaintive note of the mopoke or Australian cookoo, answered by the still more mournful cry of the wild owl from the low swampy ground on their right; while from the clear blue sky above, unflecked by a single cloud, the pale full moon shed a radiance as clear, and far softer, than that of day, over the mellow Australian landscape, and on the face of the lovely girl who cantered along by his side.

At last the white chimneys of the station were

visible some two miles ahead, and the sight of them aroused Frank from the half-dreamy reveries into which his companion's beauty had caused him to sink, and recalled him to the desperate work she had cut out for him.

"What is your name, my dear young lady?" he asked.

"Georgie Mortimer," was the reply.

"Well then, Miss Mortimer, I want you to tell me how these bushrangers are disposed. Are they all within the house, think you?" asked Frank.

"No, four are inside and two are keeping guard—one under the verandah in front and the other in the courtyard at the back," was her reply.

"And you really think that these are all?"

"I do, and, what is more, I know exactly where they are placed. The man in the courtyard I had some difficulty in avoiding, and just as I was going off he discovered and fired a pistol after me. One ball tore up the sleeve of my dress, but the others flew very wide of the mark."

"Really, Miss Mortimer, you are a perfect heroine," Frank could not help exclaiming, "but upon my word I wish you were fifty miles away now. You had better await my return here. You must not thrust yourself into needless danger."

"But wherever you go I go," was the reply; "you, a stranger, are about to risk your life for the sake of my parents. I should be a pretty kind of a daughter did I let you do so alone."

"Yet, my dear girl, as you cannot aid me——"

"But you come to that conclusion without knowing me," said the fair girl. "You have two revolvers, I see. Lend me one, and you will find me useful, I warrant. I know how to use the weapon as well as you, perhaps."

"I sincerely hope that you will not shoot yourself instead of a bushranger," quoth Frank, giving her the weapon she asked for, for he was under a spell as it were; "but you must obey me as your senior officer, and not run into needless danger. Is that a bargain?"

"Yes, as long as you don't order me to run away."

"All right, but I must impress upon you that prudence and discretion are the better part of valour, and as my army is small, I must not allow my troops to expose themselves needlessly. Watch my every look and motion, then, and don't fire before I give the word."

"Very well, captain," was the roguish rejoinder.

"All right then, that's arranged. Now, where are we?"

"Yonder's the station amid that clump of trees, just a quarter of a mile away," said the fair girl.

"Then we must ride more under the shadow of the ferns," said Frank. "Keep directly behind me, and walk your horse as noiselessly as possible."

How earnestly our hero longed at that moment for a cloud to pass over the face of the moon, but there was not the slightest trace of one in the hole dome of heaven.

He glanced back the way they had come, but not sign was there of Ted or Job.

Their chances of aid and reinforcement were few indeed, so Frank Beaumont nerved himself to encounter the fearful odds as best he could.

And now the chimneys and roofs of the home station were close by.

They could hear the neigh of horses, and Frank was fearful lest one of theirs should answer them and thus spoil all chances of a surprise, but luckily they did not.

Thanks to the sheltering shadow of the tree ferns, which grew nearly up to the house, their approach would not be detected, and the long lank grass over which they rode prevented their horses' hoof-strokes from being audible.

At length Frank saw the end of this fern grove, and that it extended to within a dozen yards or so of the post-and-rail fence at the back of the sta-

tion, but at the same time he saw another sight that caused him more uneasiness, which was, the bulky form of an armed man pacing up and down, just at the extremity of the grove and between it and the house.

His cabbage-tree hat was slouched over his eyes, his long shaggy black beard flowed far down over his scarlet shirt, and his broad belt was adorned with a bowie knife and a revolver.

He saw at a glance that this fellow could not be avoided, that they could not gain the station without his perceiving them; whilst on the other hand an open attack could not be contemplated, as the report of the pistol would bring the whole band upon them.

Frank's pretty companion was too far in the rear to see him, and, not wishing that she should, he rode back a few yards and met her.

"We must leave our horses here, and proceed on foot," he said in a whisper; and, dismounting, he assisted her to alight, and then fastened both their steeds to the trunk of a fern tree.

"Now, then," he continued, "you must stay here for about five minutes, whilst I reconnoitre ahead, and see that the coast is clear. I shall not be long."

She looked at him suspiciously, but nodded assent.

"Don't move an inch until my return," he said, and, walking away from her until he got a little distance in front, he drew a long-bladed spring knife from his pocket, opened it, and gripping it between his teeth, crept snake-like through the long grass towards the unconscious bushranger.

It was a deed he involuntarily shrank from—it looked so very like murder; but he knew that the act he meditated was necessary, and justifiable under the circumstances, and that reflection consoled him.

This snake-like motion was a very slow and unpleasant mode of progression, but was a successful one.

Once only he made a noise, which was caused by his spur coming in contact with a stone.

The sentry heard it, and glanced suspiciously in Frank's direction; but perceiving nothing, he muttered in a rough tone—

"Only a possum, as I live. I'm getting as skeered as a cat since I shot the trap on the Monaroo plains. A drop of brandy will set me to rights."

As he spoke, he drew a spirit flask from his pocket and raised it to his lips.

Frank was at the time only five or six yards from him, and, availing himself of this favourable opportunity, he sprang forward; a short, sharp struggle took place, but Frank triumphed, and sheathed his knife in the bushranger's heart—not one word being uttered during the deadly struggle.

Frank caught the body in its fall, and dragged it many yards into the bush, so that the young girl's eyes should not rest upon it in passing by.

Then he hurriedly retraced his steps, to find her somewhat terrified at his prolonged absence.

He did not inform her of what had occurred, but, with a few whispered words of assurance, told her to follow him, for that there was no sentry at the back of the house now.

They walked on until they gained the post-and-rail fence which enclosed the yard at the back.

Here Frank again reconnoitred, and finding the yard empty, and no lights in the back windows of the house, they went on, but creeping very cautiously, and keeping under the shadow of the fence, for discovery now would have been fatal.

When they gained the door they listened breathlessly, and heard bursts of laughter and loud voices within, with cries of—

"Your health, old gentleman, and yours too, Mother Mortimer, and many thanks for your hearty welcome. I trust you may always have as honest and jovial boys as us to eat your cold meat, and drink your wine, spirits, and beer."

This speech was followed by uproarious applause, and then another voice shouted out—

"Let us unbind the governor, and make him dance a hornpipe atop of the table."

"Agreed!"—"Good!"—"Capital!" were the answering shouts, and for a minute or so the jingling of glasses, and the mingled volley of shouts, laughter, and imprecations were tremendous.

Amid this dim, Frank and his fair ally crept into the house, and the beautiful girl led our hero by the hand, through two or three rooms, until they reached one which was only divided from that occupied by the revellers by a thin partition, in which was a little square of glass, though which they could plainly see all that was passing in the adjoining apartment.

A stranger sight could not very well have been beheld.

The room in which the bushrangers feasted was furnished with carpets, lounges, ottomans, and rich lace curtains, and the many articles of vertu scattered around presented a strange and ludicrous contrast to the odd assemblage it contained.

The table was spread with every variety of food and liquor, while empty and broken bottles and glasses strewed the floor.

On the velvet-cushioned chairs and elegantly carved couches sat or reclined, in every attitude of ease and disregard of appearance, rough and ferocious looking men, with tangled, uncombed hair and beards, and mahogany-tinted complexions, dressed in the rough bush costume, consisting either of cabbage-tree hats, coloured shirts, and cord pants, with long boots reaching above the knee, or broad felt hats, red or blue jumpers, and moleskin continuations.

Most of them had their brawny throats bare, and wore silk scarves around their waists, with revolvers and knives thrust in them.

These worthies were smoking most zealously, the short black pipes being seldom removed from their mouths unless to spit about the carpet, or to drain deep draughts of wine.

One had a quart basin before him, another a huge Venetian glass goblet, a third preferred a decanter pure and simple, whilst a fourth seemed bent upon trying the capacity of every vessel capable of holding a liquid.

But not so Blue Cap, who had evidently assumed the leadership of this gang of desperadoes.

He sat at the head of the table in an arm chair, with his muddy boots dangling over the back of an ottoman, and the sleeves of his jumper rolled up to his elbows.

He drank little, and chiefly amused himself by chaffing the squatter and his wife, who were seated on either side of him at the table, for, with his usual grim humour, he had caused them to be strapped down in separate chairs, and placed in a position where they should seem willingly to preside at the festive board.

Mr. Mortimer looked anything but pleased at the disappearance of the treasures of his cellar.

His stiff gray hair almost stood erect, like the quills upon the fretful porcupine, and his jolly round face was purple red with bottled-up passion.

The old lady looked angry and nervous both, but tried to smile and take things easy, as she fancied that course to be the best policy under the circumstances.

The two maid servants were the most terrified of the group.

They were seated on chairs placed back to back, with a thick rope encircling their waists and another their wrists, their arms being passed backwards between the top and middle bars, and thus brought together.

In their manner, they were united almost as thoroughly as the Siamese twins.

It was evident that they were suffering from ex-treme terror, for they were trembling violently, though they did not dare to utter a sound.

It did not take Frank a tenth part of the time to notice every incident of this scene that it has taken us to describe it.

He had only time to take a hurried glance around ere the bushranger who had proposed the horn-pipe drew his knife, severed Mr. Mortimer's bonds, and a second having by this time cleared a place in the centre of the table, the old gentleman was hoisted up, passed safely over the bottles and glasses, and told to begin his performance.

Frank could tell, by the hard breathing of his companion, that she felt deeply this indignity offered to her father; but our hero had no desire to open an attack before such a step was absolutely necessary, as every minute's delay gave a greater chance of Ted Hogan and Job Short arriving to share the honour and the danger.

This he intimated to Miss Mortimer, who nodded approval at his prudence.

Events soon hastened a denouement, however.

The worthy squatter, who had at first been too angry to comply, and too alarmed to refuse to dance, at length became more heated to harness, and getting too near the edge of the table, capsized it, and in company with wine, spirits, grog, and crockery, went crashing to the floor.

And what a crash it was!

What a ruddy lake poured over the carpet!

What cries ensued from the women, and what curses from the men!

The voice of Blue Cap soon quelled all other noises however.

"Stash that row, yer fools," he roared. "Hold your tongues, yer she cats, or I'll give you something to holler for. And you, you tarnation old ass. I'll have a drop of yer blood for every drop of spirits yer've spilt. Out with yer knives, my boys, and prick his tough hide for him. He's clear spoilt our feast."

And as he spoke, Blue Cap with one kick launched the wine-saturated and half-dazed old man half way across the room.

Almost simultaneously with this act, and just as Frank was about to take the initiative, Georgie Mortimer brushed by him, raised her revolver, and without pausing a moment to take aim, fired it through the little window, full at Blue Cap's head.

Frank saw the villain clap his hand to his right shoulder, and heard him howl like a wounded bear, but he saw that he was not dangerously wounded.

The other bushrangers sprang to their feet and drew their weapons, so Frank fired hastily in amongst them, and, seeing that they were about to send a volley, hap-hazard, against the partition, he hurriedly dragged his companion to the ground.

He was right in his conjecture.

The bushrangers fired their revolvers, and the bullets tore through the lathe-and-plaster wall, and whistled above their heads.

"Stay here, I entreat, I command you. Do not move hand or foot," said Frank to his beautiful companion, for he was resolved that she should not get under fire, if he could prevent it.

Then, perceiving in the gloom the handle of the door, he resolved on a ruse de guerre, and walking into the adjoining apartment, he exclaimed in a firm and authoritative voice—

"Throw down your weapons, or you are all dead men. The six troopers behind that partition will shoot you down, if you offer the least resistance."

It was worth a good deal to watch the bush-rangers' countenances at that moment, for Frank's fearless bearing had had the desired effect.

They never doubted the truth of his assertion, yet they evinced no disposition to lay down their arms.

"Why the devil don't the traps show them-selves?" said one.

"Why the deuce should they, when they can

bring you down just as surely, whilst concealed themselves," quoth Frank.

He knew that bravado alone could carry a point now.

"And if we do yield, will you ensure us our lives, and a fair trial?" asked another.

"Fools, will yer believe the lying young thief?" yelled Blue Cap, with a frightful oath. "'Tis the bullet or the halter, and I choose the first; so here goes."

He raised his revolver as he spoke, and covered Frank with it, but ere he could draw the trigger, there came another shot through the little window, and Blue Cap, with a yell, dropped his weapon with an oath.

The bullet had carried away his right thumb.

"There, my lads," cried Frank, taking advantage of this demonstration, "you see the fate of the only man who dared raise his pistol against me. Now, are the rest of you going to be sensible, or shall I give the signal for your massacre?"

"Let them be shot, sir—let them be shot. The rogues deserve burning. Look at my wasted wine, and the way they have treated me," said the old squatter.

"No, no, don't make our peaceful home such a scene of ruthless slaughter. Take them away," sobbed the old lady, who, pale and trembling, sat still bound in her chair.

The servants only increased the confusion by their screams.

"Mr. Mortimer, we dare not shoot them if they surrender. They must be fairly tried and condemned. Madam, they seem to have had their dessert already, though no doubt the next they partake of will have less wine and sweetmeats to flavour it, said Frank.

Then changing his tone and manner as he turned again to the bushrangers, he exclaimed, "Now, my gallows birds, is it to be surrender or sudden death?"

"Well, hang it, I suppose we've no choice. I don't want to be shot down like a dog, so here is my barker," said a muscular fellow, handing Frank his revolver.

No doubt his example would have been followed by the rest, but just as Frank extended his hand to receive this first tribute of submission, a voice shouted—

"What on earth are you about in here, surrendering to a gal and a boy? Out on you for white-livered curs."

And the door being burst open with a kick, a bearded rascal appeared in view, holding in one hand a revolver, and with the other dragging in Georgie Mortimer by the hair of her head.

Frank saw then that the game was up.

He tried to draw his revolver which he had returned to his belt, but ere he could do so he was felled to the floor by a blow from one of the bushrangers, and in a twinkling was bound hand and foot.

He looked round and perceived that Georgie Mortimer was lying at a little distance from him, in the same helpless condition.

What next they would have to encounter Frank knew not, though he pretty well guessed that his doom would be death, whilst a fate, far more terrible in all probability, overhung the brave and lovely girl, whose love for her parents had strengthened to encounter such perils as she had done that night.

He could hear her sobs—sobs that were not wrung from her by the cords that cut her delicate arms and ankles, but through her heart bleeding for the sufferings of those whom she loved more than life.

Much as Frank longed, he was unable to help or sympathise with her.

Lying on his back, helpless as an infant, he was constrained to listen to the narrative of the bushranger whose entrance at so inopportune a moment had spoilt his ruse de guerre, and brought them to such a miserable strait.

This ruffian had been on guard under the verandah in front of the station.

Having no tobacco in his pouch, he had run round to beg some of his mate, who had been posted as sentinel in the rear.

Unable to find him, he had halloaed and coo-ee-eyed, but this being of no avail, he had in the clear moonlight tracked his footsteps, and discovered his dead body in the bushes.

This had alarmed him, for the knife wound was so broad that he feared it had been made by a trooper's sword.

The whinny of one of the horses had next attracted his attention, and aided him to solve the mystery.

He quickly found them, saw that they were only two, then noticed the human footprints, and plainly perceived that one was a woman's.

He had then tracked them back to the station, entered by the back door which they had left open, discovered Georgie crouching behind the partition, and dragged her into the adjoining apartment just in time to undeceive his mates, and turn the fortunes of the day completely against the conspirators.

Long and loud was the laughter of the rangers, as Red Tommy as they had dubbed him, spun his yarn.

Immediately he had ceased, dark and lowering brows was bent upon both, and Blue Cap, still nursing his right hand, shouted—

"What shall we do with them, lads? Blood for blood's my creed. Let's hang 'em both. Hang 'em, and take cock-shies at 'em I say."

"Hang the boy by all means, if you like; but the gal's mine. I'll make her Mrs. Peter Dargan," cried another ruffian.

"Dash it, no, that's not fair; she's no more yours than ours, Peter. We'll cast lots for her. She is worthy of any of us. A brave girl like that deserves to be a bushranger's wife. We will bury the boy alive," said a third.

"Burying or hanging is too good for the likes of him," grumbled a fourth. "I second friend Blue Cap's motion. Let us hang him by the heels to the lamp crook, and take flying shots at him from the other end of the room. Whoever, first two rounds, sends a ball through his head nearest his right eye, shall have the gal."

"Good! Good! Bravo for Big Mike!" they all cried.

The resolution was carried nem. con., and, with a thrill of horror, Frank glanced up at the lofty ceiling.

There, sure enough, was the hook, which had evidently been hung there for the purpose of supporting a candelabrum.

Little did the man who fixed it in its place guess what a burthen it was one day destined to bear.

Frank tried to think that the bushrangers were jesting, but another look at their ferocious countenances dispelled the last ray of hope from his own.

He turned towards his companion in misfortune, who was as pale as marble, and her eyes full of tears.

He was going to whisper a few words of encouragement, when the harsh voice of Blue Cap turned his thoughts.

"A rope! A rope! Where are we to get a rope?"

"I know—I saw one in the kitchen, long and strong enough to hang them both by," quoth a ranger.

"Hurrah! Then just bring it here, matey. Let's get this thing over, and fix who's to have the gal, and then we'll hunt up some more lush," cried Peter Dargan.

"Ah! Ah! We'll drink to the lad's long journey, and that he may engage us snug quarters in the next world, by the time we want them," laughed Red Tommy.

"Me lad, how do yer feel yerself? Young leddy, how do ye do, at all, at all?" inquired a ruffianly looking Irishman, squirting some tobacco juice over over Frank's face as he spoke.

"Wretch! hold your tongue. If I was free of these cords, I would thrash the whole lot of you," roared our hero, and managing to give the last speaker a kick on the shins, that made him howl lustily.

He glanced fiercely at Frank, and handled his revolver, as though to put an end to him then and there.

But in a voice, hoarse as a raven's, Blue Cap shouted to his mates, who by this time had found the rope, and brought it into the room.

"Reeve a noose there; this fellow's neck is itching for a hempe collar. Here, Tommy, clap a chair on the table. Now another on the top of that, and you will be able to reach the hook. That's right, my hearty; make it safe. Now, Mike, have you finished the slip noose? You have? That's right, then. Now you other fellows, slip his feet into it, and run him up. Look alive now. Look alive, will you?"

They did look alive, and in another minute Frank's ankles were tightly caught in the noose, and up he went with a run.

"Pull with a will, my hearties. Yo, heave ho!" screamed Blue Cap, dancing and capering around the room in high glee, amid the threats of the station owner, and the prayers and supplications of Georgie and her mother.

But threats and prayers were alike unheeded.

Up, up he still went, until at last he swung like a pendulum, equidistant between floor and ceiling.

"That's right, mates. Let him swing. 'Twill require a better shot to win the gal. Are you all loaded. Pat Hennessy, I depute you to fire for me as well as for yourself; the shunk has put my hand out of order. I'll have to lie close and practise with my left for a bit. Now Carrotty Tom, stand by him and set him swinging afresh, as each man steps forward to fire. And you, my fine fellow, say your prayers if you know any, for in another minute you'll be no better than a dead possum," and Blue Cap laughed consumedly.

How can I paint poor Frank's agonised feelings at that moment.

Pray he could not.

The horror of his position made him forget all that he had ever known.

He felt a rough hand give him a push.

He felt himself swinging to and fro.

And then he heard a wild scream, followed by a loud report, and a tingling as though a piece of red-hot wire were held against his ear.

Next he heard Blue Cap's croaking voice ejaculate—

"A miss, by George! Hennessy. That shot was your own, mind. This time you fire for me, so see that you score a hit, or I'll test the thickness of your Tipperary skull."

Again there came the sharp click of a pistol lock, and another hearty shove from the hand of Red Tommy, followed by the loud report of a revolver, but this time, to Frank's surprise, it was followed by a shriek of agony and a heavy fall within the room.

A strange hope suddenly fluttered within his breast.

He tried to turn his head round, but could not.

"Bang! bang! bang!" came more shots. Another scream—a moan—a wild cheer—the crashing of glass and wood—a shout of "Murderer of my brother, I have you now!" and Blue Cap's answering cry, "Stand firm, men. We are still three to two. It's the gallows or the bullet, remember. Return their fire, can't you. Fight it out to the death."

Then Frank felt as though a whole river of blood were rushing to his head, and he swooned away.

* * * *

Over what followed we draw a veil, and take up the thread where Bluecap turned to see how Peter and Pat were getting on.

Pat was down, and as dead as the saint he was named after, and poor Job Short was just in the same condition, with a bullet through his lungs.

Then, as he looked, down went the trooper, too, and Blue Cap muttered a yell of frantic delight.

But the cry was premature, for it was a shot through the thigh that had caused Hogan to fall, and that didn't hurt his shooting powers, as Peter Dargan found to his cost, when, a second later, a bullet pierced his right shoulder, and his revolver fell from his relaxed grasp.

Both he and Blue Cap were now powerless for mischief as far as their right hands went, seeing which Ted pulled himself up off the floor, and drawing his sword, for he had fired away every charge in his revolver, he upraised himself somehow against the wall, and bade them "Come on, if they were men."

But Blue Cap and Dargan had no stomach for the contest.

"We will take off the lad," said the former, with a demoniac grin; "he can't prevent us, and we can torture him at our leisure."

With his knife, Blue Cap cut Frank down, and then the two maimed men dragged him out of the room.

In vain Ted Hogan tried to prevent them.

His wounded leg might have been off for all the good it was to him.

Had he left the supporting wall he must have fallen, and then the villains would have made short work with him.

So he merely brandished his sword, and indulged in vague threats which they did not care for one whit, and five minutes later he saw Blue Cap dash past the window at a gallop, with poor Frank hanging limp, and apparently lifeless over his saddle pommel.

And that was the last glance that he caught of our hero for many a long year.

CHAPTER XXIII.
THE DETECTIVE OFFICE, SYDNEY.

FIVE years have now passed away, and all that while the heroes of our tale have made little noise in the world, and Blue Cap has disappeared as though he had never had an existence—disappeared in company with Frank Beaumont, who, like the bushranger, has neither been seen nor heard of since the night when his mortal foe dashed off at a headlong gallop, with his body lying limply across the pommel of his saddle.

Rewards have been offered again and again for the discovery of one, and the capture, dead or alive, of the other, but without avail.

They have been added to and added to until hundreds have swollen into thousands, but still without result.

And strangers have buried the dead, and Marrang has passed away to a cousin of our hero, who, by this time, has flattered himself that his inheritance will never be disturbed, which doesn't seem indeed to be at all likely now, for the reward bills have long since been pasted over in the towns, and been washed by the rain from off the trunks of the great trees that border the various bush tracks, whilst even the police have given the matter up in despair.

Ted Hogan was wont to affirm that, but for the bullet through his leg that he received at the close of the desperate struggle recorded in our last chaper, he would never have given up the pursuit until the accursed bushranger had been stretched dead at his feet. But that bullet had put the brave trooper *hors de combat*, and into Goulbourne Hospital for six weeks in addition.

When he came out he was no longer fit for the mounted service, his maimed leg having lost much of its former power to grip the saddle, and so he was transferred to the detective branch of the service, and this business, as a rule, seldom took him out of the great cities.

He has long given up the thought of avenging his brother; he has long ago come to the conclusion that Blue Cap must have perished in some mysterious manner, in swimming a swollen creek, by being thrown from a vicious horse, through being lost in the Mallee Scrub, or, perchance, from a snake bite, or the sting of a triantelope spider.

We shall soon see whether he was right.

In a private room of the Detective Office at Sydney sat the Inspector-General of Police.

The table before him is littered with letters, charge-sheets, telegrams, and other documents, and the walls are decorated with bright steel handcuffs, neat ebony staffs embossed with gilt crowns, sabres, and revolver-pistols.

The inspector-general is scratching his head with the feather end of his long quill pen, evidently in search of an idea. At last it seems to come to him, for he picks up a little bell off the table and rings it violently.

It is promptly answered by a constable.

"Send Hogan to me," says the inspector, curtly.

The man salutes and departs.

Five minutes later, our old friend Ted enters the office.

He is clad in an unassuming suit of grey, and is very much altered in appearance from when we saw him last, for his figure is square and set, making him look shorter than he used to, and he has cultivated whiskers, which are glossy and curly, but do not by any means add to his good looks.

"Hogan," says the inspector, "sit down."

Hogan sits down accordingly and prepares to listen.

"I want you to go up the Turrent way, Hogan."

Hogan nods as if all ways were the same to him.

"Very well," says the inspector, interpreting his look; "you will draw ample funds for the journey, and start at once. A pedlar, called Levi Moss, has mysteriously disappeared between an inn called the Cornstalk, standing close to the Three Mile, and the town of Turrent, and as it was known, through some drunken admission or other that he made in his cups, that he had jewellery of considerable value in his pack, and money to the amount of a hundred-and-fifty pounds in his pocket, it is to be feared that he has been murdered and his body made away with."

"Did he make these admissions at the Cornstalk?"

"Yes, and before a miscellaneous company."

"And he admitted that he was going on to Turrent?"

"Yes, and he set out for that township at nine in the evening, but seems never to have reached it."

"Can you give me a clear description of the man?"

"Still better, I can give you his likeness. Here it is; his wife has just brought it. It seems to be a very tolerable photograph. One thing it doesn't show, though: the man has lost a finger off his left hand. The third finger it is."

"And is there any reward offered for his discovery?"

"His widow will give a hundred pounds if you find him alive, and Government the like sum if you discover him dead and succeed in arresting his murderer."

"The sum in either case is little enough."

"True, but then duty is duty, and besides this bush shanty, the Cornstalk, is, I am informed, a house-of-call for bushrangers, cattle-duffers, and all the rest of them, so that you may be able to kill two birds with one stone if you are only careful."

"Thanks for the hint. I'll depart at once."

"You'll be too late to catch the day mail."

"No I won't; I've a good ten minutes to spare."

"Very well, nothing more remains to be said. Keep me well informed of what goes on."

"I will — in cypher when it is important. Goodday."

And Ted Hogan abruptly quitted the officer.

"Well, if any fellow in the force can unravel the mystery he can," muttered the inspector as he rubbed his hands, and then he bestowed his attention on other subjects.

CHAPTER XXIV.
THE CORNSTALK INN—THE BUSH.

THERE is, perhaps, no more beautiful mountain scenery to be met with in the world than that which may be found by an adventurous traveller amidst the wilds and fastnesses of the Shoalhaven gullies.

By an adventurous traveller, I say, for none but such, or a stockman who cares little for risking his neck, would venture over the range of precipitous mountains, through a gorge in which the Shoalhaven river pursues its silent way, fed on the north by the broad Kangaroo Creek, which has its rise in the inaccessible heights of the ranges of the same name, and on the south by the noisy Warringong Creek, which skirts that tremendous range of lofty mountains, starting from the very banks of the Shoalhaven, and running in a curve, tending southwesterly, until it joins the western point of the dividing range at the Jingera Mountain, noted as being the haunt and place of refuge of outlaws, bushrangers, cattle-duffers, horse-stealers, and all the other classes of "conveyancers" belonging, or, rather, incidental to this wealthy portion of the grazing district of N.S.W.

Sometimes travellers who want to make a short cut from the coast districts to the more inland towns of Bong or Berrima venture along the steep and dangerous roads which cross the ranges, and now and then a more than ordinarily adventurous packman scales these heights, with his horse-load of clothing, jewellery, cutlery, and tobacco, and if he have the good fortune to get back without being stuck up, he returns to the busier haunts of men well repaid for his venture.

Generally, however, these mountains are kept sacred to the hoofs of the mobs of cattle and horses driven, lawfully or unlawfully, as the case may be, to market or elsewhere.

At the time of which we write, there dwelt in a little hollow, formed by the dip or shoulder of one of the highest peaks of these ranges, a man known by the soubriquet of Billy-the-Bull.

He was a big, powerful fellow, long-haired, and bearded and whiskered like a pard. In short, his piercing and savage eyes looked out from a face that might almost as well have pertained to a gorilla as a man, so hair-covered and repulsive was it.

He declared himself an Irishman, and that he had been sent out "on account ov the throubles," though those who knew him best had heard him admit, in his cups, that the "trouble" which had caused his involuntary emigration from his native land was for something in connection with a slight mistake made by himself and two other gentlemen in fancying that another person's house was their own, and that the proper way to get into a dwelling-house was

A SHORT, SHARP, AND SILENT STRUGGLE TOOK PLACE, AND FRANK SHEATHED HIS KNIFE IN THE BUSHRANGER'S HEART.

stealthily through a window, in order not to awaken the family.

It was not, however, a safe subject to talk about in Billy's presence, and was a particularly dangerous one to jest on, for Billy had the temper of the very deuce, and when he became enraged, lost all self-control, and would as soon knife any one who had offended him as not.

Billy had a friend and neighbour called Jacky Cain, who kept a small public-house, standing a little way back from the road—one of those bush inns which are scattered over the country on which travellers stumble so unexpectedly.

It was not, however, occasional travellers that Jacky depended upon for the sale of the fermented and spirituous liquors in which he dealt, although he was always glad to see them, philosophically thinking that "all was fish that came to his net."

But he infinitely preferred the flash overseer or the rowdy bushman who had just had his year's wages paid him, and was going in for a "*bust.*"

This was the guest whom he delighted to honour.

This was the man who, from the day he staggered into the bar, and handed over to Jacky his thirty or five-and-thirty one-pound notes, telling him to "let him know when that was knocked down," for whom he had the pleasant word and the ready smile, whose interests he protected against the travelling jewellers and hawkers, who otherwise would have made him a victim.

Jacky Cain knew full well that every pound spent on these gentry was one less for him, and so whenever they opened their packets and displayed their tempting wares, gaudy jumpers, flash bandanas, and duffer watches, he plied his lodger with drink until he became so helplessly intoxicated as to be unable even to talk, and then he conducted him off to bed, into which he tumbled him without ceremony, boots and all.

But it was whispered that Jacky Cain had other means of "winning an honest penny" besides that of fleecing unwary travellers and stockmen out on the spree.

In no part of the world perhaps, certainly in no part of Australia, is "cattle duffing," as it is called, carried on to a greater extent than among the Shoelhaven gullies, if we except, perhaps, the far-famed Jingera Mountains, before stated to be the head-quarters of bushrangers and other loose fish.

Certainly in more than one transaction where the rights of meum and teum with regard to horses and cattle had been forgotten or ignored had the names of Jacky Cain and Billy-the-Bull been unpleasantly mixed up with the affair, although there had never yet been anything beyond general suspicion attached to them, and in no instance had there been sufficient evidence to bring any such charge directly home to them.

There appeared to be a kind of moral certainty in the district, however, that when Jack Thomas, of Menangh, lost seven head of cattle one day, and when Mr. Cox, of Billingh, had a chesnut horse and grey filly "lifted" one night, as also when Nannong was nearly weeded on another occasion, that Jacky Cain and Billy-the-Bull had something to do with it.

Yet in every one of these cases, as in many others, there was a link wanting somewhere in the chain, and it was impossible to bowl them out.

For the rest Jacky Cain was a man well-to-do in the world, having five or six thousand acres of the best pastoral land in the district, besides a joint share with his partner, Billy, in a run somewhere lower down the range—a run on which, by the way, the police were in the habit of making a raid occasionally whenever any cattle were missing.

But Billy and Jacky were too old birds to allow their tails to be salted, and managed their little arrangements with too much skill to be trapped.

Jacky had an eye and love for a horse, and always rode a good one, whereon he was invariably to be seen at every race and sporting meeting in the country, whereat he bet freely and generally luckily.

The forenoon of the same day on which Hogan the Detective left Sydney, three men were in the bar of the Cornstalk, for the Cornstalk was Jacky's hostelry. That is to say, there were four men there, but one of them being a fencer who had just finished a job for the landlord, and was of course taking it out in lush, and therefore blind drunk, as he had been for five days already, and would be for six or seven more, unless indeed delirium tremens set in, and either hurried him out of the world or sobered him for awhile; and he cannot be counted.

There were three, however, besides him, namely, Jacky, his partner Billy-the-Bull, and a stranger, not a bad-looking young fellow but for the cunning expressed in his twinkling blue eyes, with fair hair, and dressed in a jaunty bush costume, consisting of a finely plaited cabbage-tree hat (one of Larry Finn's best make at four-pound-ten, a bottle o' rum, and half-a-pound o' Barrett's twist, and heap at that); a shepherd's plaid coat and vest, and a pair of light blue trousers strapped with moleskin. He sucked the hammer head of his riding whip, and was all over a bush dandy of the first water.

Very different looked Billy-the-Bull in his shabby old Panama hat pulled out of all shape and battered and weather-stained in every part. A ragged blue jumper, open at the chest, clothed his upper, and a still more ragged pair of moleskins his lower man, his feet being shod in old muddy Blucher boots worn all out of shape.

He was in the act of rubbing a pipeful of tobacco which he had just cut up from a fig which lay on the bar counter before him, and looked the very picture of an old and incorrigible scoundrel, though he did call himself a squatter, and was reputed to be worth twenty thousand pounds.

Jacky Cain was leaning over at the other side of this bar, looking at the pair with anything but amiability and attired in his usual manner, Bedford cord vest and trousers, and in his shirt sleeves.

Any disinterested party looking on that group would have decided in a moment that there was some knavish piece of work going on, and that the parties thereto had disagreed and come to a dead lock.

After a short pause, however, the young man ceased sucking the head of his whip, and broke out as follows:—

"Well, cuss me if ever I seen two sich onreasonable cusses in my life! Don't I tell you that the cattle's as right as the mail?"

Billy-the-Bull held up a finger as a warning that he was going to speak; he then carefully shook the particles of tobacco into his left hand, whilst with the right he took the pipe from his mouth and flourished it impressively as he said—

"Look 'ere, young feller, me and Jack is two poor men is me an' Jack, but if thare's one thing as we walleys far more nor another, it's bein' honest, ain't it, Jacky? Now here's you, a young cove as we doesn't know much on, comes to us and sells us a few head o' cattle—not but what we got 'em cheap enough. Oh! yes, bless you, we'll acknowledge hat, and not but what you may be quite respectable. Well, so far so good, we gets a bit of a bargain and you're satisfied. Well, now, you comes agin with a lot more o' the same sort, and nattrel enough we wants to know where they comes from. Nattrel enough we axes that, because, you see, we're onex perienced and might easy be tuk in, and if we was—mind, I say, if we was—to buy anythink what hadn'e been come by fair and square, oh dear! wouldn't that be a precious go?"

The young man moved about restlessly for a moment, and then, speaking under his breath, said—

"Well, if you won't buy them I must only drive 'em somewhere else. I daresay somebody else'll have 'em if you won't."

"Oh, certainly," replied Billy-the-Bull, with a grin, "you may find plenty o' people to buy 'em and ax no questions, but then you see me an' my pardner's honest men, is me and my pardner, and we couldn't think o' havin' on 'em without knowing where they comes from—leastways," he continued drily, "at the price you ax."

Jacky Cain, who had become rather impatient during this long colloquy, broke in upon it at this point, by informing the chafferers that they " wor both a pair of fools," and asking them why they didn't "come to the point at wanst, and not be a blowing there all day."

" Look here," said he, " I'll tell you what we'll do, young man. Ye'll take two pound five a head for 'em all round, an' thot's the most ye'll get. Sure, man, we know you got 'em on the cross as well as you do yourself, and it is a mighty good bargain ye're making. Take them anywhere else an' ye like, and it's the inside of Gullom Jail ye'll be inthroduced to afore ye're much oldher, me lad—tak my word for that."

After some more discussion of the same nature Billy-the-Bull and Jacky Cain became purchasers of seventy head of fat cattle of mixed brands, at a price not more than half their value.

"The quicker we put our project into execution now the better," said Jack, when the young man was gone.

"We will set out with to-morrow's dawn," replied Bill.

And then they took leave of each other.

CHAPTER XXV.

IN SEARCH OF PASTURES NEW.

BETWEEN the Sachlan and the Bogan rivers on the south-east and east respectively, and the wide channel where the mysterious Darling rolls its vast volume of waters in long placid reaches, or through immense marshes silently on to the monarch of Australian rivers—the Murray (the Millewa of the aboriginal) lies an immense track of country extending over four degrees of latitude and three of longitude—a track of country stony, grassless, treeless, lifeless, silent as the grave, desolate as Sahara.

In the summer an arid desert, in the winter an interminable swamp, a country totally unfit for human habitation or occupation, where the only sign of vegetation is an occasional patch of salsolaceous plants or a thick impenetrable belt of Mallee Scrub, and where save in the rainy season water is unknown.

Unknown? Not quite, for to the weary and thirsty bushman there is a never-failing source in the supply which nature has wonderfully provided for this desolate region in the very heart of the Mallee plant itself.

Known only to the experienced bushman, to the savage native of these pathless regions, and to the parched bird whose instinct guides its drooping wings to the hollow tree, in whose recess it will find wherewith to quench its thirst.

It was noon on a hot day in October. The sun was shining forth in his full strength, and there was not a breath of air stirring to temper the heat of his rays, which, striking on the white and burning sands and the rough stones, rises when reflected back into the quivering air with double their original intensity.

Standing in the midst of that solitary plain, and looking round, nothing was to be seen but one vast expanse of sand—white, hot, arid.

Not a blade of grass was there to refresh the aching eye with its greenness, not a tree, not even a rock to shelter the traveller (if there ever should be one) from the fierce solar rays within its welcome shadow. Not a drop of water to cool his parched lips, nor a breath of wind to fan his fevered brow.

The sky was blue, the beautiful bright blue of an Australian summer—the beautiful bright blue that has formed a canopy to the death-bed of so many of the gallant explorers of the mysterious inner desert—the blue into whose illimitable depths the glazing eyes of the patient Wills, the gallant Gray, and the chivalric Burke, and noble Leichadt had looked as they finally closed on their ill-starred expeditions and on all earthly things.

Painfully toiling across the white and arid plain, their jaded steeds plodding slowly along with hanging heads and drooping ears, were two travellers—wearied, sullen and silent.

Mile after lengthened mile had they passed without an interchange of a word, and ever and anon as they darkly eyed each other askance, it was with looks of scarcely concealed distrust, if not with openly expressed dislike.

And yet these two travellers are partners—partners not only in business matters, as holding betwixt them a cattle and sheep station on the Shoalhaven, but also partners in many deeds which would hardly bear the scrutiny of the police.

They are, in fact, Jacky Cain and Billy-the-Bull.

A strange place to meet them out in these uninhabited wilds and journeying in such an unfrequented direction.

Still here they are urging onward their tired horses silently and sullenly, until their shadows lengthen out behind them more and more, and the sun becomes larger and larger as he sinks in the west.

"How much further on is this water-hole you spoke about?" at length asked Jacky Cain, apparently becoming tired of the long silence.

"About four more miles. I told you we'd be there by sundown, and so we shall," was the reply, and for a time they both again relapsed into silence.

"In my opinion it's a fool's errand altogether, and whatever made me believe yer blarney and start on it I dunno know. Wanst let me get back to the Cornstalk, and the devil a bit any body'll ever get me out again anyhow," at last grumbled the first speaker, talking at his mate.

"Look 'ere, Jacky Cain," replied the elder of the two, "you and me's gone into this 'ere bisness together too far for one of us now to draw out. It wouldn't be safe for neither on us to cut it—leastways not just at present."

"And why for no?" asked the other.

"Why for no? Well, I'll tell you why for no," was the chuckling reply. "Becos you and me knows too much of one another's bisness. You're very clever, Jacky Cain, you are, and you've contrived to dodge the traps for a long time; but if I liked to say the word I could put you where you'd be found when wanted, and no questions axed. Maybe you might do the same by me, but that's nothin'; anyhow it's better to stick together."

Jacky Cain gave a short, insulting laugh, and then, with a sneer, replied—

"You think I'm in your power, old fellow, do you? But you're mistaken! You think you could put me into quod, do you? Ha! ha! ha! that's a good joke. But I'll tell you a bit of a secret, Billy. I know that of you that would put the rope round your neck, ay, and hang you, too, as high as Haman."

Billy-the-Bull gave a cry of terror as, reining up his horse with a jerk that almost threw the jaded animal on his haunches, he became almost livid with fright, and cried—

"It's a lie! It's a lie! I never done it! You can't prove it!" and then suddenly regaining some degree of composure, he added, "What do you mean, Jacky? What do you mean? You shouldn't frighten an old man like that. But there, you're only joking."

And he tried to laugh, but only succeeded in gasping out a few hysterical sobs.

"Divel a joke in it," was the response. "You didn't think I knowed so much of yer, you mane old villain, did ye?"

"Look 'ere, Jack," said Billy-the-Bull, in an insinuating tone, "I always acted fair by you, and if I did pick up a stray calf, or kill a few sheep not exactly my own, it's only what you've done yourself many a time as well."

"It isn't a few sheep they'll hang you for, Billy, and well you know it," was the response. "But rein up nearer while I tell you something I never tould ye before. Whisht, now, whilst I whisper," and in a low tone he hissed in his mate's ear, "I know that ye were once known as Blue Cap, the Bushranger, and I know what became of the pedlar as well."

The old man, for old he was through drink and dissipation, who had trembled to that extent that he could scarcely sit upon his saddle, no sooner heard and comprehended the words that his companion uttered, than, with a wild cry, he sprang upon him, clutching at his throat, and endeavouring to drag him from his horse.

The younger man, who was, however, very much the stronger now, and who, although taken partially by surprise, was not totally unprepared, bent backwards in his saddle, and catching him by the collar and shoulders, hurled him from his horse on to the hot sand, where he lay pale and convulsed, his teeth clenched, and his lips vainly attempting to articulate.

No man living would have served him that trick five years previously.

"Hands off, an' ye plaze, Masther Billy. Don't thry thim games on me, for I won't have 'em," said Jacky Cain, as the other lay panting at his horse's feet. "Get up, now, for I didn't mean to hurt ye, and wouldn't so long as yer kept yer hands to yerself. But I only want yer to understand, in a friendly way like, that it's Jacky Cain who has Billy-the-Bull in his power, and not Billy-the-Bull who has Jacky Cain."

The old man hoarsely gasped out a few unintelligible sentences, and apparently thoroughly cowed, raised himself and slowly got upon his horse, the while staggering like a drunken man, and, hanging down his neck, he let the reins fall upon the neck of his weary steed, which slowly and painfully moved forward, following his companion, who went on ahead, occasionally looking round at him with a curious and half-contemptuous expression.

CHAPTER XXVI.
THE CAMP BY THE GREEN SWAMP.

MEANWHILE the character of the country had somewhat changed; the flat plain had taken a dip to the westward, and cropping out of the deep covering of sand were occasionally small beds of alluvial and fluvial deposit, showing the course of a creek, which, in the rainy season, was of some magnitude, but which was now completely dried up.

The horses, however, by their pinched-up ears and eager steps, appeared to detect the presence of water at no great distance, and presently the travellers came in sight of a swampy water-hole, the only one for miles around, and at which they had prepared to camp for the night.

On arriving at the soft, boggy borders of the swamp, the old man, roused by the inquiries of his companion, twice or thrice repeated, directed him to head round it until he got to a place where, the alluvial deposit having drifted out to a considerable distance, there was some scanty feed for the horses and a few dry sticks to make a fire.

The sun had sunk below the boundless expanse of barren desert when the travellers reached their halting-place, and the light evening breeze began to spring up and sigh mournfully through the few stunted box trees that grew on the small oasis on which they were encamped.

The old man dismounted from his horse, and crouched fearfully under the shade of the trees.

His companion, after having vainly tried two or three times to rouse him to make himself useful, grumblingly hoppled and unsaddled the horses, producing the wherewithal to make the evening meal from the saddle-bags on his own horse.

He then proceeded to make a fire.

After having done so, he turned to the old man, who still sat in the same position, staring into the fire, the lurid gleam of which, as it flared and flickered, played fantastically on his unnaturally ghastly countenance.

"Come, Billy," said he, "don't sit there as av ye'd seen a ghost, man. Sure I meant no harm, and yer secret's as safe with me as though nobody knew of it but yerself."

The old man groaned and hid his face in his hands, and the younger one continued—

"There's not a soul knows of it but myself, for I never breathed a sound of it to anybody. Why would I? Such friends as you and I always wor, Billy, and more betoken that you told me all yerself, as one may say."

The old man raised his head, and staring dreamily at his companion, said—

"How? I told you? It's a lie! I never told you!"

"But I say you did, or what kims to much the same thing," retorted the other.

"Impossible!" cried Billy, energetically. "When did I, or how could I have told you, when I never dare even to whisper it unto myself?"

"Faith," said Jacky, laughingly, "it was a mighty loud whisper, a pig's whisper, as one may say. Take my advice, ye ould fool, and don't eat heavy suppers, nor sleep so sound of a night, for 'twas in your dhrames that you tould me."

The old man gave an agonised cry and threw his arms wildly over his head. It was then observable that a couple of fingers were missing from his right hand.

Jacky continued—

"Ye remember the time I slep' at your place about a month afther he—you know who I mane—was missed. He called at the Cornstalk as he was passing, but didn't like to stop, on account of the bad characthers as was hanging about the place, and bekase he had a tidy lot o' money about him. Begorra! I think he'd a done betther av he had stopped. But no, 'he must be getten on,' he said, and as he axed me av I could tell him a dacent rispectable place to sleep at, and knowing nobody more dacent and rispectable than yerself, I recommended him to stop with you; and he never was seen afther he left yer house."

He paused for a second and then continued—

"So whin I wint down to yer place I kep my eyes open and my ears too, and by-and-by, when ye wer asleep, I heard ye talking and walking in yer dhrame, and I folly'd ye from one place to another till ye stopped at the ould dhry well beyant the stockyard—a mighty cunning place it was too, and one it would take a stranger a very long time to find. Whin the traps wor up my way about it a axin' me which road he tuk from my house I didn't tell 'em all I knowed. Why should I, whin I knowed that hinceforth whin I wanted a note or two I'd only to mention the circumstance to ye and I'd git it."

The old man, who had never ceased rocking himself to and fro whilst Jacky Cain was giving this long explanation, now looked up, and said in a tremulous, yet husky voice—

"He tempted me with his gold, Jacky, or I wouldn't ha' done it. Rolls and rolls o' notes and bright shining sovereigns in plenty. He'd a bottle o' rum with him, and he drunk and I drunk, and then he began to count over his money, and fell asleep before the fire counting it. The bright yellow gold sparkled in the firelight, and the devil tempted me, and—and," he continued, whilst his face became livid with contending passions, and his voice sank to a hissing whisper, "I throttled him as he slept."

"And did he offer no resistance?" asked Jacky Cain.

"Oh yes," came the choking reply. "He woke and tried to shake me off; but I had him fast, and by-and-by his face blackened and he fell backwards, but I never let him go while the breath of life was in his body. So then I hid him in a sack, and dropped him into the old well—down, down, deep with an awful plunge into the water at the bottom. But you won't betray me, will you? You wouldn't betray your poor old friend and partner, would you, Jacky?"

"Betray you, not I; though I daresay I should still get a thousand pounds for it if you really were Blue Cap, as another night in yer dhrames yer let out that you was. But I ain't a sneak nor a traitor, and divil a word'll ever pass my lips, unless indeed ye thry to ride rough-shod over me agin, as you did to-day, for you know, Billy, dear, I can't stand that," replied Jacky, with a grin.

By this time the tea in the tin billy on the fire began to boil, and the two travellers began to cut into the food that was spread before them.

But the old man, notwithstanding the repeated invitations of his companion, ate but sparingly, and though Jacky Cain, being desperately hungry, did ample justice to the damper, salt beef, and tea, there was something in his friend and partner's face that caused him a vague feeling of uneasiness, not to say actual alarm.

CHAPTER XXVII.

THE MURDER BY THE CAMP FIRE.

AFTER supper, and as they sat together over the fire, smoking a pipe, preparatory to "turning in," Jacky Cain attempted to get up a conversation relating to the business on which they were journeying so far from the haunts of civilisation, which was in reality for the purpose of taking up a piece of good country, on a creek, or one branch of the Darling River, flowing into a swamp in the wild unknown district, between that river and the distant barren range of mountains.

There they proposed to make a plant of the cattle which, coming into their possession unlawfully, they were unable safely to dispose of in their own immediate neighbourhood,

This they had agreed to do, chiefly because the police, instructed by the numerous squatters, who were continually losing cattle, had begun to keep a look out on the doings of the pair—rather more sharp than was agreeable.

Jacky Cain, who seemed to have his own reasons for conciliating the older man, then tried to argue the point as to whether, supposing the country which they had come out to see was all that was represented, it would be practicable to drive a large drove of cattle over the bare and inhospitable region which they had passed and had still to pass, devoid as it was, for so many weary leagues at a stretch, of both grass and water.

All was, however, of no avail; the shock to the old man's nervous system, at the discovery that his crimes, which he had supposed buried within the recesses of his own conscience, were known to another, had so shaken his intelligence that he was totally unable to carry on a lengthened conversation.

By-and-by, Jacky Cain grew tired of the old man's taciturnity, and putting as large a log as he could find upon the fire, he wrapped himself up in his blanket, drew his saddle under his head, and composed himself to sleep.

For a time he lay watching the immoveable figure before him, sitting staring into the fire, the hard, stony expression of his face now and then revealed by the fitful glare of the blaze, until at last, lulled by the ceaseless hum of insect life in the air, and fatigued by his day's journey, he fell unconsciously asleep.

Not, however, without trying many a time to shake off the drowsiness which overcame him, and taking his revolver in his hand ready for use; for much as he held his companion in contempt, he felt a kind of vague alarm at his singular behaviour.

Soon night spread her pall over the scene, the pale stars which glittered in countless myriads in the firmament were overcast by the large clouds that blew up from the south-east, and the moon, which had not attained her first quarter, shone at intervals from between the masses of driving cloud, casting a faint, sickly light on the surrounding desert.

The few stunted box-trees waved blackly and gloomily in the light wind like funeral plumes, and still the old man sat crouched over the fire, muttering to himself, and still the young man slept a troubled sleep.

Could it be an innate warning of impending danger that caused him to tumble and toss in his uneasy slumber?

Could it be that the dismal boom of the bittern, the lonely cry of the native cat, and the harsh note of the frog in the swamp sounded in his ears and rang at the windows of his dulled senses like alarm bells calling on him to awake?

Once he dreamed a fearful dream, that a huge snake was crawling—crawling—crawling over his body, and drawing back its head to strike with its venomous fangs; and he struggled in his sleep; but those fiery eyes, and that forked tongue playing about like red lightning, ever came nearer—nearer, until he awoke with a start, in the cold, grey, semi-darkness, only to see the fire smouldering low, and the old man still crouching over it, apparently asleep; and he got up, raked together the ashes, turned the logs and lay down to rest again.

Then he slept once more, and dreamed still of danger. This time he was riding along inaccessible precipices and rugged shelvings, when his horse bounded into an unfathomable gulf and he felt falling down—down—down until again he awoke with a start and in a cold perspiration of terror, and thought he would walk down to the swamp and bathe his throbbing temples in the cool water.

But he lay still and dozed off again, and the boom of the bittern, the cry of the native cat, and the croak of the frog in the swamp sounded in his ears fainter and fainter, until at last he sank into a profound and dreamless sleep.

Midnight had come, and the dark clouds grew darker and denser, as they coursed before the light breeze across the firmament of heaven, the breeze that surged fitfully through the black boughs of the overreaching trees.

The fire had again smouldered low, and from the swamp and far as the eye could reach to the westward across the plains from the distant, arose a thick, white, streamy blanket of pearly mist.

The old man crouched over the fire, apparently sleeping. Apparently, for nothing was farther than sleep from his thoughts.

His mind bent on one object, could see but that object—the new danger which threatened him, and to sweep that danger from his path was the sole subject of his cogitations.

The surest, the safest, and the clearest way was to kill Jacky Cain as he slept.

To kill him—but that was not sufficient. What was he afterwards to do with the body?

If he threw it into the swamp it might be found, for occasionally, although very seldom, travellers wandered that way in going to the outlying stations about Menindie, thus taking a shorter cut than by travelling round by Mount Burke, which lay far to the northward.

If he buried it in the sand the dingo and the native cat would rake it up and leave it bare to the eye of heaven and man.

What, then, could he do with it?

Ah, a thought! Five or six miles to the southward there was a dense belt of Mallee scrub, into which the foot of the white man had never penetrated. If he could but bestow the body there it would be safe. And why not?

The old man slowly raised his head and looked around.

In the dull, red gleam of the fire he could dimly see the outline of his victim, and above the moaning of the night wind could hear his heavy, long-drawn breathing.

He slept soundly—very soundly.

The old man raised himself slowly from his crouching position, and cautiously gliding through the grass, he dragged himself over the sand towards his prey.

Suddenly the sleeper moved uneasily, and in an instant Billy-the-Bull had resumed his old crouching position over the fire.

Will he awake? No.

He had merely turned in his sleep; turned so as to present a fairer aim for the deed by bowie knife, which the old man held naked in his left hand and hidden under his coat.

He had merely turned, and the moon breaking at that instant from behind a cloud, shone whitely on the sharp outline of his face.

He was smiling in his sleep.

Did the old man relent? No.

He savagely, but noiselessly, chuckled as he saw the breast of his victim exposed, and again silently glided towards him.

But Jacky was armed. He might awake and struggle hard for his life.

Yes, and it was better to make sure.

The revolver was clutched firmly in his right hand, the hand nearest to him, and he could not deprive him of it without waking him.

Rapidly, quietly, and with a steadiness of hand that was surprising, Billy took the kerchief from his own neck, wound one end of it through the trigger-guard, and loosely, but securely fastened the other around his victim's leg, which lay uncovered by the blanket.

Still he slept on. In vain the bittern boomed his warning note, in vain the native cat sounded his discordant screech, and in vain the frog in the swamp croaked his dismal cry.

In vain—alas for him, in vain!

In the fitful firelight there is a sudden gleam, then a cry—a hoarse, faint cry—then a struggle, another stab, and an agonised yell of "Oh, you blood-thirsty villain!"

To it a voice, thick and husky, responds, "You know too much—you must die."

There is a flash, and a report, and the booming bittern takes wing, and the native cat hides in a hollow log, and the blue crane that stood in the midst of the swamp dreamily on one leg, with his head under his wing, seeks a quieter resting place.

Then there is a groan, an effort to rise, a heavy fall, and a sudden silence. And when the moon again breaks from behind a cloud, she shines on a white, upturned face, and on a crimson pool, which the greedy sand is drinking up, as it trickles, slowly and heavily from two unsightly gashes in the breast of a motionless human form.

CHAPTER XXVIII.
THE DEAD MAN'S RIDE.

THE sun rose in his majesty of might on the vast sandy plains, where a few hours before the weary travellers, who camped by the green swamp, had crossed, and as his red beams shot straighter and straighter across the plain, so rose the veil of white mist which had covered the sleeping earth, higher and still higher, and the cool night wind dies away as the heavy dew, which hangs on the sparse grass round the borders of the swamp, evaporates under the growing heat, and the air begins to quiver above the parched sand.

Not a sound is heard, save the short nibble of the two hoppled horses at the crisp grass.

The fire has burned itself nearly out, and only an occasional puff of faint white smoke tells of the presence of fire among the dull embers.

By-and-by, in a clump of underwood growing near the swamp, is heard a sound as of something moving.

The bushes are parted, and cautiously a white face peers forth from the opening.

Slowly a form emerges from the hiding-place, and hurriedly looks around as though afraid of human witnesses in that dreary place.

It is that of the old man, who muttering to himself—

"He knew too much, oh! yes, he knew too much," goes down to the fire, and stands irresolutely gazing on the unmoving form that lies covered up beneath that tossed, tumbled, and blood-stained blanket.

Beneath his shaggy eyebrows his eyes burn fiercely, and the innumerable lines in his face express firm will and determination, although he cannot yet summon up courage to disturb the silent sleeper.

"Shall I leave him where he lies?" he says, in self communion. "No, it would not be safe; and yet to touch him after what I have done. Bah! I was not so chicken-hearted once, and as it must be done, why, the sooner the better."

He stooped down and rudely snatched the blanket from the face of the dead man.

It was white and ghastly.

The teeth were clenched, and the eyes open, but totally lustreless.

Too surely the two stabs in the breast had done their work.

They had been sharp, sudden, and deep, and death had been almost immediate.

His body had become cold and rigid, and one of the limbs, which the old man raised and let fall, dropped with a dull thud on the sand.

But the old man had work to do.

He emptied the dead man's pockets, unbound the treacherous handkerchief which had prevented his using his revolver, and threw it, saturated with blood, on the smoking embers.

He next caught one of the horses, put on his bridle, and, after a weary struggle, succeeded in throwing the body across the animal's back.

He then took off the hopples and started to bestow the corpse in the distant Mallee scrub that loomed darkly and drearily in the distance.

Across the burning plain slowly and painfully he toiled, guiding the horse with one hand, and with the other steadying the horrible burthen that lay supinely across its back.

The sun had risen high in the heavens before he had reached the scrub, and into its darkest recesses he plunged at once, crashing through the dead branches and rotten sticks, and forcing a way through the thick prickly undergrowth.

Then there was a sudden pause.

He had reached a small open spot surrounded with more than usually dense vegetation, and with a dull and hollow sound he allowed the swinging body to drop upon the earth.

The horse sprang aside in terror, but the old man spurning the corpse with his foot, hissed between his teeth in bitter and malignant tones—

"And you've got my secret, and would betray me, would you, Jacky Cain? But you'll never do it my man, for ye're safe enough now till the Day of Judgment, and the ants and native cats are welcome to yer ugly carcase; anyhow, theirs are the only eyes that'll ever look upon ye now. Ye can't say I didn't give ye a ride to yer funeral, and that's more than the hangman would have bestowed on ye," and Blue Cap chuckled villanously as he turned to leave the spot.

At this moment, sounding strange and weird-like in the silence, rose the harsh and uproarious scream of a laughing jackass that was perched on the branch of an adjoining tree, as if in mockery of the old man's words.

And as it rose peal after peal in the quiet morning air, Blue Cap shook his clenched fist in the direction whence the sound come, muttering half aloud—

"If I had yer neck in my clutches, yer mocking devil, I'd sarve ye as I sarved the hawker, I would, I would. But mum—enough of that, I mustn't think of it or I'll be killing myself for knowing it, like I did him as lies there cold and stiff—ay, cold and stiff."

So saying, he caught the horse that had begun to quietly nibble the grass that grew near, and retraced his steps to the last night's camp.

All was as he had left it.

There lay the blood-stiffened blanket, there the saddle on which the murdered man had pillowed his head, there the pistol, its muzzle still begrimed and blackened with powder, and there the fatal knife with which the horrid deed had been perpetrated.

Hastily he gathered together the evidences of his crime, and piling them on the embers, gathered a few sticks and made a fire.

Slowly slowly it blazed until he piled more wood, and more' still, when in a very few minutes, the blanket, the handkerchief, and the dead man's hat had perished in the flames, and the knife lay red-hot and undistingnishable amidst the glowing ashes.

The horse he then led down to the swamp and washed off the dark stains from his sides, and saddling him and the other horse, he mounted his own, and leading the second, took a last look at the spot, and started backward by the route they had come across the boundless plain, revolving what he should do next, and how he might get home without raising suspicions, or being observed.

And his victim, what of him?

Shall he lie there, unhouselled, uncharnelled, washed by the driving rain, beaten by the pitiless wind that sings a mad song of triumph through the waving branches of the thick Mallee scrub?

Shall he be eaten by ants?

Shall wild cats fight and snarl over him as they tear his flesh?

And shall his bones bleach and whiten in the summer's sun and winter's storm, until the day of doom?

Or shall the mocking laugh of the noisy bird that sounded through the silence when the old man left the place be prophetic, and that pallid corpse be made terrible and damning evidence against the murderer?

Let us wait by the place where the fire smoulders low on the border of that green and slimy swamp.

Let us watch the old man with the fierce eyes and the gloomy brow as he toils across the heated sand, until his shadow, merged into that of the two horses with him, becomes smaller and smaller, and at last is lost in the quivering air.

Still, let us wait, watch, and listen.

See, from the broad west, where the reddening sun begins to sink in a firmament of fire below the horizon, their shadows lengthening over the wide plain, comes a band of black hunters seeking a resting-place for the night.

They have marched all day across the blighting sand, and come to search the thick belt of Mallee to the south for game, but they know of this stagnant swampy pool, and will camp by it for the night.

There is a sudden halt, for the keen nostrils of these sons of the wilderness have scented the smell of the burnt embers that even yet are smouldering below the patch of timber, and they fear danger.

See how cautiously they divide, and how noiselessly they crawl through the bushes, until they obtain a full view of the swamp, darkening in the growing thickening twilight; then, when they see all clear, the sudden, low, penetrating signal of "All right!" calls them together.

"Whitefellow fire," says one of them, looking at the embers. "Whitefellow sit down like it long 'o that to-day,"

"Yowi," (yes) is the reply of another.

"Ah-h-h!" cries a third, as with his eyes glistening like a fire-ball, and his white teeth chattering with terror, he points to a black stain on he sand.

The others gather round.

There is a loud and continuous chattering in the native tongue, which is kept up around the fire until late into the night, when beneath the gathering clouds that drive across the pale shining moon, the swarthy hunters sink one by one into a troubled slumber.

The first beams of the morning sun shot redly over the wild waste of white sand that surrounded the green swamp, gilding with a rosy tint the ripples on the water caused by the faint breeze that, blowing nightly from sundown until morning, was gradually dying away. But long before his beams came slanting athwart the horizon, and while yet the east was tinged with rosy streaks, precursors of his coming, the blacks' camp on the border of the swamp was in motion.

CHAPTER XXIX.

BLACKFELLOW ON THE TRAIL.

THE early bird whose search for the proverbial worm led him that way came to grief that morning, as the blacks were abroad, and having knocked over a score or so of honey-eaters in the Banksias, and half-a-dozen or so of dozing ducks on the swamp, were making, amidst a very Babel of what they very appropriately term "yabber-yabber," preparations for a grand pita, or feast, prior to following up the trail of blood which they had discovered.

Nothing can be done in a black camp without a grand "yabber," or great consultation, in which everybody expresses his opinion upon the whole matter under consideration with a volubility and a strength of lung which would drive many of our members of Parliament mad with sheer vexation and envy.

One great peculiarity of these consultations is that everybody, men, women, and children, with the occasional assistance of half-a-score of curs of various sizes and degrees of manginess, give tongue at once.

Talking it can scarcely be called. Singing it certainly is not.

There is no "honourable the speaker," in flowing robes and big horsehair wig, with look severe, to curb the fluency of any honourable member, and to stop the flux de bouche which, while it lasts, is to all intents and purposes a real, downright, original, con furio Dutch chorus, and no mistake about it.

After eating, the blacks gather their household goods together and make a move—not, however, in the direction leading directly to the Myall scrub, to which they are bound, but following the forward track, on account of its having the marks of "whitefellow foot," as well as the horse trail, and also the occasionally congealed black drops that showed that the body had been carried that way, rather than the more recent backward track which otherwise their instincts would have taught them to take in preference to the older one.

The track was a perfectly easy one, and they followed it rapidly and without a fault until, led by the one who strode foremost, acting as a kind of chief or leader, they forced their way through the thick undergrowth into the heart of the scrub, and there, lying in a wide open space, they came upon the stark and stiff corpse of the murdered man, covered with hundreds of buzzing flies.

They turned the body flat on its back to see whether they could recognise the features as those of anyone they knew, and amidst much talk and gesticulation, came to the conclusion that they did not know him, which, indeed, as he had never been in that part of the country before, and came from so distant a place, it was not likely they would.

They, however, did not leave the body until they had stripped it completely naked, each of them taking whatever struck his fancy most or whatever they could best get hold of.

And then they departed, striking off to the eastward, well satisfied with their morning's work.

One of them, however, who had been at one time in the native police force, and who had, as is the wont of these people (getting tired of a regular life, and longing for his old free-and-easy existence in the woods), simply thrown off his uniform and wandered away towards the far west one fine morning, without beat of drum, where he had been welcomed back by his tribe, or those of it whom rum and disease had not carried off, and had lived the old nomadic life ever since.

This one, true to the habit grafted on his natural instincts, after possessing himself of the blue shirt or jumper worn by the dead man, set off from the tribe to follow the back trail, and thus return to the rum and civilization, for which he had felt a hankering for some time past.

When he arrived at the camp he paused awhile in order to puzzle out the strange tracks which had been made, talking to himself all the time, his soliloquy being in the following strain:—

"Two fellow come like it long a land. Plenty baked* that yarraman,† sit down longe fire. By'n-by gib it knife; my word, that fellow him go bong!‡ Get him yarraman, put him long a bush, like it in Myall down a yonder, where this fellow get it budgeree jumper. Come back that fellow. Get him 'nother one yarraman, then him go 'way. Bail me think I find him. I find him by'n-bye, no fear."

He then picked up the remains of the morning's feast, took a long drink of the water in the swamp, and started off at an easy, swinging pace across the yielding sand, his head bent forward, and his eyes cast downward, so as not to miss a trace of the footsteps of the horses, which had in many places been almost obliterated by the high winds that had blown the fine sand about into ridges and furrows in all directions.

It was easy enough to trace him the first day,

and to his first camping place by a branch of the Bogan river.

Yet still the marks were perceptible to the tutored eye of the savage, and he followed them unerringly, although as he got farther and farther on they became more and more difficult, inasmuch as the tracks of other horsemen began to cross, and in one instance, for a short distance, went in the same direction.

By close observation, however, he kept on the trail, although occasionally having to retrace his steps and make a fresh start.

At length, when painfully deciphering step by step the tracks of the horses he was following from those of others which had gone in the same direction, he suddenly came across a recently dropped horseshoe, which had evidently been cast by one of the horses he was in search of.

Picking it up with a cry of delight, he exclaimed—

"Aha! now me find him longe all the way, I believe!"

And he thereupon increased his pace almost to a run as he rapidly traced the track by the now peculiarity of the hoof-prints.

* * * *

In the meantime, Blue Cap, guided by the marks he and his partner had made in coming, leisurely made his way back across the sandy waste, and camping at the same place as they had done the night before, made the Bogan river late in the second day, leaving the former track, however, on its banks, and crossing at a much higher point than they had in coming.

This he did with the intention of making the main cattle track from Fort Burke, so that it might appear, should he meet any person, that he had come from that direction, it being his intention to cross the plain, and get to Maitland, where he thought he might sell the horses without any danger of their being identified, at the same time as he put those who might see him, and who knew him, on a wrong scent as to the direction whence he had come.

Keeping, therefore, a north-easterly course, and leaving his horses in the scrub near the small township of Cannonbar whilst he purchased a fresh stock of provisions, he skirted that township and made across the dreary country known as the Macquarie Marshes, until he struck the road, after four hard days' travelling, below the township of Walgett, on the great north-western road, at which township he arrived late in the evening, having apparently come from Fort Burke, or some of the stations in that district.

Putting up at the Bunyip Hotel, he pretended to be very tired, and asking to be roused early in the morning, so as to escape from all interrogatories, he went to bed.

To bed, but not to sleep, for, hardened as he was in crime, his nerves were not what they were, and the foul crime that he had last committed haunted him day and night.

Not that he repented of the deed, or wished it undone, but fear of the consequences kept him awake.

His victim and late companion had spoken to him of his talking in his sleep, and that was enough to deter him from yielding to the drowsiness which he could scarcely keep from overpowering him, and as often as he felt himself falling off to sleep, so often would he wake again with a guilty and terrified start, as if he felt the hand of justice upon his throat.

At length, however, exhausted nature could stand no more, and despite all his endeavours, he sank into a profound slumber, tossing and tumbling in his troubled dreams, until, with a loud cry of terror, he was awakened by the knocking of the groom at his chamber door the next morning, and

---

* "Baked:" fatigued. † "Yarraman:" horse. ‡ "Go bong:" die.

opened his eyes to see the sunlight streaming cheerily into his room, and to hear and smell the grateful preparations for breakfast going on in the kitchen.

CHAPTER XXX.

THE HORSE WITHOUT A SHOE.

"THAT'S a comical old cove in number four," was the observation made by the groom of the Bunyip Hotel, Walgett, as, having roused Billy-the-Bull in the early morning, he made his way into the kitchen and stood with his short pipe in the corner of his mouth, his hands employed meanwhile in rubbing the necessary quantity of tobacco for his matutinal smoke.

John Chinaman, the cook, speaking amidst the music of the colonial organ—Anglice, frying-pan—said languidly—

"Yah! yah! no muchee good! What he do, eh?"

"What he do, John? why, when I went to knock him up he sets up a squeal like a stuck pig. Oh, Lord! I reckon he frightened the seven senses out o' me. He must ha' had a horrid dream last night, that old cove."

Meantime the subject of these remarks lay in bed blinking in the bright sunshine, and conversing with himself as to whether he should start at once, or wait for breakfast and rest for a few hours before he resumed his journey.

His habitual caution and his natural niggardliness inclined him to prosecute his journey without delay, whilst his aching joints, tired out with the unwonted exertion he had taken, and more than all, the grateful aroma arising from the kitchen on the other side of the yard—so refreshing to the nostrils of a hungry and weary man—tempted him to linger awhile on the road, and, at all events, to have the benefit of a full meal.

Whilst he lay unable to decide, the sound of the hissing in the kitchen and the rattling of the cups and saucers became louder, and by-and-by the cheery voice of the landlady calling to him, "Now then, old man, come on, breakfast's ready," decided him upon staying.

Hastily tumbling out of bed, he shuffled on his clothes, and giving his face a rub with the wet towel, and his matted hair a shake, he smoothed it with his fingers, shambled into the sitting room, and grunting a mumbled response to the hearty "Good morning" with which he was greeted, sat down to the morning's meal.

What havoc he made, his appetite sharpened as it was by his long ride and sojourn in the bush, amidst the ham and eggs, the sausages, and the fried potatoes, and what cups of tea he swallowed, it boots us not to tell, further than to say that he took care to have the full value of his half-crown for breakfast, if he had not had it out of his half-crown for bed.

The landlady poured him out cup after cup of tea, and helped him to heap after heap of edibles in silent dismay, whilst Charley Kelly, the landlord, after watching him awhile with something like astonishment, remarked drily—

"I say, mate, I reckon you intend going on to Coonanbarabran before you feed again?"

But the old man merely mumbled something in reply, and attended to his eating.

When he had quite finished he cut himself a pipe of tobacco, and calling for a glass of brandy, drank it off and slowly wandered off to look at his horses.

"Well, I ham jiggered!" said Charley Kelly. "If that cove hain't got a twist it's a pity! I'd rather keep him a week nor a fortnight, anyhow. I wonder where he came from. Wherever 'tis they haven't given him much to eat lately, I'll go bail."

Mrs. Kelly turned up her nose in reply, muttering something about "a dirty old bushman, not fit to sit at a decent table," and then went off to look after her household duties.

Meantime the old man had filled his pipe, and after lighting it, had gone to see after his horses, and given orders that when they had had their feed they were to be saddled and brought round.

Watching them eat their feeds of corn and begin to munch the armfuls of hay which were thrown to them, he turned away and walked slowly up the yard, thoughtfully smoking away at the dirty black little pipe which he held in the corner of his wrinkled mouth.

As he turned out of the slip panel to go into the house again he met the grinning face of a blackfellow, who, covered with dust, and weary and travel-worn, stood in the verandah of the inn looking wistfully into the bar as if waiting for someone to offer him a drink.

The black, touching his hat as the old man passed him, said to him in a supplicating tone—

"You gib him glass rum?"

But Blue Cap passed by unheedingly, scarcely looking at the savage.

Had he done so—had he but glanced at the garment he wore—he might have seen that which would have driven the blood from his cheek and made him blanch with terror, for there, full on the breast, and plain to be seen, were the two clean cuts of the deadly knife, and a blackened and stiffened daub covering the whole of the left side of the chest.

He might have seen that which would have caused him to hurry that poor benighted blackfellow into the bush on the other side of the road, and buy that jumper and his silence at any price, and would have taught him that all his care, all his cunning, all his secrecy, were in vain in the face of the great principle that "blood will have blood."

But no, it was not to be.

The sword of retribution had been bared, and although the avenging angel had placed the hilt in another hand than that of the savage, it should not be sheathed until terrible vengeance had been taken, until the prophetic warning of the laughing mocking-bird in the scrub had rung again upon the old man's memory as the debt was paid.

The blackfellow turned away slowly as his eyes followed the shambling steps of the old man into the house, and then he sauntered down the yard into the stable, the place where blacks invariably make for.

There was no one there, and the two horses turned up their dark rolling eyes to look at the intruder.

"Ha! two yarraman! Me see him foot," he ejaculated as he stooped down and lifted up the feet of the horses one after another until he came to the one from which a shoe was missing.

At this moment the groom came in, and seeing him, called out—

"Now then there, you blackfellow, what are you doin' along o' them horses?"

"That fellow he lose him shoe; you know, eh?" said he, replying to one question by another.

"Lost a shoe, has he? Well, you go and tell the old cove in the bar, and maybe he'll give you something to drink for lettin' him know," said the groom.

And the black thought this very good advice.

Bungy, for the silent tracker is an old acquaintance of ours, started to go, but with a dim idea that something better than a glass of rum might come out of the affair, he stepped back, and taking off the dead man's jumper, rolled it up, and threw it aside into an empty dray. He then walked into the bar, and with a grin and twinkle of his large eyes, said—

"Master, one yarraman belong 'o you; he lost one

fellow shoe. Me take him to blacksmith's, eh?"

"What are you staring at?" said the old man, finding the black's eyes fixed on him scrutinizingly. "Yes, take him and get the shoe put on if there's one off, and I'll give you a nobbler when you come back."

"All right, master," was the reply of Bungy, and he went back and led the horse away, having impressed the features of the old man indelibly on his memory, besides taking a mental note of the brand and general appearance of both the horses.

The lost shoe was replaced, Bungy got his nobbler, and by-and-by the old man rode off; the black, who had determined to keep about the hotel for a few days, and help amongst the horses, not putting on the jumper again until he was gone.

In the course of the next day the groom remarked the cuts and the bloodstains on the garment and said in a half bantering tone—

"Why, Bungy, what a flash shirt you've got. Somebody been giving you knife, eh?"

Bungy's eyes flashed as he rejoined in a sullen and consequential manner—

"You know that old feller come here by'm-by yesterday, long o' two yarraman?"

"Oh, yes, rather," was the reply.

"Some one day me tell you somethin' 'bout that feller. Brother belong to that feller give me this shirt. He lie along a scrub; he get it knife."

"What do you mean, Bungy? I don't understand you," was the puzzled rejoinder.

"Me tell you by'm-by, to-morrow, next day then," and beyond that no more could be got out of Bungy.

Meanwhile, Blue Cap, unheeding or unthinking of the danger which impended so near to him, rode on down the road at an easy pace, determining to travel on horseback as he was until he reached Maitland, on the high road for which township he was.

Stopping at the necessary hotels on the road and making easy stages, he in three days more arrived there with his horses in good condition.

Flattering himself that he had succeeded in baffling all trace should there ever be, as was most improbable, any search, he sold the horses at the great weekly sale in the yard at East Maitland, and taking the steamer from Morpeth, sailed the following morning for Sydney, the capital of New South Wales.

There he stayed for a few days striving to drown the remembrance of the deed he had committed by a course of drunkenness and debauchery in the low haunts of vice which are to be found in that as in all other great cities, until at length, feeling anxious to know how his place was getting on in his absence, he took his passage in the steamer to Shoalhaven, and thence made his way over the mountains in the direction of his own house, which he had left empty and fastened up until his return.

But what has become of Hogan, the detective, all this while? Perhaps in the ensuing chapter we all see.

CHAPTER XXXI.

INTRODUCES A LITTLE SWAGMAN.

THE Cornstalk Inn, the hostelrie of Jacky Cain, situated in the dip or hollow of one of the mountains of the Shoalhaven range, had not been left to take care of itself during the unavoidable absence of its master.

The business was carried on by the wife of that worthy, a little, thin, sharp-eyed, peaked-nosed, shrewish woman, with a vixenish look, and a most uncertain temper, added to a loud, high-pitched voice, the tones of which might be heard all over the house from morning until night, rating the servants when she could get any to stop with her,

or the customers in default of a more legitimate object for her vituperation.

She was in truth an arrant scold, and it was said that Jacky Cain, unable to stop the continual nagging to which he was subjected, even by the very summary process of knocking her down, at length, like a sensible fellow, had let her chide on, merely, when it became unendurable, putting on his hat and taking a walk into the bush as soon as the house got too hot to hold him,

Until now his absence had created no suspicion, even though he had said nothing about his departure further than that he was going out on business and should not be back for a day or two, for he was in the habit of going away for oftentimes more than a week at once, and never by any chance mentioned either where he had been, or the business he had been about, notwithstanding the frequent and loud reproaches and lamentations of the wife of his bosom, that he "could be after no good leaving home for so long."

The only satisfaction he had ever given her was when, on one occasion she made more noise than usual, and slightly ruffled the equanimity of his temper he told to "mind her own business, and hold her jaw, if she didn't want a stockwhipping," a warning which, notwithstanding her ill-humour, she had the good sense to take.

On this occasion her husband had already been away for more than a week, and she had heard neither of nor from him, neither did she know even when he had started, further than, having got up early one morning, she had missed a saddle and bridle out of the stable, and had not seen him since.

Many had been the inquiries after him, for business happened to be pretty brisk, inasmuch as half a dozen bushmen in the neighbourhood had just been paid off, and the Cornstalk being the first public house they had come across on the road to Sydney, for which place they had started, they had naturally enough gone in, and were "knocking down" their earnings as fast as ever they could.

On this particular occasion, not only was the bar occupied by them, but there were also several other persons congregated round, getting intoxicated as fast as ever they could conveniently manage it.

First and foremost there were the half dozen choice spirits spoken of, who had recovered from the effects of the "spree" of the previous night by sleeping it off under the verandah, in the stable, or wherever else they might find a resting place, and who had already got into the singing state again.

Then there were two stockmen, who had turned the cattle they were driving into the paddock behind the house, and a teamster and his mate, all of whom had vowed a vow that they wouldn't move that day anyhow.

And besides these there was a swagman, or travelling bushman, a dapper little fellow, with his blankets over his shoulder, and his boots, moleskin trousers, and jumper, old, worn, dusty, and travel-stained, who had just dropped in to take a drink and inquire about any work in the neighbourhood, and who had found the company so good that he couldn't make up his mind to leave it, the more particularly as "he had a few notes left and was determined to see them out before he turned to again."

He was a smart little fellow, as merry as a cricket, and what with his yarns and his songs, had been declared by the unanimous voice of the company to be a "brick," a "trump," a "tulip," and a "good fellow."

It was about two in the afternoon when the little swagman arrived, and as two good hours had elapsed since that, the whole party were of course in an advanced state of intoxication and were loudly discussing the sticking up of Marrangong Station by three bushrangers, three days previously, and which the teamster and his mate, having come up that way, had been the first to bring the intelligence of.

The little swagman appears particularly interested, and the teamster who has told the tale half a dozen times before during that and the preceding day, and told it each time differently is (his imagination rendered fertile by the fumes of the liquor he has taken) giving loose to his fancy, and describing the circumstance, as though he had been an eye witness, which by this time it is highly probable that he may conscientiously believe himself to have been.

"' And so says they,'" he is saying, "' we must crack this crib,' and at it they goes. First thing as they does they goes to the hut at the bottom of the paddock, and there they sees two men a just going to turn in Bill the Splitter, and another. So they kills them two, and then away they goes to the house."

Here the narrative was interrupted by one of the bushmen, who had been dozing, and who had suddenly woke, up declaring that he was "a man as didn't care a cuss for nobody, and if anybody had anythin' to say agin that, why, let 'em come on and have it out."

There is a general cry for him to "shut up," amidst which, after vainly calling for somebody to "come on," he falls asleep again.

"When they gets to the house," continues the teamster, "they bustis in the door and tries to get into Mrs. Fraser's room, but that gal as lives there she heard them a comin', and, without saying a word, she blazes away at 'em through the keyhole, a killin' two and woundin' two more first shot. By this time it's a reglar pitched battle, she firin' and they firin', till at last all her powder's done, when away she cuts through the winder into the bush, shootin' one and giving another the knife as tried to stop her."

"Well, that's a rum yarn, and I don't believe a word on it," said Mrs. Cain, who had, with the inquisitiveness of her sex, been listening with a half-contemptuous expression to the narrative of the teamster. "Who told you all that, I should like to know?"

"Who told me?" says the teamster, defiantly. "Why Bill the Splitter told me—there!"

"Why, you fool, you told us that he was killed first going off," was the response. "Liars should have long memories, liars should."

"Tell the yarn yourself, then, next time, as you seem to know so much about it, and let's have some more brandy, and don't stand grinning at a fellow like a Cheshire cat," said the irate teamster.

He made a slight mistake, however, when he addressed the landlady of the Cornstalk in such terms, for the reply he got was a pewter pot thrown at his head, which narrowly missed him as it winged its flight through the window.

"Come I say, missis, none o' that," said he.

"Who are you calling names then, you rough you?" replied she. "I'll teach you to take advantage of a poor woman when she's left alone to take care of herself. Cheshire cat, indeed!"

The teamster declared that he meant nothing, and the sleeping bushman, waking up again under the impression that a fight was going on, hit out at the first man he came near who, happening to be one of his own mates, knocked him down under one of the benches at the other end of the bar, where he composed himself contentedly to sleep again, calling for a song.

The little swagman thereupon proposed that, in order to make things comfortable, they should have another drink, and he would sing them a song, an offer that was accepted with acclamation by the whole company, who insisted upon repeating every verse as a sort of Dutch chorus, every man singing in whatever key or tune best pleased him.

The song over, the swagman turned round to his communicative friend, the teamster, and asked him whether "any of the coves who had stuck up Marrangong were known?"

"Nobody seems to know nothin' on 'em," was the reply; "but Bill the Splitter he says as he'd know 'em again and old Andrew, the shepherd, says as he saw, some coves knocking about the same day, but he 'can't say as he'd know 'em again if he was to see em, cos why, his sight ain't so good as it wos."

"Did they get anything worth while, did you hear?" asked the swagman.

"Well, you see, sir," is the reply, "nobody knows but the missis, and she says not; but lord, it's hard to tell. Come, blow this yarning—my throat's dry. Let us have another drink."

But by this time Mrs. Cain concluded that they had had enough, and bade them turn out and sleep in the best place they could.

The little swagman, however—and it was wonderful how a man so helplessly intoxicated as he appeared to be should have his wits about him so far as to ask for a bed—would not be put off.

"No, no, missis," said he, "you don't turn me out into the road like that, after taking my money. Find me a bed somewhere, can't you?"

"Yes," sneered the landlady, "you're a fine fellow to go to bed anywhere, you are. You shall have a bed soft enough. Here, Joe, take him out and throw him on the top of the dungheap." And, as she spoke, she seized one of the drunken men, and lifting him as easily as she would have done a child, she carried him out of the place.

"Yes, Joe," said the little man with drunken stolidity, "you throw me on the dungheap."

Joe, the barman, groom, and man-of-all-work, however declined to tackle the swagman, but remaining in his place behind the bar, during thea temporary absence of Mrs. Cain, he offered a gigntic fellow a drink if he would carry him out for him.

The man consented, and advanced with the intention of doing so, and had succeeded, after some trouble, in getting the little swagman upon his feet, when, balancing himself for a moment, he delivered a blow from the shoulder so full and true between the eyes of the astonished giant that that worthy went crashing down into the midst of a heap of empty bottles that lay in one corner.

"Yes, Joe," the little fellow repeated, pointing to the prostrate man with drunken gravity; "you throw me on the dungheap—do. I'd like to see you do it."

Joe objected to having anything to do with so "houtragious a customer," and so, turning round to the astonished Mrs. Cain, who had re-entered the shanty, and steadying himself by the table, the swagman continued—

"Come, mother, no gammon with me, you know. I must have a bed somewhere. I don't care where it is, but no dungheaps, you understand."

The landlady, a little more civil than she had been, said there were no beds for him and he'd have to sleep in the stable. There was an empty stall, or, if he liked to climb up into the loft, there was plenty of hay there wherein he might make himself comfortable.

"All right," said he, "good night;" and shutting the door after him with a loud bang, he staggered away in the direction of the stable, the mistress of the house directing Joe to go after him and see that he did not set the place on fire lighting his pipe.

He, however, followed at a distance, and after watching the swagman roll himself up in his blankets in the unoccupied stall, betook himself off to his own bed in the kitchen, first telling that all the company were asleep—one in an empty dray, two under the verandah, two in the travellers' bed

THE GIANT WENT CRASHING DOWN INTO THE MIDST OF A HEAP OF EMPTY BOTTLES ON THE GROUND.

room, and one in the stockyard—after having carefully put up the slip-rails after him.

By-and-by a light might have been seen going from room to room, as Mrs. Cain saw that all was right, and then, after glimmering for a short time through the drawn blinds of her bedroom behind the bar, it was extinguished, and the Cornstalk and all about it were soon buried in deep and profound slumber.

CHAPTER XXXII.

THE SWAGMAN NO SWAGMAN AT ALL.

NOT quite all, for half an hour or so after Mrs. Cain had extinguished her candle the little swagman, who had rolled himself in his blanket, and gone off into a heavy and noisy sleep, gradually allowed his stertorous breathing to subside, and gently raising his head, listened for a moment ere he sprang lightly up, and creeping along by and in the shade of the stable, darted nimbly into the bush, and gaining the creek, knelt on the bank and plunged his head into the clear, cold water, holding it there a moment, and then allowing the water to drip from his crisp dark hair and moustaches before he wiped his face.

"Pah!" said he to himself, "a fellow needs something to brighten up his wits after drinking the infernal stuff they half poison you with at a bush inn. If I hadn't contrived to throw away three parts of the drink I got without being noticed, a nice headache I should have had in the morning, as nice an one as I expect that fellow Joe'll have. Lord, how astonished he was when I gave him a touch of 'old Lanky' between the eyes;" and the swagman laughed noiselessly at the remembrance. "Now, let's see what's to be done next. I should like a good look at this place, so that I might know my way about, if need be and so that—— Hallo! what's that?"

The sound which had disturbed his ruminations by the creek was that of the patter of horses' hoofs higher up the road than where he stood, and farther from the house, the road crossing the creek at a point about thirty yards above him.

"Travellers," said he to himself, "and at this time of night—that's queer. I hope they're not coming to stick up the shanty, for if they do that'll spoil my little game. However, I must get back to my crib, for it won't do to be seen here."

So saying, he retraced his steps, and regained the empty stall in the stable.

After waiting a long while in expectation of hearing the travellers ride either up to the door of the inn, or along the road past it, and there being no sign of their approach, he cautiously knelt down by the side of the doorway and looked out.

In the light of the moon he saw two men standing talking in the road in front of the house, one gesticulating violently and pointing to the inn, and the other apparently disagreeing with some proposition made by his companion.

They, however, spoke in such low tones as not to be heard.

"Come," said the little swagman to himself, "this is a rum start anyhow. Things are getting warm in this quarter. I must find out what those two coves are up to. I suppose they've left their horses in the bush."

At this moment the two men—the first one having apparently overcome the scruples or fears of the other—began to move slowly in the direction of the spot where he lay concealed.

So, rapidly wrapping up his blanket, he hastily, yet silently, scrambled up into the loft above, at the same time drawing an old sack over the hole, so as to conceal it.

The rafters above were crazy and rotten, and he had to lie perfectly still to prevent their creaking, but as he had his head over the opening, he was able to hear perfectly well every word that was said beneath him, for the two men, instead of stopping at the door of the inn, cautiously passed it, and came into the stable to consult further.

"Do you know the signal to let him know who it is?" asked the shorter of the two men.

"Never fear," was the reply. "He told me himself plainly enough. 'Knock twice,' says he to me, 'and then scratch twice on the side window behind the bar, and I'll hear you, no matter how lightly you do it.'"

"I wish this job was over, and we away at the other side o' the counthry. I don't feel safe here at all, after that affair the other night at Marrangong Station, and I'm sorry we ever went into it," said the other.

"Never say die, old fellow," was the answer in a voice rather more loud than cautiously, and which was decidedly that of the youth who in chapter twenty-four was bargaining with Jacky Cain and Billy-the-Bull for a better price for his cattle. "We must stick up that place again, and as for that girl who withstood us so bravely, she shall be my queen."

"Whisht! not so loud, Bob," said his companion; "there may be someone about, and it's better to be cautious. Come on now. Let's go and rouse up this cove, that you say will buy the cattle, and then get quit of this part of the counthry."

"Come along then, and keep dark," was the reply, and the two men left the stable together.

No sooner had they gone than the sack was removed from the entrance to the loft, and a pair of sharp blue eyes, as different as light from darkness to the mooning, lack-lustre, meaningless orbs they were half an hour ago, carefully scanned the half-dark stable below.

"Oh! oh!" said the little fellow in the loft to himself, "you're there, are you? So you're the beauties that stuck up Marrangong, eh? Who is that tallest fellow, I wonder? I seem to know the voice—both voices, but his particularly. I must have another look at them, and hear a little more—but how? Let me see."

He hastily took out of his swag a bright little revolver and a small ornamented staff, with a crown on the top (for the swagman was Ted Hogan the detective and none other), and stowing them away on his person, he swung himself down into the stable lightly and noiselessly, excepting a slight creaking, which was, however, unperceived.

Looking round, he saw that there was in the brick wall of the stable a square opening, having a door over it which fastened inside.

Carefully drawing the bolt, he swung the shutter back, and creeping through the opening, landed on the dungheap outside.

Making a wide circuit round the back of the kitchen, which stood behind the main building, he got to the other side of the house, and contrived to ensconce himself in the dark angle of the chimney, about three or four yards from the corner of the house, and in such a position as to easily hear all that might pass.

He had scarcely reached his hiding-place when the two men, who had again stopped to consult, and thereby given him time to get round, approached the window, one of them giving clearly and distinctly the signal spoken of.

For a few minutes there was no response, and then the lower part of the sash was cautiously lifted a few inches, and a voice whispered—

"Who's there?"

"It's me, Jacky, you know—Bob Loveridge—all right. Come about a few cattle I've got to sell," was the whispered reply.

"Speak low, young man, and mind what you say, for Jacky isn't here at all; but it's all the same thing," said the voice from the window.

"Then who are you?" asked Bob with an oath.

"Keep quiet, can't you?" replied the voice from the window. "There's a lot o' strangers about, and you might wake up some of 'em, only I fancy they're all too drunk. Jacky's not at home at present—hasn't been for more nor a week. I'm his wife, and I don't know when he'll be back, so, if you want to see him, you'll have to call again. But what's your business with him?"

"Our business is with him, not you, or with the old man his partner, and we must see one or the other to-night," was the reply.

"Oh, well, if you must you must, and the best thing you can do is to go and see the old man, as you call him. So good-night to ye, and good luck go with ye," said the woman with a spiteful sneer, and annoyed at not being fully entrusted with the business the two men had in hand.

"But hold on, mother," said the young man. "I say, be a little reasonable, can't you? Where does the old cove live? and which way do you ride to get there, for I don't know?"

"You won't get there this night anyway," was the reply, "and when you do you'll find his place about six miles higher up the creek—an old ramshackle hut, about a quarter of a mile from the left-hand side of the road. You'll see it from the back, and find it easily, because 'tis the only building for miles around."

"You wouldn't let us have a drop of brandy, mother, before we start?" asked Bob's companion.

"I wouldn't let you have anything at this time of the morning to save your lives; so be off with you—and take my advice: if you've got any friends as know anything about the sticking up of Marrangong, you'll tell 'em to sleep with their eyes skinned, and clear out of this side of the country afore they find it's too late," and with a spiteful laugh at their evident discomfiture, she slammed the window down, and went back to bed.

"Well, this is a rum go," said Bob Loveridge to his companion. "Jacky Cain not at home after all our trouble. There's nothing for it now but to go on and find old Billy-the-Bull. We'll lose no time about it neither, for that old woman's warning is not to be despised, I can tell you."

The other man turned away, swearing at the obstinacy of the landlady, who would not give them anything to drink, and Bob and he made the best of their way to the road, where they again stood consulting what was best to be done, thus giving the detective the opportunity to slip back into his place of concealment, without being seen.

"Whether now to follow up the trail," said he to himself, with his eye to a slit between the slabs of which the stable was built, "whether to follow up this trail and nab those two coves for bushranging, or to wait awhile and stick to the lay I'm on, I don't quite know."

"Bob Loveridge, Bob Loveridge," he continued, a minute later; "I know the voice, but not the name, and yet I can't call him to mind. Who the deuce can it be? By heavens!" he ejaculated suddenly, as a conviction struck him; "I know! Oh! oh! so it's you is it, master? Well, I know you now, anyhow, and I'll have you when I want you, but I must see a little more of this neat little game you are up to here first. Billy-the-Bull with Jacky Cain for a partner; well, I heard something of that before, but I didn't make much of it. I must introduce myself to this Billy-the-Bull as soon as possible. Six miles further up the creek is it, missis? Thank'ee. I'll find it, never fear, and to do any good, I must be there before daylight, so here goes."

And packing up his blankets, he slung them over his shoulder and started along the road, skirting, however, the edge of the bush, so as to keep well under its protecting shadow.

CHAPTER XXXIII.
THE HOME OF BILLY-THE-BULL.

WHEN Ted Hogan started after the bushrangers, it was his intention to keep up with them as much as possible, and to arrive at the hut of Billy-the-Bull as soon after them as he could.

Not having a horse, and not daring to use one even if he had, for fear of discovery, he had of course no hope of being beforehand with them, as he would have liked to have been, in order to overhear the conversation between them and the innkeeper's partner—a conversation which he had no doubt, if it did not throw any light upon the matter to investigate which he had come up to that part of the country—namely, the mysterious disappearance, and presumed murder of the hawker, who had been traced from the township of Terrara, on the Lower Shoalhaven, from various huts and stations along the road to the Cornstalk Inn, and of whom no further trace was to be found—would give him further information as to the sticking up of the Marrangong Station, and probably the future intentions of the bushrangers and cattle-duffers, which he might be able to turn to profitable account in many ways.

Whether to leave the business he had in hand for a time, and by following out the clue which had been so unexpectedly thrust upon him, lodge the bushrangers in the hands of justice, and so reap the reward of two birds in the hand, instead of a problematical one in the bush he scarcely knew, and so was sorely puzzled how to act.

He knew from experience how dangerous it was to have two things in hand at once, and how much more likely he was to attain his object, by giving it his undivided attention, and was therefore disinclined to turn aside, either to the right hand or to the left, in search of anything that did not bear directly or indirectly on the matter in point.

Besides this, his professional pride had been somewhat aroused by the manner in which the job had been given into his hands.

The police who had been on the alert for so long, were completely at fault, and could find neither trace nor clue.

They had made a bungling raid on all the settlers and squatters in the district, and had thus created a general storm of indignation against themselves, without doing the slightest bit of good.

Correspondence had passed between the more influential residents and persons high in office, the subject had been discussed in the Legislature Assembly, and although no positive vote of censure had been passed upon the head of the police department, still it was tacitly understood that the officers of that force, who had had the matter in hand, had acted indiscreetly, and that their proceedings had savoured more of the nature of a lawless inquisition, than the prosecution of a legitimate and cautious investigation.

Harsh words had passed in high places; it had been hinted to him when he received his orders, and was informed of the nature of the service required, that it was at the express wish of the high official authority, that the best, sharpest, and most wary officer in the detective force should be sent upon the errand, and that no pains or expense should be spared, in order that the mystery might be unravelled.

"I can't do two things at once," muttered Hogan to himself as he carefully threaded the green bushes which skirted the road. "If I follow these chaps, there's no telling where they may lead me, and while I am looking after them, the other thing may slip through my fingers. No, no, it won't do; I'll stick to them fellows as long as it does not interfere with the other matter, then I'll first learn where I may lay my hand on 'em when I want 'em, and then they may go for the time. This precious partner of Jacky Cain, I've somehow got a strange longing to see him, though I daresay I shall not be able to get anything out of him that will help me. Yet a chap does see queer things sometimes, when he don't expect 'em, just by keeping his eyes open. Hallo! what are those two coves up to now, I wonder?"

The concluding exclamation was caused by the two men whom he was so cautiously following, suddenly stopping, and commencing to talk in loud tones.

It appeared from what he could understand at the distance he was obliged to keep, that they had come to high words in consequence of one of them, who was called Jack Last, wishing to go back and make the landlady of the Cornstalk give them something to drink, which Bob Loveridge strenuously opposed, wishing to get down to the place whither they were bound as quickly as possible.

Jack Last, however, would not be persuaded, and insisted on going back to the inn, which was still only a few hundred yards away, rather than take the chance of getting anything to drink at the end of their journey.

"I tell you I don't care a fig, if there was fifty men at the place," shouted Jack defiantly. "My throat is parched, and I'm shivering with cold and ague, and I don't go another foot afore I gets some brandy or summat."

"Don't be a fool, Jack," pleaded Bob Loveridge—"don't be a fool, but come along down to the old man's place, and we'll get as much as we can drink. Think of the danger of our being seen at the Cornstalk. Why, if we were seen there, Jacky Cain would refuse point blank to have anything to say to us about the cattle."

"Bother the danger, and Jacky Cain, and the cattle, and you too. I've said it, and I'll stick to it. Let us go and get some brandy, and then I'm your man. I'm not going to ride six or seven miles furder, afore I have summat to drink."

"Well, a wilful man will have his own way, I reckon," said Bob; "but remember, if anything comes of it, it ain't my fault."

"All right," replied Jack Last, "I'll hould you harmless. Come along, I tell you; we'll find a way to make the old hag give us a drink, or we'll put a fire-stick in her roof."

The bushrangers turned back, and the detective, crouching close behind a thicket of tea-tree, allowed them to pass him on their way back to the bush inn.

He then followed and watched them, and after considerable altercation with the landlady, he saw them go in at the back door, which was opened for them.

"So much the better," said he to himself; "this leaves me a clear road. If I had only a horse, now? Ah! a good idea!"

Whatever this idea was, he soon acted up to it, for stepping rapidly through the bushes in a line with the road, he went in search of the bushrangers' horses, which they had left tied up.

He had nearly passed them, when a whinny from one of them on hearing his footsteps recalled him, and making his way through the trees, he came upon them hidden in a clump of bushes.

For a moment he considered whether it would be prudent for him to take one of them, and so ride to the place to which he was bound, but reflection told him that the horse being missing, might arouse the suspicions of the bushrangers, and he therefore decided not to do so.

Before leaving them, however, he examined the valise, which was strapped before the saddle of one of them, and finding under it and likewise strapped into a kind of improvised holster, a revolver capped and loaded, he took the liberty of taking off the caps, he dipped the weapon into a neighbouring waterhole, and carefully wiping it dry, he replaced the caps, and again fastened it on the saddle, muttering with a grin smile—

"It might come to fighting, and if so, it is as well to make it all right."

In order to gain a little more time, he also took off the bridle of one of the horses, and turned him loose, breaking the check strap, to make it appear as if it had been done by accident, and leaving the reins still hanging to the tree.

Next, taking out his knife, he carefully severed the stitches of both animals' saddle-girths, leaving them depending upon a few which he left uncut, so that if the riders urged their horses, at anything beyond an easy pace, they would give way, and let saddle and bridle come to the ground.

Having taken these precautions against being too suddenly disturbed, he started along the road at a brisk walk, which in the course of a short time brought him to the turning, and there, still keeping in the shade of the bush, he crossed the paddocks which intervened between the road and the homestead.

As he neared the hut, the moon broke forth from behind a cloud, and whilst it rendered his steps more cautious, it revealed to him the extern appearance of the place.

It was a long, low, ramshackle wooden building, or rather pile of buildings, most of which were in a ruinous state. Some roofless, some doorless, and all leaning and propped up by slabs and saplings, without the support of which they appeared ready to fall to pieces.

One portion, however—the one nearest to him—seemed to be patched up at different times, and with different materials, varying from pieces of bark and tin, to portions of old gin cases and fencing, from the nearest stockyard.

The whole place seemed the very impersonation of neglect and desolation, and, but that the doors and windows seemed securely barred or otherwise fastened, there was no sign of its being a human habitation at all.

Carefully and noiselessly, for fear of disturbing some sleeping dog, the detective crept up to the gable of the house.

Not a sound, save the slight rustle of the night wind through the gum-trees.

Not a sign of life.

He went round to the back.

There was a dilapidated kitchen, with an open door, containing nothing but an empty fire-place, and one or two rude cooking utensils.

He placed his hand upon the hearth.

It was stone cold, and even damp, and the camp oven upon the hob was red with rust.

In finding this out, he disturbed something, which fell with a clang upon the bars of the fire-place.

He held his breath and listened.

Not a sound—not the cluck of a fowl, not the bark of a cur.

Was, then, the place deserted?

Hush! Mingled with the sound of horses' hoofs coming up the road, where the old dray tracks had left the earth harder than in the surrounding paddocks, he heard voices in converse, and in an instant had darted out of the house, and into an old ruined woodshed, the slab walls of which swayed to and fro with every breath of wind.

He had only just reached it in time, for a moment afterwards the two men whom he had left at the inn rode up, and, rendered pot-valiant by the liquor they had taken, dismounted, and fastening their horses to a fence, knocked boldly at the door.

There was no reply, and with a loud curse, one of them began to kick lustily at it.

Still no reply.

The echo of the blows rang hollowly through the house, that was all.

"Well," at last ejaculated Bob Loveridge, "if this isn't the rummest go I ever cum across, may I be cussed! The very devil's own luck I should call it. First Jacky Cain's not at home, then I lose my horse, next my girths break, and I get rolled in the road, and now to cap all with there's this old fool not to be found. What the devil is to be done, Jack?"

"I know what I shall do," replied Last. "I shall break into this place, and find summat to ate and drink, and then I shall have a good sleep, for I'm dead bate wid the cowld."

Bob agreed with this proposition, the more so as he too was tired, and thoroughly disgusted with the series of disappointments and misfortunes which had happened to them; but suggested that they should try to find some hay or corn for their horses, which were nearly knocked up.

On searching the entire of the outer premises, however, they could find neither one nor the other, save a few handfuls of mouldy straw, which they well knew their horses would not touch.

They had therefore no alternative but to take off their saddles and bridles, and turn them loose into a paddock, where there was however plenty of grass, so that the poor animals had the chance of refreshing themselves after their day's work, a privilege which was denied to their masters, for after bestowing considerable trouble in forcing an entrance—a feat which was only accomplished by forcing the back door down off its hinges, their search proved entirely fruitless, for beyond a heap of potatoes in a corner, and few pieces of broken and mouldy damper, they could find not a single thing to eat.

Their search had nearly, however, led them to discover more than they had calculated on finding, for after rummaging the kitchen, Jack Last turned into the very woodshed where Ted Hogan lay concealed under a sheet of bark.

He looked round, but seeing nothing in the eatable line, turned away swearing at their ill fortune.

They, however, succeeded better in the matter of sleeping, for finding a heap of blankets, and a couple of possum rugs, they lighted a fire in one of the rooms, and wrapping themselves warmly up, soon fell into a profound slumber.

CHAPTER XXXIV.
THE SEARCH—THE WOOLLEN GLOVE.

TED HOGAN lay still for a few minutes after Jack Last had left the woodshed, and until all appeared quiet inside, and then, slowly and cautiously raising himself up, he breathed feebly, and whispered to himself—

"By George! a near squeak that. A little more light, and my game would have been spoiled."

He was, however, puzzled how to act.

He had determined that he would not devote any attention to the two bushrangers further than such as might assist him in his investigations, but they appeared to be thrown into his power at every turn.

Now he had them safe, unarmed and asleep, and it almost seemed like throwing a chance away not to avail himself of the opportunity of effecting their capture.

A smile of grim humour flitted over his face as he thought of the astonishment which would be depicted in their countenances if he should saddle their horses, ride over to the inn, make known who he was, bring back with him one of the bushmen, and wake them by informing them that they were his prisoners.

Then he thought how he would like to capture them both, single-handed as he was, and he pictured himself creeping into the room cautiously and noiselessly as a ghost, handcuffing them together as they slept, and allowing them to have their sleep out, and then to awake to find him standing over them with a loaded revolve and themselves completely helpless at his feet.

It would be a glorious thing for him to do and he could not resist the temptation to try it.

"I'll give them a fright," he chuckled. "A sort of foretaste, at all events, of what will happen to them. Perhaps," he added, grimly, "it will serve as a warning to turn them from the evil of their ways."

He cautiously struck a match, lit a candle, and stuck it in a convenient corner, and then shuffled noisily with his feet amongst the litter on the ground.

The sleeping bushrangers started.

The dream that haunts the slumbers of all such criminals was realised—they were tracked down!

They knew Ted Hogan, and they knew that to move would be the signal for his finger to close on the trigger of the revolver, and hurl them both into eternity.

The detective only stayed to note, with a grim smile, the look of terror on their white faces, and then, swift as thought, he blew out the candle, and then slipped out of the hut.

"Ha! ha!" he chuckled, silently, "they'll think they've seen a ghost, for no one ever knew Ted Hogan to loose a prisoner once he had him within reach of his revolver. What a fright the fools will be in."

And indeed they were.

The sudden appearance and disappearance of the detective had led them to doubt the evidence of their senses, and after a half-sleepy, half-surly discussion, they guessed that it must have been a dream, and so growled themselves to sleep again, leaving Ted Hogan to wonder whether he had done a foolish thing in letting the two men go free.

But no, he had other and more serious work to do than the capture of a brace of embryo bushrangers, or, at any rate, so he looked at it in a professional point of view.

To him it was left to solve the mystery of the disappearance of the hawker, and all other things must be subservient to that.

He concluded, therefore, that, having found out the hut, he would keep an eye on it until the owner, whom he doubted not would return in a day or so, came back, in the meantime taking up his quarters at the Cornstalk, and endeavouring, in the character of a swagman on the spree, to pick up such information as might finally lead to the development of the mystery.

In the meantime, the scoundrels who were sleeping in the house might escape for the present, as knowing their haunts, he had no fear of being able to lay his hands upon them if ever he wanted them, and he determined that if he brought his present search to a successful termination, they should receive his next delicate attention.

Rolling his blankets, which he had hidden outside when he approached the house, round him, he cautiously and silently started on his journey back to the inn, intending to reach there by daybreak, and to take a good long sleep on his bed of hay in the stable.

Cautiously picking his steps past the gable of the house, he suddenly started, ejaculated a muttered oath, and catching at a slab which supported the end of the hut, the blood flushed into his face and he staggered as if about to fall, and then he blanched white—white as a corpse—and the big beads of sweat stood out thickly upon his pallid brow.

What was it that caused him to stop, to gaze, to stoop and pick up some article as if he had found a treasure, and to hurry back past the kitchen, into the scrub, as if he were fearful that someone might snatch it from him?

What was it that caused him to sit hidden in the bush, and, wrapped in his blanket, hour after hour anxiously waiting and watching, watching and waiting, for those laggard bushrangers to depart, and ever and anon to take forth his prize, and gazing upon it with a stern, sad, abstracted air, to return it into an inner pocket with a sigh of relief?

And when at last they did awake, and, so slowly as appeared to him, saddled their horses and rode off, what was it that caused him to go to the hut and commence to search with a scrutiny as if he were searching for hidden gold?

What had he seen?

By the slanting gable, there, in the full, broad moonlight, what had caused his heart to knock at his ribs, and the cheek of the strong-nerved and ready-witted detective to turn ashen pale as that of a schoolboy seeing something move in the churchyard after dark?

What?

Only an old woollen glove!

CHAPTER XXXV.

WHAT THE DETECTIVE SAW IN THE GLOVE.

IT was only a common woollen glove, such an one as there were plenty of others like in every store in the country.

It had been trodden under foot in the mud and dirt, and had been rained on until there was left no appearance of any distinctive hue, if it had ever possessed such, and altogether it presented the appearance of a highly dirty and exceedingly disreputable member of the glove family.

It could not possibly, then, possess any appearance by which it might be identified, unless, indeed, it were that its late wearer were so notorious for his filthy habits, that its very dirtiness was its peculiarity.

Stop though.

That shrewd and astute officer would not treasure it up as such a prize if there was not something more about it than appears at first sight.

Let us look over his shoulder as he takes it out of his breast pocket for the twentieth time, and scans it so narrowly that one would almost imagine he was reading a curious tale written in its very web, and let us examine it a little more closely.

We see that it is a left hand glove, worth, say, a farthing, and that it is much worn inside the fingers as if through carrying a stick.

Well, so far it might suit the character of a hawker's glove, which, we doubt not, he is mentally trying to make it out to be.

So far, so good; but so as well it might suit fifty other persons of totally different callings.

So it might.

Ah! but look here!

You perceive that the ends of all the fingers save one are frayed and have holes worn in them.

The one that has not is the third, and you may observe that from where the second joint of that finger might be supposed to come, to the finger of the glove, is flat and unstretched, as though it had never been worn.

Well, that is something, certainly; for it will be remembered that Hogan was told at the detective office in Sydney that the pedlar, the mystery of whose fate he was to unravel, had lost that identical finger of his left hand.

And so, having found this one link, Ted had gone to work, and had searched the whole of the house from cellar to ceiling, inch by inch, slowly, patiently, unweariedly, but he had found nothing—that is, nothing more.

But that did not matter.

He had one piece of evidence which, to him, at first (not afterwards), appeared almost conclusive.

That is to say, arguing from the point that the glove had at one time belonged to the hawker which, by the way, as Ted *afterwards* saw clearly enough, was taking a good deal for granted, notwithstanding his having been known to have disappeared in the district.

Well, then, the glove being, or having been, the hawker's, that is to say, if it had been the hawker's, it was not likely, in the first place, that he would have sold it to anyone on the place, as it had evidently seen some service, and had been the worse for wear for a considerable time.

Then, again, it was not at all probable that so careful a man as the Scotch hawker was known to have been would have left it behind; and, finally, as it was not worth stealing, why you see the detective, by thus taking a very wide stride of imagination, came to the conclusion, not that the hawker had been murdered there, but that he simply might have been.

But by whom? and for what? and if so——

Where was the body?

Where were the proofs?

Ah, all that in good time.

That is the difficulty!

That is what we have to find out.

One thing at a time.

What comes first.

The body!

No; let us first find evidence of the crime!

Thus, then, to the search.

Such a search as shall leave no place unexamined—shall leave no place disturbed—shall leave no mark or signal to arouse the suspicions of the guilty victim, around whom the subtle and imperceptible, yet powerful, net of circumstantial evidence is fast closing.

Such a search was consummated, but nothing further was discovered that would throw any additional light upon the matter.

Day after day was the examination proceeded with, the detective leaving not a place unsearched where, by any possibility, any evidence of the crime might be hidden, not only in the house, but in the stable and the other outhouses connected with the building, and even in the bush adjoining.

He took long walks in the locality, and yet, by some fatality, missed the old well, supposed to be dry, which lay in a neglected spot at some distance beyond the stockyard belonging to the hut, which was situated about two hundred yards away.

Rightly judging from the continued absence of both, that the journey taken by Billy-the-Bull had something to do with that which had taken Jacky Cain also from home, he, after satisfying himself with his search at the hut of the former, took up his residence at the Cornstalk again, in his old character of a swagman, accounting for his absence by saying that he had been higher up the river looking for a job, and had been unable to get one; and stating his intention of waiting until something turned up, or, at all events, until he had "blued" his money, a proceeding which the landlady seemed no way averse to, but relaxed her grim features into something as nearly approaching a gracious smile as they were capable of expressing, telling him—

"He had better stay until Jacky came home, as he would be able, no doubt, to tell him where he would be most likely to obtain work."

But in the meantime, and whilst Ted Hogan was waiting somewhat impatiently at the Cornstalk for the appearance of the landlord, and as he thought for at the same time the coming of the old man he so much wished to see, Billy had, by coming down the road along the river, and thus avoiding the inn, got safely home.

But he had been somewhat startled at finding the backroom door forced off the hinges, and had made a closer examination, in order to discover who it was that had visited the house in his absence.

But finding nothing beyond the signs of a person having slept there, he concluded that it had been some way-farers, who, seeing the place empty, had concluded it deserted, and had so forced their way in for shelter during the night.

He therefore resumed possession of his tenement, and took a walk over the ranges to a hut where a man who looked after the stock he had on that run lived, and with whom he had left his few household utensils when he went away.

What, then, was the surprise of the detective, when one day, thinking that he would go down to the house and see that all was right, he leisurely strolled up to it, and found that the windows were open, and that there was a smouldering fire in the kitchen, and other signs of life about the place.

He quietly and noiselessly walked on into the bush, and concealing himself behind a clump of tea tree, waited for the appearance of someone.

Nor had he to wait long, for presently, leading a horse laden with half a sack of flour, a quantity of potatoes, and other things, an old man, whom he at once concluded to be the master of the house from the description of him he had from time to time received, with an air of indifference and unconcern, at the inn up the avenue.

The detective, with all his readiness and power of adaption to circumstances, was rather taken aback at this.

It was evident from the signs about the place that the old man had been at home before, and still the innkeeper had not returned, neither had there been any intelligence from him, and he must either give up the idea upon which he had been working, namely, that the absence of one was connected in some way with that of the other, or find out the object of the journey, and what had become of Jacky Cain.

After some reflection, he determined on his course of action, and skirting the bush, made his way back to the inn, where, telling the landlady that he had heard of a job at a distance, he paid his bill and took his departure the following day, in his assumed character of a swagman.

When he arrived at the house of Billy-the-Bull, he found things pretty much the same as they had been the previous day.

Walking boldly up to the door, he knocked, and the next moment confronted Billy himself, who came to see who was there.

With all his look of cunning and hardened assurance, the old man looked slightly perturbed; but the open and innocent face of his visitor reassured him, and in a querulous tone he asked him what he wanted.

The detective, or rather the swagman, for he looked the character to the life, with an affectation of a foolish simper, replied that, "he was a cove in want of a job, and thought he'd call and see if he could give him one, or tell him where one was to be had, as he must know what was going on in the neighbourhood."

The old man replied that he had no work for him, nor did he know of any, and appeared inclined to shut the door in his face, but the swagman asking him to allow him to boil his pot of tea upon the fire, he, after a minute's consideration, consented, and gruffly bade him come in.

The swagman did as he was bidden, after leaving his blankets at the door, and placing his billy upon the fire, he sat down to wait for its boiling, and for the old man to speak.

He did so at last.

"Which way have you come?" asked he.

"Up from Nowra way," was the reply. "I stopped last night at the public house on the hill above, the Cornstalk I think it is—and talking of that, they say the master's been a missing from there, this last fortnight or more."

The old man moved about uneasily, and in a husky voice, replied by the monosyllable, "Ah!"

"Yes," resumed the swagman following up his lead, "the missis is getting quite uneasy, and can't tell what to think on it. She says as she hopes as he ain't bin and got lost in the bush, nor murdered like the hawker."

This last was a chance shot, and one which was made more on impulse than with a purpose, but it told with immense effect.

The old man's face, or such of it as the swagman could see, looking as he was out of the corners of his eyes, became for a moment perfectly livid, and his knees trembled under him; but, recovering himself in an instant, and seeing the swagman's back turned towards him, and that individual to all appearance intently watching the tin pot on the fire, he forced a short laugh, and said—

"That's a comical idea, that is, mate. Who does she suppose would murder her husband, and what for?"

"There, now master, that's just what I said to her," said the swagman, turning round upon the old man with a beaming smile of confidence, and following up the hit he had made. "Them there's the very words as I said to her myself this blessed morning as ever was. Says I to her, says I, 'Missis,' says I, 'what's the use o' going on like that there? Who could have murdered him, and what for? He didn't take away much money with him, did he?' says I. 'None to speak on,' says she. 'Very well then,' says I, 'who do you think would go for to be such a fool as to do that, 'cos we very well knows' says I, 'as sooner or later murder's sure to be found out, because you know it allus was.'"

The last few words constituted another well-directed shot, but the old man was not be hit twice in the same place, and although he perceptibly winced, a fact that the swagman did not fail to notice, he gave no further sign of inquietude, but bidding him look sharp and get his breakfast over, he left him to his own company and went out of the room.

CHAPTER XXXVI.
BILLY-THE-BULL'S WHITE HAT.

LEFT alone, the expression of the face of the detective underwent a complete metamorphosis, and to the open and half-foolish look of the swagman, succeeded the stern and thoughtful aspect which he had worn after finding of the glove.

He was considerably puzzled, as the possibility of another murder having been committed by the old man had never presented itself to his imagination before, and although he had guessed correctly enough that the absence of the two partners had something in common, he had never doubted but that when the one returned, the other would not be far behind.

From the effect which followed the few words which he had, however, let drop, more without meaning than otherwise, his suspicions were aroused that the murder of the hawker was not the only piece of villany of which the old man was guilty, and that on the eve of the discovery of one crime he had stepped upon the threshold of the finding out of another, not less atrocious in its nature than the former.

Little did he guess, however, that he was on the portal of discovering yet a third, that would interest him far more deeply than the others, and enable him yet to keep a terrible oath, made in a moment of anguish, oh, ever so many years ago.

He had not recognised the once terrible and formidable Blue Cap, the murderer of his brother, in Billy-the-Bull, and it was no wonder—so changed in aspect was that individual by an habitual indulgence in ardent spirits, more than by increasing years. But the time was to come for all that.

The more he speculated upon matters, the more

he became impressed with the notion that Jacky Cain would never return home, and that Billy-the-Bull knew the reason why.

But to find a motive.

It could scarcely be avarice, for although that was one of the old man's vices, so he had learnt, yet the temptation was surely not sufficient.

What then could it be? Perhaps revenge!

He would find it out in time, if possible.

He quietly revolved the matter in his mind, as he sat drinking his tea before the fire, and having again assumed the vacant look of the swagman, he waited the reappearance of his host.

Billy came in at length with a morose expression upon his countenance, and crossly bade him "look sharp and get his breakfast done, and be off, for he didn't want him to be stuck there all day long."

"All right, master," was the reply of the swagman. "I'm off in a minute. So you really can't give a fellow a job, eh?"

"No, I can't," was the surly answer.

"May be it might be worth your while," urged the swagman. "This old place o' yours wants a bit o' patching up, and I'm a bit of a carpenter myself. There's that door there now as has tumbled off o' the hinges. I'd put you that to rights in an hour, and charge you nothin' for the job, except, it may be, a feed or so."

Billy sadly wanted the stranger to go, yet still this was a chance that he did not like to miss.

As he had said, the old place was sadly out of repair, and a carpenter was a godsend in that part of the bush.

The temptation was enhanced too by the cheap rate at which the swagman had offered to work, and by the reflection that it would not take him long to fix up a few things which were needed; so that, after his habitual caution had had a struggle with his avarice and the latter had prevailed, he concluded to have the work done, and intimated as much to the swagman, telling him at the same time that he must be long about it, for if he were, he would not have it done at all.

"No fear, master," was the reply; "get me a few nails and a hammer, and I'll soon have that job jobbed."

Billy got him what he desired, and would then have left him to do his work by himself, but the swagman found it necessary to have someone to hold the door whilst he put a bar across it, and fastened on the hinges, and then to hold it in its place whilst he set it up, and to do so many little odd things, that he did not get a chance to leave for a moment.

And then the swagman was such a companionable fellow, and told such funny little yarns, and sung so many snatches of odd songs whilst he was at work, that once or twice the old man relaxed the cross expression of his facial muscles, and allowed himself to be betrayed into a grim smile, and at last suffered himself to be drawn into conversation, although his remarks were short and snappish.

The swagman was not to be deterred from talking by this, but kept up a brisk conversation, in which he took by far the greater part, trying the old man every now and then with a question which, although apparently quite innocent in itself, might lead him to speak of circumstances that might give an idea as to where he had been lately.

He was not, however, to be caught, and gave few but monosyllabic answers.

"When I was down in Sydney," said the swagman, "I remember a comical thing as happened to a friend o' mine. He was a knowing cove too, was Bill. Bill the Cockney we used to call him.

"Well, he'd just come down from the town, where he had made a decent pile, and he met some fly chaps in a public-house in Pitt Street, so nothing would do but they must have a throw of the dice.

"Bill could see that he had got into a nice school,

but he thought he was quite knowing enough for them.

"Howsomever he couldn't make headway nohow, he kept on losin' and losin', and couldn't see how it was done for all his sharpness, not a bit of it.

"At last, however, one of the chaps bungled it, and then Bill see it in an instant.

"By this time, he had lost about thirty pounds, and the coves—three on 'em—was still winning.

"Well, he never says a word, but he hauls all the money as he had, about another fifty pounds, out of his pocket, and down he slaps it, just like a man as was getting to play desperate.

"No sooner was it covered, three to one it was too, than he draws back, and lets out with his left, knocking the fellah as had just thrown down on his back in a corner o' the room among the cheers, and with his right up he grabs the bank notes as lay on the table.

"'Now,' says he, "'the whole three on you, come on here, and I'll teach you to try it on with me.'

"When the chaps seen as it was no go, and that he'd bowled 'em out, they wanted him to give 'em back all the money, only what he had lost, but 'No,' says he, 'if you wants it, why fetch a policeman.'

"They didn't see that though, and at last they went away, looking very sheepish indeed.

"Well, Bill he comes to me in great joy, telling me what wonderful things he had done, and how he'd bowled out the sharpers, and made about a hundred pounds by it, so the first thing he shows me was the dodge.

"It was uncommon simple, to be sure. There was a little slide in the side of the box, so that the thrower could force it up with his thumb, and see the dice inside.

"Then we looks at the notes, and with the exception of what he had put down himself, blow me if it worn't all flash money.

"So, uncommon blue as Bill looked to be sure, Gad, I couldn't help but laugh at his long phiz. Whenever we used to want to take a rise out o' Bill arter that, we only had to ax him if he'd seed any more card sharps, and he get as mad as a hatter.

"Yes, a funny place is Sydney. I always stops at the Blue Pig myself, in Parramatta Street. Do you know the Blue Pig, master?"

"No," was the reply. "I've never been to Sydney."

"Never been to Sydney!" said the swagman with affected astonishment; "well that is queer."

"Never for the last ten years or so, I mean."

"Ah! that was before my time," said the swagman, and finding that he had gained nothing by his question, he changed the subject, and the door being finished, asked what was the next job?

The old man hesitated for a moment, and then asked him whether he would put a lock on a door.

"A lock! Of course he could—half a dozen of 'em if necessary."

"Come along here then, and put this on," said Billy, taking a new lock out of a cupboard, and leading the way to another room, evidently the old man's bedroom, on the door of which he directed him to fasten it.

The swagman looked hurriedly round the room as he entered, but, save that the bedding which he had last seen in the other room had been moved into it, it presented the same appearance as it had done on his previous search.

He, however, saw hanging up on a nail near the bed, a bran new hat as it appeared, and requesting the old man to get him a chisel, in order to adapt the door to the lock, he took advantage of his momentary absence, to examine it.

The hat was a common felt one, but the swagman looking inside said to himself with a low chuckle, and a transient smile of satisfaction—

"Oh the old fox you've not been to Sydney this

ten years, haven't you. We'll see that by-and-by."

He had scarcely time to replace the hat in its original position, and to get back to the door, before the old man returned, but when he did so he found him absently playing with the lock.

"Come, look sharp," said he, "and get this job finished; I'm not going to have you here all day."

"All right, master," was the reply, "I'll have the lock on in no time," and setting to work, he had it fitted in a space of time, that even the old man could find no possible fault with.

The two then went into the other room, and the old man producing a lump of corned beef and a damper, set the swagman to make tea, whilst he laid the table, a proceeding which did not take up much time, as it consisted merely in laying a couple of plates and tin pannikins, and the same number of knives.

When all was ready Billy-the-Bull bade his guest turn to, and the pair made a hearty meal of the rough fare before them.

At its conclusion the swagman, picking up his blankets, bade his entertainer good day, thanking him for the job he had given him, and saying as he crossed the threshold—

"May be I'll be travelling this way again, one o' these days, and then if you want any more locks putting on, or anything, I'll be very glad to do it for you, master."

Words that, had Billy-the-Bull known the deep significance of, would have made him wish to see any person in the world, rather than the insignificant and foolish looking little swagman.

CHAPTER XXXVII.
THE BACKWARD TRAIL.

IF you want to feel all the discomforts of an Australian summer, without any of its concomitant and redeeming comforts and enjoyments, its glare which makes your eyes ache, its intolerable heat which makes your head ache, the feeling of lassitude which makes your limbs ache, and induces a general despondency which makes your head ache.

If you want to feel an atmosphere that appears positively to bake you, a dusty, sandy wind that blows from every point of the compass at once, and which renders the immaculate white shirt collar, which you put on in the morning, a mass of perspiration and grime.

If you want your skin to look as if you had not washed for a week, and to feel an intolerable itchiness and flabbiness, and to be half devoured by thousands of ferocious flies that follow and torment you beyond endurance.

If you want all this, and without a single redeeming feature, just take a walk along that part of George Street, Sydney, known as Brickfield Hill, on a hot wind day.

A hot wind in Australia is a very serious matter.

It penetrates into every pore of your skin, conveying dust and discomfort wherever it touches.

And where does it not touch?

Shut yourself up within doors, fasten every crevice and every opening, and it shall find you.

Like a Scotch mist, it pervades every place.

But in the bush, although you may be scorched by it, you can, unless you are in a very bad country, out of which every man keeps, unless indeed he cannot help it—in the bush, I say, you come across an occasional creek, where you can lie down under the golden wattles, and whilst smoking your pipe, go into a half doze to the music of the cicadas or colonial locusts, that abound overhead.

Or if you are at the other end of Sydney, you can, by stepping down to the Circular Quay or Wooloomooloo Pier, take a boat, and on the bosom of the most beautiful harbour in the world can enjoy the soft cool breeze that comes stealing over the surface of the bright blue water, kissing the ripples that glitter in the sunbeams like mimic waves of molten gold.

But in the midst of Brickfield Hill there is no hope.

Nothing, but either by a superhuman effort to defy the hot wind, and the sand, and the flies, to do individually and collectively their worst; or to plunge headlong into the body of a stuffy and grimy bus, and seek the pleasant, albeit somewhat dusty, fields of Newtown or the Glebe.

But for a man who has business to do on a hot wind day, upon Brickfield Hill, let us compassionately sigh, "Poor fellow!" and pity him.

Such might have been the reflections of Detective Hogan, as, three days after he left Blue Cap's retreat among the Shoalhaven Ranges, he slowly strolled down the part of George Street South referred to, and 'phewed' and sighed, and wiped the beaded drops from his melting brow.

He was a swagman no longer, but, in a neat suit of dark grey, he has assumed the character and appearance of a well to do farmer, or a station superintendent.

We notice one thing, however, namely that his hat is considerably the worse for wear, and judging from the speculative manner in which he looks into the windows of the various shops as he passes them, we should think that he was about to exchange it for a new one.

So it would appear, for stopping before a window in which a goodly array of hats and caps of all kinds and descriptions are placed, he gazes for some time with an abstracted air, until the proprietor—who has been dreamily lying on the counter, wondering whether anybody in the world were fool enough even to come out to buy anything on a day like that, and whether he had not better go for a sail or a swim, or to lie under the trees in the domain or anywhere else out of that sweltering shop—suddenly awakens to the surprising fact that a man looking very like a customer is standing outside and looking in at his window.

He goes to the door, smoking part of the profits, for he is in the tobacco and cigar line as well, and courteously invites the stranger in.

"Do you want anything in my way to-day, sir?"

"Have you got any hats like this?" is the reply of the would-be purchaser, at the same time pointing to the dilapidated wide-awake on his head.

The proprietor looks as if he would like to ask his customer if he called that thing a hat, but the day is too hot for much talking, so he signifies assent, and reaches down a dozen or so.

The customer is hard to be suited, but mentions that a friend of his, an elderly gent, bought a hat from that very place about a week ago, and he wants one exactly like it.

The proprietor does not remember the old gentleman, but will call his boy.

The boy remembers the old gent from the description given him, remembers, too, that they had not a hat that would fit him, and that they had to send one into the workshop to get it altered.

Indeed! then the customer will take one that he picks out, and have that altered to fit him.

So he goes out at the back, and seeing a little square room built up of sheets of corrugated iron, puts his head in, and asks pleasantly—

"Is this the workshop?"

"Yes," says a young man, lightly clad in a paper cap, a pair of thin cotton trousers and an under shirt, which, as it is his only upper garment, is on this occasion not an under shirt at all, and who is wielding a large flat iron, nearly red hot—"yes, this is the workshop; come in."

Despite the heat, which, like the fiery furnace, is ten times hotter than before, for, regardless of the broiling sun, and the baking wind outside, a fierce fire burns in a flat-topped stove at the end of the room, he steps in and explains what he wants, particularly impressing the young man with the fact that he wants it done just like his friend's was done, the old gent as was there a week ago.

The young man remembers the circumstance very well, and will attend to it; "will he wait?"

"Oh, yes, I'll wait; but my word, isn't it hot here?"

"Well, yes, it is warm," says the young man, and Jim his mate, working in the corner, asseverates that "it's as hot as fire."

The customer hazards a conjective that "a drop o' good beer, if it was good, would do nobody no harm on a day like that."

The young man shuts one eye, and looks scientifically along the leaf of the hat, as he "guesses it wouldn't," and Jim in the corner sighs, as he piteously wipes the beads of perspiration from his forehead, with the corner of his apron.

"Then we'll have some," says the customer, and forthwith the boy Tommy is summoned, and despatched to the Australia Felix Hotel, where the young man affirms "there's as good a drop of ale to be had as any in Sydney."

By-and-by the beer is discussed, and the liberal customer begins to talk again about his elderly friend.

The young man is communicative, and remembers what a hurry his friend was in. "He wouldn't wait for his hat, but had it sent home."

"Sent home, eh?" says the customer; "ah that's just like him. He did tell me where he stopped, and recommended me to stay there too, but I've forgot the place. How lucky I came in here."

The young man agrees that it is lucky, and so it is so far as the beer is concerned, and Tommy is again summoned to tell him where he had taken the hat for the old gent the week before, and Tommy's memory happens to be good.

The job being by this time finished, the purchaser mounted his new hat, throwing the old one ignominiously into a corner, and marched out of the shop, into the hot wind again.

CHAPTER XXXVIII.

AN INN IN THE BACK SLUMS.

HOGAN made straight for the address the boy had given him, that of a low pothouse in one of the narrow streets or lanes, off the lower end of George Street, near the wharves, and on arriving there, stepped quietly in, and with a significant look at the landlord, who stood behind the bar serving what is familiarly termed "stringy-bark,"* to a set of blackguardly looking men and women, he called for a nobbler of gin.

"Jack," said he in a whisper over the counter whilst the landlord was serving him, "I want a minute's talk with you."

Jack assented with a look, and calling his wife into the bar, stepped out of a side door, the detective following him in a few seconds.

"Jack," said the latter, when they were alone, "you had an old cove stopping here a week since, that I want to know something about."

Jack, with a cunning leer, protested that "there hadn't been no old coves a stoppin' there, leastways not as he recollected."

"Look here," said the detective, "you had better try to recollect, because I'll have it out of you one way or another, and if you don't like to tell me freely and fairly, I'll find a sure way to make you open your mouth, never fear."

The landlord thereupon assumed a bullying tone, and surlily said that "he knowed nothing about it; it was no business of his, and he didn't meddle nor make in nobody's business but his own."

"Listen to me, Jack Smith, and then please yourself. You know me, and you know that what I say I'll do, or if you don't know it you ought to.

I don't want to do you any harm, but suppose this old cove has been playing a game that will bring his neck into a hempen necklace, and suppose I find out that he's been hiding in your house, and that you refuse to give information concerning him, that would place you in queer street, wouldn't it?"

Jack admitted that he hadn't looked at it in that light, and in a considerably less assured tone, asked—

"What is it, then, the old 'un is wanted for?"

"Never you mind that," was the reply; "maybe he's a friend of yours, and I don't like back-biting, you know, or saying anything that's painful."

Jack declared with a fearful oath that he never saw the old man before, that he knew nothing about him—neither where he came from, nor where he had gone to; but that if it was anything serious, dared say he could direct the detective where or from whom to inquire, only his name must not be mentioned in the matter.

"I believe you, Jack, and will take your word," said Hogan, after a moment's pause. "The old man is wanted for murder—no less. You may stare, but it's true. Now you can please yourself whether you tell me anything or not; but I'll bowl him out some way, never fear."

"Murder, is it?" said the landlord, with a frightened look. "Oh, that's a different affair altogether. I'd no idea it was such a serious charge as that, or you know very well I wouldn't have hesitated a moment, Mr. Hogan, because——"

"None of your palaver, Jack Smith," was the interrupting retort; "and now you take a fool's advice, that the less you say about this matter the better for yourself, you understand?"

Jack, completely cowed, said that he understood that well enough, and promised not to say a word about the business the detective was on, at the same time telling him that during the time the old man had been staying at his place, he had talked very little, and had certainly said nothing about his goings or comings. That a parcel had come for him from a shop down Brickfield Hill, he forgot which, and that he had spent much of his time with a woman who lived in a narrow back lane on Gallow's Hill, and who could perhaps tell him more if she was so inclined.

"Inclined!" said the detective, with a short, dry laugh. "Who is the woman?"

"Nell Brown. You know her," was the reply; "but mind, she's a regular tiger when she's roused."

"Pshaw, Jack, you don't know how to deal with women. I'm not afraid of her sort, anyway. It's well for you that you've told me the whole truth, old fellow; for I know you have, by a way of my own. And I know where that parcel came from too, and what was in it. And now let me again advise you to keep your mouth shut."

"Close as a rat trap, Mr. Hogan," said the landlord, as closing his lips he smacked them with his open palm, thus signifying that whatever was inside that, stayed there, "and now come and take a ball* at my expense."

The detective, who had reasons for keeping friendly with this man, as with others of his class, so long as it suited his purpose, followed him, and having drunk his small modicum of gin, with a knowing glance at the landlord, bade him good day, and walked out unconcernedly, leaving him standing gazing after him admiringly.

"Who's that cove, Mr. Smith?" asked one of the ragamuffins at the bar. "He's a cool card, he is; I wonder what he's up to; no good I should say."

The landlord informed the questioner, with a string of oaths, that the "cove in question was a friend of his, and that he, the questioner, had better mind hisself and not be shoving in his jaw where it wasn't wanted—leastways if he didn't want

---

* Colonial ale.

shoving outside the bar door into the street, he had."

To which the curious and observant one, having spent all his money, and being trusted to the extent of another pint of "stringy," replied in all humility that "he hoped no offence," and "that if he'd knowed," etc., etc.

CHAPTER XXXIX.

NELL BROWN'S BOWER ON GALLOWS HILL.

IN the meantime Ted Hogan, proceeding up the narrow street in which the tavern was situated, and then up another almost as steep as a house roof, turned at last into a dirty lane, or rather blind alley, which consisted of two rows of ricketty looking brick houses, of three stories in height.

It needed but a glance to tell him that he was in a very hotbed of vice and crime, a very den of Cacus.

The pavement of the alley was broken and rugged, with a stagnant pool of foetid and miasmic water in the centre.

The houses themselves were in the very last stage of shabbiness and disrepair, the windows were broken and stuffed with dirty rags, or left for the foul and pestiferous wind to have free ingress and egress.

Every door was open, and at most of them was a group of dirty, frowsy women, and two or three men of various ages, all engaged in loud slangy and blasphemous conversation with their neighbours; and standing by, listening with deferential admiration, or playing in the filth of the gutter, were about twenty children, girls and boys, dirty, ragged, and vicious the veriest scum of the city.

But the entrance of the detective into the court treated as much consternation amongst the noisy denizens thereof as the throwing of a stone into a frog pond does amongst its inhabitants.

The moment his face was recognised, the loungers at the doors, or at least the male portion of them—the thieves, the pickpockets, the housebreakers and magsmen of the city—slunk away and disappeared incontinently.

All but one, who, having made a haul the night before, was of course in a state of semi-drunkenness.

He came staggering up the yard, pot-valiantly exclaiming—

"Ah! Hogan, my prince of traps, how are you? Give me your flipper, old fellow."

He was followed by a youngish woman, who in vain tried to induce him to turn back, but he doubled his fist, and struck her in the face.

The detective took no notice of this cowardly act until he came close up, when he suddenly launched out the blow that had so astonished the bushmen at the Cornstalk Inn, and, before he knew where he was, the drunken bully lay on his back in the midst of the putrid pool in the middle of the court.

The detective then turned round to the woman, who stood silently wiping the tears and blood from her face, and he said to her not unkindly—

"Polly, my girl, I would have taken up with a man, at any rate, and not with a thing like that. Let him lie there; it'll do him good."

He was passing on, when she called after him in a trembling voice—

"Mr. Hogan, have you seen poor Fred lately?"

"I saw him the last time I was at Cockatoo,* and he asked after you, Polly."

"Well, give him my love when you see him again," said the girl. "And, I say, Mr. Hogan."

"Eh?" said the detective, waiting for her to speak.

---

* A penal establishment on an island of that name.

"Don't say anything about—him," she petitioned, pointing to the wretch who lay in the gutter.

"All right, Polly, I won't," was the reply; and, crossing the alley, he walked composedly into one of the houses as though it had belonged to him.

Passing down the lobby and up the stairs, he was confronted at the door of one of the rooms by a big, brawny woman of about thirty years of age, with a red face, and a voice husky and rough from the constant use of ardent spirits.

Her features, though coarse and repulsive, were regular in their formation, and showed that at one time she must have been a handsome young woman, before gin and foul disease had wrecked her constitution, and left her a bloated, loud-mouthed wanderer of the midnight streets, steeped in vice and fallen into the very lowest abyss of sin.

This was Nell Brown, the woman of whom the landlord had bade the detective beware.

"Well, Nellie, my beauty," said Hogan to her as he stepped up to the door she guarded. "I've just come to pay you another visit, you see. Why you're looking as handsome as ever, I declare."

"Come, none of your Charley pork with me, Mr. Hogan," she replied, with, however, the gratified smile of vanity on her lips, which even the grossest flattery never fails to excite in the sex.

"Upon my honour and conscience, Nellie, you're a credit to the neighbourhood; and, though that isn't saying much, yet, such as it is, it's true," replied Hogan.

"Ah! you might have said so, if you'd seen me once," she said; "when I was young, and afore I took to the drink."

"You must ha' been a real beauty then, Nell, and no mistake," he answered.

"But come," she said, suddenly altering her tone, "you didn't come here to make love to me, I know that very well. So let us have no more of this gammon. What do you want?"

"I want to talk to you seriously, Nell, about a bit of business; so come, let's go in, and sit down," replied Hogan, moving towards the door.

"You can't go in there," replied the woman in a hoarse and flurried voice, stretching her arm across the door as she spoke.

"I can't, eh? and why not?" asked the detective with a frown, looking her full in the face.

"Well, you can't," she returned, doggedly.

"What, is it because you've got that little whelp, Bill Rogers, in there, that the police are after, about that sailor's watch?" said he, contemptuously. "Lord, if that's all, don't make yourself uneasy. I don't want him. I wouldn't have him at a gift. I guessed well enough where he was; but he's a friend of yours, Nell, and so I said nothing. I didn't want him. If I had, I should have had him; and you know that well enough, Nell Brown."

She looked at him for a moment, as if undecided how to act, and then said, earnestly—

"On your honour, don't you want Bill Rogers?"

"On my sacred honour," he replied.

"Well, then, Mr. Hogan, he is there; but, remember, if you play me false, I'll have my revenge on it, if it's forty years to come."

"Get out of this, you young whelp," was the salutation of the detective, as, conducted by Nell Brown, he entered the room in the dilapidated house in the disreputable lane.

The individual to whom these words were addressed was a mean-looking young man, who sat on a low stool near the chimney, his elbows on his knees, and his head between his hands, looking disconsolately into the empty fireplace, and solacing his loneliness by smoking a short pipe.

He was dressed in a shabby suit of greasy and dirty flash clothing, in which he might, from their appearance, have slept ever since he first inducted his carcase into them.

This hair was long and unkempt, and his face, dirty, greasy, and sallow, had the mark of vice and

TED HOGAN, THE DETECTIVE, GIVES THE BUSHRANGERS A TASTE OF WHAT HE HAS IN STORE FOR THEM.

few cunning legibly imprinted upon it. He had become notorious as one of the cleverest, and most daring of Sydney thieves.

The young fellow, hearing the salutation of the detective, turned round with a start, and seeing who it was that addressed him, darted a fierce glance at the woman, and embellishing his remark with a garland of oaths, said—

"So you've sold me to this infernal trap, you wretch."

"Don't be a fool, Bill," she replied, "and don't cry before you are hurt. The gentleman doesn't want you, or he wouldn't have come in here so quietly."

"Look here, Nelly, my beauty," interrupted the detective; "you are a lady I admire very much, but you've one fault, and that is, not believing what I say. I tell you what I told you before, that if I wanted him, I'd have him, whether you liked it or not; but I don't, and so, you young whelp," he continued, turning round to the young fellow, "get out of this, for Nell and I want to have a little private conversation."

The fellow looked relieved, and after a few whispered words with Nell, walked sullenly out of the room.

"And now, Nelly, my dear, I want to talk to you about an older sweetheart of yours—a very old sweetheart in every sense. That is to say, if you have no objection; and if you have, why, then I shall talk about him just the same, you know."

"Who do you mean?" asked the woman, sharply.

"Whom do I mean?" he replied in a cheery voice, "why whom should I mean, but that venerable old cove who was here about a week ago, spending his money like a prince—that particularly nice, lively, clean old man, you know."

"Bah, the niggardly old wretch! What about him?"

"Oh, nothing—that is, nothing particular, as he is a friend of yours. I shouldn't like to say anything to hurt your feelings, but he's a nice old man for a small tea party, he is."

"He's no friend of mine, and I know nothing of him, nor nothing do I want to know; so if that's all, Mr. Hogan, why you've driven your pigs to quite the wrong market," she replied.

"I don't think so, Nelly, my love—indeed I don't think so," he said. "I don't want to know much—I'm easily satisfied, I am. Lord bless you, I only want to know where he came from last. Surely he told you that?"

"He told me nothing about it, and if he had, I don't know as I should split on him," was the reply.

"What, not if it was made worth your while, my dear?" he said coaxingly. "Come, Nelly, be reasonable; you're not a bad sort, and you and I have always been good friends—you know very well that you might have a worse friend at a pinch than Ted Hogan the D. Now tell me, didn't this old man happen to mention anything about where he'd been, or didn't he happen to give you some little keepsake—some little love token, that you could show me? or didn't he leave something behind him, such as a watch or a purse, or in fact anything else?"

The woman looked irresolute, as she asked—

"What do you want to know for? I must know that before I tell you a single word."

"Nell Brown," said the detective in a whisper, grasping her by the wrist, and looking sternly into her eyes. "No gammon with me. I can see that you are inventing a lie to throw me off the scent; but you had better not try that game on. Now, mark what I say, that old man is guilty of murder, you understand—of murder—ay, of two murders in all probability—and I must and will have him; so you may judge whether I'm in a humour to be played with."

The woman turned ghastly white, and repeated the word "Murder!" staring into the detective's face the while, as though she doubted whether she had heard aright.

"Yes, Nell, of murder," he repeated solemnly. "Now, will you tell me all that you know?"

"Well, Mr. Hogan, I'll do all that I can for you, but you are ——"

She paused, and the detective took up the sentence.

"I see you want me to make it worth your while. Well, that's fair enough. Come, I'll make a bargain with you. There's that young whelp who has just gone outside—he's sure to be nailed sooner or later, clever as he is, and when he is nailed, you may judge from the down that the police have on him that he'll get Cockatoo, as sure as eggs are eggs. Now, when he is nailed, I'll just drop a word in the right place—and you know, my girl, a word from me goes a long way sometimes."

The woman reflected for a minute, and then said—

"I'll trust you, Mr. Hogan, but if you sell me ——"

"There, there, Nelly, that'll do. You trust me, and you'll do well. Sell you! Pooh, nonsense, what should I sell you for? But mind you, don't sell me," and his eyes again resumed their threatening look.

"No fear of that," she replied, and sinking her voice to a whisper, she continued—

"When the old man was here, he only stopped one night. He was a mean old wretch, and his pocketbook, why—I—I—" and she smiled deprecatingly, without finishing the sentence.

"Pinched it, I suppose," said the detective doing it for her. "I won't say quite right, because that wouldn't sound well coming from me, but I don't mind going so far as to say, 'serve him right.' My dear Nell, what next? Go on."

"There was nothing in it worth anything," she went on.

But the detective interrupted her, by remarking derisively, ' 'Oh, of course not. No notes, I suppose? Oh no, certainly not; but yet there might have been a cheque or two, eh?'"

"Not even a cheque," she replied firmly, "but there was this," and going to the cupboard she produced from thence an old, greasy, well-worn pocketbook, which she handed over to the detective, who opened it, and began carefully to examine it.

Whilst he was doing so, a rap came to the door, and the voice of the young man who had been sent out of the room, was heard speaking hurriedly and excitedly—

"Nell," he said, "here's the traps coming down the yard. They're after me, I'm sure."

The woman's eyes blazed with fury, and darting at the detective, she seized him by the collar, ejaculating—

"You infernal wretch, you've sold me!"

"Quietly, Nelly, quietly," he replied, forcing her off by a dexterous twist; "I've done nothing of the sort. Here, you youngster, come in here quick, and get under that bed, and be sure that you lie quiet, and don't sneeze nor cough."

He needed no second bidding, and was but just in time, for hardly had he ensconced himself in his hiding place, when two policeman came rapidly into the room.

"Hallo!" said the foremost of them, surprised at the appearance of the detective. "What are you doing here? I thought you was——"

"Hold your tongue," broke in the detective, "and learn to keep your thoughts to yourself. What do you want here?"

The sergeant, for such he was, took him on one side, and after a short colloquy, called his companion off, quitted the room, and began to search the other part of the house.

"You have had a close squeak of it this time,

my covey," then said the detective in a low voice to the young fellow in hiding; "if I hadn't been here, you'd have been grabbed for certain. You'd better lie still awhile, and make tracks after dark."

"Nelly, my dear," he continued, turning to the woman, "don't be quite so handy with your fists next time, until you are sure it is proper to use them, and don't accuse folks without reason."

She made no reply, and he resumed his examination of the pocket-book.

There were a few unimportant papers, which he, however, carefully put back after reading them, and at last, in one of the pockets, he came across a document, which, the moment he glanced at it, he saw just what he wanted.

"Ho! ho! Mister Billy-the-Bull, I've got you again, have I?" muttered he, carefully reading the papers, which was the account for the sale of the two horses by the auctioneer at Maitland, and which contained their brands and descriptions.

"Nelly, my princess, I'll just keep this pocket-book, and slope as soon as those two fellows up stairs have gone. You keep quiet, say nothing, and if I work out this job right, as I fancy I shall, there's a five-pound note for your information."

The woman promised silence, and began to apologise for her hastiness, but he cut her short by saying—

"Never mind, my beauty; mistakes cannot be avoided occasionally, you know; so go and get me a noggin of gin, and a drop of something for yourself."

She had no sooner brought it, than he tossed it off, and shortly afterwards took his departure.

CHAPTER XL.

THE BLACK HUNTER AND THE WHITE.

THE next morning the detective, after a long night passage o'er a troubled ocean, was in Maitland, and trace by trace, and step by step, day after day followed backward the trail, until it brought him to the inn at Walgett, where, it will be remembered, Blue Cap rested on his downward road, after leaving the cross-country route which he had taken from the Bogan river.

On arriving there, he put up his horse, and walked carelessly into the bar, switching his whip, and calling for a nobbler of gin.

As he stood there sipping his liquor and complimenting the landlady, he suddenly put down his glass, and, walking to the door, satisfied himself by a look at something which caused a grim smile to spread over his face.

Turning round, he said to the landlady—

"How long have you had that blackfellow here?"

"What, Bungy?" she replied, "Oh, I don't know exactly; about two or three weeks I should think."

"Thank you," he replied, "he's an old acquaintance of mine on two occasions. I must go out and have a good yarn with him."

So saying, he quietly left the bar, and the next moment was conversing with the blackfellow.

"Well, Bungy, what are you doing here, eh?"

The blackfellow's eyes rolled in their sockets, and his teeth chattered with terror, for the last time he had seen his interlocutor he was in the native police, and as he had deserted therefrom, he had some fears that the detective had come to arrest him.

"Why, Bungy," said Ted, "you don't seem to be glad to see an old friend. Come in and have a nobbler. I want to have a chat with you."

"By'm-bye me tell you," said the black, in great trepidation.

And he followed the detective into the bar, where, receiving a glass of rum, which was ordered for him, he gulped it down at once, and then said—

"You come along a me, Mas'r Hogan. Me tell it you like it whitefellow."

"What you want to tell me? Why you run away from the police, eh? Well, fire away. Hallo! Bungy, who gave you that flash shirt? What! has somebody been giving you knife?"

"Baal,* him gib it knife a this fella. You come along a me," was the reply.

"Bungy's always muttering about that blessed shirt," said the landlord, from behind the bar. "I'm jiggered if I don't think he's been killing somebody in it, and then taken to wearing of it himself, as a kind o' penance like."

The black's terror now became more unconcealed, and the detective, wondering what it was that he had to impart, but not dreaming of the truth, followed him outside into the yard.

"You know by'm-bye yesterday, plenty week, eh?" asked the blackfellow, as they walked on.

The detective nodded in acquiescence.

"One fella, cobbon old, plenty wrinkle, he come long a grog shop, long two yarraman," said the black, earnestly.

Ted Hogan stopped, stared, and pointed at Bungy, as he asked, eagerly—

"And that shirt? It belonged to the murdered man?"

Then the blackfellow, in the long roundabout manner peculiar to his people, told him the entire story.

How they had found the fire, and traced the body, and how he, wearing the garment the murdered man had worn, had tracked the murderer to the hotel where he had spoken with him, and would swear to him again wherever he saw him.

The detective listened without interruption until he had finished, when he asked, calmly—

"Do you think you could find the place again, Bungy?"

"Yowi, me find him long a myall scrub, 'bout a green swamp, you know," was the reply.

"Then you shall take me there, Bungy," said the detective. "But, first, I will try to lay my hand on the horses, and I think I know where one of them is to be found."

CHAPTER XLI.

THE LAST LINK BUT ONE.

THE glorious mid-day sun is careering across a vault of lovely blue, flecked with fleecy clouds which course over it like the foam on the summer sea.

A fresh, cool breeze comes up from the south-west, tempered in its course from the inner desert far away, by crossing the snowy peaks that shine up a like a white cloud on the horizon, and throw faint hazy light into the blue depths above.

A wind that sings its low song of happiness through the loftiest branches of the stately gum forest, and murmurs a soft measure over the grassy downs beyond.

Between the shadeless open forest and the nearest range of purple hills, lies a clear, open flat, encircled by undulating ridges, with drooping wattles, heavy with golden blossoms and rich perfume, and carpetted with fresh, tender grass, and here and there the tall, white, leafless, naked trunk of a massive gum, looking like the bleached skeleton of some huge guardian giant standing still to survey the scene below.

Further away, and bounding the prospect to the south, where the ridges show grey and bare, and run up in terraces of scarped rock, rises a solitary, lonely, flat-topped hill, with glowing rifts, overhung with gigantic ferns, and a noisy creek bubbling on its way over a bed of slate and quartz shingle.

A lonely hill, treeless and shrubless, save where the crimson and white species, and the yellow

---
* Baal: No.

furze, bloom and blossom amidst the huge masses of basaltic rock.

A lonely hill, left as a monument of some forgotten throe of the pent-up giant that tosses and tumbles in billows of fire and molten matter beneath the crust of earth on which we stand.

A strange scene is being enacted under the shadow of that long hill, and one which is surely enough to waken the wonder of the ancient denizens of that dark olive forest.

For "plenty white fella—plenty white fella, may cobbon flash belong a that fella—plenty budgeree yarraman, murry mickey, like it one big corroboree; my word, plenty nobbler, plenty p'ta gib it bla' fella," as the natives would exclaim.

Yea, where of yore stood the gunyah of the swart aboriginal, where his brood of young savages tossed and tumbled over the tangled grass, and hunted the wombat up the trees and the wallaby through the fern, has been constructed by the pale-faced and brawny-armed white men a framework of saplings, and hewn and sawn timber, decorated with flags and gaudy streamers, which flutter and rustle in the breeze.

And where, a quarter of a century ago, nought was to be heard save the whoop and the "Coo-ee" of the black hunter, now rise the strains of the merry "Cornstalk" polka, played by that modern institution, a German band, and echoed back with wonderful distinctness from the hollow caves and lonely glens of that great volcanic hill opposite, it rises half way up to the very clouds, and seems to frown in dignified disapproval upon the scene.

It is the district races!

Yes, it is the district races, and from all parts of the country, far and near, have come to that universal gathering—in carriages, in dog-carts, spring-carts, drays, but mostly on horseback—the inhabitants.

From far and wide—from Goulburne plains and Lake George up in the north; from the widely-spreading Manewo country, which reaches in rich rolling downs to the boundless Pacific in the south; and from the Limestone, Molonglo, and Murrumbidgee districts in the west.

From the rich and powerful squatter, whose domain embraces an area larger than many a German principality, whose flocks wander over many plains, and whose herds roam in semi-savage freedom on a thousand hills, and who comes with his wife and his two beautiful Australian daughters in the handsome, new, two hundred guinea barouche, drawn by a pair of greys of his own breeding, that would fetch five hundred pounds at Hyde Park Corner any day in the week, down to Mick the hutkeeper, who has walked that morning from the slopes of the Tinderry mountains, a good twenty miles, with his handsome and faithful colley dog, that money would not buy, at his heels.

There, too, is of course "our member," radiant with good humour, and blazing in all the glory of a steward's scarlet coat.

Our member, who talks soft nonsense and describes the dresses at the last Government House ball, to the young ladies; the scandals and the "goings on" of their sons, Charlie, Tom, or Jack, at Sydney; and whom he, knowing dog, warmly defends to the elder ones.

Footrot, the Impounding Act, the wool market, dipping for seals, the drought in the north, the estimates, pleuro-pneumonia, and who has been touched by the great failure of A. B. & Co., with the squatters; rust, protection, the Land Act, and rotation of the crops with the farmers.

Breeding, pedigree, handicapping, and the evils of light weights and short distances with horsey men; and every other imaginable topic with everybody else, and who takes six to four in tens on the favourite from a betting J.P., bets an even fiver with toss for pick of horses with Joe Burrows the

sporting publican, and goes into half-crown sweeps with half the small settlers in the district, being for the time "all things to all men," and as great an authority on horse-racing and agricultural and pastoral matters as he must be, to hear the familiar way he talks of the ministers by their abbreviated proper names in the House of Assembly. What a shame, thinks his auditors, that those jealous newspapers never report him.

There, too, is the young squatter, the very beau ideal of a bush dandy, mounted on a thoroughbred horse, and clad in well-fitting cords and top boots, a dark grey coat, and a well worn and finely plaited cabbage-tree hat, who makes a book on every race, and lunches at the carriage of his sire, so well supplied with everything good, and wherein the young ladies, his sisters, make rash and reckless bets of gloves—bets which they never dream of paying if they lose, but rigidly exact if they win, the losers taking their taper fingers betwixt their own, ostensibly to measure their fair and delicate hands, and thinking the gloves cheap at the price.

There, too, is the gallant young Cornstalk bushman, long, lean, and brown, with the straight yellow hair, and the incipient moustache, riding the half-bred bay colt, anything but handsome, but great after cattle, and a "plum," at timber, escorts his sweetheart (the daughter of the next settler, four miles down the creek), who rides the long-tailed mare with the foal at foot, and whom he treats to thin ginger bread and lemonade with the air of an emperor.

Outside the grand stand, and in close proximity to the nearest drinking booths in its rear, on the stalls of the tag-rag and bobtail who attend the races, the proprietors of "under-and-over" tables, "ring-the-bull" games, dirty, disreputable looking Aunt Sallys, and last and worst of all, the seedy innocents who earn a living by the manipulation of three greasy cards, and whose stock-in-trade appears to consist of the three cards aforesaid, an empty gin case, and a pocket full of flash notes on the Bank of Elegance, together with a brace of accomplices—one a hard-faced, broken-nosed ruffian a cross between a dog fancier and a prize fighter, with a touch of the fifth-rate horsedealer, who has matriculated in half the gaols at home, and taken degrees in half a dozen colonial prisons; and the other, a lank, rowdy, pasty-faced young blackguard, partly sham-auction-duffer, and partly Pitt Street bully.

Amidst the noise and riot, the half-drunken horsemen galloping recklessly through the crowd, the loud-voiced men who offer incomprehensible odds, make all kinds of mysterious bets, and enter them in small pocket-books, with an air as who should say, "There, thank goodness, that's all right," and who, more mysteriously still, always appear to win, for, however the race may go, you are sure to find them at the next meeting loud-voiced and cheery as ever, ready apparently to bet any way, and to any amount.

Amidst these and the quiet little parties of six or eight, making up a sweep on the next race, o drinking the winnings of the last with noisy glee at the nearest booth, walks a quiet, unpretentious little man, with a jolly round face, a fresh complexion, dark crisp hair and whiskers, and little sharp, restless eyes, that appear to have the faculty of abstract volition, and to see everything at once.

He is dressed in a suit of dark grey clothing, and looks like a well-to-do farmer, or a retired jockey, or a publican, or a super on a station, or a betting man, or in fact from his appearance, anything you like to name.

The great feature in his general "make up," is quiet knowingness.

His dress is of the quietest cut and material, and yet it is worn with a kind of jaunty air, that imparts to it a character that the nattiest of horse-trainers might strive in vain to assume.

His hat is a plain white one, such as there are scores of others similar to on the course, but it is set on with an intuitive, yet humble cock, that is almost laughable in its shrewdness.

The very stick that he carries under his arm, a common eighteen-penny oak sapling, looks in keeping with the man, and the horse's head carved at the top (in honour of the occasion no doubt) has a kind of cunning leer, and a wide-awake grin on his wooden face.

In and out, sauntering dreamily along, or scanning the beauties in the saddling paddock with what old Scott would have called a "judgematical eye," going into a small sweep, or betting a crown on his fancy, he lazily and apparently carelessly moves to and fro, now in the grand stand, with all the power of those brilliant eyes concentrated on—the race? No, on the mass of faces below. Now in the inside of the course, peering upward through a small lorgnette into the grand stand, or into the betting yard, yet always carelessly and apparently aimlessly.

At last he goes to a bar with Bob Magrath, the lively butcher, with whom he makes a crown bet, and loses.

Over the nip of brandy, he says condescendingly—

"Nice lot of horses you seem to have here?"

"Middlin'," is the reply. "Wait till the next race, and see my filly Miss Mary. Bless you she's the nicest little thing the whole country round."

"Is she?" says our friend; "I'd like to have a look at her. I'm fond o' horses, I am."

"So you shall, then. Come along," says Bob in a friendly tone, "and if you don't say she's the prettiest mare on this course, why, I'll eat her, saddle and bridle in—there."

The two elbow their way though the crowd to where Miss Mary, a neatly made bay filly, with a switch tail, and a coat like satin, stands turning back the whites of her eyes, and threatening destruction to the unduly familiar. How is it, I wonder that horses owned by butchers have always more or less the devil in them?

"Look out for her heels," is the caution given to our friend by her owner, as he sweeps the rug from her quarters, and spreading his hand in the direction of the filly, bids him—

"Look there!"

Our friend cocks his "judgematical" eye in a manner that profoundly impresses the butcher, and pausing ere he speaks, he buries his chin is his left hand, and laying his head on one side, says severely to him, at the same time transfixing him beneath his gaze—

"You know a good horse, you do, and how to bring him out too."

The butcher simpers an acknowledgment to the soft impeachment, and in reply says—

"You ain't a bad judge of a horse yourself, I should say, now."

"Hum! tolerable," is the reply, and after another pause, and a scrutinising walk round the stall—keeping at a tolerable distance all the while though—our friend suddenly asks—

"Did you ever see Veno?

"Never," says the butcher with the air of a man who had been suddenly found out. "Never had that luck."

"Ah, she was a sweet 'un, she was," says our friend solemnly. "Do you know now, mind, it may be my fancy, but do you know that there filly reminds me very much on her."

"What, of Veno?" cries the butcher.

"Of Veno!" is the reply, sententiously definite.

The butcher's heart is thoroughly won. He smiles beamingly on our friend, and asks him whether he owns any horses himself.

"A—ah! no, not exactly—that is, not just now," is the reply. "He had bred a good many on 'em, but he was rather out o' that line just at present,

unless he could pick up summat very cheap," and then he asked the butcher suddenly, whether he had bred her himself.

No, he had bought her some time since at the Maitland weekly sale. Bought her cheap, as one might say, and another nag with her of not nearly so good a sort, and that he'd like to turn a penny by. Not but that it was worth twice as much as he gave for it, for both poor critturs was very poor then—nothing but bags o' bones, in fact.

"Been ridden a long way to market, perhaps," says our friend carelessly.

The butcher was inclined to think that they had, and "the old file as they belonged to seemed to be very anxious to be rid of them at any price."

Then he was led on to describe the personal appearance of the old man, and to confess that the other nag was hoppled not far off in the bush, and our friend he wanted to buy a nag on the cheap, and was taken to see him, and offered Bob Magrath five pound in advance of what he had given for him at the auction sale, but not before he had peeped into his pocket-book, and studied a strangely mumbled-jumbled hieroglyphic, the exact counterpart of which was on the off flank of the nag he had bidden for.

The bargain was struck, and sealed by a drink as such bargains usually are, and then our friend proposes that they should have another, and then he would go and try to get a bet on with somebody, for he wanted to back the filly, and he couldn't think of asking her owner to bet against her.

At this the butcher swears he is a brick, and proposes a sweep, which is agreed to, and then introduces him to a number of jolly individuals who are engaged in a general "shout" at the Royal Oak booth, and with whom, by his witty sayings and entertaining conversation, he soon becomes so great a favourite, that he finds it rather difficult to get away from their charming society.

At last he succeeds, however, and then he rides away on his new purchase, a horse that has carried the dead as well as the living.

On his arrival at the hostelrie where he has been staying for a day or two past, he stables, grooms, and feeds his nag, nearly every one being away at the races.

Then he goes straight to his room, and, unlocking his little carpet bag, discloses, carefully wrapped up in his spare Crimean shirt, some singular travelling companions for so jolly and companionable a little man.

There is, first of all, carefully capped and loaded, a bright little six-shooter revolver, scarcely bigger than a child's toy, but deadly as a rifle. Then, stranger still, a pair of bright handcuffs, and, last of all, a small ebony staff, with a pretty gilt crown on the top.

Look at the little man now. The look of bonhommie has totally gone, and is replaced by a stern, thoughtful expression, habitual to the countenance of Hogan, the detective, when in a state of repose.

CHAPTER XLII.
BILLY-THE-BULL HAS VISITORS.

THE wary avenger then took a sheet of paper, and upon it wrote a few words—very few, but remarkably pregnant of meaning. They were as follows:—

"I am running him to earth on another scent and have the links of evidence almost complete. In the case of the pedlar, there was moral proof but none whereon to convict. On committal for one he may confess the other. More in a week or so from

D. H."

This he enclosed in an envelope to "The Chief of the Detective Department, Sydney," sealed it, and enclosed the whole in another envelope, which he addressed to a private friend in Wooloomooloo, the enclosure to be delivered by hand, and a receipt taken.

He then took his letter to the post-office, asked whether there were any there for William Brown, received one, put it in his pocket, and leisurely walked back to the inn, quiet shrewdness playing in every line of his face as he occasionally muttered to himself—

"One horse I have, and the other I can clap my hand on whenever it is wanted."

The next morning the detective, and Bungy, the black tracker, started at daybreak, the former having hired a couple of extra horses, one for Bungy and one for the swag, and ere night they were far advanced on the route for the crossing of the Bogan river.

* * * *

Billy-the-Bull, in the cool of that very evening, sat at the door of his hut smoking his pipe, ruminating meanwhile on the events of the past few weeks—ruminating, perhaps repenting, although but little penitence appeared in his hardened countenance and vicious-looking eyes. He was roused from his reverie by the sound of horses' feet coming pattering up by the stockyard and across the home paddock.

He could make nothing of them except that they carried strangers, and muttering a curse at being disturbed, he waited for them to come up to the door.

"Hallo! old cock," said the foremost of the two horsemen; "you don't appear to recognise old friends, blessed if you do."

"Who are you? I don't know you, nor don't want to, as I know on," was the ungracious reply.

"Well, come, you might be a little civil, anyhow, you know, if you're nothing else. Hang me if I know what's coming over the country," said the former speaker, who was none other than our old acquaintance, Bob Loveridge, who, with Jack Last, had again been over to the Cornstalk, and again been disappointed in not meeting with Jacky Cain, and who had, therefore, come on again to the hut of Billy-the-Bull, hardly, however, expecting to find him at home.

"What do you want here?" asked Bill, doggedly.

"First thing as we want," replied Bob, coolly dismounting, "is a feed, and then we want a little talk with you. We've been up to your pardner's place, but he's not at home, and not expected, from what we can make out. We thought he was away with you somewheres, because we've been here before. However, that's no matter; you'll do as well."

The old man was rapidly getting into a bad temper at his hospitality being thus coolly demanded, and indulged in some expressions more forcible than polite, and which we omit, but which were to the effect that he desired certain portions of his body at the antipodes of the North Pole, if they got anything to eat or drink there.

"Come, come, Billy, it's no use trying to carry on that game with us," said Bob Loveridge, turning his horse loose in the home paddock whilst he spoke; "we've got a way of forcing people to attend on us, if they won't do it quietly; but we want to be friendly if you'll let us, because it will be the best for all parties—won't it, Jack?"

Jack Last cursed Billy for an old fool, and was about hinting that it would be the worse for him if he did not turn civil, when he was stopped by Bob, who at once explained their business, and asked the old man if he was willing to buy the cattle they had lying hidden in the ranges, at the same time recalling to his recollection the dealings they had previously had together.

Billy-the-Bull then grumblingly asked them to come in, his cupidity being aroused by the chance offered to him of making a bargain; and after much chaffering, and frequent appeals to the rum bottle which he at last produced, the cattle were bought, and arranged to be delivered at the other end of the run on the morrow.

CHAPTER XLIII.
THE ABDUCTION.

HEATED by the spirits he had drunk, and excited at the prospect of receiving a large sum of money from Billy-the-Bull for the cattle he would be able the next day to drive upon the run, Bob Loveridge proposed that they should turn out of their direct road for their hiding place, and see how things were going on at Marrangong station, that they had stuck up some time before, and Jack Last, after some dispute, agreed to do so.

Leaving the track they were following, therefore, they skirted the Marrangong Creek, and coming out into the open forest at its head, got a full view of the station, which lay directly beneath them.

As they watched in the bright moonlight, that luminary having risen half an hour before, a young lady came out of the house, attended by a big dog, apparently for the object of taking a walk in the cool of the evening.

"By the lord," said Bob Loveridge to his companion, in a hoarse and husky whisper. "That's the girl as lives with her aunt, and as shot Jim Benny. I'd give all that I possess to run off with her into the bush. What do you say to trying the trick on, Jack?"

"Don't be a fool, Bob," was Jack's reply; "that gal's a regular Tartar. They do say as how she was mixed up with bushrangers afore the other day, and that her father and mother was killed by Blue Cap and his gang, ever so many years ago—not before she'd settled a whole pile of them however, blazing away with a revolver in each hand, as hard as ever she could. Mortimer's her name, and tiger cat's her nature, so what would you do with her when you'd got her?"

"Do with her? Oh, lots of things," growled Bob.

"Why, man alive, she'd take the three of us to watch her, and then she'd give us the slip somehow. My opinion is, you'd better come along, and let's get back to the hut where Jim's waiting for us, and for his supper too, and wondering the while what the deuce has become of us, I'll go bail."

"But look, Jack—look at her. She's coming this way. By George! I've a good mind to—and, if you'll stick by me, I will, too."

"Will what?" growled Jack Last.

"Why, carry her off, you fool, to be sure—carry her off with us to the hut, and from there up and away with her to the Jingera. I know a place there where we'll be safe enough, and from where she'll never find her way out."

"Are you really mad, Bob?" was the reply. "Why, man, we'd have the whole country after us in no time. Devil a doubt about it."

"Mad, Jack? Well, yes, I am mad—mad with love and revenge. Hang the danger; I don't care. Will you help me, or won't you?"

"Don't be a fool, Bob. Come along, and leave the gal alone, can't you?" was Jack's answer.

"Jack Last, will you do it? Because I don't care a cuss whether you help me in this matter or not. I'm bound to try it, though, even if she shoots me down like she did that dog, Jim Benny, the other day."

"Well, Bob, I don't like it, but I'll never forsake you, old pal; and, as you're determined, why, here goes," said Jack Last.

"Give me your fist, Jack. You're a brick, and

I'll do as much for you one of these days, see if I don't," replied Bob. "Come on here quietly down the hill, and we'll meet her at the foot. If the dog makes any row, knife him, and I'll look after the girl."

"All right, Bob," was the reply. "But just think again twice afore you go slick into the matter."

"Think! I cannot think—my brain's on fire, and I must and will have her!" And so saying, he darted through the underwood, so as to cut off the young girl's retreat, followed closely by Jack Last.

While all this was going on, Georgie Mortimer—for it was indeed she—tempted by the fineness of the night, had almost unconsciously wandered along the flat open bush towards the foot of the ranges, wrapped in sweet maiden meditation, and had got quite beyond the cleared ground into the shadier forest, unconscious of the danger which was impending, until a low growl from her faithful four-footed companion recalled her to the recollection of where she was, and to the imprudence of being out so late and so far from home.

Still, she had no fear of being beset, and thinking that the growl of the dog was caused by his having seen or smelled a snake, or some other noxious reptile, she looked around, and seeing nothing, turned round and began slowly to retrace her steps homewards.

The next moment she was alarmed at hearing a noise as of some persons rapidly crashing through the underwood, and, with a beating heart, she quickened her pace, her dog still growling and snuffling uneasily by her side or at her heels.

She had not gone far before, at a turn in the path, she came in full view of two men standing one on each side of the footpath, as though waiting for her.

As she neared them, the taller of the two stepped forward before her, and called on her to stop.

"Who are you, and what do you want with me?" she asked, in a trembling voice.

"Who we are, my beauty, doesn't matter. What we want is your own pretty self, to come with us and live with us in the wild bush—the Queen of the Forest."

Georgie's heart beat with a sudden throb; but summoning her courage to her aid, she, in as steady a voice as she could command, bade the men stand back and let her pass.

"Stand back!" repeated Bob Loveridge, with a savage laugh. "That's what you said to Jim Benny when you shot him. But it was a bold deed for a gal, and you've won a sweetheart by it, my lass, and one that'll never let you know what it is to want anything while there's a station in the country to stick up."

Jack Last broke in here, and bade him fetch the girl along, if he was going to, and not stand blarneying there all night.

Bob thereupon rushed up to seize her, but Carlo, who had been standing snarling at the two ruffians, sprang forward, and, with a loud growl, met him by seizing him by the throat before he was aware of it—thus giving Georgie an opportunity of slipping past, which she did, running forward as rapidly as she was able, calling loudly for assistance the while.

Jack Last, leaving Bob Loveridge to get rid of the dog, followed her however, and she, in her terror, getting out of the path, and being encumbered by her dress, which kept catching in the scrub, was soon overtaken, and as she heard the steps of her pursuer rapidly gaining on her, fell forward in a deep faint.

At the same moment, Bob Loveridge, with a loud volley of curses, succeeded in getting a knife from his pocket, and ferociously stabbing the hound again and again in the side, the gallant beast at length fell backwards from his throat, with a loud yell upon the grass, which, already

stained with the blood of the man, was soon saturated with that of the poor animal, who lay and struggled in what appeared to be the throes of death.

Bob did not wait to see his canine antagonist die, but binding a handkerchief round his own bleeding throat, rushed off to the assistance of Jack Last, who was vainly endeavouring to recover Georgie from her swoon.

The creek was not far distant, and by means of a few drops of cold water carried from it by Bob in his hat, she was soon brought to herself, and for a moment stared wildly about her, without being able to make out where she was.

She soon, however, recovered full consciousness, and, with many tears and entreaties, begged the two rascals to allow her to go home, promising that if they did she would never say a word about the subject to anyone.

The only reply she got, however, was a surly command from Bob, whose temper had got considerably ruffled by the encounter he had had with the dog, and who was suffering no small amount of pain from the wound, to "get up and come along, or he'd make her."

This, however, she point blank refused to do, until, seeing the man determined, and about to remove her by force, she rose with an air of dignity, and bade them stand back, and not lay one of their ruffian hands upon her, rather than suffer which she would walk to wherever they wished her to go, and trust to heaven to deliver her out of their power.

Marching one on each side of her, and leading her past the place where the hound lay stretched, panting and bleeding, on the sward, the faithful animal whimpering faintly, and trying to get up as he saw her pass at a short distance—a sight that almost caused her courage to give way again—they conducted her through the intricacies of the bush, to the place where they had left their horses.

"Now, look here, my beauty," said Bob Loveridge to her, when, weary and footsore, she arrived with them at the top of the hill—"look here; we've had some trouble with you already, and we don't mean to let you go; so you'd better make your mind up to come quietly. You've got a good ten mile to go from this, and go you shall. You can ride if you like, and if you won't do that, you can walk; and if you won't walk, we'll carry you. So now you know."

Georgie appealed to them for the love of heaven and as they were men, to let her go; but, seeing that her prayers were of no avail, she sat down at the foot of a tree, and defied them to take her.

"Kill me, you may," said she; "but you shall never take me hence alive."

"Oh, my lady," said Bob; "won't we? We'll see that, though. Come on, Jack; we shall only have to carry her, that's all."

The two villains seized her roughly, with the intention of forcing her along; but with all the strength in her body, and with all her womanly weapons of defence—her nails—she resisted to the utmost, until, unable to struggle any longer, she again sank exhausted and insensible to the ground.

The two men looked at each other for a few moments, as she lay hysterically sobbing at their feet. They were neither of them improved in personal appearance by the tussle they had just come out of so victoriously, Jack Last bearing five lines ruled like a music stave down his face, from his forehead to his chin, and Bob Loveridge lugubriously feeling a sore place in his head, whence a large handful of hair had been torn out by the roots.

Jack Last was the first to speak—

"Isn't she a tiger to fight, Bob? What the devil are we to do with her now?"

"Do with her? Why, lift her up on my horse, to be sure. He'll carry double, and let's get away afore she comes to herself, and we have any more bother with her. Hang me, if I don't like her all the better for that spurt of temper."

"Lord! what a row there'll be when Jim Benny sees her," said Jack, with a chuckle.

"Jim be hanged," retorted Bob Loveridge. "Jim had better keep a civil tongue in his head, or it'll be the worse for him, I know. But come, let us get the girl away from this."

Georgie lay perfectly insensible, her long, yellow hair streaming down in golden wavelets over her pale face, and her breath coming heavily and irregularly, and broken by spasmodic sobs.

With some considerable trouble they succeeded in raising her from the ground, and in lifting her upon the saddle of Bob's horse, that worthy mounting behind her and supporting her in his arms, and Jack Last having got upon the other horse, they carefully and slowly picked their way down the side of the hill, making with their prize for a ruined hut, wherein their wounded companion, Jim Benny, lay anxiously awaiting their coming.

CHAPTER XLIV.

THE ESCAPE FROM THE HUT.

IT was a long and wearisome ride from the brow of the hill to the dilapidated hut, and the rough motion of the horse, coupled with the difficulty he felt in keeping the insensible girl in her place on the front of the saddle, rendered it anything but a pleasant one to Bob Loveridge.

Arrived on the road, which was tolerably level, he spurred his horse however to a canter, and although the double load it had to carry bore heavily upon it, still the gallant steed sped along at a sweeping pace, so that in less than an hour and a half the hut was reached.

A pile of blankets and rugs was hastily thrown down in a corner, and Georgie, still in a deep faint, laid upon them, Bob, with a savage chuckle, saying—

"Let her lay there; she'll come to, soon enough. And now we must tell Jim Benny what we've done. Lord, what a row there will be at Marrangong by this time. But we'll be off afore daylight, and then let 'em find us if they can."

Jim Benny, who sat in a dark corner nursing himself gloomily, and hardly as yet recovered from the effects of his wound, here wanted to know, with many objurgations, "What the matter was—what they'd got there—and what they'd been up to?"

"Great things, Jim, my hero," said Jack Last. "By George, we've brought a particular friend of yours home to see you. She was mighty particular asking after your health, so we brought her along with us to see for herself."

Jim thereupon wanted to know "what the, &c., &c., they were talking about," until Bob Loveridge explained what they had done, and intended to do; when, with a ferocious laugh, he slapped that worthy on the back, calling him "a brick and a good fellow," and swearing that he'd stick by him as long as he lived.

"Only to think," said he, "as the gal as gev me pepper, and whom I had sworn to be revenged on, should be lying here in this hut at my mercy. Oh, my lady," he went on, shaking his fist in the direction of the corner where she lay, "I'll make you remember it—I will so!"

Bob Loveridge did not exactly see things in that light, but thought it better to say nothing just then, as he perceived that Jim had been making free with the rum bottle, and knew that when he was in that state it was sometimes dangerous to cross him.

The precious trio then sat drinking and smoking over the smouldering logs, Jim Benny becoming more and more obstreperous, and Bob and Jack finding that 'twas as much as they could do to keep him quiet.

It was probably to this cause that Georgie Mortimer owed her safety up to the time she came to herself, which she did in the course of about an hour after she had been taken into the hut, awaking with a sigh and a start.

Luckily for her the three ruffians were at that moment engaged in loud and angry dispute relative to the sale of the cattle that lay up in the ranges to Billy-the-Bull, Jim Benny contending, with drunken pertinacity, that they ought to have got a much higher price for them, and Bob Loveridge and Jack Last vainly endeavouring to convince him that they had made a good bargain.

For a few moments after she recovered her senses, Georgie lay in a kind of half stupor, trying to remember where she was and how she had got into that strange, noisy place, until her memory coming to her aid, she suddenly remembered the manner in which she had been attacked in the bush, and concluded that she must have been removed to the place where she lay whilst in a state of insensibility.

She raised her head, and could just see the dim outlines of the three men as they crouched over the dull, smoky fire, and could barely distinguish that she was in the interior of an old bark hut.

Her first thought was of escape, and she partly raised herself in order to look for any means.

Alas! escape was hopeless. The door certainly lay near her, and the men sat with their backs towards her, but then it was barricaded with heavy slabs that it was impossible to move without noise.

The fire was smouldering low, and the bush lamp had just gone out, leaving a stench noisome enough to poison anyone but a half-drunken herdsman.

"Get some wood to put on the fire, Jim," said Jack Last, "and let's have a light on the subject."

"Get some yourself, and be hanged to you!" answered Jim Benny; "I don't move out of this place this night, not if I knows it."

Jack got up, grumbling that "the least Jim could have done was to have kept up a good fire against they came home;" but knowing that it was of no use talking to him in his then present state of drunkenness, said no more, but felt his way to the door in order to get the wood himself.

Before he went out, however, Bob Loveridge called to him to look at the girl, and see whether she was all right.

She had the presence of mind to lie back and feign insensibility, and he, after looking at her, and listening to her breathing, replied that "she didn't seem likely to come to for a good while," and asked whether he had not better throw some water upon her face and bring her round.

"No," shouted Bob, savagely, for he was annoyed at what Jim Benny had said respecting her, and did not dare to show his spleen. "No, cuss you, leave her alone. She'll come round quite soon enough, I dare say. Go and get the wood, and shut the door after you."

Jack cursed them both for a pair of cantankerous fools, and unbarring the door, went out, pulling it to after him.

The moment he had gone, however, a slight puff of the night wind forced it partly open again, where it hung, gently swaying to and fro noiselessly, upon its leathern hinges.

Georgie's heart leapt in her bosom, as she saw the means of escape thus left open to her.

If she had but the time.

There was scarcely a moment to do it in, but yet it must be done now or not at all.

The two men were crouched over the fire with their backs turned towards her, in deep converse, and by the crashing of sticks outside, she could hear that the third ruffian was not yet coming back.

Rapidly and silently she rose, and in an instant had darted outside the door and round the hut.

At the same moment she heard the approaching footsteps of Jack Last, staggering under the weight of a heavy log and a bundle of brushwood.

She crouched closely in the corner formed by the angle of the chimney, and as the ruffian went by, some of the twigs brushed over her face.

Had he looked for a single instant, he would have seen that face as it gleamed in its whiteness through the obscurity; but no, he staggered onward round a corner of the hut, and the next instant a light figure shot swiftly over the clearing, glancing like a scintillation across the gloom, and plunged into the darkness of the bush beyond.

CHAPTER XLV.

BILLY-THE-BULL WALKS IN HIS SLEEP

DARTING from bush to bush, and from tree to tree, weary, faint, and frightened, did Georgie Mortimer continue, regardless of the danger she incurred of hopelessly losing herself in the intricacies of the dense forest which stretched away on every hand, to put a greater distance between herself and the ruffians in the hut, whom she knew must, ere long, discover her flight, and attempt to discover her retreat.

This they did—sooner, indeed, than she anticipated—for a quantity of light, dry honey-suckle leaves and cones being thrown on the smouldering logs, and a lighted match applied to them, created such a glare in the hut, that the whole interior was brilliantly illuminated, and Bob Loveridge, turning round to see whether the light might not have disturbed the, as he supposed, still insensible girl, perceived that she was gone.

With a loud and savage oath, he jumped up, knocking Jim Benny, who was arranging the logs, clean into the fire, amidst the blazing brushwood, and bounded through the still open door into the darkness outside.

He ran round and round the hut, but could see no trace of the fugitive.

"What the deuce is the matter with Bob?" asked Jack Last, in a half-drunken tone, as he sat composedly on the floor, for he, too, had been upset by the impetuosity of the bushranger.

"Blessed if I know," replied Jim Benny, picking himself up out of the fire, and blowing his scorched fingers very ruefully.

"Why, dash my wig!" exclaimed Jack, after a glance round, "if the gal ain't gone."

"That be hanged for a lie," said Jim Benny, raising himself, and looking round to the heap of blankets, when, seeing that it was so, he commenced a volley of blasphemy, that was only stopped by his throwing himself into a violent fit of coughing.

Bob came in at this juncture, and in a towering rage demanded how the girl had escaped, to which Jack Last replied in equally strong language that he didn't know, and Jim Benny lay back upon the floor cursing and coughing alternately.

Bob, however, and Jack, who were comparatively sober, hurriedly left the hut in pursuit, leaving Jim to choke himself or recover as he thought best, and that worthy having coughed and cursed until he was black in the face, wisely thinking that he had done all that he could, crept over to the blankets, and tumbling down amongst them, was soon fast asleep.

The other two, after a few random dashes into the scrub on either side, went to work in a more scientific manner.

Forgetting in their hurry that she did not know a foot of the way, nor, indeed, in what part of the country she was, they rapidly ran along the bush track in the direction of Marrangong station, narrowly examining the bush on either side of the way.

Nothing, however, could they find, and when at last they returned, thoroughly wearied with the pursuit, the grey light of early dawn had begun to show itself over the distant eastern hills, a rudely dragging the blankets from off their sleeping companion, they, amidst muttered anathem sought the repose of which they stood so much need.

In the meanwhile, Georgie, plunging deeper deeper into the recesses of the bush, had completely eluded pursuit, but in doing so had totally lost herself.

It was past midnight when she escaped from the hut, and she had partly walked, partly run, onward until the light grey tinge in the clouds over the eastern sky warned her that morning was approaching, and reminded her that she knew not where she was.

The air felt damp and chilly, and she was fatigued and footsore, but keeping her left hand to the grey dawn, and turning her back upon that noblest constellation of the Australian sky, the Southern Cross, which, by this time, shone faintly in the leaden-looking firmament, she made for the north, judging or guessing that she had come in an opposite direction.

There was not a sound to break the deep silence which reigned around her.

The wind had died out, and even the busy hum of insect life had ceased as the rapidly growing light over the tops of the dark olive and funereal swaying trees betokened the coming day.

By-and-by a rosy streak between the tall trunks of the gum trees told that the sun was rising in his strength, and ere long, and whilst she yet struggled painfully along through the tangled grass and bushes, the atmosphere began to lose its chilliness, the stormy mists to rise from the damp earth, and the birds to chirrup and flutter in the red sunbeams that shot in arrows of light through the heavy foliage.

The Southern Cross had faded out from the sky, and the sun was beating down in fierce splendour upon her aching head, when, reaching the bed of a creek, where, partly dry, the water lay in small pools, and long, shallow, detached reaches, and a clump of shady wattles grew, offering shelter for her wearied and sinking frame, she, after commending herself to the care of Providence, lay down under the grateful and aromatic shade, and, thoroughly worn out, soon sank into a deep and refreshing slumber which lasted many hours, so that when she woke, the sun had attained his meridian.

She sat for a long time reflecting what course to pursue until, trusting to chance, she rose and moved onwards.

Hunger, which she had not before felt, began now, however, to visit her, and this she attempted to allay by chewing the tender purple leaves of the sarsaparilla plant, whose black berries and long creepers hung in almost every tree, and by eating bunches of the sour native currants, which grew in abundance.

Hour after hour she wandered on, up hill and down gully, now skirting the edge of a deep morass, and anon crossing the bed of a dry creek, until the sun sank low again in the western heavens, and she found herself lost in the trackless bush.

Still she felt but little fear, and bravely wandered on ever to the northward, until late in the night she came across a deep gully, at the bottom of which flowed silently and slowly a fine creek, whose clear waters shone like silver in the starlight.

This creek she determined to follow down, judging that upon its banks would most likely some shepherd's or settler's hut be built, where she might obtain shelter for the night, and be directed the right way home.

As to where she was she had not the slightest notion, but boldly striking off along the course of the creek, she followed it down for many a long and weary mile.

At length, when her aching limbs almost refused to carry her further, she came suddenly across a clearing, at the further end of which, glinting whitely in the moonlight, stood a rambling hut and a number of outbuildings.

She paused, and looked at the place, her heart beating strangely, and yet she knew not why.

The place seemed to her to have a weird, wild appearance, and to almost speak of some weird, wild deed of villany which had been perpetrated within its nearly dismantled walls.

Endeavouring to shake off this uncomfortable impression, she slowly crossed the paddock, making for the house, and was approaching the stockyard fence which lay between it and her, when she saw the door slowly open, and the figure of a man emerge therefrom, coming directly down the slight slope as if to meet her.

A presentiment of evil hung heavily and chillily over her heart as she saw him coming down towards her, but, to her surprise, she perceived as he neared her that he bore away to her right, and did not seem to notice her in the slightest.

She stood still and watched him as he passed within a few feet of her, walking with firm footsteps and an evident familiarity with the way he was going.

As he neared her, the moon shone out fully on his face, which was white and ghastly, and her heart throbbed wildly as she remarked the diabolical malevolence and ruthless ferocity imprinted on his every feature.

His eyes were wide open, but were fixed and stony, nor did he seem to use them as guides to his feet, but their strange inward look and deathlike expression chilled her very blood with horror.

Impelled by a curiosity she could not master, and despite her fatigue, she carefully and noiselessly followed him.

Striking across a small patch of scrub, he gained another and a larger stockyard, the fencing of which was pulled down in many places, and crossing this, he reached another part of the bush.

This, however, he skirted for about twenty yards, and then suddenly stopped.

Georgie, who stood concealed in the scrub, watched him with a growing feeling of alarm and wonder.

Had he discovered her?

No!

He stooped down, and picking up a stone, he threw it down an opening in the ground, and then appeared to be listening intently.

Georgie saw the action, and in a few seconds heard a hollow sudden plunge which smote her to the very heart.

She still stood rooted to the spot, however, and saw the old man next tie a bundle on to a long rope and lower it down the cavity.

The rope was nearly all payed out, when a voice that sounded scarcely human came up out of the cavity, and frightened and appalled by the shrill, unearthly sound, Georgie turned away and rapidly fled from the unhallowed spot.

Fortunately for her, however, in doing so, she, after a walk of half an hour or so, struck the road, and immediately afterwards found out where she was by certain marks that she recognised.

Re-invigorated by the knowledge that she was within three or four miles of home, and nearly prostrated though she was by the unwonted exertion she had gone through, and by hunger and want of the rest to which she had been used, she hurried along the road, scarcely feeling the exhaustion that was creeping over her.

At length the long wished for roof of the house appeared in sight, sleeping calmly bathed in the soft radiance of the full moonlight, and standing forth clearly marked above the dark, thick foliage of the passiflora which enveloped its lower part.

As she neared it, her pent-up feelings sought to relieve themselves, and she burst into a paroxysm of tears and sobs for the first time since she had escaped.

Whilst doing so, her attention was attracted by something moving at a short distance from her in the bush, and observing it more narrowly, she distinctly saw the shadows of two men flitting from tree to tree, so as to get nearer the path which she must follow to gain the house.

For an instant she was almost paralysed by this new danger, doubting not that they were her captors watching for her return.

But in this trying moment her presence of mind did not leave her, and taking advantage of a shady part of the road, she slipped into the bush, again making a detour, and coming out on the open ground in front of the house.

Her pursuers, however, missing her from the road, and judging what she had done, ran along it, and skirted the bush with the intention of intercepting her.

But having, fortunately for her, overshot the mark, she got a considerable start of them, and terror lending her wings, she flew rapidly across the lawn, screaming at the top of her voice for assistance.

The two villains, for it was none other than Bob Loveridge and Jack Last, who, heated with drink and passion, had determined to try again to recapture her, pursued her with brutal curses, and she, despairing of assistance, for no sound answered her call, and her wearied limbs failing her, she fell, with a loud shriek, into a fit of deep insensibility, just as she heard the footsteps of the first ruffian close behind her, and felt his hand seize her dress.

As, however, he did so, the crash of branches was heard, and the next instant two horsemen came thundering through the bush at full gallop, into the other end of the open.

Seeing this, the two scoundrels who were at the moment trying to lift Georgie Mortimer up so as to carry her to where they had left their horses, let her fall heavily to the ground, and darting into the nearest point of the bush, were soon beyond pursuit.

CHAPTER XLVI.
HOW THE RESCUE CAME ABOUT.

FOR a short distance the horsemen followed the two ruffians into the bush, but without catching sight of them, so they returned to Georgie, who still lay insensible on the green sward before the house.

Georgie's rescuers were an uncle and a cousin, Mr. George and Mr. Harry Miller, who had arrived at the station on the previous afternoon, on a short visit.

They bore her into the house, the servants, who had heard her screams and the shouting, having by this time opened the door, and Mrs. Beauvey having thrown on a dressing gown and come out of her room to see what the matter was.

Georgie was laid carefully down upon the sofa, and restoratives being applied, she soon came to herself.

Mrs. Beauvey, who had been seriously ill ever since she had been missed, laughed and cried by turns, whilst old Mike, the Highland shepherd, who had been out all day on a quiet expedition of his own in search of his lost favourite, leaving his flock of sheep under the care of his knowing little colley dog, Pincher, and had not long ago returned, was behaving generally like an amiable old lunatic, getting into everybody's way, and vowing deep vengeance against the villains when he caught them.

"I reckon it was the same coves as stuck us up the other day (old Mike always spoke of himself as forming part and parcel of the establishment, though he lived in a hut five miles away, and had seen nothing of the late sticking up), and the same coves as I see the day afore yesterday. Ah! if I'd only knowed what they was after! Howsomever, may be I'll drop on 'em one o' these fine days, and then we'll see if they will get away so easy."

Mr. Miller, however, recommending quiet both for Georgie and Mrs. Beauvey, the house was soon cleared, the servants and old Mike retiring to the kitchen to smoke the calumet of peace, and talk over the exciting events which had happened of late, the two ladies seeking the rest of which they stood so much in need, and Mr. Miller and his son Harry, sitting up for awhile to consult as to what should be done in order to bring the marauders to justice.

Early the next morning the household was astir, and Georgie rose at her accustomed hour none the worse for her involuntary trip, save that she still felt a little foot-sore and had a kind of general vague impression that the entire affair had been an unpleasant dream.

On meeting at the breakfast table she related the whole of the circumstances in connection with the abduction, and in return her uncle Miller informed her how her absence had been discovered a little earlier than it otherwise would.

It appeared that Mrs. Beauvey and the visitors, doubting nothing that she had gone to rest, had sat up rather later than was their wont, and were just about thinking of finishing their whist and retiring to their rooms, when they were suddenly startled by hearing the low whine of a dog on the verandah, and two or three faint scratches at the door, as if caused by the same animal.

On going outside, they found the hound Carlo lying across the doorway, bleeding from a deep wound in his side, and vainly endeavouring to stagger to his feet.

They immediately staunched the wound, and their suspicions being aroused that all was not right, as they knew that the dog always followed Georgie wherever she went, Mrs. Beauvey went to her bedroom to see whether she was there.

With a choking sensation in her throat, and a feeling of terror in her heart, she perceived that Georgie was not in her room, and that there were no signs of her having been there, and the two men, on hearing this, immediately saddled their horses and set out to endeavour to find out her whereabouts, for that foul play had been had recourse to they now felt no doubt.

It was easy enough to discover the place where the struggle had occurred, by the track of the dog, which was marked with blood the whole distance, and near to the place where he had fallen when he was stabbed the bushes were broken and bent as if a hard struggle had taken place there.

But beyond that it was impossible to find any further trace, as the ground was dry and hard, and intersected by cattle tracks and out-paths in all directions.

After a brief conference, therefore, they separated, agreeing to meet again at the house if unsuccessful in their search after two or three hours.

Harry Miller rode up, and his father rode down the road for several miles, but of course finding no trace of Georgie.

It was early dawn before Mr. Miller senior reached Marrangong station, and about an hour afterwards the sharp canter of a horse was heard coming up the home paddock as Harry returned.

"Well," asked the father, as the younger man sprang from his jaded horse, "have you seen or heard anything of her?"

"No," was the desponding reply; "have you?"

"I have not," said Mr. Miller senior. "I cannot find the slightest trace, nor can I imagine where she can have been carried off to, if carried off she has been, of which I think there is very little if any doubt."

Harry swore a fierce oath that he would never rest until she was recovered, and proposed that they should, with fresh horses, resume the search, and with the aid of all the men on the station, scour the whole country round.

But the father pointed out how necessary it was for him to take food and some natural rest in order to fit him for the labours of the morrow, when a regular and systematic search should be organised.

Although with wild impetuosity he at first refused, and wanted to start again at once, still, after a time he saw the excellence of the advice, and yielded to it.

He ate sparingly, and throwing himself on a sofa, attempted to sleep; but sleep would not visit his eyelids, woo it as he would.

He could but think of the fair girl whose love he so longed to win, dragged perchance through the rugged scrub, her golden hair torn from its bands, her beauteous face scratched by bushes and brambles, her limbs failing her, and she in her anguish and terror calling for aid, whilst he lay there inactive; and with a deep groan and an agonised sob, he sprang from the couch and walked to and fro across the room and into the bush, which lay calm and dark in the bright moonlight outside his French window.

Directly the sun was up he roused the whole house by his impatient call, and the search was at once renewed.

It seemed as if nothing could tire him.

Hour after hour, and weary mile after weary mile did he and his father thread the intricacies of the surrounding forest, until, at last, the remonstrances of the latter were turned into a point blank refusal to go any further without first having partaken of food, and resting the horses, which had begun to droop their heads from hunger, thirst and fatigue.

After about an hour's rest, and some tea and damper, they again sought their saddles and set out.

Twice they had heard distant footsteps in the bush, and as often were disappointed, coming across some of the men from the house also on the search.

At last, after wandering about the whole day, and far into the night, they sadly and wearily turned their horses' heads homeward, determining to claim the assistance of the mounted police, and have the whole country round thoroughly scoured and examined.

It was not until nearing the house that they first heard faintly through the bush the cries for help.

They knew not whether it was the voice of Georgie, or whether the station had again been stuck up in their absence.

Nor, in sooth, did they pause to think.

Digging their spurs into their jaded steeds, and reckless of the danger from tree stumps and dead timber, they dashed on to the rescue.

As we have already seen, they were but just in time, for had they been but a few seconds later, our heroine would again have been dragged into the bush, and carried off to the cave in the rugged and almost inaccessible mountains lying away to the west, where pursuit would have been an almost impossible and hopeless task.

THE BUSHRANGERS STARTED, TURNED, AND SAW DEATH GLARING AT THEM FROM THE MUZZLES OF THE PISTOLS.

CHAPTER XLVII.

TED HOGAN STRIKES HIS FIRST BLOW.

THREE weeks after the scenes recorded in our last chapter, and when their incidents had been well nigh forgotten in the neighbourhood, except by the persons most interested, the landlady of the Cornstalk, who had by this time begun to be exceedingly uneasy at the absence of her liege lord, and to think of advertising him in the papers, was astonished by the simple and good tempered face of the little swagman beaming cheerily on her in the doorway, and bidding her good morning.

"Well, missis," said the little man, "what's the news? You don't look lively."

The missis shook her head, and sighed heavily.

"Nay, missis, surely not so bad as all that," resumed he. "Why, good gracious, whatever is the matter?"

"My poor, dear old man!" she replied.

"Well, what about him?"

"Ah, dear, dear," she answered, "I don't know. He's never come back again. I'm afeard he's gone and died, or something."

"Nay, surely not. Come, don't take on so," said he, wheedlingly. "Take a little drop o' gin to drive away the blues, hot with sugar. Co-o-me, now, do, there's a dear creature."

The landlady drew a still deeper sigh, and solaced herself with a drop of gin as the swagman had recommended.

"Feel better after that, now don't you?" he insinuated.

She shook her head despondingly, as if to say that nothing would, or could ever induce her to smile again, and asked him where he had been for so long a time.

He told her that he had been jobbing about, and was now come to stay a spell at her pleasant hotel, at the same time producing from his pocket a handful of notes, which wonderfully tended to dispel the gloom upon her face.

"By the way," said he, "you've had some comical goings on in this quarter lately, I hear—running off with gals, and that sort o' thing."

"Ugh, the villains!" she ejaculated, with all the spite her features were capable of expressing; "I should like to catch 'em at that game with me, I should so. And let me catch 'em, that's all.

As if Providence, desirous of accommodating her in that particular, had immediately attended to her, the clatter of the hoof strokes of two horses was at this moment heard coming along the road, and the next moment the two ruffians, laughing loudly, rode up to the door, and coarsely demanding to know whether Jacky Cain, whom they denominated "the old bloke," had yet arrived home, called for some brandy, and, seeing the little swagmen standing meekly at the bar, ordered him, with an oath, to come and hold their horses.

The little man, after a moment's hesitation, came out with an obsequious smile, and assisted them to dismount, Bob Loveridge wantonly giving him a rap over the fingers with his riding whip, as he held the stirrup, and the little man saying as he received it, "Ah, gentlemen will have their joke. Don't hurt me, sir; I'm only a little 'un," a plea which so amused Jack Last, that on going inside the bar, he ordered Joe to "take the little beggar a glass of brandy."

The two men then went into the back parlour, and the swagman gently walked the horses from before the open door.

But what was Joe the odd man's astonishment, when, taking out the brandy, he saw no longer a mild and inoffensive looking little bush traveller, holding horses for the sake of a nobbler, but a man with a stern, dark, and determined countenance, and the dull mooning look in his eyes replaced by the fire of intelligence and shrewdness.

He nearly let the brandy fall, as he stared in blank amaze at the transformed figure of the swagman.

"Come here, you Joe;" whispered the latter in short, sharp, commanding accents; "throw away that brandy, and look at me."

Joe obeyed instantly.

"Do you know who I am?" said the little swagman; "of course you don't though. Well, I'm Hogan the detective; I suppose you've heard of him?"

Joe's lower jaw dropped as he began to think over his numerous peccadilloes, and he echoed—

"Hogan the detective—oh lord!"

"Now mind me, Joe; you see this little plaything?" said Hogan.

The little plaything was a small six shooter, with a bright polished barrel that shone like silver in the sun, and Joe intimated that he did see it.

"I suppose you know what it is?"

"Well, yes, I reckon I do," replied Joe hesitatingly.

"I'm glad of that, because if you don't do exactly what I tell you, and make no noise about it, I'll send a bullet through your brains as sure as life."

Joe smiled a sickly smile, and tried to say something, but the detective stopped him by a gesture—

"You see yonder big tree," said he, pointing to one down the road; "you go to that tree, and call out 'Bungy.' Not too loudly, mind, so that those fellows in the house can't hear, do you understand. You see it's about forty yards from here, and as I can kill a pigeon at sixty with this little thing, why you'd better not try to sell me."

Joe thought so too, and obeyed the instructions with the utmost caution, stepping as though he had been walking amongst eggs.

He was rather startled, though, when from behind the tree in question, in answer to his call, a grinning black face suddenly popped up, and for a moment he thought that the word which the detective had bidden him utter, was a charm to raise the devil.

However, Bungy, who had been left in hiding there, whilst Hogan went into the house in the character of a swagman, reassured him, by asking him in true blackfellow language—

"Mas'r he say, me come 'long a you, eh?"

On being answered in the affirmative, the two stole softly back towards the house.

In the meantime the detective had taken the two revolvers carried at the saddle bows of the bushrangers' horses, and giving one of them to Bungy, he directed him to go round to the back of the house, and prevent the escape of the bushrangers, should they or one of them attempt it; and ordering Joe to follow him, he fastened the horses up to one of the werandah posts, and went into the house.

The bushrangers were smoking and drinking brandy and water, when he got into the room.

Bob Loveridge and Jack Last were seated at a table.

Hogan walked boldly in, followed by Joe, and without saying a word, turned and locked the door after him.

The bushrangers started and turned round.

Then, confronting Bob, who had risen from his chair in mute surprise, Hogan said—

"The game's up, Loveridge; you're done for, my lad. So you may as well give in quietly at once. I'm detective Hogan, and here's my warrant!" pointing to his little six shooter as he spoke.

Meanwhile Jack Last turned to the window behind him, but upon being met by the grinning face of Bungy in the aperture, with the muzzle of his own revolver pointed at his head, he sank back upon the seat.

"Trapped like a bandicoot," said he, whilst Bob Loveridge, suddenly drawing a knife, made a rush at the detective, but was met by the unexpected blow from the shoulder, which had so astonished

Joe on a former occasion, and which sent him sprawling on his back in the fireplace.

"Don't cut up rough, my beauties," said the detective composedly," and you, Joe, just put these bracelets on that fellow down there, whilst I manage the other one."

The door being locked, he went over to Jack Last, who sat still muttering deep curses, and scientifically slipped the handcuffs over his wrists, an operation to which he submitted with surly indifference.

Bob Loveridge, however, was not so easily vanquished, for, determined to have a fight for it, he struggled and kicked in a most ferocious manner, inflicting several wounds on Joe, who was clumsily endeavouring to take hold of his hands. At length a howl from that worthy, caused by Bob having got the fleshy part of his arm between his teeth, and bitten it through, took the detective to his assistance, and cleverly catching the arms of the struggling ruffian, he handcuffed his hands behind his back.

"Now, gentleman," said he, "I'll trouble you to come along with me," an invitation which they both declined point blank, Bob, declaring that he would not move from where he was, and Jack swearing that if they wanted him to ship they'd just have to carry him.

The detective seemed in no way put out, but unlocking the door quietly, ordered Joe to go and put a horse into one of the drays, and as the gentlemen didn't seem inclined to walk, they should ride; and in a few minutes the conveyance being ready, the bushrangers were placed on it, and Joe directed to drive them to Marrangong station, the detective and Bungy riding one on each side, on the horses of the captured men, and Mrs. Cain standing out in her verandah, and watching them until they were out of sight.

CHAPTER XLVIII.
GEORGIE MORTIMER AND THE DETECTIVE.

THERE was not a pleasanter party in the whole of Australia than that which sat down to the evening meal at Marrangong station, on the day upon which the incidents mentioned in the last chapter occurred.

The shearing time was well nigh over, and the stay of Harry Miller was drawing to a close.

In fact, he had made up his mind to start for home several times during the week, but had always found something to detain him, endeavouring to persuade himself that his presence was still necessary for the proper carrying out of some piece of work or other, so that had not an imperative message from his father recalled him to a sense of his duties, it is hard to say whether the bright eyes and pleasant smiles of his cousin Georgie, would not have detained him for another month.

As it was, the young folks were very happy in each other's society, and the long walks and rides through the dim bush, to pay a visit to old Mike the shepherd, to see the limestone caves, or to watch the sun rise over the far distant purple hills, were sources of unmingled delight to the two hearts which in the heyday of youth beat in union.

Mr. Miller had left the station a few days before to pay a visit to some neighbours living at a distance, and Mrs. Beauvey, Georgie and Harry, were the trio who sat round the table.

Georgie sat demurely pouring out the tea, and presiding with that easy grace which invests young ladies with such a charm when in similar circumstances. In fact, it is questionable whether the hearts of as many gay young bachelors have not been entrapped by the mysterious rites and solemnities of the tea table, as by any other means.

Mrs. Beauvey was watching the young people pleasantly, and Harry, being of a turn of mind more practical than sentimental, was busily engaged in stowing away a piece of peach pie, which the fair hands of his cousin had manipulated in the morning.

They were suddenly startled in the midst of their quiet meal, by hearing the rapid gallop of a horse up the lawn in front of the house, and the next moment a sharp and loud rap at the door.

On opening it, Harry Miller was confronted by the sable face of Bungy, who advanced into the middle of the room, and with a grin that expanded his wide mouth from ear to ear, showing a set of teeth that would have sent many fine ladies into ecstacies of envy, so white and regular were they, he delivered himself thus—

"Mas'r Hogan, him one trap, come along just now, by'm-bye, he got him two fella along a dray, you see."

"What?" shouted Harry.

"Yowi, I believe," said Bungy, sententiously, and rolling his eyes around the room with that peculiar, childish inquisitiveness which characterises the aboriginals when they see anything new.

"Bushrangers!" cried Georgie, in alarm; "what does he mean?"

"I hardly know," replied Harry Miller; "but I'll go out and see."

This was, however, rendered unnecessary by the dray—driven by Joe, and containing the two villains closely guarded by the detective, who, having failed to induce them to talk, in hopes of getting something out of them regarding the grand object of his mission, had also relapsed into silence—appearing in sight at the bottom of the cleared ground.

The whole family, servants included, amongst whom the news had spread like wildfire, were by this time assembled under the verandah, watching the singular visitors who were approaching the house, and Bungy, having in vain attempted to get some one to attend to him as he asked "nobbler blandy," coolly walked over to the sideboard and helped himself to half a tumbler full, which he gulped down at once, without so much as winking over it.

In a few minutes the suspense of those gathered in the verandah had ceased, for the dray being driven up to the front of the house, the detective rode forward, and singling out Harry Miller, said to him—

"Are you the master of this place, sir? Marrangong, I think it is called?"

"This is Marrangong. I am not the master, but this lady is the mistress," replied Harry, indicating Mrs. Beauvey by a wave of his hand. "However, any business you may have here may be transacted with me."

The detective took him on one side, and informing him of the important capture he had made, and of the fact that these were the two ruffians who had stuck up Marrangong, asked that they might be lodged in a safe place, where he would leave Joe and the black fellow to watch them, as he had another important capture to make in the neighbourhood, showing at the same time his authority as an officer of the detective police.

Harry Miller, on the part of Mrs. Beauvey, immediately consented, and invited him in to join them at the tea table; but the detective politely but firmly declined, saying that he must complete his work before it was possible that the news of his being in the neighbourhood could have spread abroad.

He then set about securing the prisoners, and with the assistance of Harry Miller and some of the station hands, placed them in the stable, firmly barricading the door on the outside, and leaving them bound, handcuffed, and helpless within, lying on a bundle of straw in an empty stall.

He then instructed Joe and Bungy to keep strict guard until he returned.

This done, he went inside the house for the first time, in order to pay his respects to the ladies, and on Georgie's mentioning that she recognised the two bushrangers as the men who had carried her off to the hut in the forest—

"Carried you off, young lady?" said Hogan, who had not heard of that last exploit of the two worthies whom he had in charge. "You don't mean to say that they dared that outrage?"

"Indeed they did," replied Georgie, "and it was only by the greatest good fortune that I was enabled to escape."

"By George!" exclaimed Hogan, with a dim recollection that he had seen the lovely girl before, "they have more pluck, and"—he added, with a comical smile and side glance at Harry—"better taste than I should have given the rascals credit for."

But seeing that the young gentleman did not seem pleased with the freedom of his remark, he added, addressing Georgie—

"Jesting apart, young lady, I should be greatly obliged if you would favour me with the particulars of the matter. It might give me a clue to some other things I want to find out."

Georgie readily complied, detailing the whole of the unpleasant adventure from beginning to end, the detective sitting, leaning with his elbows on the table, listening attentively, and absently stroking the lower part of his face with his left hand, as was his custom when in deep thought.

He never interrupted her, nor moved a muscle of his countenance, until she came to where she saw the old man come from the house towards her, as she stood at the bottom of the stockyard, near the ruined house, when he slightly moved and asked her to describe the old man more particularly.

She did so, and he with a slight smile ejaculated, "Ah!" relapsing into silence again.

When, however, she mentioned the old well, and the singular act she had witnessed there, he struck his fist on the table with a loud oath, which caused Georgie and her aunt to start in alarm, and jumping up he cried in excited and triumphant tones—

"That's it, that's it, I have the villain now upon both charges! Excuse me, ladies, but I must go at once. Good night to you. Good night, Mr. Miller. I shall be back here in the morning, with yet another prisoner—a cold-blooded murderer."

"Murderer?" they all cried, staring at his white and excited face; but he did not reply, and snatching up his hat which he had thrown carelessly on the sideboard, he rushed wildly from the house, leaving them looking aghast into each other's countenances.

From the house he went direct to the stable, and ordering Bungy to saddle him one of the horses which he had taken from the prisoners, he went to see that they were all safe.

"What are you going to do with us?" asked Bob Loveridge sullenly.

"Leave you here till morning, and then take you off to Braidwood, my lads," he replied. "In the meantime, I'm going to see an old friend of yours, whose company you'll have down to-morrow—old Billy-the-Bull, I mean."

"What's he been up to?" asked Bob Loveridge anxiously, fearing that the cattle-stealing episode was coming to light.

But Hogan was not inclined to satisfy his curiosity.

"You'll find that out quite soon enough, my hearty, never fear," he answered; "in the meantime, I'll tell 'em up at the house to send you down some tucker, for I don't want to starve you, and then you'll be comfortable for the night. But mind," he added threateningly, "no nonsense, or it'll be the worse for you; you can't escape, so you'd best not try it on, but make up your minds to take it easy."

Bob assented with a surly grunt, and Jack Last mentally consigned him to a place worse even than Braidwood Gaol.

He, however, took no further notice of them, but, giving strict injunctions to Bungy and Joe, mounted b's horse, and rode off in the direction of the dilapidated house of Billy-the-Bull.

CHAPTER XLIX.
TRAPPED AT LAST.

IT was a long and weary ride in the fall of the day from Marrangong station to the residence of Billy-the-Bull, and Ted Hogan, as he galloped under the swaying branches of the lofty gum trees, felt the depressing influence of the gloom that surrounded him.

The night wind hummed its melancholy song through the foliage, and the clouds, which had been coming up from the south all the evening drove rapidly over the dull firmament, presaging a wild night.

Ted Hogan pressed his horse on at a more rapid speed, so as to reach his destination before the storm burst.

On his arrival at the bottom of the stockyard which was situated between the bush and the house, he dismounted, and quietly leading his horse round through the scrub to the back of the premises, left him in a half ruined outhouse, whilst he leisurely walked up to the front and knocked at the door.

The old man, who was sitting crouched over the fire, gloomily smoking his short pipe, rose and went to see who it was who sought admission, and on opening the door was met by the cheerful face of the little swagman, who had a few weeks before put the lock on his bedroom door, and who looked up to him with a smile as he said—

"I told you I should be coming round this way again, and would give you a call, so I've just looked in to see whether there's any other little job I can do for you."

The old man scowled upon him with his evil eyes and replied in a surly tone that he "had nothing for him to do," at the same time attempting to close the door.

The swagman, however, placed his foot in the opening, in such a manner as to prevent its closing, and in supplicating tones said—

"You wouldn't go for to turn a poor fellow out into the bush on a night like this, would you?"

"Go and find a place in the kitchen at the back, or in the stable, or anywhere else you like. I've no room for you here, that's certain," answered the old man snappishly.

"But look here, master," pleaded the swagman in a doleful voice, "I'm blessed hungry, can't you give us a pot of tea and a bit of damper?"

"No," shouted the old man savagely, as he found that he could not shut the door, "get out, or it'll be the worse for you."

"I've got a few shillings left, and I don't mind paying for it," said the swagman ready to cry.

Billy relaxed the grim expression of his countenance, as the little fellow said this, and opening the door replied in a more kindly voice.

"Oh, that alters the case. If you're willing to pay for it, of course you can have a feed here. I can't afford to be giving tucker to everybody on the road."

"All right, master," was the answer; "I'll pay you," and so saying, the swagman entered the house.

A moment's glance round the inside of the room showed him that the back door was barred, and he rapidly turned and bolted the door after him, and then sprang before the entrance to the bedroom.

The old man turned round on hearing the noise, to see what was the matter was.

Where was the swagman? and who was that

stern-browed man confronting him, with the firm mouth and the eyes that glowed like live coals?

Billy-the-Bull felt that the time was come, and in a harsh and husky voice shouted—

"What the blazes do *you* want?"

"William Daley, alias half-a-dozen other names, alias Billy-the-Bull," replied the other in a loud voice, "I arrest you in the name of the Queen for the murder of Patrick Connor the hawker, and also of John Cain, the landlord of the Cornstalk Inn on this road, and here is my warrant," at he same time holding up a sheet of paper which he had drawn from the bosom of his jumper.

The old man became sickly pale as the detective finished speaking. The room swam round him, and he fell heavily upon the floor in a deep swoon.

"Much better thus," said Ted Hogan to himself, as, stooping over the prostrate form on the floor he quietly handcuffed him, knowing that when he came to himself he would most probably be violent.

He did not attempt to recover him, however, but allowed him to come to himself naturally, which he did after a little while, awaking with a long, deeply-drawn sigh, and staring round the room for a few moments with wild and haggard eyes.

"What's all this about?" he said at last, as, trying to rise, he found his hands encumbered by the handcuffs. "Who are you and what do you want here?"

"I'm a detective officer," was the reply; "my business you know already, so you'd better keep yourself quiet until morning."

"It's a lie," he shouted with a howl like that of a wild beast, at the same time madly struggling to wrench off the irons that held his hands—"it's a lie. I never did it. You can't prove it," and he struggled unavailingly until the blood flowed from his wrists.

"We'll see about proving it, by-and-by," replied Ted Hogan gently. "Just you be quiet, for it's of no use struggling; you can't escape, and if you tried it on I should shoot you; so lie still and I'll give you some blankets."

"Take off these bracelets," said the old man sullenly. "Take 'em off I say. You can't prove anything agin me, you can't."

The detective made no reply, and Billy after a short pause, asked in a quieter manner,—

"Where are the proofs that you talk of?"

Ted Hogan turned round on him with a stern, uncompromising look, and said—

"You'll know all about it soon enough, never fear. If it'll ease your mind though, I don't mind telling you where the proofs are. They are at the bottom of the old well at the back, and in the myall scrub near the Green Swamp. I've seen Jacky Cain's corpse."

The wretched murderer turned perfectly livid at this. He tried to speak but his tongue clove to the roof of his mouth, and with a deep groan he fell back on the floor in a paroxysm of terror.

The detective covered him with a rug, and all through the livelong night kept watch over him as he lay, sometimes weeping, sometimes screaming out horrid blasphemy, and sometimes begging his stern and silent guardian to release him.

Insensible to all this however, as he was to the howling of the wind outside, and the banging of doors, and rattling of window frames in the ricketty old building in which he was seated, the detective sat silent and immovable as a statue, smoking his short cutty pipe, and only giving signs of life when he shifted to refill it or to throw another log of shea oak or red gum on the fire.

CHAPTER L.

THE RESCUE.

SUDDENLY, however, the detective's attention was attracted by Billy-the-Bull commencing to talk in his sleep.

At first he only uttered a disjointed word here and there, between groans and gnashings of his teeth, but presently, as he tossed and turned, and clenched his manacled hands, whilst the great beads of perspiration stood out upon his brow, his utterances grew more connected and cohesive, forming themselves into intelligible sentences.

"I didn't kill *him*. They cannot say that I wasn't merciful once. Ah! ah! ah; saved him alive for five years—and fed him regular, too. But then I killed his father, mother, and sister, and it ain't lucky to destroy a whole family. Well, he's worse off down in the old well than if he was buried once for all under the turf."

He relapsed into silence again, and Ted Hogan bent over him with a face as pale as his own, hoping that he would speak again.

He had not to wait long.

"No, I didn't spare the boy to become a madman, and a madman he is at this moment. Would that I could have served the infernal trap the same way. Let me see, Hogan he was called, and I smashed his brother's brains in. Ah! ah! ah! I killed the hawker and Jacky Cain in a cleaner way. Ha! ha! ha!"

"Merciful powers! it's Blue Cap," exclaimed Ted Hogan, a great spasm crossing his features. "Fool that I was not to have recognised him before, and yet can it be? Five years seemed to have added twenty to his age. He was a fine stalwart middle-aged man, and now he is old and grey. Can it really be Blue Cap?"

"Blue Cap! who says that I am Blue Cap?" exclaimed the old man suddenly awaking and looking fearfully around him. "Blue Cap has been dead and buried many a day."

"Liar, *you* are he," rejoined Ted Hogan. "You are he beyond a doubt, and I am the brother of the trooper whom you slew aboard the convict schooner in Twofold Bay. I made a vow then that I would slay you with my own hand, and heaven has delivered you into my power in order that I may keep it. The reward is for your body alive or dead, and dead it shall be. Blue Cap, wholesale murderer that thou art, die the death of a dog!"

He raised his revolver to fire, but another revolver was raised quicker still to a chink in the outer wall of the hut, a malevolent watery grey eye glanced along the barrel, taking what was meant to be a deadly aim at the detective's head, and crack went the weapon before he could pull his own trigger.

Lucky it was for Ted Hogan that he sat in a dim and uncertain light, or his career would have been put a stop to there and then.

As it was the bullet glanced by the side of his face, taking the upper tip of his right ear off, stunning him for a few seconds, and burying itself in the opposite wall.

The room spun round him as he heard a rush at the door, and saw Bob Loveridge, the bushranger dash in.

He, however, raised his revolver again to despatch Blue Cap; but rendered dizzy by the blow of Bob Loveridge's bullet, he missed his aim, even though he discharged his weapon within a couple of yards of the old villain's head, and almost at the same moment, the aged ruffian struck him violently on the head with the handcuffs with which his wrists were pinioned—very much as he had struck his brother five years ago, only not with half the strength—and knocked him down insensible.

And now to inform the reader how this unfortunate rescue came about.

Joe and Bungy, who had been left in charge of

the two bushrangers, after keeping watch over the stable for two or three hours, began to get sleepy; and the hands on the station, amongst whom the capture had created no inconsiderable degree of excitement, plying them with grog, had rendered them less careful than they otherwise would have been.

In the middle of the night, therefore, Bungy proposed that he should go to the men's hut, and see if he could get a bottle of rum and some tobacco, whilst he left Joe in sole charge.

This was agreed to, and the blackfellow trotted off, promising to be back soon, and warning his companion to keep awake.

He had scarcely gone, however, when Joe, overcome by fatigue and the liquor he had taken, dozed off, and was soon in a profound sleep.

The two bushrangers inside, who had heard Bungy depart, and who judged from the nasal music outside that Joe was fast asleep, knew that this was their time for an attempt at escape; and the younger of the two, by a trick he had learnt during his sojourn at Cockatoo (namely, by striking the handcuffs sharply and in a peculiar manner upon a stone), caused the spring with which they were fastened to fly back, and his hands were thus freed in an instant.

Jack Last, however, having his hands secured behind him, was not so successful, and after several attempts gave it up as a bad job; cursing his companion—who was busy looking after his own safety—for a coward and a cur in leaving him, and threatening to awake the sleeping guard outside.

This, however, Bob Loveridge effectually put a stop to by striking him over the head a blow with a spade, that knocked him totally insensible and nearly split his skull open.

He then scrambled up to the hayloft, and wrenching the staple out of a worm-eaten door that overlooked the back of the stable, opened it, and dropped noiselessly upon the dungheap outside.

The guard at the front door still slept soundly, and there was no sign of Bungy's return; so, rapidly saddling a horse that stood under a shed, and taking the revolver which the blackfellow had left in the hands of Joe, he rode off at a rapid pace in the direction of the house of Billy-the-Bull.

Hatred and black revenge were gnawing at his heart, and his sole thoughts were how to wreak a summary vengeance on the detective and at the same time get clear away.

He knew that the officer had gone to arrest the old man, and as he rode along beneath the giant trees which swung to and fro in the tempest that howled amongst their branches, he chuckled with fiendish glee at the diabolical scheme he had invented and arranged.

Leading the horse as near to the house as he could without being heard, he—the sound of his footsteps being quite inaudible in the roaring of the wind—carefully sought that chink in the wall that from a prior acquaintance he knew would give him a full view of the interior of the house, and having found it he peered through, and saw the detective in the act of taking aim with his revolver at Blue Cap, as he sat up manacled on the ground.

How he turned the tables upon the police officer, we have already narrated to the reader.

CHAPTER LI.

RUN TO EARTH AT LAST.

"THERE'S many a slip 'tween the cup and the lip," is an adage not more trite than true. On this particular occasion, detective Hogan found it so to his cost.

He had, after no inconsiderable degree of toil and ingenuity, succeeded in bringing home the crime, which he had been sent to investigate, to the right party. He had discovered the whereabouts of the body, and not only that, but had fixed another horrible crime on the perpetrator, making the discovery, in addition, that he was the famous bushranger who, for five years, had so mysteriously disappeared from the scene of his former atrocities. He had also captured two out of a band of three embryo bushrangers, cattle-duffers, and housebreakers, and had done all, so to speak, single-handed.

And now, in the very moment of his triumph, an unsuspected accident had occurred, which had broken the strongly woven web of his plans. One stitch had given way, and the entire fabric was ravelled.

Not quite, though, for the detective, although rendered dizzy by the concussion of the bullet and stunned for a few seconds by a blow on the head inflicted by Blue Cap with the handcuffs, soon came to himself.

The room span round and round him, and his aching head appeared to be rising—rising—rising with the rapidity of an unballasted balloon, until partially recovering his senses, he began to remember where he was.

Outside he heard the clank of iron upon iron, and as he rose a sudden snap proclaimed the fact that his prisoner's handcuffs had given way.

Staggering to his feet, and scarcely able to stand, he unsteadily made his way to the door, arriving there just in time to see Blue Cap and Bob Loveridge, whom he thought he had left safely fastened up in the stable at Marrangong, in the act of mounting—Blue Cap having found the horse which he had ridden hither, and had placed in the outhouse at the back of the premises—and Bob Loveridge on another one.

As he reached the door, still holding himself up by the posts, Blue Cap trotted off down the paddock, calling upon Bob to follow him.

The sight recalled his wavering energies, and with a bitter imprecation at his ill fortune, he snatched his revolver from underneath his woollen shirt, where it it had been concealed (his own private and trusty little revolver, which he had not yet called into use), and with an uncertain hand fired at Blue Cap, that worthy replying with a laugh of contempt, as he turned round in his saddle, and saw him at the doorway unable to stand steadily.

At the same moment Bob Loveridge, riding past the door, returned the shot, but it had been better for him if he had not attempted it, for owing to the restiveness of his horse, he fired wide of his aim, and Ted Hogan, steadying himself by a tremendous effort, fired point blank at him, and shot him through the body.

Bob Loveridge, with a loud shriek, pulled his horse back upon its haunches, reeled in his saddle, tried to steady himself and fell heavily backwards upon the ground, clutching the short dewy grass with his crooked fingers, and groaning deeply in his death agony.

The detective, now rapidly recovering from the dazed condition in which he had been thrown, ran as well as he could towards the fallen man, whose horse was plunging violently and endeavouring to break loose from the hand which so convulsively clutched the rein, and after, with some difficulty freeing the brute, mounted him and set off in pursuit of Blue Cap, who, seeing what had happened, had forced his horse to the top of its speed, and was now flying over the open space which lay between the house and the bush.

Swaying to and fro from side to side on his horse, which, frightened by the incidents which had just taken place, and by the voice and heel of the man who bestrode him, he bounded along at a tremendous rate over the open ground in the wake of the flying murderer.

The tempest which had been brewing the whole

evening had burst forth in all the terrific grandeur of an Australian thunderstorm.

The wind howled in wild gusts amidst the lofty trees which were thinly scattered in the bush through which the two men were madly flying, the artillery of heaven bellowed almost incessantly, and the bright light bolts, which shot in fearful splendour across the leaden sky, lit up almost every instant the gloom, dazzling the eyes of both man and horse, and leaving a void of black darkness.

Still guided by the glimpses which he caught during the flashes, and dimly discerning Blue Cap throught the gloom, when the interval was longer than usual between them. Hogan kept on the track of the fugitive, who had lost all idea of whither he was going, and rode recklessly onward, urging his horse to the very top of its speed.

Presently a vivid sheet of lightning streamed across the heavens, and at the same moment a clap of thunder, which seemed to rend the very firmament in twain, pealed through the air, causing both horses to swerve, and both riders to shut their eyes and hold their breaths in turn.

There, right before them, just as had happened during a very similar race five years ago, smitten by the electric fluid, crashed a giant iron bark down—down—down, with a shock which shook the very earth, and sent the splinters and wrenched-off branches flying in all d rections.

Fortunately for Ted Hogan, the flash of lightning which had so dazzled the eyes of the horses, had caused Blue Cap to turn off from the road he had hitherto been pursuing, almost at right angles, so that by making a slight detour round the wide-spreading branches of the tree that now lay prone upon the earth, and cutting off the angle, he lost but little distance.

At this moment, just again as they had done five years ago, a few large warning drops, precursors of the coming rain, fell heavily on the leaves overhead—then a thick pattering—and the next instant it came down in a perfect deluge, drenching both pursuer and pursued to the skin, in a moment.

Still they kept on their headlong course, urging their flagging steeds, whose flanks heaved and fell, and from whose nostrils the white breath streamed convulsively.

Neither had as yet gained any advantage. They had ridden about six or seven miles, and had maintained about the same relative positions as when they started. Their horses were, however, becoming rapidly exhausted, and it was evident that the race must soon be decided.

Neither of the men spoke. They both looked stern and determined, and the baleful light of hatred and mortal terror shone in the old man's eyes at each successive flash of lightning.

Just then his horse stumbled and nearly fell, but with almost superhuman exertion, he kept him on his feet.

This slight accident, however, retarded his speed, and the detective was slowly drawing up with him, when suddenly catching its foot in the root of a tree, the horse he bestrode staggered forward a few steps, and fell with a heavy crash to the ground, hurling its rider over its head, whilst at the same time the animal coughed up a column of blood from its mouth and nostrils, and with a spasmodic gasp stiffened out and died.

Blue Cap heard the crash, and looked round with a loud laugh of fiendish delight, at the same time as the detective, scrambling to his feet and with a loud oath, pointed his revolver at him, and pulled the trigger.

There were still three chambers loaded, and he snapped them rapidly in succession at the flying object before him, but they all missed fire.

They had become thoroughly wetted by the drenching rain, and the powder would not ignite.

With a cry of despair, Ted Hogan hurled the pistol in impotent rage and fury after the old man, and then sank exhausted on the grass.

At this moment a bright sheet of flame spread over the heavens, and Blue Cap screamed aloud in an agony of terror, and tried but in vain to stop the wild speed of his maddened horse.

The wild wierd note of a laughing jackass rang in his ears for an instant (was it the prophetic bird of the Green Swamp?), and the next, Ted Hogan saw a wild figure on horseback showing blackly against the blinding light, spread abroad its arms, and disappear apparently into space.

And so they had, for rider and horse had plunged headlong into that yawning and horrible gulf, through which, a thousand feet below the swollen flood of the mighty Shoalhaven river, rushes like a stormy sea.

Pale with terror at the frightful fate he too had so narrowly escaped, Ted Hogan crawled to the brink of the frightful chasm, and attempted to pierce the darkness below.

But he could see nothing—nothing but the boiling as in a cauldron of the black and seething waves, and hear nought but their sullen rush and roar against the vast rocks, at the base of the terrible precipice; and he turned away sick at heart, with the cold perspiration streaming from every pore, and silently and slowly made his way backward through the darkening bush.

CHAPTER LII.

THE CAPTURE IN THE BUSHRANGER'S HUT.

TED HOGAN did not recover his self-possession for a good five minutes after the clear comprehension of the terrible fate that had overtaken the murderer of his brother.

That he had been dashed to pieces in his fall there could not remain a doubt.

Nay, in all probability the rapidity of his fall through space had destroyed life before his body came in contact with the ledge of rocks at the bottom of the abyss.

And how near he had been to sharing his awful fate !

Had not his horse fallen dead, he would assuredly have done so.

The maddened animals would have taken the leap almost together.

Thankful for his almost miraculous preservation, Ted Hogan, as soon his strength somewhat returned, set out on his backward journey towards the hut; for he knew of no place of shelter nearer, and as Blue Cap's body was of as much value dead as alive, it might safely be where it was until he chose to go for it; but Bob Loveridge, unless mortally wounded, might get off scot free, and Jack Last escape him still easier, by reason of his whole bones.

It was no easy matter to retrace his way on such a night of pitchy darkness and blinding lightning.

He did so by the simple expedient of turning his back on the wind that, during the whole chase, had been in his face, and trusting that it hadn't suddenly veered round, he stumbled on and on mile after mile, as though he had been in a dream, until at last he fell over something, which turned out to be the body of Bob Loveridge, stiff and cold in death.

"Two hundred and fifty pounds lying about in that manner !" murmured the astute detective, as he picked himself up, and waited for the next flash of lightning to show him the position of the corpse more distinctly.

When it came, he continued—

"Yes, a thousand pounds in the valley of th' Shoalhaven, two hundred and fifty here, and another two hundred and fifty, perhaps, at Marrangong, or perhaps waiting to settle my at Blue Cap's hut. But I'll have him—I'll have him; and one thousand five hundred pounds ain't bad as the times go. No, not at all bad as the times go."

This soliloquy and connection, together with the conviction that he must be near the end of his journey, even though he couldn't see the hut in the gloom, gave the detective fresh strength and spirits.

His keen dark eyes flashed with their wonted fire, as he drew forth his revolver, and carefully reloaded it in every chamber.

"Now, Mr. Jack Last, I'm ready for you," he muttered, as he replaced it in the breast pocket of his jacket. "Bedad, if you're lying in wait for me and it comes to a shooting match, we'll just see who can shoot the longest and the straightest."

He gave utterance to a queer little chuckle as he resumed his course; waiting, whenever he was in doubt, for a lightning flash to show him the way to his goal, the bushranger's hut.

At last he espied its low dark outline underneath the darker foliage of the red gums.

'Twas all now plain sailing.

He reached it, and passed through the wide open door into its interior, a hand on his revolver-stock the while.

He listened.

All was as still as the grave.

Perhaps there were many graves, the detective thought, beneath the hard earthen floor upon which he stood.

With dawn he would find a spade, and dig for the skeleton of the hawker.

He knew where the old man kept his rugs and blankets, and the position of the cupboard that contained his food.

Ted was as handy in the dark as any cat, and hungry as a hunter, for he had not partaken of food for many hours; so to the cupboard he went first, and opening the door, felt and found a hunk of bread and a piece of cheese within.

Taking one in either hand, he devoured them to the uttermost crumb, and then his appetite was appeased.

"He did keep a bottle of whiskey here, too," he soliloquised, and again his hands went to work above the shelves.

Then there was a sharp click, and a yell of pain.

Ted Hogan had unwittingly got a finger or two of his right hand inside a rat trap, which closed with a spring, and held them as in a vice, nearly nipping them to the bone.

The pain was excruciating, and the yell therefore excusable.

He withdrew his hand, and the trap along with it. Whilst attempting to free himself from the latter, he felt something cold against his forehead, and the descent of a heavy hand upon his shoulder.

At the same time a voice hissed in his ear—

"I've waited for you a long time, matey. I know'd you'd turn up here some time or other. You didn't expect to come across me instead of the old man, did you? He's safe enough in the hands of the trap, depend upon it, and 'twould be a devilish deal more pleasant for you, were you along with him."

"Come, come, master, don't be angry with me, because I've helped myself to a piece of your bread and cheese. Your door was open, and nobody answered me, when I asked if anyone was in, so of course I thought as you was out, and if I've made myself too much at home, why I axes yer pardon. I was main hungry and tired, or I wouldn't ha' done it," said Ted, in an assumed voice, for he knew who his interrogator was.

"That ain't the voice of Bob Loveridge, the d—— scoundrel who struck me over the head with a spade, and left me to die the death of a dog, after we had been mates for five years. It's lucky I'm an amiable patient kind of a chap, or I should

have blown out your brains, in mistake for another man's, and I'm hanged if I could have put 'em in again. Now, since you ain't Bob, tell me who the devil you are?"

"I'm only a travelling swagman, on my way to the Turrent for the sheepshearing. I'm an honest body, and no thief or housebreaker. I can pay for what I've eaten. I wouldn't have come into your house, indeed I wouldn't, hadn't I thought you was from home, and been well nigh starved. I should have put a half crown down on the table, before I left in the morning, to pay for what I've had, indeed I should," whined Ted piteously.

"Well, you are a green 'un, and no mistake," laughed the bushranger. "What's yer name, and why did yer yell out?"

"Jim Brown's my name, and I hollered because I put my fingers into your cursed old rat trap, which pinched 'em to the bone, darn it. However, there it is, off at last, darn it," and as he concluded the machine fell clattering to the floor.

"I aren't the proprietor of this place, any more nor yourself, so I think we'd best make ourselves comfortable, for I don't fancy, somehow, that he means to return just yet; and as for my mate, I expect he's nabbed agin, or if he ain't, I can settle with him one time as well as another. Let's make ourselves at home, eh?"

"With all my heart," echoed Ted; "but it's beastly dark, isn't it. If one of us had a match, and if we could find a candle or a lamp, it 'ud be more cheerful. I want something to drink, and I don't fancy feeling about for things no more—there might be another of them rat traps set about the place, and they're hard biters they are."

"All right," was the reply. "I'll strike a light in a minute."

Ted clapped his bleeding right hand into the breast pocket of his jacket, and the lacerated fingers closed around the stock of his revolver, though the agony nearly made him faint

Jack Last, for it was indeed he, struck his match, and shading it with his hand, searched the cupboard until he found a candle, which he slowly and carefully lighted.

"There, we shan't get into no more traps now,' he said with a chuckle, as he stuck it into a clay candlestick, and then held it up to have a look at the face of his companion.

"I'm afraid you've put your foot in a worse one than I did my fingers. Jack Last, you're bowled out again, my boy. Ah! stop that. Attempt to put out that light again, and your life expires quicker than the flame. D—— it, sir, move a hand an inch nearer to the butt of that revolver that I see protruding from your pocket, and you'll never live to pluck it forth. Put that candlestick on the floor and sit down beside it. It's no good calculating the chances of my missing you, my game cock. I've six barrels loaded, and I'll drive a waistcoat button into your pocket with each bullet, and never a fluke amongst them, and all before you can exclaim Jack Robinson. You'd better stand it quietly, old fellow. What can't be cured must be endured, you know," said Ted Hogan smilingly.

"What a cursed fool I've been, and the game all in my own hands too!" exclaimed Jack Last, gnashing his teeth in impotent fury.

But the levelled revolver of the detective, and the keen black eye glancing along the level with such deadly aim, overawed him, and he did as he was bidden.

With his left hand the detective drew a pair of handcuffs from his pocket, and threw them into the bushranger's lap.

"Clap your fists through them," he said curtly.

"I can't, they're too small," growled Jack Last, sullenly.

"Oh, yes, you can. Unclasp them, then thrust

your wrists through, and click them together with your teeth. Instinct will show you the way, or at least it had better do so. Don't jerk the key out, for I've to manage a slippery eel like you with one hand remember," smiled the little detective.

"It's too bad to force a fellow to handcuff himself."

"Oh, if you prefer my shooting you dead, only say the word, and I'll be only too happy to oblige you. You are worth quite as much to me dead as alive, and would be infinitely less trouble."

Ted looked so much as if he meant it, that Jack Last yielded to the inevitable, and did as he was bidden.

Then Ted walked over to him, and holding the muzzle of his revolver against his forehead with one hand, he turned the key in the handcuffs with the other, pocketed it, possessed himself of the highwayman's revolver, thrust it in one of his own pockets, and then said, with a dry laugh—

"Now we are on excellent terms, and perfectly understand each other."

"I wouldn't mind so much if that infernal villain, Bob Loveridge, sat beside me," said Jack Last, savagely.

"He will never sit, stand, or walk beside you, my friend. Bob Loveridge has cheated gaol, hulks, and gallows."

"How? What do you mean?" asked Jack Last, eagerly.

"Why, that he is as dead as King Pharoah. I didn't like to cheat Jack Ketch of his lawful prey, but if I hadn't shot him he'd have shot me, and a fellow's generally rather fond of his own life, or, at all events, I am," answered the detective, grimly.

"And he fell by your hand? Tell the truth now."

"He did, and fell like a man, as far as brute courage went."

"Then I forgive you the evil turn you've done me, from the very bottom of my heart. I suppose you're waiting here to nab the old man, Billy-the-Bull I mean, on his return?"

"Billy-the-Bull will never return, unless he comes as a ghost. I've just returned from hunting him to the death."

"Why, what had he done, poor old blokee? He hardly deserved that for dealing in cattle on the cross, did he?"

"Do you know who Billy-the-Bull was once?"

"No. I'm jiggered if I do. Bob introduced me to him."

"Well, he introduced you to an historical personage, did Bob, and what is more, to a ten times greater villain than himself. Did you ever hear of Blue Cap, the Bushranger?"

"Who hasn't? But he mysteriously disappeared years ago."

"If I hadn't blown off two or three fingers from his right hand, so that he could never use knife or revolver again with any certainty, he wouldn't have done so. He funked the trade after that, and took to the safer one of cattle duffing under the name of Billy-the-Bull. But he couldn't keep his hands clear of blood for ever. A travelling pedlar at last fell his victim. I shouldn't wonder if his body lay just under us now. His last victim was Jacky Cain, of the Cornstalk Inn hard by, and his first—his first this side the great herring pond, at least—was my twin brother. That's seven years ago now, and I swore that he should die by no other hand than mine. I had to wait a long while."

"But at last you had your revenge, eh?" ejaculated the bushranger, with eyes that flashed with excitement.

"No, I had not," replied Ted Hogan, solemnly. "A higher Power, who has said, 'Vengeance is mine—I will repay,' claimed him from me, and preserved my life to me at the same moment by a special miracle in my favour."

And Ted proceeded to give his prisoner a full account of the manner of Blue Cap's death.

"Well, I'm right glad that such a bloodthirsty old devil has had a free pass to another world," said Jack Last, when he had concluded. "But," he added, with a sigh, "it strikes me that it would have been a good deal luckier for me, master, if you'd gone along. I'd not be tripped up like a bandicoot now, at all events."

"Come, come, don't growl at what can't be helped. Perhaps it's lucky you're nabbed before you've gone on from bad to worse. That fellow, Bob, would have led you to the gallows in the end as sure as eggs. As it is, you never having taken life, it'll only be Cockatoo, and in time a ticket-of-leave. Then you must turn over a new leaf, and work on the square. It pays best in the end."

"Well, I believe it do, and I believe that you're not a bad sort either, for a trap, I mean. Next to your company, I'd like that of a whiskey bottle. Do you think there's one about? I know 'twas old Billy's favourite tipple, and he won't want any more of it, that's a very sure thing," quoth Jack, philosophically.

"And that being the case, I think we've as much right to it as anyone else," laughed Ted. "You just sit quietly there, my boy, and I'll take a little tour of exploration. Don't attempt to give me the slip, though, for with those things on you can't do it, and if you tried it on I should be forced to shoot you."

The hint was taken, as Hogan could see by the man's nod, and dejected glance. Taking up the candle, he searched every cupboard therefor, and found a greater abundance of good things than he had expected to constitute Billy's larder.

There was a kangaroo pasty, scarcely touched, a damper, a piece of cold jerked beef, and some biscuits. Nor was the whiskey bottle conspicuous by its absence. There it was, and nearly full. Jack Last hailed its appearance with a smile of satisfaction.

"Now," said Ted, as he laid the things out on the floor, "eat your fill and drink your fill too. I don't care how drunk you get, for you'll be all the happier, and a precious deal more easy to manage. You may not have a chance of such another blow out for years, so please to make the most of it."

Jack did not require much pressing. He was just the fellow to follow up the principle of keeping the spirits up by pouring spirits down, and after he had made a most hearty meal on the kangaroo pie, jerked beef, and damper, he took to the whiskey bottle most kindly, Ted Hogan feigning to drink his share, but only feigning, as the reader may be sure.

Jack, in fact, now got talkative, and insisted upon narrating to his captor and acquaintance some of his past experiences, and as Hogan did not care to go to sleep, and desired still less to talk himself, he signified his acquiescence, and lighting his pipe, leaned back against an empty rum puncheon, and refilling Jack's pannikin, told him to shoot ahead.

CHAPTER LIIL
AUTOBIOGRAPHY OF A BUSHRANGER.

"I WAS not always a bushranger. I was a squatter once and tolerably well off, but I was half ruined by a drought, and a flood completed it, drowning my sheep and cattle by thousands, and carrying my house and farm buildings away along.

"I had been for two years comfortably settled, with a nice lot of cattle and sheep, when the people south of me began to complain of drought. I had enough feed and water; the question was whether it would last.

"I called my bullock driver, Bald Faced Dick, into consultation. He was laid up at the time with a broken leg. Dick strongly advised my looking for a new station to the nor'ard.

"The sheep would do for months, he said, but he thought we were rather overstocked with cattle. I had a good deal of confidence in Dick's judgment, for he was a 'first fleet,' that is to say, he had come over with Governor Phillips in the first fleet; had seen everything in the colony, both good and bad; had, it was whispered, in early years fled from a flogging master; and lived, some said, with the wild blacks, though others averred 'twas with a party of gully rakers (cattle stealers). He swore horribly, and was dangerous when he had drunk too much rum, but he was a thorough bushman, and by the stars or sun, or by the fall of the land, could find his way anywhere by night or day, understood all kinds of stock, and could make bullocks understand him.

"He knew every roving character in the colony, the wealth of every station, and more about the interior than he chose to tell to all.

"With all his coarseness, he was generous and good-natured, and when well paid, and fairly and strictly treated, stood upon bush honour, and could be thoroughly depended on.

"For a present of ten pounds, he obtained from a friend of his (or at least so he declared) a description of a country hitherto unprospected, and with first-rate feed for cattle. Men like this, who can neither read nor write, have often a talent for description, which is really astonishing.

"Having heard a minute detail of the 'pack,' and studied a sort of map, drawn on the lid of a tea chest with a burnt stick, I decided on exploring in company with Dick, and, if successful, returning for the cattle and drays, and taking them up all loaded for founding a new station.

"We only took our guns and tomahawks, with tea, sugar, a salt tongue, and a small damper ready baked, being determined to make long marches, starting early, camping at mid-day, and marching again in the evening, as long as it was light.

"Our first stage was only 25 miles, to young Marson's cattle station. Marson was a cadet of a noble family, and having lived too fast at home and in India as a subaltern, had been sent out with a fair capital to Australia, under the idea that a fortune was to be had for the asking, and no means of expense to be found open in the bush. What money he did not leave in the bars and billiard rooms of Sydney, he invested in a herd of six hundred cattle, to look after which he engaged four men—one because he could fight, another because he could sing, and all because they flattered him.

"With these fellows he lived upon terms of the most perfect equality, with a keg of rum continually on tap. Then lastly, for want of better society, he made his hut the rendezvous of a tribe of tame blacks, who were only too delighted with such a host.

"We found him sitting on the floor, in a pair of trousers and a ragged shirt, unwashed, uncombed, pale faced and red eyed, surrounded by half-a-dozen black gins (women), a lot of dogs, poultry, a tame kangaroo, and two of his men.

"The floor was littered with quart pots, lumps of fat, and fragments of damper.

"Outside the hut the relations of the black ladies had made a fire, and were cooking a piece of a fine young heifer.

"What with the jabbering of the gins, the singing and swearing of the men, and the yelping of the dogs, it was no place for a quiet meal, so we only stayed long enough to drink a pot of tea, so as not to offend, and passed on to camp an hour, under the shade of some golden wattles on the river's bank.

"Marson, with the assistance of his black friends, soon consumed his stock. The next time I met him he had changed his name, as well as his occupation. He was Bob Loveridge, cattle duffer and occasionally bushranger. I needn't tell you any more about him—you have finished his history yourself.

"Our course, after leaving his station, and after crossing the dividing range, lay over a flat country, all burned up as far as the eye could reach—a perfect desert of sand.

"The chain of pools which formed the river after rain, was nearly choked up by the putrifying carcases of cattle, smothered in fighting for water. The air was poisonous, the horses sank fetlock deep at every stride, the blazing sun was reflected back from the hot sand with an intensity that almost blinded our half-shut eyes.

"After three hours of this misery, we struck into a better country, and soon came to the camp of a squatter, who had been forced forward by the drought.

"He had marked out about twenty miles along the river for his run, a pretty good slice I thought, when, before turning back, he said—'There, that is all that I require.' But it was no business of ours, as we had views much further afield than that.

"For three days we pushed on, making from thirty to forty miles a day, without seeing anything exactly to our mind.

"We rode over sand plains dotted with scrubby brushwood, then up precipitous hills, now leaping, now clambering down and up, and now making a wide detour to avoid dry gullies and ravines, passing occasionally breaks of green pasture, but insufficiently watered for our purpose.

"Sometimes our way lay along mountain sides, sometimes up the dry bed of a mountain torrent.

"Sometimes huge boulders interrupted our course, sometimes the gigantic trunks of fallen trees. More than once we had to steer through a forest of the monotonous, shadeless gum, with its lofty, dazzling white trunks, festooned with the brown curly bark of the previous year, and its parasol-like but shadeless branches, where crimson green and snowy parrot tribes shrieked and whistled among the dark ever-green leaves.

"It is impossible to conceive anything more gorgeous than the plumage of these birds, as they fluttered in the sun; but I confess, that on serious thoughts intent during this portion of the journey, they were more often associated with my ideas of supper than in any other form.

"The evening of the third day we found ourselves obliged to camp down with a scanty supply of brackish water, and no signs of any living thing near us.

"The next day was worse.

"A land of utter silence and desolation, where it seemed as if mountains had been crumbled up and scattered about in hills, hillocks, rocks and lumps.

"The dry earth cracked, and yawned in fissures in all directions.

"Failing to find water, we camped down parched, weary, silent, but not despairing.

"The next morning the horses were gone.

"I cannot find words to describe what we suffered in the subsequent twelve hours. I had walked till my feet were one mass of blisters, and was ready to lie down and die ten times during the day; but somehow I found strength to walk, always chewing a bullet.

"At length, at nightfall, we found our horses; and nearly at the same time, to crown our delight —water!

"At the sight of this, we both involuntarily sank down on our knees, to return thanks for life saved.

"The next morning, after a scanty breakfast, we set to work, and by dint of cutting away with axe and jack knife—at the expense of our clothes and skins—through a brigalow scrub for half a mile found our way into a gap, through which our track lay, and which we had missed.

"It led straight to the dividing range.

"After crossing five miles from the foot of the range through a barren track, our eyes and hearts were suddenly rejoiced by the sight of the wished-or land.

"A plain, covered with fine green barley grass as high as our heads, and sprinkled over with the myall scrub, which cattle and sheep will eat and thrive on, even without grass.

"Such was the delicious prospect before us.

"A flood had evidently but lately subsided, for lagoons full of water were scattered all about.

"A river, running at the rate of five miles an hour, serpentined as far as the eye could reach, from which the water fowl fluttered up as we passed.

"The eagle hawks were sweeping along after flocks of quail, and mobs of kangaroo hopped about on all sides like rabbits.

"There was no sign of sheeps' or of cattle hoofs anywhere; but it was evident that the aborigines were numerous enough, for several paths were worn down where they were in the habit of travelling from one arm of the river to another. We could trace their footmarks of all sizes, and thereupon we instinctively unslung our guns and examined the priming.

"Altogether I thought I had discovered the finest place for a cattle station in the colony; but I found out afterwards, that the first appearance of a new country before it has been stocked, is far from being depended on.

"We formed a camp in an angle of the river, so as to have protection on three sides, and then ventured, in spite of the danger, to light a fire, and to cook some game.

"Oh! how delicious was that meat!

"As I lay near the river's edge, peeping through the tall grass, I saw the horned emus, that now rare and soon to be extinct bird, come down the slopes on the opposite side to drink in great numbers.

"A sure sign that white men were, as yet, strangers to those plains.

"We spent some days in examination, and during our explorations, met with adventures with the blackfellows that I will not now relate.

"I marked a station with my initials, and in returning, made out a route practicable for drays, by which a month later I retraced my way with a large herd of cattle, although not without enduring more than I could till before dawn.

"Our horses having picked up their flesh during a fortnight's spell on the green plains, we got back at a rattling pace; but before arriving home we met with an adventure that is worth the narration, and which I shall never forget with life.

"It was the first station we reached after crossing the 'barrens' that separated our newly discovered territory.

"A hut had just been built for the stockman, a big, strong Irishman, more than six feet high, a regular specimen of the Tipperary chicken.

"He had been entertaining us with characteristic hospitality, and we were smoking our pipes around the fire, when the hutkeeper rushed in without his hat, and shouting—

"'Tom! Tom! the blacks are coming down on us all around, as hard as they can run. Shut the door!—shut the door, like lightning!'

"Tom banged it to, and put his shoulder against it, while the keeper was pulling up the bar, and Dick and I were getting the lock cases off our firearms. Unfortunately the door was made roughly of green wood, and had shrunk considerably, leaving a gap or fissure between each slab.

about thirty blacks hurled a

volley of spears that made the walls ring again, and then advancing boldly up, one of them thrust a double jagged spear through the door slap into Tipperary Tom's throat.

"My back was towards him at the moment, for I was busy putting a fresh cap on my carbine; I heard his cry, however, and turning, saw him reel and fall into the arms of the hutkeeper.

"I thrust the barrel of my piece through a hole against a blackfellow's chest, and fired at the same moment as my man did.

"The two niggers dropped, the rest retreated, but turned back and caught up their dead friends.

"Then Dick flung open the door, and gave them the contents of his other barrel.

"Then he shoved the hutkeeper's musket into my hands, and I gave them a charge of buckshot.

"Three more fell, and the rest, dropping their friends instead of picking them up this time, disappeared across the river.

"All this was the work of five minutes only, and directly they had gone we turned our attention to the wounded stockman.

"The spear had entered just under his chin, and came out at the back of his neck some three or four inches. There was no great flow of blood, but he was evidently bleeding inwardly.

"He was perfectly calm, but said he knew he was going to die.

"We cut the end of the spear short off, but did not dare to take it out. The hutkeeper got on a horse, leading another, and rode off for a doctor who lived a hundred and fifty miles away.

"He never stopped, except to give the horses a feed two or three times daily, during the whole distance.

"In the meantime, poor Tipperary Tom made his will, disposing of a few head of cattle, with a mare and a foal; and also signed a kind of dying declaration to the effect that he had never wronged any of the blacks in any way.

"The weather was very hot; mortification set in, and he died two days after receiving his wound.

"The outrage was reported to the Commissioner, but no notice was taken of it, although we were paying a high tax for the protection of the border police at the time.

"Five years have elapsed since we thus fought for our lives—since I read the burial service over the poor murdered stockman.

"A handsome verandahed villa now stands where stood the slab hut. Yellow corn waves over the Irishman's grave, and while cattle and sheep abound as well as white men, women and children, there is not a wild blackfellow within two hundred miles.

"With myself, however, a bad flood finished what a drought had begun.

"My horses, cattle, and sheep, were all drowned, and Bald Faced Dick with them. My house was carried away, and I was left penniless, homeless, and almost naked.

"Well, I had a hard fight with starvation, and cattle duffing, and bushranging, in partnership with Ted Marson, alias Bob Loveridge, as just sufficed to keep body and soul together.

"This is my history, and here comes the dawn, and visitors with it."

CHAPTER LIV.

THE UNEARTHING OF THE PEDLAR.

JACK LAST did not relate the experiences recorded in our last chapter exactly as we have done, but in a much more roundabout manner, interspersed with frequent attentions to the whiskey bottle, and hiccoughs innumerable, as a kind of drunken punctuation to his discourse, the full stops being remarkably frequent.

TED HOGAN, STEADYING HIMSELF BY A TREMENDOUS EFFORT, FIRED POINT BLANK AT BOB LOVERIDGE, AND SHOT HIM THROUGH THE BODY.

By the time that it was all told, the redoubtable bushranger was as harmless as a turtle-dove, and as incapable of standing, without support, as a prize turkey with his legs tied.

In short, he was just as our friend, Ted Hogan, the detective, wished him to be.

He had noticed the approaching visitors to the hut, and when the door was opened, and Bungy the black, in company with Joe, the odd man at the Cornstalk, came in, both looking very penitent and woe begone, he tried to stagger to his feet, failed in the effort, rolled over on to his back, gave utterance to an oath or two, and then growled himself off to sleep.

Then Bungy, in his pigeon English, began to stammer forth a long string of excuses for having kept such careless watch, throwing the chief fault, however, on Joe's shoulders, which that worthy metaphorically shook off with a curse or two, declaring that Bungy only was to blame.

"There, there, you're both tarred with the same brush, but you see I could do very well without you," replied Ted, pointing towards the somnolent bushranger; "you needn't be looking around for his mate—he lies as dead as Julius Cæsar, down in the hollow, and Billy-the-Bull, as you call him, is, if possible, deader still."

"Dat bery much dead, Mas'r Hogan—bery much dead indeed. Good job dat," muttered Bungy.

"A better job than you think, old snowball," said Ted, with an hyena like laugh; "but look up some spades both of you, and find me another. We have two or three hours of sexton's work here, and must all bear a hand."

"Sexum's work—what dat?" asked Bungy, curiously.

"Never mind, you'll know all in good time," replied Hogan, who knew the superstitious fears of the Australian blacks, and was sure that Bungy would no more help dig for dead bodies, than help to bury living ones.

Spades were soon found, and the trio went to work with a will.

"No pomtatoes nor nuffin else here, what for dig then?" Bungy would exclaim every time he stopped for a brief rest, but the detective would always reply with a smile, "Go ahead, Bungy, and you'll find out at last," whereat the black would briefly ejaculate, "My word!" and dig and delve for another five or ten minutes, like a very mole.

At last he ejaculated, "Something bery hard here, Mas'r Hogan."

"Up with it, then; perhaps it's a big gold nugget," was the reply.

"My word!" exclaimed Bungy, more energetically than ever, "plenty nobbler rum that buy, eh? plenty nobbler red rum, my song," and at it he went again.

But when, five minutes or so later, he pitched out of the hole, in which he had got down waist deep, a human skull, and saw its earth-filled eye-sockets and mouth turned towards him, he uttered a yell of fear, and throwing down the spade, was up and out of the hole in a twinkling.

"Ah!" said the detective, leaving his hole for the deserted one of the black, "Bungy has found the treasure after all."

"Shall I leave off digging?" asked Joe, the odd man.

"No," replied the detective curtly; "there may be more."

He spoke no more, but worked away as though he was digging for a wager, tossing out legs and feet and ribs at every stroke of his spade, and yet never stopping to examine either, and evidently in search of something more important still.

Joe could not help frequently stopping to look at him, wondering what he could be so eagerly in search of, and once or twice the blanched black face and wildly rolling eyes of the affrighted blackfellow were visible at the window.

At last, however, the detective uttered an exclamation of satisfaction, and took out of the hole a fore arm, with the hand attached.

He carefully wiped it with his pocket-handkerchief, and whilst he did so a grim smile crept over his countenance.

Then he drew from the breast pocket of his jacket the old glove he had found outside the hut so many weeks ago, and carefully drew it over the skeleton hand.

"The pedlar, without a doubt," exclaimed Ted; "the glove fits, the proper finger is wanting, the evidence is complete, the last link is welded into the chain."

He twisted the hand from the arm, and, gloved as it was, thrust it into a side pocket of his coat.

"Joe," he then said, "I'll give you five shillings to re-inter those bones and fill up the grave; I've got all that I want."

"Whose bones be them that you've dug up, master?"

"A travelling hawker's, whom Billy-the-Bull, alias Blue Cap, the bushranger, murdered ever so many months ago."

"What, him as was never seen aftre he left the Cornstalk, and that there was such a fuss made about at the time?"

"The same. I was sent down into this district on purpose to discover his body, and arrest his murderer, and I've done the one, and as good as done the other. Billy-the-Bull's limbs lie scattered about like that skeleton's, at the bottom of the Shoalhaven gulf, and I daresay by this time the jackalls and the native dogs have picked his bones just as bare," and Ted proceeded very nonchalantly to light his pipe.

Whilst he was smoking it, lazily and half sleeply, watching the while Joe's operation of re-entombing the scattered skeleton and filling up the grave, he heard the rapid thud of galloping hoofs coming down the glade outside, and looking through the window, he saw Miss Georgie Mortimer and her cousin riding towards the hut as fast as ever their horses could set hoof to grass.

"What's in the wind now, I wonder?" quoth the detective. "Only idle curiosity, I suppose. It's very strange, but I can never look into that girl's face without thinking of poor Frank Beaumont. I wonder where the villain Blue Cap left his bones? In some far away lonely gully or patch of scrub, I'll be bound, and perhaps after subjecting him to horrible tortures too."

Ere he had finished this half uttered, half mental soliloquy, Georgie Mortimer and her cousin had dismounted, thrown open the door, and entered the hut.

Georgie's face exhibited traces of strong excitement.

She was pale even to the lips, and her eyes were unusually bright.

After a hasty and anxious glance around, and a shudder as she noticed the nature of Joe, the odd man's, employment, she laid her hand on Ted's arm and exclaimed—

"The old well! the old well! have you searched that yet?"

"It is not needed, young lady; I have found all that I require here," replied the detective, pointing towards the grave.

"But Frank Beaumont!" gasped Georgie—"Frank Beaumont, who defended us all so gallantly, and who was carried away wounded, across that bushranger's saddle, five years ago, he is down that well! He is down there alive!"

Ted Hogan gazed inquiringly into the excited girl's eyes.

He saw the deep earnestness of their glance.

He turned almost as pale as herself as he responded—

"Good heavens, what makes you think so? It is a mad thought. It cannot be—the well is half full of water, you heard the stone splash into it the other night, you said so. How could human life be sustained for one hour, leave alone five years, in such a place? It is impossible, be assured."

"No, no," was the eager reply; "half way adown that old well there is a hole in the side, leading to a deep excavation, and in that horrid cave the young and chivalrous Frank Beaumont has lived and pined for five long weary years. I know it. I saw it all last night in a dream. The packet that I saw the old man lower down was his food, that was repeated in my vision, and I saw the unhappy prisoner come to the edge of the subterranean and haul in the parcel. Tell me, Mr. Hogan, will you humour me to the extent of searching the old well through?"

"I will, indeed, my dear young lady," replied the detective, "and I pray Heaven that your dream was a soul-inspired vision."

CHAPTER LV.

THE FINDING OF FRANK BEAUMONT.

"COME, sir, let us see into this," said Ted Hogan to Harry Miller, Georgie's cousin; "it seems to me an impossibility, and yet Heaven may have sent the dream, and guided the young lady's steps to this spot the other night, for high and inscrutable reasons of its own. Let us lose no time therefore."

Surely Georgie's enthusiasm and faith were alike catching, for the usually calm and emotionless detective was now seemingly as excited as herself in the matter.

"Come along, Joe, the dead man's bones can wait, and halloa out to Bungy to follow us. We are going across to the old well—you know where that is. Now Miss Mortimer, now Mr.—Mr.—Mr. What's-your-name? what's to be done, had best be done quickly. Not that I expect to find anything, but still stranger things have happened, and may happen again. Give the young lady your arm, she looks as though she would faint by the way. Me? oh, I'm all right enough. Do I look pale? all I want is rest and loss of blood, I assure you. Now, off we go."

So spoke Ted Hogan, as unlike his usual self as it is possible to conceive, and having spoken, he led the way, passing out through the back door, crossing the stock yard with hurried and uneven strides, and then striking across the small patch of scrub that lay beyond.

The old well was soon gained, and Ted Hogan taking up a pebble cast it down, listening to the thrice repeated rebound and then the hollow splash in the water at the bottom.

"It's very deep," he said, "and," he continued, leaning over the brink and peering down, "very dark and awful looking. I shouldn't wonder if it was full of foul air too, for such old wells often are. I'm sure no human being could live down there. I'm convinced that we are come on a wild goose chase."

"No, no, don't say that—for God's sake don't say that," cried Georgie, clasping her hands together. "If no one is down there, from whence could have come the dreadful voice that I heard ascend from its depths when that horrible and murderous looking old man lowered down the parcel?"

"Did you hear such a cry? You never mentioned it before," exclaimed Ted, another ray of hope lighting up his countenance.

"I had forgotten it until this moment, my mind is so confused," replied the fair girl; "but I did hear it for all that."

Ted Hogan made no reply, but examined the windlass roller and the rope that was thereto attached, very carefully.

"The roller's all right, but the rope is so rotten

that it wouldn't bear the weight of a child," he said, thoughtfully. "Joe and Bungy, go and hunt me up another rope. There are sure to be some lying about."

The two men started on their mission, and the detective placing his hollowed hands to his mouth shouted down the well—

"Is there anyone there? If so, answer. We are friends."

But no reply came up the well, save a hollow echo.

"You see there is no one there after all," said Ted.

"Yes, yes, there is. Halloa down again. He will yet answer."

Ted did as he was requested, and this time he sprang back with surprise, and something very like terror, so awful and wild-beast-like was the yell that answered him.

"There is something living down there, but it is not a human being," said the detective, with a shudder.

"Yes, it is. I know the voice. It is Frank Beaumont's; but he has gone mad. He is a raving lunatic!" exclaimed Georgie, falling on her knees and clasping her hands together.

"I trust to Heaven that you may be wrong," said Ted Hogan, fervently; and then he bellowed down the well again—

"I am your old comrade, Hogan. Are you Frank Beaumont?"

But the answer was the same, an unearthly yell that bore scarcely any resemblance to the human voice.

And now, Joe, the odd man, returned with a long rope—a new one—that he had found on the top shelf of the cupboard.

Bungy followed after him, looking childishly curious.

The rope was soon attached to the windlass roller.

The other end was fastened around the detective's waist.

Again the wild-beast-like howl came up from the watery abyss.

"I should not like your job, master," said Joe.

"Shall I go down?" exclaimed Georgie Mortimer, impulsively. "He risked all for me and mine. He would never have been in his present awful position but for meeting me that night in the bush. Let me descend, Mr. Hogan."

"My dear young lady, nor for worlds. If he is mad he might tear you to pieces, fancying you to be Blue Cap. Besides, it will require no small amount of strength to bring him to the surface, especially if he resists," said Ted.

"Oh, yes, so it will," acquiesced the lovely girl. "I can plainly do nothing. Go you down, and Heaven prosper you."

"Joe and Bungy, stand by the windlass handle and lower away," said Ted. "Keep sharp eyes for my movements below, for I may want you to haul me up at a moment's notice."

He said no more, but mounted on to the well parapet, and stepped over the brink into space.

Joe and Bungy slowly lowered him down—down—down!

"Stop!" they presently heard him shout, and looking down, they saw him swaying to and fro like the pendulum of a clock.

Then he seemed to pass through the walled side of the well out of sight, for they could only see the reflections of their own terrified faces in the still, glassy waters, far—far—below.

The fact was the detective had swung himself into the mouth of the cavern that opened to the left, about fifty yards below the earth's surface.

He now proceeded down it, the rope still encircling his waist, and a knife in his right hand, for he was still very uncertain as to what kind of an habitant he should find in that strange subterranean.

He was not for long left in doubt on that point however.

Low moaning, growling sounds saluted his ears, much more like those of an animal than of a man.

Ted thereupon paused, drew a fusee case from his pocket, and struck a wax vesta, which he held aloft.

The light showed him a hole rather than a cave, for its entire dimensions were only those of a small room.

Its walls, floor, and roof were of battered earth, there was not even a stool by way for furniture, and its solitary tenant was in reality a haggard, emaciated object, clad in rags, with hair and nails of enormous length, and great wild eyes, in which there was too surely the gleam of madness.

A more horrible specimen of mortality, Ted Hogan in all his experience had never seen.

He looked at the last gasp of starvation.

In places where he was naked his bones almost protruded through his skin, and even beneath his rags they were painfully apparent.

His face was that of an old man, wrinkled and stubbly bearded; his red glaring eyes were deeply sunken in their sockets; he was as loathsome in appearance as he was ugly, and as ugly as he was loathsome.

"Are you Frank Beaumont?" asked the detective.

A snarl like that of a wild beast, was the only reply.

"I am come to take you from this place," said Ted.

Almost ere the words had escaped his lips the madman was upon him, mouthing, jabbering, gnashing his teeth with fury, and crooking his long talons for the attack.

But though his intentions were deadly, he had no more strength than a child, so prostrated was he by his long confinement and want of sufficient sustenance.

Ted Hogan seized him, and threw him with ease, and when down, he hadn't the strength to rise to his feet again.

The detective unfastened the rope from his own waist, and secured it around that of the madman.

Then he dragged him to the brink of the well, and pushed him over, calling out to Joe and Bungy to haul him up, and then to lower the rope again for himself.

They were not long in doing this, but when the rope came down again, it hung with vibration in the middle of the well, and the detective perceived that to gain it, he would have to spring into space from the edge of the subterranean.

It required some nerve to attempt and succeed in this, with such an awful depth to drop in case he failed, for the clear cold water sparkled a hundred feet below him, and if he fell he would rebound again and again against the sides of the well, ere he dropped into it stunned and senseless, when he would of course sink like a stone.

He never hesitated for a moment, however, and luckily the leap was a good one, and he caught the rope with both hands.

"Haul up quickly," he shouted to Joe and Bungy.

They did as they were bidden, but Ted was heavy, the working gear rusty and out of order, and the work was necessarily slow and laborious.

Meanwhile the detective, who could not succeed in getting a coil around either leg or arm, grew weak in both hands and wrists, and the sweat sprang in great beads to his brow, as every instant the conviction grew stronger in his mind that he could never hold on until he reached the top.

"Haul up quicker, quicker!" he shouted again.

But they could not haul quicker, and a moment later, Bungy, perceiving Jack Last creeping around an angle of the hut, intent upon an escape, involuntarily let go of the iron handle, and darted off in pursuit.

Georgie's cousin seeing this, flew to reinforce Joe, but he came an instant too late.

Joe had glanced over his shoulder to see why Bungy had darted away, and the iron handle slipping out of his grasp, revolved like lightning, owing to the heavy weight dependent on the rope, struck him a heavy blow under the chin as he sought to regain it, that knocked out half his teeth and hurled him back insensible to the ground, whilst Ted Hogan with the velocity of light, luckily still grasping the rope, like grim death went down to the bottom of the well.

The next minute, dazed and giddy, he found himself afloat in icy water, that set his teeth chattering, and seemed to benumb every faculty.

The top of the well looked no larger than a crown piece, and an immeasurable distance above his head.

A sudden cramp in his hands caused him to let go his grasp of the rope, which immediately wriggled out of his reach.

Then he indeed felt that it was all up with him.

Meanwhile Harry Miller was calling out to Joe, who had risen to a sitting attitude, but seemed to be unconscious of what was going on, and to Bungy, who, being unarmed, was afraid to advance on the bushranger, despite the fact that he was handcuffed, to take charge of the windlass handle, whilst he went down, and endeavoured to rescue the detective from a watery grave.

"Be quick," he said, "or it will be too late! No man can keep himself afloat in that icy water more than a few minutes. I will let myself down the rope, and bring him up with me."

Then Joe, the odd man, spat out a couple of teeth and sullenly returned to his duty, and Bungy hurried back at a run, delighted to get quit of his gigantic and determined looking opponent by order, and therefore without any imputation on his courage—for Bungy's vanity was as great as his cowardice.

Both of them seized hold of the windlass handle again, and whilst Georgie Mortimer bent over the haggard, emaciated, and still unconscious Frank Beaumont, endeavouring to arouse him from his death-like swoon, her cousin threw aside his collar, necktie, coat and vest, and prepared to descend to the rescue of the detective.

"You'll never bring him up—you're too slight to have the strength," said a voice at his elbow, and looking round, he saw Jack Last, the bushranger.

"I must. No one else will try," was the reply.

"I'll try, if you'll let me. I'm as strong as a bull, and if the rope's tough enough, I'll have him up in a twinkling."

"How can you do anything with those handcuffs on, and besides you are far from sober. I can manage very well."

"You couldn't lift him up out of the water, were it to save your own life as well as his. I can though, so be the task mine. As to these bracelets, a blow, and they are gone; see!" and he struck them a sharp click against the stone parapet of the well, that somehow or other snapped the hard iron as though it had been earthenware.

"Now," he exclaimed with a laugh, "not a moment to be lost."

With the severed fragments of the handcuffs chain still dangling from either wrist, he took a firm grip of the rope with both hands, threw a leg around it as well, and with a warning to Joe and Bungy to wind up steadily, and without jerking, directly he halloaed out to them from the bottom of the well, he began a rapid descent.

He went down with a gyratory movement, like a corkscrew, and was almost immediately lost to sight in the inky depths below.

Then there was heard the hollow splashing of water, and in duller tones the bushranger's voice apparently speaking words of direction or encouragement.

It was an anxious moment, but presently the almost painful suspense was somewhat relieved by a hoarse shout of "Haul up—slowly does it!" from below, and then round and round went the windlass handle, beneath the nervous grip of the excited Bungy and the stoical Joe.

It seemed as though the two heads would never appear out of the darkness, and more than once the anxious spectators expected to see the stout rope snap in twain, with the double burthen that it was dragging upwards.

The wooden roller around which it wound itself sometimes bent too in an alarming manner, and, altogether, neither George nor her cousin expected to see Ted Hogan and his chivalrous rescuer make good their escape from the jaws of death that every moment seemed about to close upon them.

But their fears and doubts were happily now at an end.

The heads of the two men showed, then their bodies.

They both had hold of the rope, and the bushranger's arm was thrown around the detective's body, as additional security against his falling, for 'twas evident that his strength was almost gone.

Up, up, up—higher, higher, higher still.

At last their feet were on a level with the well parapet, and Harry Miller shouting to Joe and Bungy to stand steady at the handle, bent forward, and with his utmost strength dragged them toward him until Jack Last's feet rested firmly on the stone parapet.

A minute later both were in safety.

Then Jack Last shook the water off him like a sagacious Newfoundland, and Ted Hogan sat down on the grass, for he was too weak to stand.

"Here, take some of this, my fine fellow; 'twill soon set you right," said Harry Miller, producing his brandy flask.

Ted Hogan did so, and felt considerably better.

He had to take another pull before he could speak.

Then he turned to Jack Last, and said heartily—

"You have laid me under a deep obligation, my man. What prompted you to risk your life to save mine, I do not know, but the motive must have been as noble as it was foolish. I'll never forget it to the day of my death, but for all that Ted Hogan, the detective, must do his duty, and that duty will oblige him to rearrest you directly he is strong enough to do so. You had better, therefore, get away whilst he is too weak to rise and his revolver is water soaked. Yes, you had better get away, and carry his everlasting gratitude with you before he follows it up with a pistol bullet. I don't think anyone else will interfere."

"I don't think they will," added Harry Miller, "or, by George, if they do they'll have to tackle two instead of one. Away with you, my good fellow. Mr. Hogan gives you sound advice. Don't let the grass grow under your feet, and if you think fit to borrow my horse for the first stage of your flight, you'll find him just down by the creek—a bright bay, five year old, with white stockings, and a long tail—that'll bear you like the wind for a fifty-mile stretch."

"Thank you very much, sir—thank you very much. I'll accept the loan of the good steed as freely as it is offered, and return it to you safe and uninjured within a week. Mr. Hogan, you are under no obligations to me. I owed you one for the shooting of my treacherous mate, Bob Loveridge, and so we are quits. I would, however, like the forgiveness of this young lady for the part I took in her abduction. If she will accord it to me before I go," and he looked hard at Georgie as he concluded.

"You have it," answered the fair girl. "I freely forgive you; but go, go, while there is yet time to save yourself."

"My strength is fast returning, and I've dried and am now reloading my revolver," added Ted Hogan, warningly.

"Then it's high time for me to be off," laughed Jack Last, and lifting his cap off his head he replaced it, turned on his heel, and walked rapidly away towards the creek.

Five minutes later they heard the sound of galloping hoofs, and thereby knew that he was gone.

CHAPTER LVI.
FRANK BEAUMONT A MANIAC.

THE bushranger gone, and Georgie and her cousin gave their every thought and attention to Frank Beaumont.

"You had better send Bungy and Joe off to Marrangong for some kind of a vehicle. It will be the only possible way of removing him, for when he gets out of this swoon he'll be too feeble to stand. I daresay he hasn't had any food for days, and five years in that foul hole would be sufficient to deprive a bull of its strength, even if not to drive it raving mad," said the detective, looking somewhat anxiously at Frank.

"I hope he is not bereft of reason," said Georgie, more anxiously still when her cousin had walked away to instruct Joe and Bungy about going for the trap. "His face has a most peculiar expression. See, he opens his eyes."

Slowly and wearily the heavy, leaden-hued lids seemed to rise, and the eyes that then glared upon Ted Hogan and Georgie by turns were certainly those of a maniac.

Never had the detective in all his experience of prisons and lunatic asylums seen in human orbs such an unutterable expression of agonized despair.

But there was no anger, none of the red light of murder that distinguishes the eyes of some lunatics.

"Oh, this living tomb!—oh, this living tomb!" he moaned, as he looked round. "When will it be over?—when will it be over?"

"It is over, Frank," said Georgie, bending over him.

"That voice, that voice, how often have I heard it in my dreams! It is not Blue Cap's," gasped Frank.

"No, it is not Blue Cap's; it is a friend's," replied Georgie.

"It is my mother's, then—it is my dear mother's."

"No, it is not your mother's," said Georgie, "but it is a friend's for all that. It is—it is a sister who speaks to you."

"A sister?—a sister?" gasped Frank, wildly. "Why, my sister was killed by Blue Cap, the bushranger. So were my mother and father. All, all, all, except myself alone. He threw me into the well—down, down, down into the deep water. He has often told me so. But my time will come one day for all that. Yes, it will come one day, and then, and then," and he went off into a paroxysm of wild raving, buffeting the air, foaming at the mouth, and exhibiting every symptom of acute mania.

"Keep out of his way, my dear young lady, and let his excitement have free vent. You have unwittingly aroused a painful memory in his poor dazed mind, and stirred up his bitterest rancour towards the murderer of his family and the persecutor of himself. In a few minutes nature will have exhausted itself, and he will be calm again," said Ted.

He was right.

Nature did exhaust itself, and Frank changed from a raving lunatic into a seeming idiot.

Poor Georgie tried hard, but without success, to awake any remembrance of herself or of that dreadful night—when the station was attacked, and after defending her and her parents, at the imminent peril of his life, he had been carried off by Blue Cap across his saddle bows—in his breast.

He could remember nothing but his long imprisonment in the gloomy vault of the well, and the face and name of his inhuman gaoler.

And this state of things continued until Joe and Bungy returned from Marrangong with a buggy, into which Ted lifted the poor imbecile, who was as light as a nine-year old child, Georgie's cousin seating himself on the box beside him.

Then Georgie got up behind, and, at Ted's request, allowed Joe, the odd man, to seat himself beside her.

"For," said the detective, "he may just as likely as not have another attack of madness on the road, and it'll be handy to have some one in the vehicle to manage him, for your cousin has quite enough to do to control those two high-spirited, half-broken-in young horses, I fancy."

"That's true enough," quoth Harry, "and I shall be very glad of Joe's company under the circumstances."

"We shall keep Mr. Beaumont with us until he has quite recovered in body and mind," said Georgie to the detective.

"God grant that he may so recover," replied Ted, fervently.

"Oh! I do not doubt but that he will recover for a single moment," responded Georgie, quickly and hopefully. "I will be personally responsible for his growing all right in the end. Good nursing, lively companionship, and an entire change of scene, must do wonders in the long run; and whenever you happen to be anywhere in this part of the world, Mr. Hogan, you must come over to Marrangong to see how he gets on."

"I shall only be too happy to do so, my dear young lady, and I am almost tempted to wish myself in my poor young friend's place, even at the risk of never getting off your hands," replied the detective, gallantly.

Then there was a lot of hand-shaking, and away dashed the buggy through the silent bush, and Ted Hogan, after watching it out of sight, retraced his steps towards the hut.

CHAPTER LVII.
AN ABORIGINAL CORROBBOREE.

ARRIVED at the hut door, Ted Hogan looked round before he entered the building for Bungy, but he was nowhere visible.

In vain he went out into the open and gazed east, west, north, and south.

In vain he shouted and "cooeyed" at the top of his voice.

Bungy had most unmistakeably decamped.

"Umph! the black rascal was afraid I should have him over the coals for letting the bushrangers escape out of the Marrangong stables, and not having Joe to bear the blame with him, he had not the courage to stay and meet it alone. Well, I daresay I can get on by myself almost as well," growled Ted, in high dudgeon.

He went into the hut, and finished filling in the grave of the murdered pedlar, afterwards filling in the other holes as well, and trampling down the earthen floor to make it look as nearly as possible as though it had been undisturbed.

This done, he ate up whatever food he found remaining, finished his flask of brandy to the last drop, washed his hands and face in the cool, bubbling waters of the creek, and then set out to look for his horse, which, being short hoppled, was soon found.

To take off these hopples and pocket them, and

thereafter to saddle and bridle the good steed, was a task of barely five minutes.

Then, with a fierce, hot wind blowing from the north, as if it came directly from the oven of the "great baker," he set forth across the plains to get down into the Shoalhaven valley.

He drew rein beside the corpse of Bob Loveridge, and pondered for a few minutes.

Then he suddenly exclaimed—

"Hang it, it must be done, or his face will soon lose all trace of humanity, and then how should I be able to prevent its identity, and so pocket my reward? No, I must cut it off, and let it get sundried at my saddle bow. In a few hours I'll have Blue Cap's to balance it on the other side."

He plainly did not relish the job, but he carried it through nevertheless.

Dismounting, he whipped his knife out of his pocket, opened its longest and sharpest blade, and with it cut the dead bushranger's head from off his shoulders, and attached it to his saddle bow by means of its long hair.

Then he dragged and hid the body away in the bush, remounted, and once more continued his course through a country where all around were trees of immense height, real giants of the Australian forest, raising their proud tops far into the hot steel-grey sky, from whose midst the midday sun gleamed like a vast globe of burnished brass.

At the roots of these mammoth trees, flowers of myriad hues grew in pristine splendour.

In their branches black cockatoos and parrots of every colour raised a deafening din, answered by the harsh crackling of the loosened bark which the grim gum trees shed annually instead of their leaves.

Occasionally, too, a great kangaroo would bound past in the distance, or some wild bullock, who, perhaps, had never called man master, or felt the burn of the branding iron.

Five miles of this beautiful and picturesque scenery, and the character of the scene changed.

Bush gradually merged into scrub, the dark and sombre mallee, void of shade, water, and all things that have life, except poisonous whips, and diamond snakes and centipedes, scorpions, and huge tarantula spiders that are almost as deadly.

It took the detective five hours to ride through this dangerous and inhospitable region, a gradual descent the whole way, and just as the sun was setting, he gained a vast plain, as level as the sands of the desert, and covered with coarse grass that in places reached nearly to his horse's knees.

The intense rays of the Australian sun had turned this grass into hay even whilst it grew, and the hard ground beneath being baked until it had nearly crumbled into powder, great clouds of dust rolled onwards like ocean billows before the fierce, hot wind, until at last both Ted and the good steed he bestrode more resembled a sculptured figure of grey granite than aught that was more human.

The sun was setting amidst gorgeous crimson clouds, with borders of mingled gold, ultramarine, and violet, and the only objects that looked cool and refreshing in the landscape were the undulating wooded heights, that rose precipitously at the end of the plain he was traversing, in some places to the enormous altitude of a thousand feet and upwards, and the river, whose waters rushed along with a husky roar at their base.

They were still six miles distant, and as twilight is of barely ten minutes' duration in a semi-tropical country like New South Wales, Ted Hogan set spurs to his steed, and never drew rein until he pulled up on the bank of the river.

An Australian horse will gallop for hours without getting blown, or showing any symptoms of fatigue. It is his natural pace, for he seldom knows how to trot or walk, and the author has heard old stockriders affirm that they have known their horses to sleep whilst galloping; but he thinks the assertion should be accepted *cum grano salis.*

Though his horse covered the six miles in thrice as many minutes, the moon had usurped the place of the sun by the time he reached the bank of the angry Shoalhaven River, and gazed across it in search of the dead bodies of a horse and man, which he expected to see lying in an almost undistinguishable heap of smashed and shattered humanity, on the other side.

First of all he ran his eyes along the face of the cliff, particularly near the top, and at last descried by the moonlight, which is so much brighter and clearer than that of our cold northern clime, what he had expected to see—namely, places where a heavy falling body had bounded against, and in so doing, detached portions of the soft cliff, which was mainly composed of sandstone.

He rode up and down the near bank of the river several times in search of this, and at last discerned it.

A portion of the top of the cliff had given way; fragments of grass and a shrub that had been nearly torn out by the roots, hung dangling over the edge; there was a kind of rain of brown earth for a considerable way down, mingled with here and there white splatches where the old face of the cliff had been struck or bumped off by a heavy descending body colliding against it.

Following down these, and the earth sprinkling, Ted Hogan noticed a dim indistinct heap, that he could not clearly make out, because it lay so much in the shadow, but he had not a doubt in his own mind but that it was the bodies of Blue Cap and his horse.

How to cross the river was the next question.

It was a quarter of a mile wide, and the current was both swift and strong.

Of the width, Ted Hogan thought nothing.

The current alone caused him uneasiness.

Could his horse stem it?

Well, nothing venture, nothing have. There was no ford nor bridge for a good score of miles on either side, he knew that well enough. Another night, and perhaps the dead bushranger might be wholly devoured by the native dogs, and then how could he be able to prove the identity of the corpse, and secure his reward?

He resolved to cross, therefore, at any and whatever risk.

Not but what he would take every possible precaution.

He rode some way up the river, and urged his horse to take the water.

He calculated that, if with every yard he was carried downwards, his good steed could make a foot in a transverse direction, it would eventually land him about the right spot.

For some few minutes he had considerable trouble in getting his horse to confide itself to the turbulent waters.

But the spur at last acted as a persuader, and the charger, with a snort, half of fear and half of rage, leaped from the bank.

For a minute or two, Ted Hogan could see nothing for the cloud of spray that rose and glittered around him.

Then he found that he was being borne along at great speed, and that his horse, powerful brute as it was, could scarcely make any head against the current.

It was a long and desperate struggle under these circumstances to reach the opposite bank, and how he managed at last to do so, Ted Hogan could never tell.

He landed as far below the point at which he had intended to land as he had entered the stream above it, and immediately his horse felt itself once more on *terra firma,* it sank to the ground, utterly exhausted.

"A minute longer, and he wouldn't have had strength enough to have made the shore at all," muttered Ted; "then the ghost of Blue Cap would have laughed at me—that is to say, if there are ghosts, and they are capable of laughing."

He walked on, leaving his horse to follow him as soon as it listed, which he knew the well-trained animal would do when it had rested awhile, with the sense and docility of a dog.

So he went on and on, and at last was directly beneath the scarred face of the awful cliff, when he began to look eagerly around for the heap of smashed and shapeless humanity.

At last he saw it. Bah! it was already half putrescent.

He approached it with a hand covering his mouth and nostrils; but he quickly removed it to give vent to a cry and a curse, for he gazed upon a horse without a rider.

Blue Cap's steed was there, smashed almost to a jelly, but Blue Cap himself was gone.

Ted could hardly believe it at first, it was too astonishing; but when he saw that not even a skeleton remained—nay, not even a single bone that had once belonged to a human being—he could no longer doubt but that, by next to a miracle, Blue Cap had survived the fall, and what was more, got clear away.

True, he might only have extricated himself from his dead steed, and crawled away to die under some bush, or within some cave washed by the river in flood time, under the towering cliff, and Ted hunted about for a long while for dried blood stains, or foot tracks leading thereto, but could find none.

And as he still continued to look, he heard a wild howling, and pattering of many feet, and a minute later perceived a troop of red-haired, fiery-eyed dingoes trotting towards him.

There was a score of them at the least.

They had evidently scented the dead horse, and were coming to sup thereon.

But he knew that, although their meal was all ready provided, they would not object to him as a first course, and that, though slinking, cowardly foes when met singly or in pairs, their numbers would give them courage, and ensure them an easy victory.

He drew his revolver, and prepared to sell his life dearly.

They saw him at that moment, and advanced with hideous howls.

Ted got his back up against a rock, and fired into their midst.

But, to his horror and despair, each cap snapped without exploding its charge.

His powder had got wet in the river.

There was no time to reload.

He must trust entirely to his sword.

He drew it, happily in time, and laid about him with a will.

Dingoes' heads and dingoes' paws and tails flew off and around him, as chaff flies about the head of a thrasher.

But his foes were all too many, and soon learnt to dodge and evade his slashes and thrusts, springing at him sideways, taking him in the rear, and practising all kinds of tricks to overcome him.

And overcome, and then devoured, he assuredly would have been, had not aid suddenly arrived, and from an unexpected quarter.

Whilst fighting for his life, and with very little hope of being able to preserve it, he heard strange, guttural cries, and saw the flashing of spears around him.

He still fought on; but his foes soon took to flight, and in their place Ted found himself surrounded by a troop of wild blacks, jabbering and gesticulating like anything.

Instead of answering them, however, he fainted dead away.

When he recovered, he rubbed his eyes, and tried to collect his ideas.

A strange scene was being enacted before and around him.

He was lying on the ground in the midst of a lot of women, most of them old and hideously ugly, who were one and all squatted cross-legged upon the grass, and making a discordant music with the jaw bones of some kind of animal, which they hit with little short sticks.

They were all naked, and were some of them possessed of really fine figures, presenting, in this respect, a great contrast to the skinny armed, narrow chested, hipless and calfless natives of the neighbouring colony of Victoria.

Ted's attention was quickly diverted from them, however, to the scene that was being enacted in front off, or rather around the camp fire that blazed up merrily in front.

For there about a score of stalwart male savages were executing a war dance, which consisted mostly of a series of frantic whirls and leaps, brandishings of spears, yelemens, nullah nullahs, and boomerangs, all the time, and then a mad whirl round and round the fire, as if it was the hub of a wheel, and the naked blackfellows were the revolving spokes.

Seen through the hazy smoke of the camp fire, these warriors of the tribe presented a strange, and almost unearthly aspect.

And no wonder, for their naked black bodies, arms, and legs, were marked with white paint in the hideous outlines of skeletons, and their faces made to resemble those of skulls, so that at a little distance, where their black skins were undistinguishable from the darkness of night, it seemed a veritable dance of death.

And what wonderful dancers those living skeletons were!

How quick in their movements, how devilishly light in their leaps and springs.

Sometimes their motions would have a somewhat ludicrous aspect, such as a score of drunken gorillas might be supposed to indulge in.

But in an instant this would change : the absurd would assume the wondrous, the wierd, the horrible, the satanic, and the skeletons would bound and plunge and leap and spin, brandishing their weapons, or beating them in time against their shields, whilst all the time the dancers' eyes glared, the great flat nostrils quivered, and the froth flew from their mouths like wintry snowflakes, so excited had they become.

They were evidently working themselves up to a pitch of fury, wherefore, or for what reason, Ted Hogan could not even guess—very probably for the murdering, and as likely as not the cooking and eating in addition, of his unfortunate self—for cannibalism is practised by the more northern tribes.

Presently the dance was over, and the dancers seemed to be holding a kind of council of war.

This did not last long, however, and as soon as 'twas over, two stalwart young savages advanced upon Ted, helped him to rise, and led him into the middle of the circle.

"Now my time has come," he thought to himself ; but determined to lose nothing on the score of politeness, he bowed right and left, and then stood calmly awaiting his fate.

One after another of the blackfellows came up to him, and asked him questions, in what he took to be the Naundir dialect, but scarcely knowing a word thereof, he could not answer them.

He tried to make them understand his English, but was equally unsuccessful.

This, however, did not seem to embarrass the armed natives very much.

Again they communed together, and the yabber-yabber became excessively vehement, so vehement indeed that the detective more than once thought the tribe would come to loggerheads, and decide the affair by a pitched battle.

But the storm gradually subsided, the waving of spears grew less vehement, the voices dropped to a lower pitch, and gradually harmony seemed to be restored.

No sooner was this the case than the detective was again pounced on, his hands bound behind him, and then his captors led him all around the camp, and whilst the women and old men hooted and reviled him, occasionally spitting in his face, the young blacks of both sexes threw stones, sticks and other missiles at him, with too good aim to be pleasant.

And then at last he was tied to a tree, the trunk of a lithe wattle sapling, a hundred paces were measured therefrom, a chalk line drawn, and on this chalked line the armed natives began to take their stand, poising their spears aloft.

Then Ted Hogan knew that for some reason or other, he was to be speared to death.

How had he aroused the anger of these natives?

In vain he asked himself the question.

The Australian aboriginals are by no means bloodthirsty as a rule.

Perhaps some squatter or other had shot two or three of their number for sheep stealing, and they had resolved to avenge themselves upon the first white man who fell into their hands.

Such things have happened before.

The law of reprisals was the *lex scripta* of the chosen people of God, why then should not these untutored blacks practice the same code?

Not that Ted Hogan moralised as we have done ; every moment was precious to him, and he made a last attempt to make himself understood, by mixing up all the native words with which he was acquainted with pigeon English, but his speech was still unintelligible.

The blackfellows shook their heads and poised their spears afresh.

Then Ted Hogan knew that it was all over with him, and resigned himself to his fate.

He closed his eyes and tried to pray—wincing involuntarily as he heard the long, slender, double barbed spears whizzing past his head.

Then a sudden pang of anguish caused him to open his eyes again.

A spear had passed through his left shoulder, nailing him to the tree against which he was bound.

"D—— it, you might make shorter and better work of it, at all events," he exclaimed bitterly, forgetting, at the moment, that his tormentors could not understand a word of what he said.

Yet, to his surprise, no more spears were thrown.

The blackfellows were once more yabbering together in a ring.

Ted thought that he distinguished a face in the midst of them, that was very familiar to him.

Another minute and he felt convinced that it was Bungy's.

Conviction changed to certainty, when, five minutes later, Bungy, *in propria persona*, came out of the crowd, which made way for him to pass, and advanced towards him.

"Bym-by all right. No savvee they fella—Bungy know better dan dat," he said, as he proceeded to draw the spear very slowly and carefully out of the detective's shoulder.

Then he unbound Ted, bade him sit down, and plucking some leaves—which he seemed to have some difficulty in finding, and which, when found, he selected with great care—he laid them over the wound, and strapped them on.

They stopped the bleeding as if by magic.

The other blackfellows then came up, and seemed to apologise for what they had done, for they grinned all over their sable faces, and insisted on shaking Ted by the hand.

He would have liked to have kicked them well all round had he only dared, but he didn't, and

Bungy signified to him by sundry winks, to take it all in good part.

He saw very well that the wisest plan was to do so, and he therefore essayed hard to smile, and grin back again, and to treat the spear throwing as if it had been a little amiable passage at arms, got up more for his amusement and diversion than otherwise.

This conduct pleased his sable captors greatly, who patted him on the back, and danced around him, disposed apparently to regard him now as a great personage.

Fires were lighted at the bottoms of small round holes dug in the ground, and wombats, wallabies, and native bears were laid thereon, to cook in their skins.

Then some of the women went forth to hunt for the great fat caterpillars that form the blackfellows' dessert, and ere long returned with a basket full of these highly-esteemed luxuries.

The dinner, or rather supper, was then served up, with leaves for plates, and wooden knives to eat with.

The chiefs skinned the animals, and carved them into small joints with their steel creases, so that thereafter wooden knives and fingers did very well.

When it came to the great white, hairless, fleshy caterpillars, Ted Hogan felt that he could very well have dispensed with such a dessert, but Bungy pressed the dish on him, and he didn't like to decline.

When he had got down one caterpillar, however, he would not have objected to a dozen, for it tasted like the most delicate beef-marrow.

Directly supper was over, Bungy was pointed out a mia-mia, or hut, made of green boughs, covered with leaves, which he was informed he and the white man could occupy.

Crossing an open glade, which the rays of the full moon rendered as light as day, casting the reflection of the tall trees upon the verdant sward, they soon reached this light, airy, and far from wind proof habitation, which stood just on the edge of a patch of scrub.

It had in it a heap of dried leaves, wherewith to form a bed, and the perfume of the golden wattle blossoms, of the branches of which tree the mia-mia was constructed, was very sweet and fragrant, but they did not tempt Ted Hogan to indulge in sleep for all that.

CHAPTER LVIII.

THE FLIGHT FROM THE BLACK CAMP—AN UNEXPECTED MEETING.

"BUNGY," said Ted, "we'll cut this as speedily as ever we can. This scrub patch is handy."

"Plenty, bym-by—one, two, three hours; bery good dat den; plenty bla' fella asleep, eh?"

"Yes, Bungy, you're quite right. We'd best wait until they are all asleep, as you say."

They waited, and in half an hour's time the black camp was as still as death.

Bungy put his head outside the doorless mia-mia, and for some time listened intently.

Then he grunted an "all right," and signed to Ted Hogan to follow him in silence.

The detective did so, and in another minute both had gained the cover of the scrub.

There they paused for awhile and listened, but there were no sounds of pursuit audible.

Encouraged by this, Bungy started to his feet, and again led the way.

He steered by the stars, and Ted Hogan felt the greatest faith in his guidance.

They stepped cautiously, for the blacks have long ears, and the cracking of a twig might have betrayed them.

No such thing happened, however. They were soon in comparative safety.

But even then Bungy did not care to converse.

A blackfellow, as a rule, only indulges in talk when seated around the camp fire.

He never "yabber-yabbers" when there is work to be done.

So they went on for miles and miles, as it seemed to Ted, who had once or twice tried to explain to Bungy that point of the river to which he wanted to retrace his steps.

"All right, Massa Hogan," was all that the blackfellow would reply on such occasions, and if pressed further he would turn sullen and make no answer at all.

In this way they journeyed on until at last they came suddenly upon a camp fire—so suddenly, that they almost stumbled over the solitary occupant before they perceived him.

That solitary occupant turned out to be Jack Last, the bushranger.

"Hullo! you black devil," exclaimed that worthy, "what a fright you have given me. I took you to be old Clootie himself. Get out of this, or I'll pepper you with ounce balls, you shivering, shiny, black-leaded abortion you."

Then his gaze suddenly falling upon Ted Hogan, a shade of anxiety crossed his brow.

"You follow me up rather hotly," he said, with something like a scowl. "And," he continued, with a sneer, "am I to take it as a compliment that you bring this ban-dog with you? I saved your life unaided. Do you require help to take mine?"

"On my soul, you are the last man that I ever expected to come across, or that since the morning I have bestowed a thought on. I'm deuced sorry that the event has happened, because as I have found you I must re-arrest you," quoth Ted.

"And do you mean to say that you have not been following my trail?"

"To convince you of that, I have but to tell you that Bungy and I have only just made our escape from a tribe of wild blacks. See, here is a doctored shoulder which one of their spears bored a hole through only a few hours ago. They would have killed me outright had not this faithful fellow, who I thought had deserted me, turned up again at a happy moment and turned aside their wrath with a few words."

Bungy grunted a kind of confirmation of this statement, nodding his head frequently.

"Then your enemies may even now be close at hand?" queried the bushranger.

"They may put in an appearance at any moment," responded the detective.

"And yet you would handcuff me so that I could neither help you nor defend myself?"

"Duty is duty. It and inclination often pull two opposite ways, but I have never yet sacrificed the one to the other, and, what is more, I never will. You saved my life this morning, and in a private capacity I am deeply grateful; but if a brother had done the same, and yet had violated the laws of which I am an officer, I should not spare him."

"You are a Spartan—in sentiment more than in action though. Spartans did not usually allow two men to attack one. When they fought they fought fairly."

"If you intend to offer resistance, I am quite capable of taking you single handed."

"Your left arm is useless, I imagine. Is your right wrist steady and your eye true?"

"As steady as iron and as true as the lightning flash," responded the detective.

"We are about equals then, for my left arm is useless, owing to a fall from my horse, and I daresay I'm just as tired and worn out as you are."

"That being the case, let us withdraw alone into the bush and fight it out."

"You might make much shorter work of me if

you wished, for I discharged every shot in my revolver in killing that old boomer yonder, and I have not yet reloaded."

He pointed towards a dead kangaroo as he spoke, one of whose hind legs had been cut off, evidently to supply the bushranger with a nourishing and succulent supper.

"You are utterly defenceless, and at my mercy then?" exclaimed Ted, with flashing eyes.

"Utterly defenceless and at your mercy, but I mistake your character greatly if your sense of honour will allow you to take advantage of my defenceless position."

"You are right," answered the detective, proudly. "An ordinary bushranger I would shoot down like a wild beast whensoever and wheresoever I encountered him; but when I meet a bushranger who is also a man, the event is so rare that I treat him as one. Reload your weapon, therefore, and take whichever side of the fire you like. At twenty-four paces we will exchange shots until one falls. Bungy shall retire into the bush until 'tis all over."

"You are a fine fellow," said Jack Last, "and I agree. But may not the sound of the firing bring our foes down upon us? The blackfellows have sharp ears."

"But how otherwise can we decide it?"

"Why, in four hours it will be daylight. Then we can mount our horses and have this duello out mounted. The dead the blacks will not harm, the living can ride away."

"But when the blacks carried me off, my horse was left behind, at the foot of the very highest peak of the Shoalhaven range. It must be miles away from here."

"Give your sable follower the necessary directions, and I'll warrant he'll have found and returned with it before you are ready to mount," said the bushranger.

Ted Hogan considered for a moment, and then he said—

"I will do as you suggest."

He called Bungy aside, and for nearly five minutes they conversed together.

Then Bungy emitted a grunt that seemed to come from the lower regions of the stomach, nodded thrice, and darted off into the bush at a swift run.

Ted Hogan returned to the fire, to find Jack Last busily engaged in cooking some kangaroo steaks thereon.

He remarked, without looking round—

"They'll be done to a turn presently, and if you're half as peckish as I am, you'll enjoy them. Because we're going to try hard to cut each other's throats with day dawn, is no reason that we should not eat, drink, and be good friends to-night."

"All right; we'll apply the principles of hostile armies to private individuals, and enjoy a four hours' truce," rejoined Ted Hogan, with a laugh.

The steaks were soon cooked, and Ted having manufactured a damper and baked it in the ashes, the bushranger and the trooper set to and made a hearty meal.

Then Jack Last produced a screwed up paper full of tea from his pocket, and Ted Hogan volunteered to go down to the neighbouring water-hole to fill the billy.

When he returned, it was set on the fire, and directly it boiled the tea was poured in and stirred round; and over this simple beverage the two men prepared to enjoy themselves.

It is almost the only drink imbibed by travellers in the Australian bush.

With their backs supported by a couple of trees, the detective and the bushranger sat and sipped and smoked for awhile in silence, each without doubt thinking of the primary event of the morrow, but calmly and without the slightest anger towards each other.

Then at last Jack Last exclaimed—

"I spun you a yarn last night; it is your turn now. I expect you are no more inclined for sleep than I am. I don't suppose we shall ever reach to the thousand and one nights; but I don't see why we shouldn't get as far as the second. 'Twill be a better trick then giving way to slumber; for if we did, your friends the blacks might surprise us, and put it out of our power to awake again."

"True," said Ted; "and as I never felt wider awake in all my life, I'll do my best to pay the debt I contracted last night. I'll tell you a bush-ranging adventure that actually happened to myself within six months of my entering the service, and about some six years ago."

CHAPTER LIX.
TED HOGAN RELATES A REMINISCENCE OF NINE SHEARERS.

"ONE beautiful summer's evening in January, I stood alone on the raised hurricane deck of the little steamer Wonga-Wonga, that was bravely battling her way against wind and tide up the most majestic of Australia's rivers, the Murray, bound from the port of Wentworth on the Murrunbidgee to the township of Echuca, for I had had a month's leave of absence, and was now returning to the police camp at Yachandandah.

"We had already been three days steaming up the stream, and not half the journey was yet accomplished; for this fine river, fondly designated by the enthusiastic colonists, the Australian Mississippi, is navigable for two thousand miles, and many thriving little townships rise at distances often a hundred miles apart upon its banks.

"I have said that the evening was a lovely one, and being an ardent admirer of nature, I had left my four fellow passengers playing whist in the cabin, and crept up on deck for an hour's enjoyment in watching the moving panorama on each side.

"The landscape that I gazed upon was beautiful, yet sad.

"The sun had just sunk behind a low range of undulating wooded hills, whose black outline was clearly defined against the violet and opal tinted western sky.

"Not a sound broke the stillness of the twilight hour save the hoarse murmur of the river as its mighty volumes of waters rolled past us, and the heavy strokes of our paddles as we laboured up stream against the current, mingled with the shrill scream of the steam from the 'scape pipe.

"On either side, at about a quarter of a mile's distance, low shelving banks rose upwards from the red surging stream, covered with forests of the sombre iron-bark, which stretched away to the right and left as far as the eye could reach in one unbroken pall-like expanse, whilst above all gleamed the steel-grey dome of heaven, cloudless, starless, moonless, lifeless.

"That view exercised no cheering influence on my mind; there was no companionship in it, for though it spoke of God it spoke not of man.

"As that red river, black forest, and cold grey sky now looked, so doubtless had they looked before human eyes ever rested upon them.

"We were far from the settled districts; no woodman's axe had ever rung in the gloomy recesses of those woods, and most probably even the black lord of the soil knew them not—for there are vast districts in Australia, as you are aware, large in some instances as European nations, where even the always wandering aboriginal has never yet lighted his camp-fire, or pitched his gunyah.

"I gazed upon this scene until I longed for companionship, and though I was sufficiently entranced to be unable to tear myself away, even the presence of the half sleeping helmsman, the only human being visible, gave me satisfaction.

"The Wonga-Wonga was a small boat, carrying a crew of only seven men, and we only numbered five passengers in the cabin.

"She was very comfortably fitted up, and being flat bottomed, so as to pass easily through the shallows, her saloon accommodation was a house on deck, the roof of which constituted the upper or 'hurricane' deck.

"We had hitherto steamed only during the hours of daylight, the numerous bends in the river and the frequency of snags rendering a prosecution of the journey after nightfall extremely dangerous.

"On this particular evening, however, the captain had said there would be sufficient moonlight to continue on our course all night, and that in forty-eight hours he hoped we should reach the little township of Wilcania.

"We were a merry party in the saloon that night, and none of us turned in until a late hour.

"The passengers consisted of an old clergyman and his daughter, a sweet pretty girl of sixteen, who had come from Adelaide; a fine young fellow, who I soon discovered to be a Riverina squatter; another young man, who was en route to join the Upper Murray snagging party, and my unworthy self.

"There was a piano in the cabin tolerably in tune, and as the young lady proved a competent performer thereon, we got through a fine programme of songs, and the short hand of the little American clock had got well up amongst the small hours before we adjourned to our bunks.

"As I was very tired, I soon fell asleep; but my slumbers were but brief, for presently I was awakened by a sharp hissing sound near me, and then a different toned hiss in reply, apparently from the other end of the cabin.

"The latter sound I felt sure was produced by a cat, and I recollected that we had a remarkably fine black one on board; but the other hiss I could not at all make out, it was so shrill and prolonged.

"I had a box of wax vestas under my pillow, and a little candle lamp hung just at my head.

"To strike the one and light the other was therefore the work of a moment, and then I beheld a sight which, although ludicrous in itself, caused anything but pleasurable feelings to arise in my bosom.

"On the floor of my cabin were two combatants, just prepared to engage in mortal strife.

"One was our large Tom cat, with his tail swollen to twice its usual dimensions, his back curved into the shape of a triumphal arch, and each one of his long grey whiskers bristling with rage; and the other was an immense snake, its body coiled up and ready for the deadly spring, its neck undulating gently from side to side, its head erect, and its eyes glittering with a curious metallic lustre most unpleasant to look upon.

"The mouth of the slimy brute was open, and its forked tongue played in and out in a style calculated to strike terror into the soul of a far mightier and more glorious adversary than an old Tom cat.

"I am convinced that of the two, I was far more frightened than poor Tommy, however, and I was debating in my mind what course to adopt for my own safety, utterly regardless of that of my feline acquaintance, when, much to my astonishment, instead of beholding the snake spring upon the cat as I had momentarily anticipated its doing, I saw the cat pounce upon the snake.

"Seizing it close up to its head, he pinned it to the floor.

"In vain its snakeship struggled and twisted and wriggled, and tried to throw its coils around pussy.

"Twice the poor cat was hurled on to his back, and severely lashed by blows from his antagonist's

tail; but he still held bravely on, and the serpent, who had been gripped in a way that prevented its using its death dealing fangs, was defunct in less than a minute, with its conqueror purring proudly over its body.

"On measuring the dead snake, I found it to be seven feet in length, and of a highly venomous species.

"It had, doubtless, been introduced on board amongst the firewood for the engines, and crept through the open window into my cabin.

"It may be readily imagined that after this nocturnal adventure, I vainly tried to get to sleep again.

"I had closed my windows for fear of another uncanny visitor, and presently the air in the cabin grew so close and oppressive that I could scarcely breathe; so lighting my candle again, I looked at the thermometer, and finding that it stood at 150 degs., I got up, dressed myself, and went up on deck, whereon I remained during the rest of the night.

"Nothing eventful happened during the day that ensued; but on the following morning the forests on either side grew less interminable, and cleared lands appeared here and there.

"The river narrowed to about a quarter of a mile in breadth, and just after dinner, while we were all sitting on deck, enjoying tobacco and conversation, we were startled by a hail from the near shore, and glancing in the direction of the sound, we saw eight or nine men standing on the bank, and signalling the steamer to approach.

"The captain was at first undecided whether to comply or not with this request; but having accommodation for thrice the number of passengers that he had on board, and inwardly hoping, I have no doubt, that they wanted to go up river, he gave directions to the helmsman to bring the vessel to the shore, and when we had got within easy hailing distance, he demanded what they wanted.

"'Is that there vessel of yours going up as far as Moama?' asked the spokesman of the party.

"'Within two miles of it. We're bound for Echuca,' was the reply of the captain.

"'What will you charge to take us nine up along wi' you?' came the next question.

"'Well, you see, I can only offer you deck accommodation, for I've no second cabin or steerage. I'll take you up on the foredeck for three pounds each.'

"'That'll do, mate. We agree to them there terms. So just come alongside this bank where the water's deep, and take us into yer boat.'

"'Wait a bit, my man. Tell me, first, how we happen to come across you in this out of the way spot? There's something very strange about it to my mind,' said the captain.

"'Not a bit—not a morsel,' rejoined the man, who seemed to be the only talking member of the fraternity. 'We're shearers, and have last come from Mr. Macdonald's station at Monewan, where we've sheared a thousand sheep in three days. We've come down on the left bank of the river all the way from the Edward, and now want to get back to the Upper Murray, where we hear there's much work to be done, and very few hands to do it.'

"'Well, your story seems likely enough, so I'll take you; but you must pay in advance.'

"To this condition the nine men readily assented, and getting alongside the bank, we took them all on board, and then backing into mid stream again, continued our voyage, the captain twenty-seven sovereigns the richer by the short detention.

"The nine strangers were all rough, bearded fellows, attired in cotton or canvas jumpers, moleskin or cord pants, billycock hats, and thick soled blucher boots. Some had shears stuck in their belts, and all of them carried sticks.

"They soon made themselves at home upon the

AS HE WITHDREW HIS HAND, AND THE TRAP ALONG WITH IT, HE FELT THE DESCENT OF A HEAVY HAND UPON HIS SHOULDER.

lower deck, and got through their ration of tea, bread, and half-cooked mutton, at supper-time, with rare zest.

"I don't know why it was, but we cabin passengers retired to bed very early that night. The clergyman's pretty daughter had a headache, so that music was out of the question, and although we essayed dummy whist, we did not find it enlivening.

"These two incidents had doubtless something to do with our dispersing so soon to our different state rooms, but I think we were all thoroughly tired out as well.

"To go to bed, however, was one thing, and to go to sleep another.

"The night was purgatorially hot, and if a scuttle window was opened for a single instant to admit a breath of air, an army of ravenous mosquitoes would be wafted in at the same time, and would commence their cupping and bleeding operations instanter, irritating their patient by their shrill trumpetings almost as much as by the plying of their sharp lancets.

"In spite of all these drawbacks to repose, I was at last on the point of dropping into a kind of restless slumber, when I was restored to full wakefulness by some one rushing headlong into my cabin.

"'Rouse yourself, for heaven's sake, and look to your firearms,' said a voice.

"I immediately recognised it as that of the young Riverina squatter.

"'All right, mate, but what the deuce is the matter?' I asked, taking my revolver from under the pillow, and examining the caps as I spoke.

"'Why, the very devil's the matter. Those nine fellows whom we took aboard to-day are no more sheep shearers than you or I. One of them has just pitched the helmsman overboard, and three others are driving the remainder of the crew below, with pistols levelled at their heads,' was the reply.

"'Stop—that's enough. You arouse the snagger and clergyman, and I'll to the captain's cabin. Away—not an instant is to be lost,' I said authoritatively.

"The young squatter saw the urgency of the case as well as I did.

"He rushed out of my cabin as quickly as he had entered it, and taking down my sword, I put it on, thrust my revolver in my belt, for I had lain down with my clothes on, and departed on my mission, as hastily as he had done on his, though more circumspectly.

"The saloon was as dark as pitch, and I had to steer my way across it to the captain's state-room, pretty nearly by guess work.

"The silence of the grave seemed to pervade the scene, and yet, as I crossed the floor in my stockinged feet, I thought that I heard other muffled footsteps besides my own, and once I could almost have sworn that I felt a hot, fœtid, tobacco tainted breath, upon the back of my neck.

"You may be sure that my revolver-stock was gripped pretty tightly in my right hand after that, but I reached the captain's cabin all right, recognising the glass door-handle by touch, a little piece having been chipped off it.

"Entering very softly, I shook the skipper gently by the shoulder as he lay in his bunk, at the same time whispering—

"'Rouse up! Robbers and murderers are aboard the ship. 'Twill take our sharpest wits and hardest knocks, to prevent them getting the better of us.'

"I had imagined that the captain would have sprang up on the instant, for I knew him to be a light sleeper, but to my astonishment he still slumbered on.

"Attributing his present sound sleep to the fact that he had been on deck the whole of the preceding night, I shook him again and again, but still there was no response.

"Fearing I knew not what, I felt over his body with my left hand.

"I found his face—'twas warm, and bathed in perspiration.

"His beard was wet with a dampness that made me shudder, and the next instant I almost screamed aloud, as on feeling his throat, my fingers sank into a deep gash, that almost swallowed them up.

"I knew then, though I could see naught, that his throat was cut from ear to ear."

"I left that cabin with a brain on fire, and an under-lip half bitten through in my fierce excitement.

"The inhuman fiends were below, then.

"I had almost run against one or more of them on my way to the captain's cabin, whither they had unfortunately preceded me on their errand of murder.

"Where should I find them now?

"In that opaque darkness I might grapple a friend as likely as a foe, and to pause an instant to ask the question would be to sign my own death-warrant.

"The silence was at that moment broken by the sharp crack of a revolver, and the flash of light revealed to me the squatter's face behind it.

"He had doubtless heard a rustle, and fired in the direction of the sound.

"But it was a silly act, as the flash showed his whereabouts.

"An answering shot produced a deep groan, and I knew by it that he was struck.

"A female shriek now rang out on the murky midnight air, and fearful that the young lady passenger might unthinkingly rush out of the state room into the saloon, and be shot down like a dog by the demons who had boarded us, I halloaed out to her to 'keep abed, as we had snakes aboard, and were hunting them.'

"Scarcely had the words escaped my lips, when I felt myself seized hold of by both shoulders.

"But I swung myself round, clutched a thick, bushy beard, dashed the muzzle of my pistol against teeth that chattered like castanets with the blow, and fired a chamber of my revolver right into the beggar's mouth.

"Something hot gushed all over me, and a heavy body fell to the floor.

"But I felt better now, even though a couple of shots, followed by a sharp, stinging pain in the left shoulder, told me that I was hit, and hit hard too.

"I threw myself on my hands and knees, knowing that a recumbent was safer than an upright attitude.

"Besides, in groping about I should know a shepherd the instant my hand came in contact with his moleskin pants, or thick, mudstained boots, and could tell the locality of his heart from that contact much surer than he could guess the position of my body.

"The ruse was a good one, and within two minutes of my putting it into execution, my left hand was on a boot, and my revolver bullet was through a body.

"But at that moment a piteous cry of, 'Father! father! where are you? What is the matter?' was audible above the sound of the firing.

"A state room door flew open, and the clergyman's pretty daughter, clad only in her night-dress, rushed into the saloon, lamp in hand, feet and arms bare, and face as pale as monumental marble.

"Poor girl, her rash action signed her father's death warrant.

"She lighted the murderous bullet to his brain!

"Nine balls were discharged at once, three on our side, and six against us.

"It seemed as though the concussion would burst the frail wooden walls of the saloon asunder.

"I sprang forward to catch the poor girl as she reeled and swooned, never ceasing my target practice whilst I did so.

"But the lamp was snatched from her hand ere the relaxed muscles suffered it to fall, by one of the ruffians more active than the rest, and instantly four pistol muzzles were pointed at our heads.

"My revolver's every charge was expended, the position in which the fainting girl lay in my arms prevented my drawing my sword, the squatter, the snagger, and the clergyman lay dead on the floor of the saloon, in company with five of the shearers, and we were as absolutely at the mercy of the four survivors as if we had been in the deepest depths of an Indian jungle, with a couple of Bengal tigers purring over our bodies.

"'Ha! ha! my gallant trap,' exclaimed the tallest of the shearers, with a sudden and diabolical laugh, 'allow me to introduce myself as Mr. Benjamin Welsh, bushranger, et cetera. Really, all policemen and young ladies who have any regard for their personal safeties should not travel aboard steamers laden with twenty-five chests of nuggets and gold dust from the South Australian goldfields. You must both of you make up your minds to a watery grave, for after we have secured the treasure, we shall scuttle and sink the steamer with the living and the dead in her. We never leave alive any who one day might bear witness against us. Ha! ha! ha! Ain't we right?'

"Before I could make any reply, a terrible shock occurred, which threw us all on to the floor of the saloon.

"Then there arose the shrill shriek of escaping steam, mingled with hoarse shouts of—

"'Back her! Half turn ahead! Slacken speed! Stop her!'

"The Wonga-Wonga staggered like a stricken deer, through a wide gap in her side the water began to rush in, and then one of the shearers who had run on deck to find out what was the matter, ran down again in still hotter haste, exclaiming—

"'Let those who can swim ashore! The Cumbersona has run into us! We are settling down!'

"'Save yourselves, boys,' shouted Ben Welsh, turning the colour of a turnip with terror.

"And as he spoke, he made a rush to gain the companion ladder that led to the deck.

"But my sword hilt was comeatable now, and I drew the weapon, and springing after him, drove it through the broad of his back till it came out at his chest.

"Then, never staying to pluck it forth, I lifted that fair young girl in my arms, and rushing out of the saloon, wherein the water was now knee-deep, we reached the deck.

"The four surviving bushrangers were by this time swimming ashore, but there was no time to think of them.

"We were dragged abroad the Cumbersona only a clear minute or so before the Wonga-Wonga plunged down by the bows, and sank below the yellow, turgid tide.

"Whether either or all the surviving bushrangers reached the shore, I'm sure I cannot say.

"We were the sole survivors of the officers, passengers. and crew of the Wonga-Wonga.

"The Cumbersona, sweeping suddenly around a sharp bend of the river, had run into us as we lay almost broadside on the stream.

"The bushrangers had surprised and locked up the crew in the forecastle forward before they had attacked the cabin, and all those poor fellows were drowned like rats in a drain.

"The next day we were landed at a small riverside township, called Wonongoloo, and travelled overland to Echuca.

"I have often thought of that fair girl since, and if I survive our duel to-morrow, I will try to find her out, and ask her to become my wife."

CHAPTER LX.

THE DUEL TO THE DEATH.

SCARCELY had Ted Hogan finished his yarn, when Jack Last exclaimed—

"Hark! I hear the thud of hoofs. Can it be Bungy already returned?"

"Yes," replied Ted; "I cannot see him, but I know 'tis Bungy from the hoofstrokes of the horse he rides. I know them as I should know the voice of a friend."

"He brings the daylight along with him," said Jack Last, pointing toward the east.

It was true—the cold grey dawn was slowly breaking.

"It is well," remarked Ted.

"We can get the affair over before the sun dazzles us with his beams," quoth Jack.

They spoke not another word until Bungy, the horse he bestrode covered with foam, plunged into the midst, man and horse of the same sable hue, equally spume-flecked and excited, for, put an Australian blackfellow on the back of a good steed, and he'll ride him straight to a climate of excessive sultriness.

Bungy sat in the saddle like a Centaur, and reined in the fiery horse with an almost imperceptible movement of arm and hand. Then he sprang to the ground.

Ted Hogan's first impulse was to see that the head of Bob Loveridge swung at his saddle bow.

Yes, there it was still, and in a better state of preservation than on the day before.

The sun had dried it and preserved it, changing the skin of the face to a consistency of leather. It looked very much like one of those grim heads cut out of cocoanuts that you may see at this time of the year in fruiterers' windows.

It was scarcely human—'twas more like the head of a thousand-year-old mummy.

And the burning Australian sun had effected this in a dozen hours.

It will repeat the process in a more remarkable manner before this tale is done.

And to a far more important personage in this veracious history than Bob Loveridge.

"Mr. Hogan," said Jack Last, in a tremulous voice, "I see what you have got there, and in a quarter of an hour from now you may have it in your power to balance that hideous trophy on the other side with another. Do you intend doing so?"

"You insult me by the suspicion, Jack," said Ted Hogan, warmly. "You saved my life at the risk of your own, and though duty now obliges me to capture or kill you on your refusing to yield quietly, that duty done I will bury you in any spot you like to point out, and what is more I will never reveal to the world where your body lies."

"Nobly said," quoth Jack Last, "but you will be burying five hundred pounds with me."

"I value the life you saved at a higher sum, so I shall still be your debtor."

"And you will really do this?" exclaimed the bushranger, with a burst of feeling.

"Assuredly, if I am the survivor, but remember I am just as likely to fall."

"True, and if it should so happen, what do you wish done?" asked Jack Last.

"Where the tree falls there let it lie," replied Ted. "I have less horror of death than of the grave. Better the wild dog than the worm."

"My feelings to a hair," responded the bushranger, with a forced laugh. "Leave me above ground, where the dingoes and the ants can destroy my identity as soon as may be, but yet where the south wind may murmur and the perfume of the wattle and the mimosa may be wafted over my bones. That is all that I ask of you."

"And all that I require in turn," answered Ted. "Is there anything more to arrange?"

"On my part, nothing, and as we had better get this matter over before the rising sun shines through those flickering leaves and dazzles our aim, let us mount."

"Stay, I will send away Bungy We have no longer any need of him. If we both fell he might conceive the idea of getting the reward offered for your head himself," said Ted.

"It is generous of you to think of this. But if sent away he may return."

"He shall not return until ants and wild dogs have done their work, anyhow."

"That will suffice as well as if he never returned at all," said Jack Last.

Ted Hogan briefly retorted, "Quite so," and beckoned Bungy towards him.

The black, who had been standing out of earshot, immediately came.

"Bungy, I am going to take this man a prisoner to Berrina, but I've other work for you to do. Return at once to the spot where you found this horse, and search all around on that side of the river for the body of Blue Cap, the bushranger. He has very likely crawled into some cave in the cliff to die. Search diligently for three days and nights, and if I don't join you by then, seek me at the old hut, and if I am not there, rejoin your tribe or re-enter the police service, whichever you choose. I have forwarded your name and an account of the important services you have rendered me to Inspector White at Sydney, who will take care of your interests and see that you are rewarded for what you have done. There is big white money to buy food, baccy, and rum on the way. Good-bye, Bungy," and the detective grasped the poor blackfellow's hand warmly, as he placed therein three crown pieces, the natives infinitely preferring these coins to gold—in fact, having a strange and peculiar affection for them.

Bungy took the money, returned the hand pressure, gazed hard in Ted Hogan's eyes for a moment, as if half suspecting that he was in some way fooling him, and then with a hoarse snort of acquiescence started off at a run.

"Now we are man to man—a fair field and no favour," said Ted, with a smile.

He looked round as he spoke, but Jack Last was gone.

"Fooled like a green schoolboy," exclaimed Ted, gnashing his teeth, "but he cannot escape me. By George, no, that he cannot!" and he sprang upon his horse.

But scarcely was he in the saddle when he saw Jack Last riding back towards him. He had only been to catch and saddle his horse, that was all.

Ted forebore to tell him of his ungenerous suspicions—in fact, he was ashamed of them. "You have made quick work of it; you must have found him close by," he said. "I have to hunt for half an hour sometimes before I come across mine."

"I had him short-hoppled, and there was good grazing and a waterhole, all within a stone's throw, that's the secret of it," was the reply; "but, by-the-by, I find that I have yet another favour to ask of you. This horse, as you are aware, is one freely lent me by Mr. Harry Miller, of Marrangong. I promised to return it safe and sound within a week. I never yet broke a promise freely given, and if I fall I trust to you enabling me to keep it even after death. Promise me this, Mr. Hogan."

"I do, on my honour," continued Ted. "Now Jack Last, is there anything else?"

"Yes, I would like to shake hands with you before we take our places."

"There is my hand, and with it I will own that I have at last met with a bushranger for whom, on the shortest of acquaintances, I have learnt to feel gratitude, respect, friendship, and admiration. Should we meet in another world we shall not be ashamed of one another."

"We will be friends and allies, for there will be no thieves or thief-takers there. You may think me a strange fellow for not leaving any farewell to distant relatives or friends, but it would be cruel to let them what I know what I was, and how I died. With you it may be different, and if I survive, I will if possible."

"It is not needed," said Ted Hogan, interrupting him. "I have no relatives living, and of the only two human beings for whom I have ever felt the dawnings of a sincere friendship, one is a hopeless lunatic, and the other I am about to try to kill. Take your place, man, take your place—twelve yards on the other side of that dying fire, dying slower than one of us will be in a few moments. Guess the distance, as I mean to do. Then wheel round, and fire shot by shot, with an interval of a dozen seconds between each for the smoke to clear away, and heaven have mercy on the worst marksman."

"Amen," replied Jack, fervently.

And he wheeled his horse round without another word.

All was done as the detective had half-advised, half-dictated.

A minute later they stood facing each other, their horses as still as though they were statues of bronze, the still smouldering fire equidistant between them.

"Are you ready?" asked Ted Hogan, in a harsh, unnatural voice.

"Quite," was the reply. "Give the word and present. Let our first fire be instantaneous."

Up went the right arm of each duellist.

Each right eye glanced along the sight

There was a momentary pause, and then Ted shouted—

"Fire!"

The discharge of his revolver followed instantaneously, and his ball knocked the bushranger's hat from off his head.

Jack Last hastened to reply, but his cap snapped without exploding its charge.

The bushranger uttered a subdued oath.

Ted Hogan noticed that his opponent's weapon has missed fire just as he was about to take his second shot.

He dropped his arm instantly.

"Your caps might be better. I'll give you half-a-dozen of mine, and we will begin again. They are of government manufacture, and never miss fire," he said.

"You are very generous," replied Jack Last "Anyone else would have regarded his adversary's weapon missing fire as providential, and hastened to take advantage of it. Nor would such an act have been exactly foul play."

"It would have been dastardly conduct towards a man who had saved my life, and whom I was only endeavouring to kill fairly as an act of duty. Come, catch this little tin box—it holds three dozen," said Ted, with a laugh.

He threw the tin box as he spoke.

The bushranger deftly caught it.

He re-capped his revolver, and was once more ready to wage the duel to the death.

"Now," exclaimed Ted Hogan, "we will begin again."

Up went both right arms.

Again and again keen eyes glanced along bright barrels.

"Fire!" for the second time shouted Ted Hogan, in a voice of thunder.

On this occasion the report of both pistols was instantaneous.

The detective felt a pain in his left cheek, as though a red-hot poker had been laid for a moment thereon, and then withdrawn at the same instant.

He perceived Jack Last reel in his saddle, and clap his left hand, without dropping the reins to his chest.

At the same instant there arose on every side the war-whoop of the blacks.

Ere its echoes had died away, much as the kilted retainers of Rhoderic Dhu arose from behind heath and gorse, to the astonished view of Fitzjames, arose scores of black parrot-plumed heads, and naked skeleton-painted bodies above the patches of tea-tree scrub that surrounded the arena of combat.

Spears and nullah-nullahs, boomerangs and waddies, yelemens and woomeras flashed in the rays of the now rising sun, and Ted Hogan found himself in a proper trap for wolves with a very small chance of escaping therefrom.

Two out of his six barrels were discharged, so that his revolver only held four lives, and the black warriors numbered four score if a man.

Well, he would sell his life at the highest price he could, and he only regretted that Jack Last might live long enough to be tortured to the death with their spears.

But whilst this painful thought crossed his mind, he heard Jack Last shout hoarsely—

"I'm not done for yet, Hogan. I'll last long enough to send some of these smutty devils to the shades before me to help you 'scape their clutches, never fear."

He spurred towards Ted as he spoke, and wheeling round at his side, continued—

"Now then, there's their weakest point, and a clear path for our horses. You shoot down from the right, and I'll knock over from the left. Then we'll ride down all others who attempt to bar our path like ninepins. Now then, away. Speed does it."

"Away !" echoed Ted Hogan, for there was no time to say more.

And with a leap, a snort, and a bound, as they felt the spur, the two horses darted forward.

Instantly the air seemed to be alive with spears and boomerangs, that mysterious weapon, that can be thrown all around a horse, and will then return to the hurler's feet, standing a couple or three hundred yards therefrom.

To use the language of Scott—

"Had all the fiends from heaven that fell,
    Howled forth the battle-cry of hell,"

the yells and howls of the blackfellows could not have been surpassed in horror or intensity, and above it could be clearly heard the hissing and humming of these primitive yet effective weapons.

How the detective and the bushranger escaped instant death, or at all events, being felled from their galloping steeds, stunned and senseless, was almost miraculous—as wonderful, in fact, as for two riders to gallop between the falling drops of a thunder-shower without being wetted.

Yet they did so escape, by dint of ducking their heads, swaying in their saddles, and otherwise dodging the deadly missiles.

And terrible was the return they made for these questionable civilities.

"Crack! crack! crack! crack!" to left, and "Crack! crack! crack! crack!" to right, sent eight grinning blackfellows to glory and opened a bloody gap for the detective and the bushranger to break through. The buffeting shoulders of the galloping steeds hurled to the earth those who hastily attempted to fill it up. The sable cordon was effectually broken through amidst yells of terror and hoarse shouts of baffled rage.

"Now you have but to ply the spur and you are safe," said Jack Last, as, a moment later, a shower of long slender spears fell and quivered in the earth behind them. "We are out of range. I've done all I can do—let it not be done for nothing."

"What do you mean, my brave, my gallant ally," said Ted, turning in his saddle.

"That I'm sped, old fellow—clean sped. Well, thank God I have died better than I have lived, though I have not been such a very bad man if you only knew all."

He never checked the speed of his horse whilst he was speaking, but, as the last words quitted his lips, they turned deathly white, a strange film came over his eyes, he dropped his reins and empty revolver to clutch the pommel of his saddle with both hands, and the next instant his steed was galloping riderless through the bush, and poor Jack Last lay on his back on the green sward, a fountain of blood bursting from his chest, a lesser stream from his mouth, and his pale white face, to which the death dew had sprung, upturned towards the sunlit sky.

The detective instantly drew rein, notwithstanding that the blacks were in hot pursuit.

"On, on," gasped the bushranger, "I am past help. They will catch you. On, on."

"I'm d—d if I'll leave you for these wretches to torture," replied Ted, bluntly.

"They—can't—torture—a—dead—man—but—they—can—a—living," was the faint reply.

"When you're dead I'll leave you, old fellow, but not a moment before. I'm not a coward, and I'm not exactly devoid of feeling. I should be both did I quit you now."

"Were—I—dead—would—you—ride—away—for—your—very—life ?"

"Why, yes, for then my staying would do you no good," replied the detective.

"Away—then—for—I—am—dead," gasped Jack Last, endeavouring to spring to his feet.

The effort was successful, the blood gushed forth from his mouth as it had done from his chest. It filled the air tubes, causing instant suffocation. Jack Last had by an effort died five minutes sooner in order to enable his slayer to escape the pursuing and fast approaching blacks. Truly he was in his way a hero and a christian, a better one perhaps than Byron's hero, though, like the Corsair, "he left his name to other times, bright with one virtue, dark with a thousand crimes."

Ted Hogan placed a hand on the bushranger's heart and pulse, and finding that he was really dead, vaulted into his saddle and gathered up the reins.

But he was too late—the foe were too close upon him. A shower of spears again darkened the air, and though they all missed him, one found the heart of his gallant charger, who, uttering a shrill scream of anguish, bounded into the air, and then came down upon its knees to roll over on to its back dead.

Ted Hogan extricated himself from saddle and stirrups in time to save a broken leg, and then he plucked his revolver from his belt.

He had forgotten that it was unloaded. Finding it so, he gave way to despair.

The slowest of the blackfellows could outrun him with ease, and here were a good score of them within a hundred yards, and others fast coming up in the rear.

It was even denied him to sell his life dearly, for there was no time to reload his weapon. Death immediate and inglorious seemed to await him.

As the blackfellows came up with their spears they plucked them out of the ground and poised them for another, a chosen and more deadly volley.

To Ted Hogan they looked like black fiends from the nethermost hell. He shut his eyes and folded his arms. At all events he would meet death like a man.

But death didn't come. The blacks yelled again, but it was a yell of surprise and terror, more than of rage, and with it Ted thought he could distinguish the rush of galloping hoofs.

Then "Crack! crack! crack! crack! crack!" came the report of pistols, and with the genuine

TED HOGAN KNEW THAT IT WAS ALL OVER WITH HIM, AND RESIGNED HIMSELF TO HIS FATE.

English cheers, and Ted opened his eyes to see half a dozen mounted troopers scattering the wild blacks to the four winds of heaven.

Five minutes later they were all gone, and in ten the troopers, laughing and chatting, and treating the whole thing as a very good jest, were back again and congratulating Ted on their opportune arrival and his consequent lucky escape.

"Now then, we will camp here," said the leader. "The dead will not smell for another hour, and I espied a waterhole behind that bush, a rare thing in these parts."

CHAPTER LXI.

WHAT OCCURRED ROUND THE CAMP FIRE.

THE camp fire was soon lighted, the rude meal was soon spread.

The troopers had been travelling all night, so that they were not sorry for a rest, and a fight before breakfast has the appetising qualities of quinine.

The jerked beef, damper cake, and pannikins of hot tea were partaken of, therefore, with rare gusto, and the occupation was too delightful to permit of conversation.

The wants of nature satisfied, however, and curiosity took the place of hunger in the troopers' breasts. The dead body of Jack Last, pierced by revolver bullets, instead of the blackfellows' spears, attracted their attention almost as much as the ghastly head that hung at the saddle bow of the dead horse.

They eagerly questioned Ted Hogan as to the double phenomenon.

"If I divert you with one tale, gentlemen, I shall expect to be diverted in turn by another," said Ted, and this was readily agreed to by the rest.

He gave his rescuers then a full and detailed account of the scenes and adventures that he had encountered during the preceding month, which excited the most unbounded astonishment in their minds, and when he had done, then came the turn of some one else. "I have the right of call," he said, with a smile, as he lighted his pipe, "so, serjeant, in virtue of your three stripes, do you take up the running."

"Well," said the party referred to, "if I don't narrate an experience I will nevertheless tell a tale as 'twas told to me, and a more remarkable one I don't think you ever heard," and, so saying, he commenced the following extraordinary narrative:—

"It was about an hour before sunset, on a beautiful day in early spring, that I rode slowly amongst the solitary heath-clad ranges of the once famous Kajunga diggings.

"For miles and miles the bed of every gully, the crest of every hill, and the broad surface of every flat, were thickly dotted with hillocks of pipeclay, heaped up near some fallen-in shaft, over the mouths of many of which windlass-legs, with here and there a windlass barrel, were still standing.

"Three years before, every hill and gully in the district were thickly peopled.

"The sites of tents and stores might still be easily traced on the ground, which where they had stood was hard and grassless, while on every side, sod or log chimneys—the latter for the most part entire, the former in various stages of decay—gave abundant proof how numerous had once been the dwelling places of the digger.

"The country through which I had for some hours been travelling is in general barren and desolate in the extreme, badly watered, and seldom affording even the scantiest feed, so that, once robbed of its gold, it has speedily relapsed into its former uninhabited state.

"The past winter, however, had been a remarkably rainy one, and under the genial influence of the spring sun, the landscape had assumed the most lovely appearance.

"The flats were emerald green with grass, while the ranges presented all the hues of the rainbow from the many coloured heaths, through which my horse made his way breast deep.

"Thousands of wild flowers sprang up on every side, whilst overhead the wattle blossom gleaming like gold amongst the delicate foliage, filled the air with perfume.

"The timber had been sadly thinned in old times by the axe of the digger, and by the frequent bush fires, but still many a noble white gum stood in the flats, and the summits of the hills were clothed with stringy bark and peppermint trees.

"Pausing on the top of a range, a little higher than its neighbours, to contemplate the beauty of the scene, my eye caught sight of something bright, glancing amongst the trees to the north, which I at once guessed to be the Kajunga Creek, on the banks of which I had made up my mind to encamp for the night.

"Giving my nag his head, he settled at once into that shambling gallop which an old stock horse will keep up for hours, and in a few minutes I reached the creek, on whose banks I found, as I had expected, very tolerable feed.

"Dismounting, I took off the saddle and bridle, and placing them on the ground beside my blanket and cooking utensils, I hoppled my horse and let him go where he would.

"Then after a plunge in the creek, I kindled a fire, made my tea, toasted my chops on the end of a stick, and having thoroughly satisfied my appetite, mixed myself a good, stiff pannikin of brandy and water from my capacious flask, and seating myself cozily on a log before the fire, lighted my pipe, and began to smoke.

"The sun had now gone down some time, and the stillness of the starlit night was unbroken, save by the rattle of my horse's hopples, as he now and then changed his feeding ground, and occasionally by the plaintive notes of the curlew, or the cry of the mopoke, the night cuckoo of Australia.

"Yielding to the potency of the grog, and the soothing influence of the honey dew, I had fallen into a semi-dozing state, when I was suddenly aroused by the sound of voices, and almost immediately afterwards three men stepped out of the gloom into the bright firelight, and with a hearty 'What cheer, mate?' commenced making themselves comfortable for the night, much after the same fashion I myself had pursued an hour or so before.

"They were evidently all diggers, for I noticed the marks of the pipeclay on their moleskins, and as they had only their blankets with them, and no tools, I guessed, as was the case, that they must be on their road down to town.

"After they had supped I produced my brandy flask, and we fraternised at once.

"We talked on various subjects—of the good old times when gold was plentiful and diggers few, of the bad new times when diggers were many, and gold, alas! was scarce; of Eaglehawk, of the Ballarat riots, in which one of my companions had lost a couple of fingers; of dodging the police in the old license; hunting days, and of a hundred other kindred subjects, which to an old gold-seeker furnish an endless fund of amusement, for I myself had handled the pick and rocked the cradle for many a day before I entered the service, and I was fully qualified to take part in a conversation.

"After some time, however, the current of talk slackened gradually, and at last we had remained silently smoking for several minutes, when one of my new acquaintances, addressing himself to another—a short but enormously powerful man, who was extended at full length before the fire, and whose face was so completely buried in hair, that only the tip of his nose and his sharply twinkling eyes were visible, said—

"'Bill, my boy, didn't you work somewhere hereabouts, once upon a time?'

"'Yes,' replied Bill; 'about a matter of three years and a half ago I worked on the old Kajunga; more by token, I had the best hole in Murder-will-out Gully, than ever fell to my share since I first handled a pick.'

"'Murder-will-out Gully!' I exclaimed. 'Well, I have heard some queer names given to gullies and flats in my time, what with Dead-horse, Lucky Woman, Pegleg, Nip-cheese, Pinch-gut, and such like—but that beats them all. Why was it so called?'

"'Well, you see, mate,' said Bill, 'I am not much a hand at pitching a tale, but as you seem one of the right sort, I'll try for once to manage it.'

"It will be four years on the third of next month since first I came on to Kajunga.

"I had been working at Fryer's Creek, in tucker holes, for some time previously, for my mate had been bad with dysentery, and of course I couldn't leave him.

"At last, however, he died, and having been told that there were some old shipmates of mine up there, I determined to come up too, and try my luck.

"Well, I soon picked up with a fresh mate, and a pretty tidy hole too, for there was gold galore in these parts then, I can tell you.

"There was a rare rough lot of diggers up here though too, as well.

"You see it was a goodish way from the old established gold fields, and the diggings were scattered over such a deal of ground that what few troopers we had up here, went pretty nigh for nothing, so that every man of us used to sleep with his loaded revolver under his head, as in the good old times at Golden Point.

"I was encamped a few miles higher up the creek, and in the next tent to us were a couple of chaps who had been digging there some time; but partly through want of luck, and partly through blowing all they earned in the grog shanties, they were pretty well always down on their luck.

"The name of the youngest of them was Charlie Smart—Smart Charlie we used to call him though, for of a Sunday he used to come out in a grey shirt all worked with scarlet silk, a great red sash round his waist, a real Panama hat, breeches, and knee boots, all which swell dunnage he had brought with him from California, where he and his brother, who was then away at the M'Ivor, had worked for some time.

"He was a very good looking chap, though he was as white in the face as a parsnip; but he was uncommon strong and hearty, and an out and out good workman.

"His mate, Alick, or Black Mick, as we used to call him, on account of the darkness of his skin, was a chap of about fifty years of age, and as ill looking a customer as you could well meet with in a day's march, even in this country.

"I have heard since that he was tried in the old country for robbery and murder. There wasn't quite evidence enough to bring the matter home to him however, though there wasn't much doubt of his guilt, so he saved his neck and came out to the colonies at Government expense instead.

"He was a gloomy, morose kind of fellow, very quarrelsome when in drink, and as unsociable as a bear, for when he was out of cash to knock down in grog, he used always to turn in as soon as ever he had swallowed his supper, never coming out to sit by the fire, and smoke and yarn like the rest of us used to do.

"Smart Charlie was quite another guess sort of chap. He would sit up half the night, as long as anyone was left to talk to, and seemed to dislike the blankets as much as Black Alick appeared to love them.

"Now, a short distance from where we were encamped, there was a grog shanty. Not one of your new fangled, weatherboarded hotels, and a grand bar all set out with swell decanters full of bad liquor, but a jolly great tent, well put up, with a good fly over it, lined throughout with green baize, and a sod chimney to it that would hold an eight foot log—as comfortable a crib, in fact, as a man could wish to set foot in, who was content to pour good stuff out of a black bottle, and to drink it out of a tin pannikin.

"It was kept by a Yankee—a fair specimen of one he was, too, and an uncommon good hand at drink, to be sure. The way he could mix a julep was a caution.

"Well, a whole lot of us chaps used to frequent this shanty, more or less, and though I never was much of a one for drink, I used to go up pretty regular of a Saturday night, and have a hand at poker or cribbage, and a glass or two of hot whiskey and water, real Scotch, and first-rate at that.

"The Yankee boys who came there, said it was nothing to Monongahela; but Charlie, who had been some time in America, said that that was all gas.

"However, as I never tasted their Monongahela, I can't say.

"Among the fellows who used the shanty—the Stars and Stripes, as we called it—was one who dropped in occasionally, who went by the name of Indian Hepe, though he was no more an Indian than you are, for his father was a Scotchman, and his mother a Mexican woman of Sonora; but he had been stolen away when a lad, by the Indians who live on horseback—Comanches, I think they call them—and had passed pretty nigh twenty years of his life amongst them.

"I have heard that he became a chief, and had raised a deal of hair in his time; but whether this was true or not, I can't say, for he was a silent sort of chap, and never said much about his past life. He had come on to California diggings soon after they broke out, and afterwards came over to Sydney, and from there to Victoria.

"We used to think him a bit mad, for he would go away with his gun, all alone for weeks, living upon what he could shoot, and when he came back to work he used to prefer spending half the night by himself in the bush, stretched out on his back staring up at the stars, to sitting by the fire and smoking his pipe like a christian.

"There were queer tales afloat of his having told some fellows' fortunes up on Eaglebank, and how all he said had come true; but that's neither here nor there.

"Well, one Saturday night—I remember it well, for we had nuggetted pretty nigh thirty ounces that day—we were all up at the Stars and Stripes.

"Alick and Charlie had been pretty well in luck that week, and they insisted on shouting all round time after time, till we all, I fancy, had taken a little more than was good for us, and even Hepe began to talk a bit.

"Charlie, seeing this, began gammoning and chaffing him about his powers of fortune telling. The Indian took it very quietly at first; but when Charlie went on too much at him, he got riled, and, said he—

"'Charlie, I can tell you something that will happen to you as sure as you are sitting there.'

"'What is it, Injun?' says Charlie. 'Speak up, and spit it out.'

"'Well, the best hole of the best rush that was ever, or ever will be on Kajunga, shall be found by you, and yet you will never handle an ounce of the gold, and what's more, those that work it will never profit by it.'

"At this we all laughed heartily, and says Charlie, says he—

"'If it's ever my lot to come across a bit of good ground, I should like to see the chap living that would jump it, and I'd not only handle the gold, but spend it too. As to profiting by it, why, that's another thing altogether; but, if I didn't, the Stars and Stripes would at any rate, whilst it lasted.'

"Hepe didn't make any reply; but he sat quietly smoking his pipe for a bit, and then got up and walked away.

"By this time Black Alick had began to get nasty, and wanted to fight everybody in the shanty, one down, the other come on, so I thought it time to make tracks for my tent, and turn in for the night.

"It seems that soon after I left, Alick and Charlie had a bit of a barney, which ended in a regular stand-up fight, and when old Stars and Stripes attempted to separate them, they both went into him like mad, and beat him pretty nigh into a jelly before the other boys could get him away.

"He was precious savage at this, as you may think, and swore that neither of them should ever have another nobbler from him, either for love or money.

"A few days after this shindy the rush to the White Hills took place, and Alick and Charlie got a capital claim dead on the gutter.

"It was so good an one that they couldn't have knocked down all they made even if they had had every night to do it in.

"But old Stars and Stripes wouldn't have them at any price, and though there were lots of grog-tents in the neighbourhood, there wasn't a drop of decent stuff to be got nearer than the town-ship, which was pretty nigh three miles off, with a rare rough road, bad enough to travel even by daylight, so they were obliged to lay by their gold, whether they would or not.

"For the first few Sundays they used to start off for Kajunga as soon as day broke, drink all day, and come reeling back just before sunset.

"But there had been ill-blood between them ever since the row, and on the third Sunday they had another fight, and Charlie drew his revolver on Alick—a bad habit he had picked up in Cali-fornia.

"There wasn't any harm done, for some of the boys who were present interfered, but there was no love lost between them from that day, and though they still worked and lived together, they seldom or never spoke, and used to grub sepa-rate,

"Alick still kept up his Sunday journeys to Ka-junga, but Charlie never went down there any more—turned quite steady, and saved up a heap of gold.

"This sort of game went on for three months or more, till one Wednesday evening, as we were sit-ting around the fire after supper, Charlie says to me—

"'We shall have washed up by Saturday after-noon, Bill, and as I and Alick don't hit it any longer, I shall start away on Sunday morning for Melbourne, and have a spree. I expect my brother Jack will get down there in a couple of weeks or so, and then we will either come up here again to prospect for the claim the Indian told me of, or try some fresh diggings. I rather think, however, I shall do the latter.'

"On Saturday night Charlie came and had his supper with me.

"'It's my last night on the old Kajunga,' says e. 'I wish you would get old Stars and Stripes to let me in. I should like to shout for the boys once more before I go."

"I went up to the shanty, and after a deal of trouble I made it all right for Charlie, but Alick he wouldn't have, do what I would, and I tried pretty hard to.

"However, I might have saved myself all bother on that account, for it seems that while I was away he came out of the tent, and Charlie, who

was as good-hearted a fellow as ever breathed, asked him to shake hands and have a nobbler, but Alick only swore at him, and went in again.

"Well, we had a right-down merry night of it, to be sure.

"Stars and Stripes brewed us some stunning rum punch, and we had lots of singing and plenty of good yarns, and were very merry without any of us getting much over the mark.

"Rather late, Indian Hepe came in, for like the rest of us, he liked Charlie, and would have been sorry to let him go away without wishing him good luck.

"Charlie shook him by the hand, and says he, as he did so—

"'Injun, I haven't found this grand hole yet, though I've had a pretty fair one."

"'Wait a bit,' replied Hepe—'you'll find it, never fear.'

"Charlie laughed, and was going to make some reply, but just then one of the boys began a chorus as long as from here to the top of Mount Lofty, and we all joined in of course, and so the subject was dropped.

"We knocked off soon after midnight, and I walked down with Charlie to his tent.

"'Good-bye, old fellow,' says he. 'I sha'n't see you in the morning, for I shall be off by day-break, and I know that you can do with a tidy amount of sleep on a Sunday morning. I sha'n't be long making town, for I mean to take nothing with me but the things I stand up in and my gold. The tent is Alick's, and if he pleases, before I re-turn, I have told him to let you have my tub and cradle and tools, and if I am not back in three months, why you are quite welcome to them. Good-night, old chap, and once more good luck to you.'

"With that we went into our tents, and in a few moments I was wrapped in my blankets, and sound asleep.

"Just about dawn I was woke up by Charlie, who was whistling away most vigorously as he made his fire and boiled the water for his tea.

"He wasn't long in finishing his breakfast, and then away he went on his journey as brisk as a bee.

"Instead of taking the main road which led to Kajunga, he passed right by our tent, and struck at once into the bush, intending, no doubt, to give the township a wide berth, which was a very sen-sible notion of his, as there was a deal of old hands and roughs loafing about it, and he carried a large lot of gold.

"As I was dropping off to sleep again, I thought I heard a slight noise, as if some one was passing our tent on tip-toe, but as I was too sleepy to give much heed, and the dog, which lay stretched out at the entrance of the tent, didn't bark, I just gave myself an extra coil in the blankets, and was soon in the land of Nod again.

"I seldom got up of a Sunday much before ten, and as my mate and I had agreed to go out on the plains that day after some wild turkey that had been seen about, and it being my week to cook, I roused out pretty early, lighted the fire, and set to work to get breakfast ready.

"I was busy frying the chops, when, looking up, I saw Black Alick coming along the road from the township.

"He had a gun under his arm, and a brace of snipe in one hand.

"'Why, Alick,' said I, 'you have been out after the birds pretty early.'

"'Oh,' says he, 'Charlie made such a cursed row this morning that he woke me up, and I couldn't get to sleep again; so I thought I would get up and try if there was anything to be got along the creek for breakfast. I have been pretty well all the way to the township, and this is all that I've lighted on.'

"'Well,' says I, 'I hope we shall have better sport, at any rate.'

"'I hope you will,' says he.

"And into his tent he went.

"Well, things went on pretty much in the old way with us for the next four weeks.

"The only thing in any way remarkable was the change that had come over Alick.

"Since Charlie's departure he never shut himself up of a night, as he used to do, but came up regularly, and sat with the rest of us till the very last man went off, and then even he did not seem much inclined to turn in himself.

"Not that he was a bit more pleasant than before, but formerly he used to speak now and then, but now he never so much as opened his mouth, but sat smoking and staring into the fire, and looking altogether as miserable as a bandicoot.

"Nobody cared about him for a mate, and indeed he never looked after one himself, but went and worked as a hatter at some surfacing which had just been struck on the side of Ironbank Gully.

"The stuff wasn't very rich, but as there was a considerable depth of it, and it was very easy washing, being quite free from clay and not requiring above two waters, he did pretty well at it.

"He had taken to save his money too, for his Sunday journeys to township were entirely dropped, and the Stars and Stripes wouldn't have him at any price, though he begged hard to be taken in.

"Well, it may have been a couple of months or thereabouts, after Charlie left us, that I and my mate were sitting one fine night, in front of our tents, doing our pipes.

"It was full moon, and pretty nigh as light as day.

"Alick had been working late, and was busy in his tent getting his supper ready, to cook which he had lighted a big fire, not far from where we were seated.

"I had just been talking to my mate about Charlie, and was wondering whether he meant to come for his things or leave them for me, when who should I see come out of the bush, just behind Alick's tent, but Charlie himself.

"He was dressed just the same as usual—grey shirt, red sash and all, but looked if possible, a trifle more bloodless than ever.

"To my surprise he passed by the tent, and though I shouted to him he took no notice, but walked straight over to the fire and sat down on a log which lay beside it, with his back towards us.

"Well, I was just going to ask him what he meant by cutting a couple of old pals in that style, when out came Alick, carrying a billy full of fresh soup in his hand, which he was going to warm up for his supper, and as he kept stirring it round whilst he walked, he did not notice Charlie, who sat quite still, looking at the fire, without even saying a word.

"Alick stooped down, settled the log, so as to make a firm place on which to set his pot, and, after placing it on the fire, he lifted up his head, and saw Charlie.

"Never shall I forget the expression on his face, were I to live a thousand years.

"For about half a minute he stood as still as though he were turned into stone—his mouth wide open, his eyes starting out of his head, and his cheeks as white as pipeclay. Then with a horrible yell, he fell head foremost into the fire.

"My mate and I rushed up, dragged him from among the blazing logs, and when we had done so and turned round to look for Charlie, he was gone.

"Well, I can tell you, I began to feel pretty scared and no mistake.

"'Ned,' says I to my mate, 'there's something wrong here; if that wasn't Charlie himself, it was

his ghost, and I'm sure if he'd been living, he would never have gone off like that, without having any talk with us and the rest of the boys.'

"'Nonsense,' says he, 'there ain't any such things as ghosts.'

"But though he pretended to laugh at the whole affair, and said that Charlie was only having a game with us, I could see by his looks that he was more inclined, after all, to be of my opinion than his own.

"However, we didn't give much for talking, for all the while we were holding up Alick, who though not very badly burnt, was yet insensible.

"We carried him into his tent, and tried everything we could think of to bring him round, but as it was all of no use, my mate proposed that he should sit up with him one half the night, and I the other.

"Well, it might have been about midnight when my mate came and woke me up.

"'Why,' says I, 'what's the matter with you? You look as white as a ghost.'

"'Get up,' says he, 'and come along with me. It's Charlie! I'm afraid it's all over with him!'

"As I couldn't get anything more out of him, I hurried on my clothes, and went across with him to Black Alick's tent.

"By the light of the candle which stood on the table near the head of the bunk, I could see Alick's features plainly.

"He was asleep, but his face was livid, and the perspiration was rolling in great beads down his forehead.

"For about a quarter of an hour he lay like this quite still, my mate and I watching him in silence. Suddenly however, he raised himself up and screamed—

"'Keep him off! Keep him off! He has come to drag me down to hell. His grave cannot hold him, and yet I buried him deep down—deep down. Mercy, my God, mercy!'

"His screams gradually grew fainter, and at last he fell exhausted.

"'Has he been taken like that before to-night?' asked I.

"'Yes, just before I came and woke you up,' replied my mate.

"'Well, you go and turn in now, and I'll stay with him until the morning. Then we'll think over what's best to be done,' says I.

"It might have been daylight when Alick roused up all of a sudden.

"He sat up, looked round the tent, and seeing me seated on the opposite bunk exclaimed—

"'Why, what's all this about? I must have been ill! Have I been ill?'

"I didn't make him any answer, and so he laid himself down again, and turning himself so that I couldn't see his face, he said after a bit—

"'Where's Charlie? Didn't Charlie come back last night?'

"'Where Charlie is, Alick,' said I, 'I think you know better than I do.'

"'What do you mean by that?' he says savagely starting up and facing me.

"'I mean,' says I, 'that you said things in your sleep last night, that want explaining.'

"'What did I say then?' quoth he sullenly, glancing up at me under his brows.

"'Never mind the exact words,' I replies, 'but I might just as well tell you, that before my mate and I, you said as much as that you'd murdered Charlie.'

"With that he dropped back on his bunk again, as if he'd been shot.

"He lay there a long while without speaking, then raising himself up, says he—

"'Bill, it's no use my keeping the matter to myself any longer. Charlie's ghost came for me last night, and though I escaped that time, it's all up with me. I feel sure. I did murder him. I followed

"FIRE!" SHOUTED TED HOGAN, IN A VOICE OF THUNDER; AND THE REPORT OF BOTH PISTOLS WAS INSTANTANEOUS.

him that Sunday morning, and shot him down in a gully, a few miles from here. I hid his body in the scrub, and in the evening I went down and buried him. But his grave was not deep enough—his grave was not deep enough. Besides, murder will out anyhow."

"'Well, Alick,' says I, 'I didn't ask you to tell me all this, but now that you have so, why, I must do my duty, you know.'

"'I know—I know,' says he. "'Let me go down with you and show you where the body is buried, and then you may hand me over to the traps as soon as ever you like, for I've been sick of my life ever since I took his, I can tell you.'

"Well, I called my mate, and sent him up to the Stars and Stripes, where he found some of the boys who had come in for their morning drink, and told them all about it, and a pretty row there was at once, as you may well think.

"Some of the Yankees were for lynching him right off, but the rest of us wouldn't agree to it, and at last it was settled that Alick should go down with us and show us the grave, and that in order not to attract the attention of those whom we might meet on the way, he should not be bound.

"It was necessary to take the greatest care in order to get him safe into the hands of the troopers, for if the news of the murder had once got noised about the township, he wouldn't have had many minutes to say his prayers in, I can tell you.

"However, we put our revolvers into our pockets, and gave him notice that if he attempted to escape, we would shoot him down like a dog.

"He led us right through the bush without even speaking, until he came to a very long, narrow gully with steep sides, and about the middle of it he stopped, and pointing to a great half-charred log, he said—

"'Underneath that!'

"We rolled away the log and began to dig, taking it by turns. It was a lightish soil and easy sinking, so that, working with a will as we did, it wasn't long before we got to the body.

"It was in a horrible state of decay, but still it wasn't so far gone but what we could all swear to it.

"We left some of the party with it, and then we started with Alick to take him to the police camp at Kajunga.

"Now the creek about a mile above Kajunga runs at the bottom of a tremendous precipice, 300 or 400 feet in height, and along this precipice lay our road.

"The scrub is very thick about there, and comes pretty well up to the edge of the cliff, so that there is but a narrow pathway of a few feet in width.

"Well, we had got almost within sight of the township when who should come out of the bush, about a hundred yards from us, but Charlie.

"It was broad daylight, and so there was no mistaking him.

"Well, I can tell you my heart beat double quick, and I don't think that any of us felt quite at our ease.

"Alick was walking by my side when he caught sight of Charlie advancing towards us. With a yell of terror he rushed across the narrow pathway and flung himself headlong over the precipice.

"He did it so suddenly that none of us could even offer to prevent him.

"I sprang to the edge of the cliff just in time to see him strike himself against a projecting granite boulder and fall with a dull splash into the waters of the creek, which closed over him for ever.

"When I looked round I saw the supposed ghost gazing over the precipice, with an expression of horror and amazement in his face.

"This can't be anything but a man after all, thinks I. So I marched straight up to him, and I

then saw at once that it was not Charlie, though the likeness was so striking that at a short distance it would have deceived anyone.

"The mystery was soon explained. He was Charlie's brother, Jack Smart, who, not finding him at Melbourne, as he had expected, had come up to the Kajunga to look after him.

"The evening before he had missed his way and got up to our tents.

"He had not replied to my welcome, because, being deaf, he had not heard it.

"Alick's extraordinary behaviour upon seeing him had led him to believe that he was amongst a lot of candidates for the Yarra Bend, so that while we were lugging Alick out of the fire he quietly sloped into the bush again.

"Having worked for several years along with his brother in California, he had taken to dress exactly in the same style, which made the resemblance between them almost perfect.

"Well, you may be sure when the news of all this reached the township there was the very devil to pay. Everybody knocked off work and started off to see the place where the murdered man had been buried.

"There had been a pretty smart shower since we dug the body up, and as a Scotchman, of the name of Campbell, was looking at the grave, he saw something bright amongst the dirt that had been thrown up.

"He stooped down and picked it up, and what should it be but a nugget of pretty nigh three ounces, a small piece of which had been washed clean by the rain.

"Well, he jumped straight into the grave and drove his pick in at once, and 'Rush ho!' was the order of the day.

Claims were marked out on every side, the corpse was left to the care of Jack Smart and the police, who had just come up, and the gully was soon alive with the whole population of Kajunga, half mad with excitement.

"I had marked out a claim about fifty yards from the Grave claim, as it was called, and was hard at work sinking for my bare life, when some one touched me on the shoulder.

"It was Indian Hepe!

"'Well,' says he, 'what I said has come true. He found the claim, but never handled the gold for all that, poor fellow.'

"Well, whether it was chance or not I cannot say, but everything he told us that night came to pass, for that was the best rush ever known on Kajunga, and the Grave claim was allowed on all hands to be the best hole on it.

"And yet those who worked it never benefited by it, for the two Campbells, who had it after working it right out, all except one pillar, attempted to take that away without putting in proper props to the roofs of the drive, which fell in on them, and they were both killed.

"What became of the gold they took out of it was never known.

"No government receipts were found either on their bodies or among their things, nor could an ounce of gold be discovered, though search was made wherever it was thought they might have stowed it away.

"My belief is that they planted it somewhere in the bush, but where, no one will ever know, for it ain't likely that pick or spade will ever be plied upon the old Kajunga again.

"'And what amount of gold do you think they both had out of their claim?' said I.

"'Well, me and my mate cleared nearly two thousand pounds a man after all expenses paid. The American hole, which was the best after Campbells', turned out I know upwards of five thousand pounds, so that I should think there must be between five and six thousand pounds lying somewhere handy, if one only knew where to drop down upon it.

But prospecting for that lot amongst all these wild gullies would be but a poor spec, I reckon.

"And now, mates, my yarn is clean spun out, and as we must be up with the sun in the morning, I shall say 'Good night.'

"So saying, he knocked the ashes from his pipe, rolled himself in his blanket, and in a few minutes was sound asleep, an example we were none of us slow to follow. And here with his tale ends mine also."

CHAPTER LXII.

ANOTHER HUNT FOR THE BODY OF BLUE CAP.

THE sergeant's tale concluded, it was time to be in the saddle again.

"Before you mount and ride away," said Ted, "I want two favours at your hands."

"Name them," cried the troopers, in a breath.

"Consider them granted," echoed the sergeant.

"I want the body of poor Jack Last there, carried away from its proximity to those naked savages, and laid at the foot of that golden wattle tree, down in the dell yonder; and I want his horse caught for my own riding. It was lent to him on the condition that he should return it within the week, and my last promise to him was, that if he fell, I would nevertheless enable him to keep his word," said Ted.

"And do you mean to say that you do not intend to claim the large reward that is offered for his head?" asked the sergeant, somewhat incredulously.

"I would sooner cut off my right hand than touch a penny of it," was the reply.

"Well, perhaps you are right, but the temptation with me would have been very great," said the sergeant. "My men shall bury him if you wish it."

"No," said Ted. "He possessed the same dread that I do of the worm and of the grave. He left his flesh as a legacy to the ants and the wild dogs, and his skeleton to the sun and the moon, the day heat and the night dew. He preferred that wild flowers should grow up through his empty eye sockets, rather than that they should be choked with foul earth. He shall have his wish, and you must solemnly promise me that, once having laid him there, you nor your troopers shall return to disturb his remains."

"Most solemnly do I so promise," replied the sergeant, taking his hand.

"Then let him be carried down and laid there at once," responded Ted Hogan.

This was done, and another half hour sufficed to catch the run-away steed, which was found quietly grazing less than a mile away from where its rider fell.

The beautiful animal was uninjured by spear or pistol ball, and transferring his own saddle to its back, on account of the holsters and dangling head of Bob Loveridge, Ted Hogan mounted, and bade his friends and rescuers farewell.

* * * *

The day grew hotter with the climbing of the brazen sun up the steely heavens. A regular brickfielder soon began to blow, and in less than an hour from leaving the camp, both horse and man were powdered thickly with a reddish dust, which the furious northern wind, blowing directly from the great deserts of the interior, hot as the breath from a blast furnace, blew against the detective's face, with such force as to cause intolerable pain from the fine, gritty, burning sand penetrating eyes, ears, and nostrils.

Around, on all sides, the straw-coloured vegetation was unvaried by the slightest tint of green, and the tall, white trunks of the gum trees, with their scanty, vertical foliage, mingled with sombre peppermint and stringy bark, formed about as dreary and uninspiring a scene as it is possible to imagine.

Before an hour had passed away, Ted Hogan's steed, at the start so fresh and spirited, could only amble silently and spectre like, black with sweat where it wasn't red with dust, its head drooped, and its tail as limp as a shirt collar without starch.

But worse was yet to come, for when they had got on a couple of miles further, and began to congratulate themselves that the clouds of mingled dust and sand had become less dense, a new nuisance arose in the shape of innumerable sand flies—small, filmy things, like the midges of England, but indescribably more lively and blood-thirsty.

They were as numerous as the grains of sand in the sterile Iron Bark ranges.

They covered the whole ground for miles, and as the solitary horseman rode on, they would rise up in swarms, and settling on his good steed's legs and breast, puncture them in such a manner as to cover the poor creature, wherever they were at work, with blood.

The animal very naturally became almost frantic under the torture, and every now and then would kick and lash out so fiercely under the infliction, that Ted, with his almost useless left arm, and his weakness from fatigue and loss of blood, could scarcely maintain his seat.

At last, however, a creek was reached, wherein Ted watered and bathed his poor nag, the cool water affording it great relief, and bringing a terrible retribution on its tiny persecutors.

It was a lovely spot, and on account of the moisture, the grass was green, and adorned with myriads of flowers. Gold and silver wattles and sassafras trees spread a pleasant shade over the scene, and numerous grass trees grew around, its great white flowers growing on rods shooting up three or four feet high from the midst of the tussocky foliage.

On these trees his horse fed with a rare relish, whilst Ted had to content himself with a piece of jerked beef and damper cake given him by the troopers on parting, which were both as dry as well could be, and required copious draughts of cold water to get them down.

After an hour's rest, Ted Hogan remounted and continued his journey, refreshed as much by the sight of the Shoalhaven cliffs ahead of him as by his mid-day halt.

In another hour he was riding beneath their shadow, with the deep, swift and silent river sweeping along on his right, an inky Styx, but without a ferry or a ferryman.

He marvelled greatly that he hadn't overtaken Bungy on the road, forgetful that the blackfellow had had a couple of hours' start of him, and that an Australian native glides swifter and straighter through his native bush than the swiftest horse ever foaled.

Bungy had, on this occasion, poor fellow, only glided to his doom.

Ted Hogan journeyed on, and on, with his eyes fixed on the inequalities of the cliffs, until he caught sight of the great white splatch and the little rain of earth and grass tufts that betokened the spot where Blue Cap and his affrighted steed had gone headlong over into space.

Then his gaze was lowered in search of the brown mound that, when he was there last, had represented a dead horse.

He was not long in detecting its outline; but when he rode up to the spot, only a white bleached skeleton remained. The wild dogs had done their work effectually.

"Bungy!" shouted out the detective, at the top of his voice—"Bungy!"

The cry was echoed and re-echoed from the high cliffs, that was all.

Then the detective "coo-ee-yed," that strange

aboriginal halloo adopted by the white men, and which can be heard miles further than any other human sound; but still no answer.

"I suppose he has mistaken my directions on the route; but he'll be here by-and-by, I'll warrant," muttered Ted Hogan to himself, and he dismounted and hoppled his horse.

"Now I will never mount and ride again until I find Blue Cap's corpse. He never could have survived that thousand feet fall—it is impossible to believe in such a miracle."

So muttered Ted Hogan the detective, as he commenced a fresh search.

He had determined that it should be a complete and thorough one. It should last hours, ay, and days if need be. Starvation alone should drive him hence without his rightful spoil.

This was his resolve; but rash vows are often made, and as often, perforce, broken.

Ted had not searched long before he uttered a cry of astonishment and delight.

He had caught sight of what resembled the outline of a human form, lying amidst some coarse grass and rushes close down to the river's side. A cloud of flies buzzed above it.

He thought at once that it must be the corpse of Blue Cap, and hastened towards it.

But as he drew near, and at last looked down upon the face of the dead, he saw, with a very opposite emotion, that it was the dead body of poor Bungy.

There he lay, blue and livid, an army of red (soldier) and white (bull-dog) ants, each species as big as English wasps or bees, tearing off his clothes, and digging their forceps deep into his flesh. The former were already rags, the latter a mass of gaping wounds and sores.

Bungy's head was swollen to enormous proportions, and in the centre of its most swollen portion, where the black flesh had turned of a pale ultramarine hue, was clearly visible a double puncture, the marks, as Ted Hogan knew well enough, of a serpent's fangs.

But the giver of them had not, on this occasion, escaped prompt and retributive justice.

There, grasped in the tenacious clutch of Bungy's right hand, close up to the death dealing head, and suffocated by the tightness of the pressure, was a carpet snake of about four feet in length, its mouth open, its forked tongue lolling out, its metallic eyes covered with a thin film.

By the attitude of man and serpent the detective concluded that the snake had struck its victim whilst he was lying down on the river's brink to drink of its cool and limpid waters as they rushed past, and that the black, knowing himself to be a doomed man, and resolved that his assassin should also perish, had clutched it as it was about to renew the attack, and in his dying agonies of a few minutes' duration only, had strangled it also out of life.

It was a horrible spectacle, and if Ted Hogan turned on his heel and walked rapidly away, it was because he sorrowed for the cruel fate of one who, despite his difference of colour, he liked, and because he knew also that he was past all human help.

It did not, however, influence or delay him in his search for the remains of Blue Cap, for the corpse of that wretch was as valuable dead as when embued with life.

Every cave, and crevice, and clift in the cliffs he penetrated and searched again and again. Every yard of soil between their towering barrier and the river for a good three miles, up and down, he traversed and retraversed times innumerable, peering with his eyes amongst grass and reeds, and the occasional bushes of leptospernun and tea tree scrub, for even a solitary bone or tuft of hair that had once been part and portion of dead humanity—but he found none.

For three entire days and nights did he prosecute this determined and ruthless search, scarcely sleeping an hour at a time, living chiefly on roots and berries. Then, at last, a great despair crept over him, and he might often have been heard to mutter to himself—

"Is it possible then, for the foul fiend to spirit away his own?"

Whether he finally came to the conclusion that it really was so, or whether growing weakness told him that if he didn't get away soon, he wouldn't have strength remaining to get away at all, it is hard to say; but, be that as it may, one evening when it grew too dark to prosecute his search further, he saddled his horse, and murmuring, "Now I must keep my promise to poor Jack Last," mounted, and turned its head towards Marrangong.

The station was a good twenty-five miles distant, but Ted Hogan rode on and on, every now and then reeling in his saddle through weakness caused by long sleeplessness, anxiety, and want of food. Arrived at the station, he had just strength enough to call to someone to come forth and take his horse, and then his sight grew dim, and he fell crashing to the earth.

CHAPTER LXIII.
FROM SHADOW INTO SUNSHINE.

WEEKS have come and gone since we last saw Marrangong station, days since Frank Beaumont had been borne thither, to all appearance, a hopeless lunatic.

And yet, despite of this, there is a picnic at Marrangong, the like of which has never been heard of before. The invitations have been sent out far and wide, and on the morning set apart for the festivities, Marrangong showed such a turn out of fair damsels and young cavaliers as an Australian station seldom witnesses.

Up and away, along the red road of triturated sandstone, washed from the rugged cliffs of the distant mountain range by a thousand winter storms, or perhaps ages ago scattered far and wide over the lower country by some wild throe of nature, when mighty masses of rock, unwieldy and vast, were upheaved from their beds, crumbled into myriads of atoms by the fiery breath of the awakened volcano, and strewn broadcast like the summer dust before the wind.

Who can tell how many cycles have passed since this red sand beneath the horses' feet, called into existence by the omnipotent "Spirit which breathed upon the waves," rose slowly and stately from the bosom of the eternal deep, and towered majestically above a silent and new-born world—since the first ray of light shot from the feebly-lit sun gleamed in glad radiance upon it, and the Maker thereof saw that it was good? or how many ages it has looked down upon primeval forest and uninhabited wilderness, until that mighty and mysterious throe of the inner and unknown world shattered it to powder.

A red road, speckled with minute dots of emery that glitter in the morning sunlight like gems upon the tawny skin of an Indian queen.—a road which winds through the sparsely grassed shrub, and is ever hidden ahead by a turn to the right hand or the left, round dense gum bushes and thick clumps of shining leaved banksia, and which ever and anon appears again further ahead, trailing amongst the trees and looking in the sunshine like a large fiery serpent lying upon the hill side.

They then, seventeen in all, young and old, than whom a happier party never started on a similar expedition, were bound for a distant dell under the shadow of the great Dividing Range, intent upon their picnic.

Place aux dames—Georgie Mortimer, saucy,

laughing, bright-eyed Georgie, whose curls dance gaily beneath her coquettish straw hat, and whose ringing laugh echoes merrily amongst the grand old trees which swing their giant limbs o'erhead— Georgie, our Georgie, light of heart and glib of tongue, at a sight of whose smiles care and grief fly dismayed like the night mist before the rising sun.

Margaret, Queen Margaret, brown haired and brunette, tall, calm, cold, stately, like that other Margaret, who, setting aside womanly fear, boldly threw down the gage of defiance to the grim king who had snatched her husband's crown; or like she of Anjou, who with imperial brow and native majesty of mien, tamed the savage robber in the wood. Margaret, whose calm grey eyes sleep in calm serenity, and upon whose thin lips ever sits a half scornful smile, save when some tale of wrong awakes her into wrath, when her eyes will light up and flash, and from her lips will issue words of burning indignation and contempt. Oh! Margaret, beloved by the good, but feared and hated by the weak and wicked.

Then Mary, merry, loving, beloved Mary. She of the golden tresses and soft blue eyes.

Then Katie, and more Marys, more Margarets, with a scattering of Eleanors, Annies, Elizabeths, and I know not what; and then the male portion of the party. Frank Beaumont, who, thanks to Georgie's and her aunt's nursing, is as sane and strong as ever, and in whose especial honour the picnic is got up. Ted Hogan also, hale and hearty, and quite got over his spear thrust in the shoulder and his disappointment at not being able to find the body of Blue Cap; Harry Miller and his father; Charlie Stuart, from Goonangle, down Michelags way; Frank Watson, just out from England and fresh from college, come out to pick up colonial experience; Ned Smith, from the Dawson River, come down to buy store cattle and pick up a wife; with sundry others, not forgetting Mr. Ballantyne, the honoured and well beloved father, magistrate and clergyman of the district, a man amongst men, and a child amongst children, a man with the tenderness of a woman and the courage of a hero.

Who could forget how, when in the streets of Berrina one day a drunken savage, the bully and terror of the district, insulted a poor and defenceless woman, and used language to her that was a shame to his strength and manhood, this worthy pastor, his right arm not forgetting its cunning, for he had been one of the best boxers of his college, thrashed the bully until he made him roar for pity, and then put five pounds into the poor box as a kind of practical apology and penance for giving way to his just anger? or how he had sat by the side of the sick and suffering in mind, body or estate, no matter of what creed or position in society, doing as his great Master had done before him, giving comfort and consolation to the sick, the suffering, and the afflicted?

These formed the party who, cantering over the sandy road and waking the woodland echoes with snatches of song, with quip and jest, and jocund laughter, were out on this picnic excursion.

After a ride of about five miles, as the towering peak of Mount Linnings, which was enveloped in the thick morning mist when they started, was gradually becoming more and more sharply defined against the sky, and the irregularities of his surface which had at the distance appeared like mere patches of grey light and purple shadow, became more and more clearly developed as they approached him, their leader, Harry Miller, who knew every inch of the country, suddenly turning off the road, led the way along a grassy gully that seemed to tend to the very foot of the range.

On they went through the scrub, brushing the lingering dew drops from the green bushes, and scattering them like molten diamonds in their path, ever and anon startling from its browsing place the great grey kangaroo, and the fleet but timorous wallaby.

On they went, mile after unnoticed mile, laughing and shouting in very lightness of heart, in the calm morning—their dogs barking and their horses whinneying in unison.

At length they reached the spot appointed by their guide for the camping ground, and truly a more beautiful spot could hardly have been chosen.

From a mighty rift in the rugged mountain wall which towered in front of them, issued a creek, which, falling noisily over a barrier of dull granite, formed a deep, dark pool, overshadowed with flowering wattles, the faint but balmy odour of which was wafted by the gentle morning breeze like grateful incense over the senses.

Below the pool the creek flowed down a green gully in a wide, shallow stream, showing a bed of granite rock beneath.

The banks shelved gradually down from the upland, and were dotted with clumps of undergrowth, the many coloured furze, the blood red waratah, the purple sarsaparilla, and the tender leaved and sweetly perfumed peppermint.

Far away below them to the north, and shining forth between the spurs of a rocky rise, lay a spreading lagoon, whose wavelets glittered in the sunbeams like molten silver, and whence rose, softened by the distance, the cry of the solitary crane, and the strange and mournful tolling of the bittern.

Led by their guide, they dismounted, and hoppling their horses, left them to graze at will on the sweet grass which sprang luxuriantly around. They then descended to the bed of the creek, and producing their stores, prepared for the more practical pleasures of the day—eating and drinking. A strange medley was there when these stores were laid out upon the grass. Charlie Stuart produced a pillow case from his saddle bow stuffed with cold fowls, a tongue and a ham. Frank Watson, from the folds of his cloak, that had loomed suspiciously large during the entire journey, drew forth an unlimited and surprising number of bottles, of forms and sizes various. Ned Smith, from a bag brought out a huge damper, a round of beef, and a cheese. Harry Miller produced no end of sandwiches, and tins of lobster and salmon; and Joe Somebodyelse a monster pie, filled with all kinds of good things, too numerous to particularise. Mr. Miller senior carried the billy and the pannikins filled with tea and sugar, and the rest had some one thing and some another; but all something.

The ladies, too, each added something to the common stock. Georgie had a large pineapple and a bottle of milk, Margaret a bag of oranges, and Mary a bonne bouche, in the shape of a packet of almonds and raisins. Spreading Ned's bag and Charlie's pillow case as a table cloth, under the shade of a spreading wattle, which effectually screened them from the rays of the sun, now beginning to pour down with intense fervour, and placing the bottles up to their necks in water, preparations were made for breakfast.

"What a sweet place to live in," said Georgie; "to have a cottage built on yonder eminence, where you could catch the sun's first rays in the morning and his last ones as he sinks beneath the horizon at night. Oh! wouldn't it be delightful!"

Frank Beaumont looked as though he would like to commence to build the cottage at once.

"And get flooded out by the winter rains, and catch your death of cold," quoth practical Kate.

"You would damp the enthusiasm of the most enthusiastic poet in the world," laughed Ted Hogan, coming to Georgie's assistance, much to the disgust of Frank, who had just turned a very neat retort which now didn't exactly suit.

"The rain would effectually do that, with

my aid, to say nothing of the floods," replied Kate.
"Why, I have seen the torrents rushing down the
sides of that mountain after a rainfall, and I can
assure you it would be no joke, particularly if you
live below high water mark.

"'The glasses sparkle on the board, the wine is
ruby bright.'"

"That is to say, ladies and gentleman—

"The billy boils upon the fire, the tea is ready
quite," improvised Frank gaily. Then, still in-
spired by the poetic muse, he continued—

"So on the verdant carpet sit, and gather to the
feast,
And whilst you eat and drink a bit, we'll—
we'll——

"I say, can anyone give me a rhyme for feast?"

Georgie suggested east, and Katie least, but
neither would work in, and Frank had to resign
his pinions amidst loud laughter.

"So fell Icarus," said Frank, pulling a long
face.

"Icarus—who the deuce was he?" laughed Ted
Hogan, who was sweet on Katie.

"A gentleman all of the olden time, who possessed wings, and who, flying too near unto the
sun, melted the wax wherewith they were stuck
on, and fell into the sea—a warning to all poets and
aspiring persons generally," said Mr. Ballantyne.

"Not unlike some of our sucking politicians who
would be ministers," quoth Ted, who, from not
having been promoted to an inspectorship, had a
spite against the powers in office.

They then sat down upon the grass around the
the improvised table cloth, amidst the ferns that
grew along the banks of the creek, and the gentle
ripple of the water over its rocky bed sounded like
sweet music in their ears.

High overhead rode the sun in his refulgent
course across the clear depths of the firmament,
and through the leafy screen that sheltered them
from his fiery beams the cool wind from the
mountain gorges whispered crisply and refresh-
ingly,

The lyre bird, whose bright plumage glistened
now and then amidst the distant trees, roused by
their joyous shouts, spread his wings and fled to
deeper solitudes. The laughing jackasses perched
in mobs upon the neighbouring trees, and there
uproariously copied and mocked their hilarity, and
the gorgeously arrayed parrots flew to and fro
above their heads, making day hideous with their
discordant shrieks, which waking up the sluggish
native bears, caused them to peep out of their
holes, with their screwed-up, comical little eyes,
to see what the matter was.

Forth from their crystal beds in the creek, where
the cold waters had gurgled pleasantly around
them, came the bottles. Pop went the corks, and
cheerily flowed the amber and creamy topped
champagne and sparkling sillery.

And lazily and slowly curled upwards the grateful
smoke, as, breakfast over, the male portion of the
party lolled back on the green sward, and dreamily
puffed the Indian weed. Dreamily, for the Rev.
Mr. Ballantyne, overcome by the warmth of the
air, soothed by the fragrance of a real havannah,
and lulled by the shimmer of the green leaves over
his head, dropped off insensibly into a state of
beatific and dreamless slumber.

When he awoke he was alone, save for the
company of a little dog, Carlo, who lay fast asleep
and dreaming by his side. Dreaming, perchance,
of fleet kangaroos and howling dingoes, for he
would bark and yelp hoarsely in his perturbed
slumbers, as was his wont when on the track of
some bounding, flying doe, or engaged in a free
fight with those pests of the poultry yard, the
native dogs.

There, too, lazily cropping the herbage, were the
horses; but his bipedal companions were all gone.

He lay for a long time in that luxurious half sleep
from which it is somewhat difficul to summon
resolution to awake, until at last, arousing himself
with a start, he went off in search of the
wanderers.

Not that they wanted him, that he knew full
well; but being middle-aged (envious friends said
getting old) and somewhat like the melancholy
Prince of Denmark, "fat and scant of breath," and
moreover, not in love, he began to want his
luncheon.

He shouted with all his might, cooeyed until the
laughing jackass brayed in reply with a ten-fold
energy, but received only an echo for an answer.

Once he fancied he heard a titter, as of the lively
Kate Cliftonville, and once he thought he saw the
gleam of a pink ribbon, like that in the hat of that
witch Georgie, but the next instant there was no
sound save the crisp rustle of leaves, no sight save
the flutter of the gaudy parroquets across the
green forest vista.

He rambled down the creek, leaving dog Carlo
in charge of the provisions, and by-and-by, his
footsteps not being heard for the splashing of the
creek over a bed of boulders, he came across the
prettiest sight he had seen for many a day.

There was Georgie—the blue-eyed, golden-haired
Georgie, the mild and modest Georgie, who could
scarcely look a stranger in the face, and certainly
not that without the tell-tale blood rushing to her
own brow and cheeks—being kissed!

Yes, absolutely and positively being kissed by
that young scamp, Frank Beaumont, whilst she,
the little hypocrite, pretended to be busily engaged
admiring a bouquet of bush flowers which he most
probably had plucked and presented to her.

The reverend gentleman turned hastily round,
but only to encounter a similar scene about a score
of yards further up the stream, where saucy Kate
Cliftonville was undergoing, and as if she rather
liked it too, the self same operation from the hands,
no, the lips of Ted Hogan, who sat with his arm
fondly encircling her slender waist.

The good clergyman did not interrupt the
innocent love making, but rubbed the moisture
from his spectacles, and softly turning back, left
them to their billing and cooing, wondering where
all the others had got to; but at last wisely
concluding that it was no affair of his, he lay
down again and dozed until they returned.

"Good gracious me, Mr. Ballantyne," cried
Georgie, who came in last, not with Frank Beaumont's arm around her waist though, "have you
been asleep ever since we went away for a stroll
in the bush?"

"No, Miss Georgie; oh, no, Miss Katie," replied
Mr. Ballantyne, with a comical twinkle in his eyes.
"Not all the time. I took a stroll down the creek
between my naps, but coming across two brace of
cooing turtle doves I thought I would turn back."

The conscious blush rose to the cheeks of both
the fair girls, and both the lovers looked rather
silly. But the kind-hearted old man turned away
with a smile, and said no more.

Then luncheon was eaten, the mid-day pipe
enjoyed, and the pic-nic party returned home along
the red road they had traversed in the morning as
happy, and four of their number much happier
than during their outward journey, for under the
shadow of the old Linnings hill and beside the
waters of the babbling creek, Frank Beaumont and
Ted Hogan had won Georgie's and Katie's consent
to become their wives.

CHAPTER LXIV.

THE NEWSPAPER PARAGRAPH.

FRANK BEAUMONT and Ted Hogan were
both staying at Marrangong, and early on
the morning succeeding the events recorded
in our last chapter, Frank came into the

detective's bedroom with a newspaper in his hand.

"Georgie and I are to be married on the 18th, old fellow. I wish your nuptials with Miss Cliftonville could take place on the same day," he said.

"Ah, my dear fellow, that is impossible," responded Ted. "Unlike your lady love, Katie Cliftonville is not an heiress, and unlike you I have to wait for my inspectorship before I can creditably support a wife."

"Would the head of Blue Cap have enabled you to marry at once?"

"A thousand pounds! I believe you, my boy. Besides, the inspectorship would have followed that as a matter of course. Confound the whole affair, say I."

"Don't be in too great a hurry to do that," said Frank, with a peculiar smile; "but just look at this picture in the 'Australian Illustrated Post,' and read the letter press relating thereto. In my belief Blue Cap, the Bushranger, is in Melbourne."

"The devil he is!" exclaimed Ted, as he took the paper out of Frank's hand.

He glanced at the picture first. It represented a bearded, half naked, mummified figure stuck upright in a glass case of some museum.

Underneath was printed—

"THE SHOALHAVEN MUMMY, FROM A PHOTOGRAPH."

"That's not him," quoth Ted. "There isn't the slightest resemblance. Besides, he couldn't be a mummy. It takes a thousand years to become a mummy."

"Stick a dead man up a tree and the Australian sun will dry him up to the consistency of leather in five days," rejoined Frank. "This Blue Cap, if his horse came to the ground first, might not have been so battered by the fall. Read the account."

Ted Hogan turned over the leaf and did so. It ran as follows:—

THE MUMMY FROM THE SHOALHAVEN.—This sun-dried relic of mortality was brought to Melbourne a week ago by a party of overlanders, and at once secured for the Australian Museum, where, during the past week, it has attracted enormous crowds. It was found in the fork of a tree at the foot of the great Shoalhaven range, five miles to the north-west of Tumberumba, and three from the banks of the river. The way in which it was fixed and prevented from falling, shows it to have been the work of aboriginals, who doubtless found the body in the bush. The remains are those of a man about fifty-five years of age, and the body is much battered and bruised, as though it had fallen from a cliff or precipice. The countenance is most repulsive and forbidding; the body is here and there marked with scars as though of pistol bullets. Two fingers and a part of the thumb of the right hand are missing. The Mummy Man has not yet been identified, but is supposed by the police to be that of some bushranger, who has eluded human justice only at last to fall a victim to Heaven's vengeance."

"It is Blue Cap without a doubt; indeed, it can be none other," said Ted. "Frank, I must start for Melbourne at once—that is to say, directly after breakfast."

"I will accompany you," replied our hero. "I can help to establish the identity of this wretch, and so help you to the thousand pounds and the inspectorship. I say, old fellow, we may yet be married on the same day."

*   *   *   *

The journey was undertaken and accomplished in perfect safety.

Ted and Frank were accorded a private view of the mummy the morning after their arrival in the metropolis, an hour before the museum was opened to the public.

Both recognised it instantly as that of Blue Cap.

There was no difficulty in proving the identity to the full satisfaction of the police authorities, and the thousand pounds were at once paid over.

The following morning Ted Hogan was also presented with his inspectorship, to which a salary of three hundred and fifty pounds per annum was attached, with a whole train of little emoluments connected therewith. At a public dinner, too, he was presented with a silver goblet, bearing a flattering inscription, and filled to the brim with golden sovereigns. In fact, he and Frank were fêted the whole time that they were in town.

And then as quickly as it was possible they returned to Marrangong, where, by virtue of special licenses, the Rev. Mr. Ballantyne united them to their fair and blushing brides.

Frank Beaumont took his bride away to his own station the day after the wedding—a station whose threshold he had never crossed since the murder of his father, mother and sister the night of the opening of our tale, and Ted and his wife started at the same time for Melbourne. He is now Chief Inspector of Police for the entire colony.

THE END.